Twice in a
Lifetime

Twice in a *Lifetime*

a novel

by Rachel Ann Nunes

CEDAR FORT™

Springville, Utah

ISBN: 1-55517-626-7
e.1

Published by Cedar Fort, Inc.
Imprint of Cedar Fort Inc.
www.cedarfort.com

Distributed by:

Typeset by Kristin Nelson
Cover design by Nicole Mortensen
Cover design © 2002 by Lyle Mortimer

Printed in the United States of America
10 9 8 7 6 5 4 3 2 1

Printed on acid-free paper

Library of Congress Cataloging-in-Publication Data

Nunes, Rachel Ann, 1966-
Twice in a lifetime : a novel / by Rachel Ann Nunes.
    p. cm.
ISBN 1-55517-626-7 (pbk. : alk. paper)
1. Pregnant women--Fiction. 2. Widows--Fiction. I. Title.
PS3564.U468 T88 2002
813'.54--dc21
                                    2002012485

For TJ.

I would do it all again.

Acknowledgments

A special thanks to Anita Stansfield, Julie Bellon, Polly Daw, Tami Bradley, and Dore Elmer for their friendship, encouragement, and support through difficult times. Ladies, I couldn't have done it without you!

Also, a thanks to the great authors on the Published LDS Authors' list. It's so wonderful to associate with talented writers who understand that it takes more than words to make a successful book.

And finally a note of appreciation to the wonderful people at CFI who have made me feel so welcome.

Chapter 1

Rebekka Massoni Perrault arrived much too early at the Parisian restaurant where she planned to meet her husband for lunch. She couldn't help herself. With news as wonderful and life-changing as she had to share, how could she be anything but early?

She was bursting with her news and felt that everyone could see it in her face. It sang in her veins and echoed on the hot August air as pungent and enticing as the smell of the fresh bread that permeated the streets of Paris. Surely Marc wouldn't be surprised at her announcement. He would take one look at her and *know*. His brown eyes would twinkle in the way she loved and his ready grin would cover his handsome face. Then he would wrap his arms around her and laugh with pure joy.

"Rebekka!"

She looked up to see her brother-in-law André Perrault emerging from the depths of the restaurant. Since Perrault and Massoni Engineering and Architecture was located across from the restaurant and down the street a short way, she wasn't surprised at his presence. Both Marc and André, as well as her own brother Raoul Massoni, the third partner in the firm, often came here for lunch, either on their own or with clients.

"Hi André." She smiled widely at him. Once she would have launched herself into his arms and shared her good news, knowing he would be happy for her. But such openness belonged to years ago— before she had chosen to marry his older brother Marc. Though André had never treated her other than a sister since the day of her marriage, she remembered when there had been more between them than friendship, a time when she wondered if she was engaged to the right brother. And because of that, she was still careful. Guarded. Just in case.

"You look beautiful today." He didn't kiss her cheeks in the customary French greeting. The innocent gesture was something else she missed, something that now belonged only to her childhood. Yet even while missing the easy camaraderie, she wouldn't take back her decision to marry Marc. The past two years and eight months had been the most happy time of her entire life. She loved Marc so completely; there was no doubt in her mind that she had made the right choice.

"Thank you." She smiled, eying her brother-in-law's finely cut gray suit. "You're looking rather nice yourself. Just finished a lunch meeting?"

His laughter was warm and his brown eyes, so like Marc's, glinted with amusement. "You guessed it. Just nailed another bid and took the client out to celebrate." He lowered his voice. "You know how they treat me here—like royalty. My client was completely impressed."

She laughed with him. André, either at this exclusive restaurant where he was so well-known or anywhere else, was always someone who impressed people. Though not quite as tall as her husband, his shoulders were broader, and his dark brown hair as every bit as thick. His attractive face was decidedly masculine, and his manner engaging. His heart was equally admirable, and over the years Rebekka had often been a first-hand witness of his compassion. She had watched him with clients, members of their church, and with Ana and Marée, his young, motherless daughters. She had especially noticed the kind and firm hand he had extended to his adopted son, Thierry, who was by birth André's nephew on his wife's side of the family. Without André's unconditional love and guidance, the eighteen-year-old Thierry would likely be living a life of hunger and deceit on the streets.

The one thing André didn't do was date, though no one who had known his wife could blame him for that. Claire's death almost three years ago had taken a heavy toll on his soul. But that was something else they didn't talk about.

"Are you meeting Marc?" André asked.

"Yes. I'm early, though. I suppose I'll have a seat and wait for him." She glanced past him at the thin, distinguished-looking maître d', hovering near at his post.

"I'll tell him to hurry. I'm headed back to the office right now."

"Thanks."

Rebekka watched him leave the restaurant before heading toward the maître d'. "Ah, Madame Massoni," he said with his small perfunctory bow. "I have your table reserved. This is a very important day for you, no? I can see it in your eyes."

"Yes. It really is. This is one of the happiest days of my life."

Later, the statement would return to haunt her.

* * *

As he left Rebekka, the old familiar loneliness hit André square in the chest. Oh, it wasn't always this hurtful—usually he could talk to Rebekka and remember that he had done the right thing in encouraging her to marry his brother. They belonged together as he and Claire had belonged together. But today Rebekka was so beautiful and . . . well, radiant, and Claire so long absent from his life that for some reason it took more effort than usual to stay aloof. Exactly why he couldn't say; he was well resigned to living the rest of his life alone.

Squinting in the bright sunlight, André shoved on the dark glasses he had begun wearing more and more of late. Not because he needed them, but because they made it easier to hide his loneliness. Sometimes he would even leave them on inside—especially when Rebekka and Marc were in the room. He would never let either his brother or Rebekka realize how much he suffered. No, he wanted them to enjoy their life together. And he was happy for them. Well, at least he tried.

How had it all happened? Well, he knew, of course, but the reality wasn't as simple as it seemed. Shortly after his wife's sudden death, his feelings for Rebekka—ones that had root in a youthful crush but had lain forgotten during his years of marriage to Claire—had briefly blossomed. Rebekka had returned his feelings, at least in part, but she had chosen to marry Marc. End of story. From that time there had sprung up between them an invisible gulf that neither he nor Rebekka would ever approach, much less attempt to cross. Yet for André the old feelings were difficult to set aside completely. Lately he had found it an increasing challenge to be in her presence, so he used every opportunity to distance himself. No matter the consequence to his own feelings, he would never allow his loneliness to hurt either Rebekka or his brother.

Sometimes the distancing worked. Most of the time he enjoyed seeing them happy together. But not today. Today seeing her waiting so eagerly for Marc made the loneliness in his heart ache. Why was today different? André couldn't pinpoint it exactly, but there had been something new about Rebekka. While always beautiful with her dark auburn hair, oval face, and slender, smartly-dressed figure, today she had been absolutely dazzling. There was an undefinable look in her gray eyes, a becoming flush on her high cheek bones, and the line of her strong chin was somehow softened. Every one of the fourteen freckles on her otherwise unblemished face seemed more appealing than the first time he had counted them years ago.

It's because she's meeting the man she loves. André felt no bitterness at the thought. He had shared a great love with Claire, and believed he would again in the next life; and he loved his brother and Rebekka enough to wish them a similar relationship . . . despite the insoluble longing that too often arose in his heart.

Fighting this inner turmoil, André walked steadily in the direction of the crosswalk. Around him he heard the clatter of feet against the cobblestones, the continuous hum of the car motors, rising and fading as they raced madly past. Frequently the drivers used their horns to warn off pedestrians or perhaps simply because they felt like it—André couldn't be sure. There was also the occasional shout from a pedestrian greeting an acquaintance. He saw that he wouldn't make the street before the light changed; the area became more and more crowded each day—with both people and cars. He didn't mind. The noise and bustle was invigorating, exciting.

He continued walking, his thoughts once again drawn to his personal life. His only salvation in the years since Claire's death was the gospel of Jesus Christ, his children, and his work. He lived for these things, and had found great joy in them. The laughter in his life had returned.

Yet he was not complete, and there was nothing he could do about it.

His family and friends urged him to date, but he felt no need. Losing Claire was heartache enough for a lifetime. No, better he stick to being a father, businessman, and friend. This, he knew he could accomplish with at least some measure of success.

Lifting his head toward the intersection in the distance, André caught sight of his brother's face on the far side. He was closer to the street than André, but wouldn't make the light this time either. Marc spied him and grinned boyishly, lifting a hand in greeting. Though Marc was three years older than André, he often passed for younger. André suspected that his brother's youthful appearance was due to his well-deserved happiness—or perhaps to the fact that Marc had married a woman nearly ten years his junior.

At the curb André waited, a crowd of impatient pedestrians gathering around him. He studied his brother's face over the cars that rushed by. He looked good. His strength had been completely regained since his third kidney transplant just before his marriage to Rebekka. With luck and a lot of prayers, it would be years before he had to face another operation. André felt gladness in his heart for the miracle of his brother's life.

A commotion behind Marc drew André's attention. Somewhere a woman shouted "My purse!" and then a small man in dark clothing shoved into the crowd around Marc. Something large flew into the street.

Brakes screeched, and there was a sickening thud. More frightened screams pierced the air.

"He's hit! He's hit!" a woman yelled in a high, excited voice. "He was pushed!"

"Call an ambulance!" someone else called.

André froze, a feeling of horror seeping into his body. He scanned the crowd across the intersection for his brother's familiar face.

He couldn't see it.

He's just helping the victim, André reasoned. *That would be like him.* The traffic had stalled, and André was carried into the street with the crowd, most of whom paused near the fallen figure.

Marc.

André was on his knees in a minute next to his brother's prostrate body. Tears wet his face, and his entire being trembled with fear. "Marc, I'm here," he said, almost unable to make his throat force out the words. "Hold on. You're going to be all right."

Marc's eyes slowly opened. "André . . ." He trailed off and then said, "Take care of Rebekka. Just in case I . . ."

"You're not going anywhere. We need you! *Rebekka* needs you."

"I always knew our time would be short." A trickle of red liquid gushed from Marc's parted lips as he struggled to speak.

"Don't say that." André gripped his brother's shoulders, careful not to raise him from the pavement or to cause more damage than the car had already inflicted.

"Please," Marc said with a groan.

Suddenly André was consumed with guilt. "Marc, it was me. *I* was the other man. That time she called off your engagement before you got married. It was me who made her confused. I didn't mean to . . . to hurt either of you."

Marc's brown eyes turned in his direction, but they were unfocused. "I know . . . I mean, I didn't know at the time, but later I saw how much you cared for her, and she for you. It doesn't bother me."

"She loves you—she always has! And I promise I've never stood between you since. Never! When I came to my senses, I even urged her to marry you. Can you forgive me?"

"For loving Rebekka?" Marc asked. For a moment, André thought he detected a trace of amusement in his brother's faltering voice. Then Marc continued with gasps and pauses between his words, "There is . . . nothing to forgive, little brother. How could you—anyone—not . . . love her? I am glad you felt that way. You're the only one I trust to take . . . care of her. I asked you once before . . . when I was sick . . . when the kidney failed . . . now I'm . . . asking you again. If . . . anything happens to me . . . I want you to make her happy. I want you to . . ."

Sirens cut through Marc's words. André crouched down and put his wet cheek next to his brother's, his mouth close to his ear. "Fight, Marc! You must fight! I couldn't be the one to tell Rebekka something happened to you. I *can't.* It would destroy her. You have to make it. Please, Marc— I don't want to lose you!"

"Promise me." Marc's voice was faint but urgent.

"Yes, of course. *Of course.* I promise." André fumbled in his pocket for his consecrated oil, hoping to give his brother a priesthood blessing.

He was too late.

André held onto his brother until the ambulance arrived. He sobbed as they drew the sheet over Marc's abruptly calm face and put him inside the ambulance, away from the interested stares of the crowd. The police began to ask questions. Still sitting on the black road, André put his head in his hands, struggling not to give in completely to the agony knifing so profoundly into his soul. Vaguely he was aware of someone pulling him to his feet and pushing him toward the sidewalk.

At last a welcome feeling of disbelief settled over him. With hands that didn't seem to be his own, he took out his cell phone and called his father, transferring part of his terrible burden.

Traffic was moving again shortly and the ambulance had driven away. André didn't go with it. What good could his going to the hospital do Marc now? Besides, there was something more important André must do, a trust he promised to fulfill.

With a heavy, aching heart he walked back to the restaurant to face Rebekka.

* * *

Rebekka heard the faint sound of sirens but wasn't really concerned. Nothing could penetrate the warm cocoon of contentment around her. Sitting at her table, she scanned the menu, thinking she would try something new in honor of this day.

She didn't know what made her look up just then, but she saw André coming toward her, his face a pasty white against the dark sunglasses. Her hand froze at what she could see of his expression.

Something was dreadfully wrong.

He threaded around the linen screens that nominally divided the tables in this section of the restaurant, giving the occupants a semblance of privacy. The crystal dewdrop chandelier overhead seemed suddenly too bright. Couldn't that be what made André so pale?

She rose to meet him, knocking over her wine glass, filled with ice water against the heat of the summer. The water turned the burgundy cloth red as the spill seeped over the neatly laid table on its way down to the matching carpet.

"Oh, Rebekka. It's—it's Marc," André said.

All the gladness drained from Rebekka's heart. She tried to peer past the glasses to see his eyes, but all she saw was a woman she no longer knew, staring back at her with a frightened expression.

"No," she whispered. "No!"

André's strong hands gripped her arms. "He was—" he swallowed with difficulty "—hit by a car." Tears cascaded from under the dark glasses, but seeming unreal. Rebekka wanted to rip off his glasses and shatter them beneath her heel—anything to see the truth beneath—but her shaking hands wouldn't obey her command.

"I'm so sorry." His lips trembled with the words. "Rebekka, I—"

She pushed away from him and started wildy toward the exit, uncaring of the interested stares of her fellow diners, peering around their screens. In two steps he caught up with her and held her back. "I have to get to Marc!" she cried. Her chest began to hurt, and she tried to suck in breath to relieve the pain. "I have to hurry. If he's hurt, he'll need me!"

"No." André's arms were like stone as she struggled within their circle, trying to free herself. Her hand flew out, unintentionally striking his face, and his glasses fell with a soft sound to the plush carpet. His grief-stricken eyes met hers, and in that moment she saw the truth she had craved.

She wished she hadn't.

A mournful cry escaped her lips—a cry of despair. She felt herself sway toward him, then gave up to the blessed darkness.

Chapter 2

In the months after her brother's death, Marie-Thérèse Portier constantly fought feelings of depression and longing. She told herself that it was only natural after such a tragedy, but her emotions ran much deeper than that. She had lost so many already—her birth parents and her sister Pauline. And the third baby that had never really been hers.

How she could lose something she'd never had was still a mystery to her, but she felt the loss of the faceless child nonetheless. And although she had long given up the idea of adoption, she still dreamed of someday finding a way . . . another child. The desire remained in her heart, no matter how latent, and with Marc's passing the old feelings had come to the surface.

At least she had her two natural children—Larissa and Brandon. Marie-Thérèse loved them fiercely, perhaps even too much. Brandon never seemed to mind her smothering, but Larissa, now fifteen and a half years old, was . . . well, difficult. Things had come to a crisis three years earlier when they had applied for adoption. Larissa had been violently opposed to sharing them with another child and had voiced her opinions loudly and without reserve. She also acted out repeatedly at school, at home, and at them—mostly hurting only herself. Afraid they would lose her to drugs or worse, Marie-Thérèse and her husband had withdrawn their papers. Larissa had to come first. It was as simple as that. Looking back, Marie-Thérèse felt the sacrifice had been worth the change in their daughter.

Not that everything was perfect with their relationship. Larissa was still a magnet for every new fad or idea to come into the schools or the media, and she continued to be very headstrong. But Marie-Thérèse knew they were making headway. Every night, she and Mathieu poured out their hearts to God in Larissa's behalf, and they both were full of hope that Larissa might just make it through the teenage years in one piece—though perhaps a rather battered one.

Yet none of this stopped the covert longing in Marie-Thérèse's heart, or the feeling that their family was not quite complete. These emotions centered on the confirmation she had received from the Lord when they had first prayed about adopting. Adoption had been right; she'd *felt* it. But giving up adoption for Larissa had also been right, hadn't it? So why was the subject still bothering her? And how could these two opposite feelings be correct?

If Marc was here, she would ask him. Or maybe the feelings would have stayed dormant inside that remote corner of her heart that she refused to let even her husband glimpse. Yes, it was her brother's death that had brought on all these emotions. Tears pricked behind Marie-Thérèse's tired eyes and she blinked them back. She had to be strong—especially while visiting Rebekka, whose grief over Marc's death went far deeper than her own.

She took a deep breath and turned her attention to her sister-in-law. "Rebekka, you need to eat." She made her voice gentle and without reproach.

Rebekka looked up vaguely from the kitchen chair she had seated herself in moments before, as though she was unsure how she had come to be there. "Oh, yeah. Eat."

Marie-Thérèse sighed and sank into the other chair, the one that Marc had typically used. "I know it doesn't seem necessary, but it is. You need your strength."

"I know." Rebekka's gray eyes were still unfocused, directed inward, but at least she wasn't crying anymore. "But there's so much to do. I— see his books?" Her hand fluttered toward a box on the floor and then to several stacks on the counter. "He loved them so, but I can't bear to have them around like they're waiting for him to come home. I don't want to ever see another science fiction book again."

"I'll take them to Brandon. He loves to read."

Rebekka smiled faintly, but without real happiness. "Thank you. I really appreciate it."

"Is there anything else I can do?"

Rebekka shook her head. "No. But I'm thankful for everything you've done. And everyone else. Your whole family, my parents, my brother—they've all been great." She met Marie-Thérèse's eyes. "Raoul's moving in here with me, you know. In a few days. It'll be good for both of us."

"Yeah, you told me last week."

"Oh, I guess I forgot. I never thought . . . I mean . . ." An ironic smile hovered around Rebekka's lips. "I guess I never imagined I'd live with my brother again."

"Well, it's just till you both get on your feet again." Marie-Thérèse knew that since the beginning of Raoul's marriage three years ago, he had been enmeshed in a continuous cycle of separation and reconciliation. At the present his wife was gone again, and moving away from his lonely apartment might do as much for him as it would for Rebekka. "Come on, now—eat. I bought the rye especially for you."

"Thank you." Rebekka's hand touched the sandwich, then paused. "It just seems so odd, me here eating, life continuing without Marc." She hiccupped a little sob. "I just miss him so much. And I feel so—so lost."

How well Marie-Thérèse knew that feeling! "It'll get better soon. It will. And thank heaven for the hope of eternity."

Rebekka nodded, her eyes dark and solemn. "If it weren't for the gospel, I don't know what I'd do."

The bell rang and Marie-Thérèse went to answer the door, expecting another member of the family or perhaps Rebekka's mother. Though no one had rung to get inside the lobby, likely a neighbor had been leaving the building and had let them in. Both families were very close, and since Marc's death, they had rallied together to help one another—and especially Rebekka—deal with the grief.

Sure enough, André was pulling out a ring of keys as Marie-Thérèse opened the door, his free arm carrying a large box. He flushed under the dark sunglasses perched on his nose. "I—these are Marc's keys. They were in his office. I cleaned it out for Rebekka today, and here's his stuff, or what I thought she'd want to keep."

Marie-Thérèse didn't reply, but pushed the door open wider to allow her brother to enter.

"I let myself in downstairs," he continued. "How's Rebekka?"

"She's holding up. She's strong."

André nodded. He seemed paler than normal under the dark glasses.

"You ought to take those off," Marie-Thérèse told him. "You look like a hit man, or something." He did as she requested, and she nearly winced at the tension wrinkles around his eyes. "You look awful."

"Thanks," he said dryly. Then he hefted the keys, his voice becoming defensive. "I'm not giving these to her. I told Marc I'd look after her, and I may need them to do that."

She knew he felt his burden keenly, and her heart went out to him. Not only did he have to help fill Marc's absence at their company, but he also had to keep his last promise to his dying brother. As much as the others visited Rebekka, André came with even more frequency. He obviously would not rest until she was happy—however long it took.

"Keep the keys," Marie-Thérèse said with a shrug. "At least until Raoul moves in."

"Where is she?"

Marie-Thérèse pointed over her shoulder. "In the kitchen. I brought her lunch, but she's not eating. She's been preoccupied with Marc's things—particularly his books."

André actually laughed, though the sound cut off much too soon. "Oh yes, his sci-fi books. He certainly had a lot of those."

"It's a good sign she's willing to part with them to Brandon. At least I hope it is."

Marie-Thérèse returned to the kitchen, with André in tow. Rebekka had still not taken a bite of her sandwich. Streams of sunlight filtered through the lace curtains beyond, casting intriguing patterns on the table. Rebekka studied them intently. She looked up distractedly as they entered. "Hi, André. Want any books?"

André set his box on the counter near the refrigerator. He took Marie-Thérèse's vacated seat and reached for Rebekka's hand—stopping just short of actually touching her. "I'd better let Brandon have them. That kid reads like there's no tomorrow."

Rebekka's gray eyes filled with tears, reminding Marie-Thérèse of rain threatening to fall from twin dark clouds. Abruptly, Rebekka burst from her chair. With several violent motions, she threw the books on the counter toward the already full box on the floor, until they stacked high and overflowed onto the tile. She kicked the box for good measure, sending more sprawling.

The next second she was down on the floor gathering them up. "I'm sorry. I shouldn't have done that. I'm just so . . . I don't know."

Marie-Thérèse and André were beside her instantly. André helped her up, while Marie-Thérèse stacked the novels. "Look, don't worry about it," André said. "Marie-Thérèse has them. See?"

"That's good." Rebekka's normal velvet voice was strained and rushed. "Take them right now, okay? Brandon will be home from school soon, right? He can start reading them today."

Marie-Thérèse looked at André. He nodded once, signaling that she should do as Rebekka wished. "I'll stay with her," he mouthed.

"Okay then, I'll be going." Marie-Thérèse put the books that wouldn't fit in the box into a plastic sack and slung it over her shoulder.

Then she hefted the box. André started forward to help her, but she waved him aside. "No, I can carry them. You stay and have lunch with Rebekka. I made plenty."

"Oh yes, I bet you haven't eaten," Rebekka said in that same forced voice. "Have some." Her eyes darted toward Marie-Thérèse. "Thanks for coming. You don't know how much I appreciated your company. And I will eat this lovely meal." As if to prove her words, Rebekka took a healthy bite of the sandwich. She chewed steadily with such a look of bleak determination that Marie-Thérèse's heart again went out to the young widow. Marie-Thérèse had loved her brother deeply, but she hadn't been married to him; she couldn't even think about how she would feel if her Mathieu had been the one to die.

Impulsively, she hugged Rebekka. "Call me," she said, knowing Rebekka wouldn't. She was too independent. No, it would have to be Marie-Thérèse who checked up on her. But that was something Marie-Thérèse understood and was willing to do.

"Thank you," Rebekka whispered. Her eyes looked at Marie-Thérèse, but were unseeing.

Marie-Thérèse escaped the apartment, her heart as heavy as the load of books she carried. Rebekka would be all right, they all would, but they would need the passage of time. Until then, she prayed that the burning light of the gospel would sustain them.

Once in her own apartment building, Marie-Thérèse rode the elevator to the second floor and carried the books inside her apartment. She left them on the counter in the kitchen where Brandon would see them as he came in for his after school snack. He would be content to have his favorite uncle's books.

Marie-Thérèse swept her light brown hair up into a ponytail and was searching in her cookbook for a quick cookie recipe that contained nothing Brandon was allergic to when the buzzer to the outside door rang. Thinking the children had forgotten their keys, she slapped the buzzer in the entryway without asking who was there. She was glad André had taken her place at Rebekka's today. On Friday her children often returned home early from school, and Marie-Thérèse liked to be at all the cross-roads in her children's lives.

A short time later she answered the apartment door, and what she saw stunned her into speechlessness. Pascale Blanc, the woman who had worked with them on their plans for adopting in the Ukraine, blinked at her, an apologetic look on her worn, perspiring face. She was carrying a huge diaper bag and at her feet was a plastic baby carrier that obviously doubled as a car seat.

"Thank heaven you're home!" Pascale exclaimed.

Marie-Thérèse hadn't seen Pascale since Brandon's food allergy accident almost three years ago, the one that had nearly taken his life. They had canceled their plans for the adoption at that time, and she hadn't expected to see Pascale ever again.

"Uh . . . what's . . .?" Marie-Thérèse pointed to the baby carrier. Her heart suddenly ached with a hurt she couldn't name.

"I need your help. Can we come in?" Pascale shoved back a lock of thick black hair that had escaped the comb at the nape of her neck.

"Well, okay." Though Marie-Thérèse hadn't yet seen any "we." Just a baby carrier whose back faced her.

Pascale smiled faintly, for an instant looking less harried and more like the calm adoption agency employee Marie-Thérèse remembered. With a fluid motion, she swooped down on the carrier and hefted it, immediately passing it to Marie-Thérèse.

Marie-Thérèse gazed down at the face of a very young baby with brown hair and a sweet, adorable face. She couldn't see the eyes because the child was sleeping, but knew they would contain the wise innocence that always accompanied newborn infants.

In her peripheral vision, she saw Pascale turn and stoop, picking up something that had been behind her. The "something" was another child—a little girl. She was older, perhaps three, and she held herself rigidly in Pascale's arms. Her face, framed by brown, shoulder-length hair, was utterly expressionless and her blue eyes hauntingly solemn. Marie-Thérèse had the impression it would be a hard thing to coax a smile from this serious creature, no matter how hard she might try.

Inside, Marie-Thérèse led the way to the kitchen. Carefully, she placed the baby carrier and its precious cargo in the middle of the table. The baby murmured in its sleep, but didn't awake. Pascale sighed with relief and slumped into a chair, allowing the bag on her shoulder to slide to the ground. Abruptly, the little girl pushed away from Pascale's lap, and in an instant had disappeared under the table.

Marie-Thérèse stifled an urge to peer after the child and instead looked sternly at Pascale. "What's going on?" She didn't mean for her voice to tremble.

Pascale sighed again more loudly. "I just couldn't think of anyone else. You see, I don't work for the adoption agency anymore. There were some problems—like people taking up to seven weeks in the Ukraine to adopt children instead of the three to four they were promised. And many others I won't go into right now. But I got tired of the game. Sometimes it seemed as if no one really cared about the children, except how much they could get for them. Not the adoptive parents, of course. They were the reason I kept at it so long." Pascale rubbed her big-boned hands across her face. "But I just couldn't take it anymore. So I decided to change jobs. I work for the government now in social services. And I do like it better—except there are still a lot of challenges. Like today."

Her voice became low and urgent as she leaned forward. "Look, the reason I'm here is because I need to know if you can take care of these two for the weekend. I don't have anyone I can really trust with them right now, and it'll take awhile to get new applicants approved."

"But I'm not approved either." It was the only thing Marie-Thérèse could think of to say.

"No, not technically. But since I went through that whole approval process with you at the agency, I know you and Mathieu are good people and well-suited for taking care of them. I'll be able to get a temporary approval for you—I'm allowed to do that in an emergency. And temporary approval is all the time I'll need. Please say you'll do it! I just don't know what else to do. The baby I could leave in quite a few places easily enough, but her sister . . ." Pascale's voice dropped to a scarce whisper. "There's been serious abuse, and I just can't stand the idea of putting her into a home not equipped to deal with that."

Marie-Thérèse's chest tightened. She should have recognized the pain behind the child's solemnness. "How . . . where did they come from?"

"They were found this morning in a room in a run-down apartment building after the police answered a report from a neighbor. They were locked in a back room alone. I have no idea how long they were there, but they were both very hungry—starving even. The baby had been crying all night, which is what alerted the neighbor. Luckily, the police broke in and found them. The baby was in a crib and Celisse—that's what the neighbors say the little girl's name is—was under it. She hasn't spoken since we found her."

Marie-Thérèse could see there was more Pascale wasn't saying, most likely because of the child crouched under the table. "Let's go into the other room," she suggested.

Pascale nodded and looked under the table. "We'll be right back, Celisse. Okay honey? Don't worry." She arose and gazed at Marie-

Thérèse expectantly.

Marie-Thérèse hesitated but Pascale didn't reach for the baby carrier, and Marie-Thérèse was reluctant to leave the infant unattended. Was Celisse inclined to climb onto the table? Marie-Thérèse wasn't willing to risk finding out. She picked up the carrier and left the kitchen, ignoring the amused smile Pascale sent her way.

In the sitting room that also doubled as the TV room, she set the baby carrier on the floor and sat in a chair across from Pascale. She fished the television remote out from under her and placed it on the end table. "Well?"

Pascale's face again took on a look of weariness. Now that the older woman's arms were free from her burdens, Marie-Thérèse noticed she had lost weight. The waist of her gray linen skirt drooped on her hips, and her white blouse looked a size too large. She wondered if social work wasn't even more stressful for Pascale than working on adoptions.

"There were feces pretty much all over the room where the children were found, mixed in with food and garbage," Pascale said. "There is evidence that Celisse at least has been kept there alone—like an animal in a cage while her mother works or goes out . . . whatever."

Marie-Thérèse digested the information slowly. "What does her mother say?"

"Mademoiselle Despain hasn't been found yet. My guess is that someone tipped her off about the police. Now we just have to wait to see if she shows up or if the police find her. Regardless, it's unlikely Celisse will ever go back there. Besides the terrible state of the room, she has cigarette burns on her arms, numerous scars over her body, and the doctor we took her to this morning said she has been sexually molested. You should have seen how upset she was when we tried to do the examination. He did only the bare minimum while she was awake because he didn't want to traumatize her any further. He actually had to give her a sedative to continue—we needed evidence for the court. He's seen a lot of our cases, but he recommended taking her to a specialist—both for her psychological damage and for her physical needs. He thinks she'll need some surgery to correct the damage." Pascale shook her head sadly, and the lock of escaped hair fell over her shoulder. With an impatient gesture, she pinched open the comb at the nape of her neck and repositioned the hair inside. "Of course, that will all come later."

The sick feeling in Marie-Thérèse's stomach had increased with Pascale's words. She could almost see the child's bright blue eyes staring at her gravely. *No wonder she hasn't spoken!* she thought. And how can anyone ever make up for what she's been through?

"From what we can determine, she's four years old," Pascale continued. "Or nearly so, though she's small for her age—more like a three-year-old. Lack of nutrition, no doubt. Like I said before, she hasn't said a word since she's been placed in my care, though she eats everything I give her. Fortunately, the baby seems to have escaped much of the abuse—hasn't cried once since we fed her. But we don't have any idea what her name is or how old she is—probably somewhere between two and six weeks old. She's small, but healthy, so it's hard to tell." Pascale's dark eyes met Marie-Thérèse's. "So can you do it for a few days? I know it won't be easy, but Celisse deserves a good home with consistency and kindness. I can't just toss her in with anyone. I'll have to find the perfect family. She's been through enough."

Marie-Thérèse took a deep breath. "Of course we'll help. We'll be glad to. And you don't have to worry, I'll take good care of them until you find a foster home you feel comfortable with."

"I can wait while you call Mathieu."

"It's not necessary. You know Mathieu—of course he'll be fine with it."

Relief etched over Pascale's worn face. "Thank you. You can't begin to know how much I appreciate this."

Marie-Thérèse tucked her hair behind her ear, thinking that it wasn't so important what Pascale thought as what little Celisse was thinking. *That poor child!*

"There's formula in the bag . . . and diapers. And a few clothes that we had at the office—what Celisse was wearing was not salvageable. Looked like it'd never been washed. What I brought is not much, and you'll have to get more to get through the weekend. We'll reimburse you, of course."

"Don't worry, I've done this before with my own children." Marie-Thérèse's mind was already racing, wondering if the outfits she had saved from Larissa's childhood were still usable. Or maybe she had some material she could use to whip up something simple on the sewing machine. "It's been a while since they were small, but it's like riding a bike, right?" she added.

"Probably."

But the moment the door closed on Pascale, Marie-Thérèse's confidence faded away. She had a baby just waking up in a carrier and a little girl who crouched in silent terror under the table. What should she do first?

She set the carrier on the table and knelt down. "Would you like a cookie?"

Celisse said nothing, but stared at her with wide blue eyes. Her back was pressed up against the wall, as far away from Marie-Thérèse as she could get.

The baby started crying then, pursing her tiny button mouth and howling as though she were being tortured by a thousand needles. "It's okay," Marie-Thérèse said, placing a consoling hand on her stomach. The infant sobbed harder.

Marie-Thérèse was still on her knees trying to quiet the baby *and* coax Celisse from under that table when the slamming of the apartment door signaled her children's arrival.

"Mom!" Larissa glared at her with piercing brown eyes. Her very short, almost black hair, sculpted around her skull with her customary gel, made her look older than almost sixteen . . . and mean. Her nose wrinkled in angry disgust. "You went ahead and did it, didn't you! You got a kid without even asking *me* how I felt! I can't believe it! And you talk about honesty! I can tell you one thing, it's not sleeping in *my* room!" With a jerky movement of her gangly body, Larissa threw her backpack to the ground. Her school books tumbled through a hem that ripped with the impact. She ran from the room, and Marie-Thérèse stifled an impulse to run after her daughter and wring her little neck.

Ignoring his older sister, Brandon shrugged off his own backpack and set it on the table. "Cool," he said, dipping his head to peer at the baby. The brown hair on his head was longer than Larissa's and fell forward with the movement. "Can I hold him? Without waiting for an answer, he unhooked the safety belt and scooped the baby out of the seat. At once the baby stopped crying. "Hey, he likes me. What a smart kid."

"She. She's a girl."

"Even better. I like girls." He stroked her soft cheek. "She sure is cute. Like Aunt Josette's babies, only smaller. Hey, this isn't so hard. But she's trying to suck on my finger. Looks hungry. Can I give her a bottle?"

Marie-Thérèse blinked away sudden tears. At least one of her children was reasonable. "Sure," she said with a sigh. "Now what do you know about getting a scared child out from under the table?"

Chapter 3

For Rebekka, the last few months had passed in alternating bouts of numb disbelief and agonizing tears. The grief was all-encompassing, like a suffocating blanket she could not remove—nor would if she could. She had never realized how a feeling could permeate every aspect of her life. Or how trite the well-meaning condolences sounded from people who did not know real tragedy—though she believed they were all sincere.

That day at the restaurant her life had ceased, though strangely the world had gone on. Bills continued to arrive in the mail, the television stations continued their programs, birds still sang outside her window. People got up, went to work, ate, and went to bed. Even her body had gone on, though at first it had surprised her that her body still demanded food, rest, and regular trips to the bathroom. It was all too mundane for any semblance of reason, and yet it was these ordinary things that helped her cling to her sanity. Yes, she believed she would one day be reunited with her husband, but at twenty-eight, the belief wasn't as comforting as she had hoped. Her heart was utterly broken.

"Eat up," André encouraged, breaking through her thoughts. He was at the window, watering the potted plant Marc had always cared for. Rebekka didn't want to point out that it was way too late. She had never remembered to water them before Marc's death and afterward there had seemed even less reason to do so. How could she care about a plant when her life was over?

"Come on," André said. "I know how you love rye bread."

She lifted the sandwich Marie-Thérèse had made and took a bite. The smell of the mustard made her stomach queasy and she dropped it to the plate. She would much rather contemplate the warmth of the sunlight through the curtains. Or maybe she should go through her bedroom and out onto the balcony to feel it better. But no, it wasn't August anymore, it was October. There might be a cool breeze and that meant the sun would feel warmer coming through the glass. She should have remembered what month it was. Why did she always think of it as still being August? Would it always be August? The month Marc died.

"Is something wrong?"

She purposely misunderstood his question about the food. "Yes, I always knew he would die before me. I mean, with him being ten years older it was likely. Or if he didn't die from old age, I thought he'd die of kidney failure. But either way I *thought* there would be time to say goodbye." Her voice had begun calmly enough but rose steadily as she talked. "So it's over just like that? No tender goodbye as I watch him struggle for breath? No time for last minute declarations of love and undying loyalty? No intense looks? No kisses to endure a life-time?" She was nearly yelling now. "No! I have nothing! Nothing! It was over, just like that!" She snapped her fingers.

"Rebekka," he groaned.

She knew he hated when she talked that way, and even felt a little sorry for him—if she stopped to think about it long enough. But she was also angry because André *had* shared her husband's last few moments of life while she had waited obliviously at the restaurant, believing her good news would insulate them from all trials.

The silence between them grew, and then he said, "I know what you're feeling, Rebekka. Claire and I . . . I never got to tell her what a difference she made in my life, and how grateful I was for her love and companionship."

Rebekka closed her eyes, unable to bear the pain in her heart or the terrible loss in his eyes. "Claire knew," she muttered.

"And so does Marc."

Rebekka forced her eyes open. "I know, but I wanted to say it! And I wanted him to remind me that he would be looking down from heaven, that our marriage was eternal. You of all people should understand that!" Her voice broke as she lifted her face to the ceiling. "You hear me, Marc? That wasn't fair. It just wasn't fair!"

"Life's *not* fair!" The words came roughly from André's lips.

She focused on his face, bleary from her tears. "And you don't think I know that? I'm not *stupid*, André. I may have been a lot of things in my life, but I'm not *stupid*."

And suddenly it was all too much. All of it—the rye-bread sandwich she had no appetite for, the powerful smell of the mustard, and the continual ache of missing Marc. She sprang to her feet and ran down the hall to the bathroom. She heaved repeatedly into the toilet, but nothing came except the single bite of sandwich she had swallowed, mixed with bitter gall. So she sobbed and heaved and sobbed some more. At long last, she wiped her mouth with trembling fingertips and sank to the floor, her back against the wall and her knees tucked close to her chest. She wrapped her arms around her legs. *That's right—hold them tightly against my heart. That way maybe it won't hurt so much.*

There was a noise, and she looked up to see André who stood watching her from the doorway. Instead of the sympathy she had expected, his face wore a stunned expression, one that held more than a hint of anger.

"So how long have you known?" he demanded.

Rebekka stared at him blankly. She tried to rise, but felt too nauseous to move. Instead, she gripped her legs more firmly.

He was unyielding. "Don't play innocent with me, Rebekka. How long have you known you were pregnant?" She didn't reply, and he slapped the wall with his open palm. "I can't believe it! I've been here twice a day since . . . twice a day!—and I never guessed!"

Rebekka squeezed her eyes shut, allowing new tears to fall. The tears turned to sobs. Releasing her hold on her legs, she clenched her fists and rubbed the pulse of her wrists over her wet eyes.

"It was that day," she said finally without looking at André. "I suspected before, but there have been so many disappointments these last few years that I wanted to be sure before I told Marc. I'd just come from the doctor's . . . Ohhhhh!"

Rebekka curled into a miserable ball on the floor, the position in which she had spent so much time these past two months. She did it without thought, perhaps as a subconscious effort to protect her unborn child. Her sobs came heavily and continuously, until she wondered if she would cry herself into nothingness.

Strong arms encircled her, and before Rebekka realized what was happening, she was cradled against André's chest. "Shush now. It'll be okay," he murmured.

She wasn't comforted. "He'll never know. I mean, not so that he can be involved. He won't be able to see our baby grow, play tiger with him as your dad did with you guys, or . . . or anything." Her sobs became a wail. "Oh, why did it have to happen?"

André didn't answer, seeming to understand there could be no answer that would satisfy her. He carried her into the bedroom and laid her on the bed. "Try not to move," he ordered. Rebekka didn't feel she could move so obeying wasn't too difficult. She couldn't remember feeling so sick during her entire life.

Shortly, André returned with a bed tray. Rebekka pried open one eye and groaned, "I can't eat that sandwich."

"Of course you can't eat that sandwich. It has too much of that gourmet mustard you like so much. It's too tasty for an expectant mother. You have to eat differently now. At least at first. Here." As he lowered the tray, Rebekka saw a plate of dry toast and a mug of warm milk. "Eat up," André said. "Or do you want me to feed you?"

What she really wanted to do was throw it at him, but something in his eyes forbade such an action; he just might actually follow through in his offer to feed her! So she brought the toast to her mouth and chewed steadily without stopping, following the bread with sips of warm milk. Miraculously the nausea began to subside.

"You have to eat small meals more often," André told her from where he sat at the foot of the bed. "And begin *before* you're actually hungry. If you wait until your stomach's growling, it's way too late. And in the morning, you need to eat a few crackers or something before you even try to get out of bed. Keep them on the night stand within reach."

"I know all that!"

"No you don't. Or you would have done it."

"That's because . . . " Rebekka couldn't finish.

André's eyes become sympathetic. "Oh Rebekka, I know it's been hard and I'm sorry. But you should have told us about the baby. Marc's baby." After a moment of silence, he added wistfully, "Marc would have been so excited."

"*Is* excited," Rebekka corrected. As if that changed things. Marc could be as excited as he wanted in heaven, but her baby still wouldn't have a father on earth.

André was apparently thinking along the same lines. "We'll all pitch in," he said, lifting his right shoulder in his customary shrug. "That baby has four uncles, two grandfathers, and a host of older cousins. He'll be just fine."

Rebekka knew that but her heart ached for Marc and for what they had lost. She sighed wearily. "Thank you, André. You've been great."

"I'm gonna be here, Rebekka. I promised Marc."

That stung, though she didn't know why. She spoke before she thought the words through: "I wonder if he would have asked you to take care of me if he knew that you were the reason I broke our engagement."

Immediately Rebekka wished she could take the words back. Tears gathered in her eyes, and this time they weren't for Marc. André had been nothing but honorable, and she had no right to say such things.

André regarded her with the air of one whose conscience was clear. "I told him that day," he said, "but he already knew. He'd guessed. No, don't get all upset. He knew you loved him. He knew if there had been something important to tell him about us, you would have told him. And he didn't blame me for . . . caring for you."

"You didn't really—at least not in *that* way." Rebekka remembered too clearly how André had been the one to take himself out of the running, claiming that he was still mourning his wife and that Rebekka belonged with Marc. By doing so, he had helped her realize that she couldn't possibly live without Marc. And so she had married him.

But now I will be living without Marc, she thought. She placed her hand on her abdomen to feel the unborn baby that was now the most important thing in her life.

André looked as though he wanted to say something about her comment, but shook his head. "Look, Rebekka, that's all in the past. We made the decision we did and it was the right one. You can't deny that."

She didn't even try. Two years and eight months wasn't a long time to be with the man she adored, but she wouldn't trade loving him to avoid the pain of his loss. The biggest comfort was that she was sealed to Marc in the Lord's holy temple. They *would* be together in the next life and for the rest of eternity. That knowledge would have to be enough; she would live for that time.

André came to his feet, reaching for the tray. "I think you might try a little salad in an hour or so, or maybe some fruit. Whatever, you must keep eating. The first three months or so is the most common time to miscarry, and you've already lost too much weight."

A new fear leapt to life in her heart. She stared at him, almost hating him for voicing the thought. Through gritted teeth she muttered, "I'm three months now. And I *can't* lose this baby."

"I know."

They stared at each other for a long moment. Standing there, he looked so much like his brother, that Rebekka longed to reach out her arms and ask him to hold her, to comfort her. But it wasn't André she wanted, it was Marc; and out of long habit, she resisted the urge to touch André. With Marc gone, André had to be even further out of her life; she would not betray her husband by encouraging a relationship with his brother.

And what makes you think André would even be interested? a nasty voice sneered inside her head. *He didn't fight for you the last time.* There had been a time when Rebekka would have laughed at such a ridiculous thought, but now everything hurt too badly.

"When is your next doctor's appointment?" André asked, balancing the tray with her empty dishes on one hand.

Rebekka's eyes wandered to the French doors leading onto her balcony. There was no light filtering directly though the sheer curtains and she remembered the balcony caught only the morning sun. *That's right*, she mused. She had always wished it was the other way around: the kitchen should have the morning sun and the balcony the evening rays. She and Marc had joked about it.

"Well? When's your next appointment?" André asked.

I don't want to answer, she thought. But there was really no choice. "I—I didn't make one before I left the first appointment. I wanted to talk to Marc to see if there was a time he . . . could come." She clamped her mouth shut and bit the inner flesh on her bottom lip to stop herself from crying again.

"Well, that's one of the first things we'd better do," he said with false brightness. "In fact, I'll do it myself. Where's the number?"

Rebekka directed André to her address book. He was good at organizing, and she could see it gave him a sense of fulfilling his duty to his brother. That was what she was now: a duty. And she had better get used to it. Even so, André was great to sacrifice so much of his time to help her these past few months. Especially today. If he hadn't forced her to remember that the life of her baby depended upon her taking good care of her body, she might have lost the one thing she had left of her husband.

André returned shortly with the date of a doctor's appointment scribbled on the back of one of his business cards and a small bowl of fresh curd cheese topped with pineapple. As he handed these to her, Rebekka grabbed his hand for the first time in years. "Thank you for everything. I really appreciate it."

An undefinable emotion flared in his eyes before they became hooded and unreadable as if he had put on sunglasses. The hand in hers returned her squeeze. "I'll always be here for you, Rebekka. I thought you knew that."

The words gave Rebekka comfort, but also a feeling of unease. What would Marc say about her holding his brother's hand in the bedroom they had shared? Yes, it was an innocent gesture, but why did his touch suddenly disturb her so?

He's only stayed this long for the baby, she thought. *And next week when Raoul moves in, I won't need André so much. Maybe not at all.*

She tried to pull her hand away, but André held on. He seated himself on the edge of the bed. "Remember when Claire died in the hospital and no one in the family knew yet? You stopped by to see me. I don't know how I would have gotten through that time without you. You were like a light in the darkest of nights. I hope I can be that for you."

She drew her hand away, smiling, but feeling extremely uncomfortable. "I appreciate that. And thank you for the food," she said, hefting the bowl of cheese and pineapple. "I'll eat it right now. And then afterwards I think I'll take a nap." She snuggled into the comforter, although with her pregnancy she was feeling rather warm. "Tell the girls hi for me, okay? Shouldn't you be picking them up?"

André glanced at his watch. "Mom got them from school today. I'm supposed to pick them up at her house in a while, though. Then we're all going to the train station to get Thierry. He's coming home to visit this weekend."

This was a topic Rebekka felt safe in pursuing. "How's he doing? Not grade-wise—he's always been a good student and I'm sure college hasn't changed that. But what about spiritually? I know you worry about him." Thierry, André's adopted son had joined the church at fifteen when André had first received guardianship of his nephew, and though Thierry seemed to have a strong testimony, there was always the chance he wouldn't make the right decisions once he was away from home.

André's smile was genuine. "Really good. It seems he's found some friends who respect our beliefs. If all goes according to plan, I think we'll have another missionary in the family next year."

"That's wonderful! We haven't had one since Louis-Géralde came back." Rebekka lifted her fork and paused halfway to her mouth. "Well, tell him I said hello and that I'll see him at church on Sunday." She looked down at her fork pointedly.

André took the hint. "Okay, I'll leave you to eat and rest, but I'll give you a call later to see if you need anything."

"I'll be fine." She lifted her chin slightly in challenge.

He grinned, very much like Marc would have done. "I know. But I'm still going to call."

Without warning, he bent and kissed her on the cheek. There was nothing untoward in the action—in the years before her marriage he had kissed her in that way a million times in greeting or in parting—but it was the first time since he had done so since her marriage to Marc. Her cheeks felt hot and tingled with his touch.

"See you," he said. "I'll let myself out and lock up. Don't worry about it. And try to think positively, okay? It's good for the baby." With a wave, he was gone.

Rebekka's hand touched her burning cheek. What did it mean?

She looked at the ceiling. "I'm being such an idiot, Marc, aren't I? André's only doing what you told him to."

Blinking away the fresh tears forming in her eyes, Rebekka focused on her unborn baby. She would do her best for him, even if that meant she would have to eat all day and restrain her grief. Her life was basically over; the baby was what mattered now.

* * *

André found it difficult to leave Rebekka. Her voice, her demeanor, her every expression held the unmistakable mark of tragedy. He wanted to comfort her more than he had ever wanted to comfort anyone; and perhaps there was some part of him that craved her comfort just as strongly. But if he took her in his arms, he didn't know what might happen. Only the years of self-discipline had allowed him to maintain a proper distance.

Marc's dead. He asked me to take care of her, to make her happy.

That doesn't mean to fall in love with her.

But if she loved me, then maybe I could make her happy.

The idea of falling in love with Rebekka was ludicrous. André had already loved her for years, first as a close friend, then as a future sister-in-law, and finally as something more. That "something" had almost caused a break up between Marc and Rebekka just before their marriage. And it was the same "something" that had increased his loneliness these past years—though he hadn't recognized it until now.

"I love her," he whispered. Even to himself his voice sounded amazed. He had been fighting the emotion for weeks now, but despite his efforts the feeling had only deepened. So help him, even now that he knew she was carrying Marc's child, he loved her. Perhaps even more. Never since Rebekka's marriage would he have even considered attempting to come between her and Marc. But with Marc's death everything was suddenly different.

He asked me to make her happy. He entrusted her to me.

I wonder how Rebekka would feel about that? Could she care for me again—perhaps even love me? I would be good to her and her baby. I could love him as my own. And I would always be there whenever she needed me.

The more he thought about it, the more it seemed the only way he could properly do as Marc asked was to marry Rebekka and become a father to her child. It was simple. Surely Rebekka would agree, and he would be free to give her all the love building in his heart.

Doubt crept over him. Was he taking advantage of the situation? Was Rebekka even interested in him as someone other than a brother? She had loved him once to some degree but had chosen to marry Marc.

You urged her to, he thought. At the time he felt there was no other choice. She had loved Marc so deeply and for so long. They'd shared more together, had more time to build a relationship, and André had realized that eventually he would lose her to Marc. Ultimately, the choice had been whether he would lose his brother as well. That was no choice at all. He would have given his life for Marc—what was a little loneliness? Besides, the confusion in Rebekka's haunted eyes had eaten into his heart. Giving her up was the only way he could help her. There had been nothing else he could do.

But now he had a second chance—and what he had come to believe was his brother's blessing. Or was he fooling himself? How well had he known his brother after all? *Yes, I'm sure*, he told himself. *I've replayed our conversation a million times in the past months and I think—know— that he wanted us to go on.*

All the way up the elevator to his parents' apartment, André thought about how soon it would be proper to ask Rebekka to marry him. Should he confess that he loved her, or let her think he was doing it to fulfill Marc's last request to make her happy?

And what if I can't make her happy? he thought. *What if she never gives me a chance? Oh, why do I feel so inadequate?*

On the fifth floor, his mother Ariana opened the door with her customary smile. "Hello dear, you're a little early. How did work go?" She offered her cheeks for his customary kisses.

"I was at Rebekka's."

Ariana's smile became wistful. "How is she?"

"Not good, but I think she'll pull through."

"It is very difficult for her . . . for us all, but mostly for her." Ariana wiped a tear from under her eye. "The girls are in the TV room doing their homework. Come on."

"Wait." André put out a hand to stop her. "I need to ask you something."

His mother's brown eyes met his. There were more wrinkles in her face than he remembered, and he wondered how many private tears she had shed for Marc, the third child she had buried over the many years of her life. But there was hope in those wise brown eyes as well, and that was enough for him.

"I think Marc wanted me to marry Rebekka," he blurted, feeling oddly like an awkward teenager again with his first crush.

"Oh, have you talked to him?" She spoke seriously, as though she talked to Marc every day.

"It was before he died. He knew about how Rebekka and I . . . well, how we felt about each other."

Ariana's brows arched in surprise. "I know you turned to Rebekka after Claire's death, and that you thought you might love her. But that was a very vulnerable time for you. Are you sure you love her now?"

André was loath to admit the truth—loath to admit how much his feelings for Rebekka had grown in the past two months. Just as he would never admit to anyone how much he had suffered when Rebekka had chosen Marc nearly three years ago. If he made such confessions, perhaps they would realize, as he suddenly had, that he had continued to care for her all along—a realization that made him starkly uncomfortable, though he didn't know why. After all, Marc was gone and André had never betrayed him.

"Well?" Ariana pressed.

"What difference does it make?"

She drew herself up to her full height. Though she only came up to André's chin, she was impressive. "Every difference in the world, André. And if you have to ask, then you'd better think about it some more. Marriage is not something to be entered into lightly. Regardless, there's a lot of time to decide these things."

"But there isn't. Rebekka—" He broke off, knowing Rebekka's secret was not his to share, though the existence of Marc's baby would bring joy to his mother and the whole family.

"Rebekka what?" Ariana waited in silence.

André shook his head. "Nothing."

"Let some time pass," Ariana counseled. "Don't rush anything. Rebekka needs time to heal. So do you. I know you miss Marc very much and want to do what he asked, but if you do make such an important commitment, you have to do it because you want to, not because your brother asked."

André didn't want to listen, though his mother had never steered him wrong before. Yet had he really any choice? While Rebekka was in a sense an available woman, he felt trepidation at pursuing her. Even if he could express his true feelings—the ones that seemed to grow stronger each day—he wasn't sure she would ever accept them, much less agree to marry him. And he couldn't go through that kind of rejection again. He just couldn't.

"Rebekka gave Marc's books to Brandon," he said, changing the vein of conversation.

"Good, that's a step." She started walking toward the kitchen. "That reminds me. Do you still have those boxes of clothes Claire saved from when the girls were little?"

He lifted a shoulder as he followed his mother. "I suppose they're still down in storage at our building, but I haven't been down there for years. They'd be pretty old. We should have given them away a long time ago."

"Well, Marie-Thérèse needs them now, and since we have time maybe we can stop by your place and get them and then go by her apartment before we hit the train station to pick up Thierry."

"Marie-Thérèse? What would she . . . she's not pregnant, is she?"

Ariana sighed. "Unfortunately no, but she has agreed to take care of two little girls for a few days until they can find them a good foster home, and the children don't have any belongings. The girls and I have already collected a box of toys for them from those I keep around here for grand-kids. That'll do until we can make it to the store. Josette did go buy pajamas for them, but I thought if your girls' old things fit, we might as well pass them on as well."

"I bet we could find a few other clothes and toys in the apartment," André said. "The girls have been growing like weeds lately."

"Well, I doubt anything they wore recently would fit. The oldest is only four and Marie-Thérèse says she's more the size of a three-year-old. Just a little bigger than Josette's David—and he'll be three in December."

Ana and Marée chose that moment to come running into the kitchen. They both hurled themselves at him. "Daddy, we're going to give our old stuff to a little girl, did you hear?" Ana said, voice full of excitement.

André hugged his daughters, who were the same size though a year separated them. As always, looking at them, with their dark hair and turquoise eyes, reminded him of their mother. There was no pain now in the constant reminder, though once it had been difficult.

"I want to give her my doll with the blue dress," added Marée. "Is that okay?"

"I think giving her your doll would be a wonderful thing to do." André kissed them on each cheek, remembering a time when he had been able to pick up both girls at the same time and "fly" them around the room with ease. Since Ana turned nine and Marée eight this year, the custom had fallen into disuse. All at once he missed it acutely.

"I want to give her something special, too," Ana said. "Only I don't know exactly what yet."

"We'll think of something." André was glad to have this to occupy his thoughts—glad for anything other than the vision of Rebekka lying alone in her room with her enormous grief and her unborn, fatherless baby. "Come on, ladies. Let's go."

Chapter 4

Marie-Thérèse sat down on the floor by the table, wondering what she was going to do. "Don't you want to come out now, Celisse?" she asked. "It's more than time for bed."

No reply.

Marie-Thérèse rubbed her nose thoughtfully. The past few hours had been filled with constant commotion, and this was the first moment of quiet. The rigid, organized part of her had been working overtime finding clothes for Celisse and her baby sister, organizing sleeping arrangements in their three bed-room apartment, and trying to convince Celisse that she was safe.

Still the child hadn't come out from under the table. Brandon had no success, and Marie-Thérèse had let her stay, thinking perhaps her sister, Josette, could do better. Josette was the mother of five boys and Marie-Thérèse figured she knew more about small children than almost anyone. Josette was as easy-going as Marie-Thérèse was nervous and uptight—especially where children were concerned.

Josette had arrived before dinner with the new pajamas she had purchased for Celisse. Marie-Thérèse's parents, her brother André, and his two daughters had also come, bringing toys and clothes for Celisse and the baby. Celisse refused to budge from her sanctuary, so Ana and Marée went under the table to give her a doll and a new brush. Celisse showed no interest, though she didn't cringe around the girls as she had when Brandon tried to coax her out. Ana and Marée had to content themselves by playing with the baby and taking turns giving her a bottle. After a short while, they left with their father and grandparents to pick up their adopted brother at the train station.

Josette had left with them, also having failed to communicate with Celisse. "I think it really has to be you," she said on her way out. "I bet she understands that you're taking care of her."

Marie-Thérèse didn't remind Josette that the children would only be with her until Monday. She couldn't even think about that; the probability of Celisse's being transferred between various foster homes nearly broke her heart.

In the end, she had let Celisse stay under the table until bedtime, even serving her three helpings of dinner there. But now it was time for bed and Marie-Thérèse couldn't just let the girl sleep on the floor, could she?

Making a quick decision, Marie-Thérèse crawled under the table and gathered the stiff little body in her arms. A acid smell of urine hit her, but Celisse wasn't wet so the smell must be coming from either her clothes or her hair.

She took Celisse to use the restroom. When she tried to help her with her pants, Celisse fought her, pushing away her hands and uttering a high, thin wail that pierced Marie-Thérèse's heart. All thoughts of giving Celisse the bath she desperately needed fled from her mind. Maybe tomorrow would be soon enough for that; maybe by then Celisse would trust her a little more. Marie-Thérèse compromised by setting the child down in front of the toilet, telling her to use it, and pointing out the new pair of pajamas Josette had purchased. Then she waited outside the door.

When the toilet flushed, Marie-Thérèse waited a little longer for Celisse to change before going inside and showing her where the soap and water was. The little girl didn't appear to know what to do with either so Marie-Thérèse opted for wiping her hands with a soapy cloth as she had done for dinner.

She carried Celisse to Brandon's room since he had volunteered to sleep on the couch. There, they had already installed a plastic sheet, fresh bedding, and a safety rail borrowed from Josette since Brandon's bed was so high. Celisse lay rigidly in the bed where she was placed, and when Marie-Thérèse checked on her later, she was asleep in exactly the same position.

The baby slept in the bassinet Josette had also brought. Marie-Thérèse and Mathieu planned to take turns with her during the night, but she was remarkably quiet—too quiet. In fact, she had cried just once since she had arrived and Brandon had quickly fixed that with a bottle. Marie-Thérèse suspected that the unnatural quiet was a sign of neglect. Why cry out if no one was there to offer comfort? Perhaps this baby had learned her lesson already too well and only hunger drove her to utter a sound. It was a wonder she had cried enough to alert the neighbor at all. If a few more days had gone by . . .

Marie-Thérèse knelt down to pray, forcing the thoughts from her head.

* * *

On Saturday morning, Marie-Thérèse hummed as she prepared her family breakfast. At last she stood back and surveyed with satisfaction the array of food she had gathered—juice, milk, yogurt, fresh fruit, and the still-warm bread Brandon had brought back a few minutes ago from the corner bakery. Something in this assortment ought to appeal to Celisse. Normally, Marie-Thérèse didn't bother making breakfast as each member of the family had different rising times and liked to eat whatever appealed to them, but today she wanted them to eat together.

"Brandon, tell your sister to come to the table, would you?" she called into the sitting room where he was watching television.

Larissa hadn't come out of her room the night before, not even for dinner or to ask to go out. Marie-Thérèse hoped a night of going hungry had done something for her attitude. Mathieu had talked to her last night and explained that Celisse and her sister were only at the house temporarily.

That alone should have made her happy, Marie-Thérèse thought with sigh. Just when life was going smoothly, something else had to come up. First Marc's sudden death and now these helpless children.

Marie-Thérèse felt guilty as the thought came. She would only have to deal with the situation until Monday, but the unfortunate Celisse would have to live with her hurt for a lifetime.

Easing open the partially shut door, Marie-Thérèse tiptoed into Brandon's room, not planning to awaken Celisse if she was still asleep. The bed was empty.

"Celisse?" Marie-Thérèse called when she didn't immediately see the child. She checked under the desk and in the closet before she became worried. Had Celisse somehow slipped out of the apartment unseen? Marie-Thérèse immediately dismissed the thought. She could be anywhere in the apartment. Perhaps she was with Mathieu and the baby. Or with Larissa. She could even be watching TV with Brandon, although she didn't seem to like him at all.

As she went toward the door, a rustling sound under the bed caught her attention. Marie-Thérèse dropped to her knees. She hadn't thought of looking under the bed since the space was so small. "Good morning, Celisse," she said, trying to sound happy. "I'm glad you're awake. Do you feel safe under there? Is that why you're there? Don't worry. That's perfectly okay. But guess what? I have some breakfast for you. I have fruit and yogurt and fresh bread, and juice. And milk. If you want, I can put some chocolate in it for you. How does that sound?"

Celisse didn't speak, but simply watched Marie-Thérèse with her sober blue eyes. A lump came to Marie-Thérèse's throat. "Look, honey,

I'm going to help you come out from under there, okay? I'm not going to do anything but take you into the kitchen to eat. All right?

"My, how did you get in there?" she said, lifting part of the bed to pull Celisse out. "Hey, maybe next time you could go under the desk instead. I could put a sheet there to make it like a secret hiding place. You would still feel safe, I bet."

Celisse made no reaction, so Marie-Thérèse put her on the bed and pulled off the top sheet. She folded it and put it over the front part of the desk. "See? Like this. That way it's your own little private space, and you can go there whenever you want. Brandon won't need his desk." There was still no reaction from the child, but Marie-Thérèse tried not to feel deflated. Celisse had been severely abused and it would take time for her to trust an adult again. "Well, let's go eat."

She stopped in her room to tell Mathieu she was ready for breakfast. He was lying prone on the bed with the baby on his chest. "Look! She's raising her head, watching me. Did you ever see anything so cute?"

Marie-Thérèse laughed and sat down at the edge of the bed. In her arms, Celisse stiffened. "It's okay," Marie-Thérèse murmured. "Mathieu is good. He would never hurt you."

Mathieu sat up, his black hair tousled from the pillow. "Hello, Celisse. How are you this morning?" He reached out a long-fingered hand to touch her arm, but she recoiled, burying her face into Marie-Thérèse's shoulder.

Marie-Thérèse tightened her hold on the child. "Don't worry, he won't hurt you. Come on, just say hi."

"No, don't make her." Mathieu settled the baby into a crook of his arm. "Celisse, we will never force you to say anything or to let anyone touch you."

"Well, except to get you out from under the table to eat." Marie-Thérèse made her voice light. "So let's go have breakfast."

"Breakfast?" Mathieu raised his eyebrows.

"Yes. We're eating breakfast together this morning."

"Good." He arose, bending briefly to plant a light kiss on her lips. "I guess, we might as well get used to not being alone," he teased, black eyes reflecting the light from the window.

"Only until Monday."

He sighed. "That's too bad. I kind of like having them around."

Marie-Thérèse stared at him. "Better not let our daughter hear you say that."

He shrugged and looked at the baby in his arms. "I didn't remember what it was like, caring for a baby."

"I know," she answered softly.

"Maybe Larissa wouldn't mind. It's been a long time since we thought about adopting."

"You can say that after how she acted yesterday?"

"You're right. But let's just wait and see, okay?"

Marie-Thérèse shook her head. "No, Mathieu. We made our decision."

"We made it once the other way, too. Things can change. I'm only saying we should remain open to possibilities."

Marie-Thérèse started for the door. "Pascale will be here on Monday. I don't think Larissa will change before then." She looked back over her shoulder. "Or me."

"What does *that* mean?" Mathieu came after her.

"Please, not now." Marie-Thérèse's head dipped toward Celisse. There was no telling how much of their conversation she understood.

"Okay, but this isn't finished."

Marie-Thérèse recognized his determination, but hers was stronger. No matter what Mathieu said, she wasn't going to become further involved with Celisse and her sister. From the experiences shared by other infertile couples, she had learned that the foster care program was even more dangerous emotionally than adoption, and Marie-Thérèse wasn't going to be a part of it.

In the kitchen, Brandon and Larissa were already filling their plates with food. "Hey, you guys, wait for us," Mathieu said.

"We are." Brandon poured himself a full cup of juice. "We haven't said prayer yet."

Larissa glanced in Marie-Thérèse's direction, but didn't meet her eyes—a sure sign she was feeling guilty for yesterday's outburst. Maybe Mathieu's talk had made her sorry for Celisse. But all she said was: "We don't have enough chairs."

"That's all right, Celisse can have mine," Mathieu said.

Marie-Thérèse set the child down on it, but she immediately scrambled under the table, huddling against the wall. She was dangerously close both to Larissa's and Brandon's feet since the table wasn't very large.

"Oh brother," Larissa said, rolling her eyes.

Brandon peered under the table. "Hey, Celisse, you don't have to go down there."

Celisse backed away from him so fast that she crashed into Larissa's legs. Larissa's face grew angry, and she kicked her away—not hard, but in obvious annoyance.

"Don't." Mathieu pointed his finger at Larissa, his voice low and calm but deadly serious. "Remember what I told you last night. This child has had enough people abuse her. She *won't* get abuse of any kind from *anyone* in this family. Now apologize this instant."

Larissa's face drained of color. She scooted her chair back from the table and squatted down a foot from Celisse. "Look, I'm sorry. I didn't mean to push you away. It just surprised me. I didn't mean to hurt you."

Marie-Thérèse had thought Larissa's paleness was because she was angry at Mathieu, and humiliated by the forced apology, but her daughter's voice was sincere. Whatever else Larissa might want, hurting Celisse was not something she had planned.

"Hey, I know," said Brandon. "We can all eat under the table. Well, at least partly. We won't fit, but we can sit on the floor and our plates can be under the table. Don't worry, Celisse, I'll stay far away from you."

"Great idea." Mathieu set the baby in her car seat and began pulling things from the table.

Marie-Thérèse grabbed a plate for Celisse. "Here, honey. I bet you like strawberries. I don't usually even have these in the house since Brandon's allergic to them. But they're very good. And how about grapes?" She put some on a plate. "Now something to drink. Would you prefer milk or juice? That's okay, you can have both, although I hope it doesn't give you a stomach ache. And a little chocolate in your milk for good measure—I've never known a kid who doesn't like chocolate milk."

In minutes everyone was seated on the floor, except Larissa who sat in her chair, which was pushed far back from the table. She stared at them as if they had all gone crazy.

"I'll offer the prayer," Mathieu said. He did so and everyone except Celisse and Larissa began to eat. After watching them for a few minutes, Celisse picked up a strawberry and a handful of grapes. She shoved the food down quickly, almost without chewing, getting in as much as possible with each motion. She drank second and then third helpings of the chocolate milk.

Larissa filled her plate and then asked, "May I be excused to eat in my room? I have some homework I need to do."

Marie-Thérèse wanted to say no, but she also wanted to give her daughter as much space as she needed. Glancing at Mathieu, she nodded.

"That's fine, Larissa," he said. "If you need any help, let us know."

"Okay." Larissa went from the room.

Mathieu made a face at Marie-Thérèse. "You think she really has homework?"

"One can only hope. I'll look in on her la—"

"Hey look, Mom," Brandon interrupted. "Celisse here took a strawberry I put on her plate! Maybe she's going to like me after all." His face radiated happiness.

Marie-Thérèse smiled. *But in two more days that will hardly matter,* she thought silently.

When everyone had their fill, Marie-Thérèse said as she always did after meals, "Plates in the sink, and the table—I mean the floor—" she laughed "—needs to be cleared." Brandon and Mathieu started working while she sat down near Celisse. "Are you done?" Celisse handed her the plate. "Good. You want to hang onto that bread? Go right ahead. You can keep it until you're hungry again, though I can give you more whenever you want."

She felt the child's sober eyes on her as she helped with the breakfast clean up. Soon the kitchen was back to normal. "I'm going to take a shower," Mathieu said, giving her a kiss.

"Right now? I wanted to try to give Celisse a bath—if she'll let me." Not for the first time, she found herself wishing for more than one bathroom.

"I can wait. Brandon and I'll take the baby here and watch a little sports or whatever's on TV. Unless you need help."

"No. I think I'd better go this one alone. She doesn't seem comfortable around you yet."

"We gotta give this baby a name." Brandon picked up the infant. "I mean, calling her baby is weird."

"She has a name," Marie-Thérèse said. "We just don't know what it is."

"Oh, Mom. What's it gonna hurt? I just want to call her something instead of baby."

Mathieu agreed. "A name would be nice."

Brandon grinned, recognizing success. "How about Raquel? There's a nice girl at school named that."

"I like it!" Mathieu slapped him on the back.

Marie-Thérèse said nothing as they left the room. *They shouldn't be naming the baby as if she were theirs to name. Even today, Pascale might call with her proper name. Regardless, on Monday the point will be moot.*

With a heavy sigh, Marie-Thérèse knelt again next to the table. "Well, Celisse, at least we know *your* name."

Celisse's blue eyes stared at her steadily without expression.

Marie-Thérèse wished she could take away her pain. It seemed like only yesterday she had been the same age and suffering over the death of her birth mother and the resulting despair of her birth father. There were so many varied emotions in a traumatized child—how could they be identified and dealt with? Marie-Thérèse was grateful she'd had her aunt and uncle—who later adopted her—to help her through the crisis; Celisse had no one. Obviously her mother had done nothing to protect her.

"I know you probably miss your mom," Marie-Thérèse said, reaching for Celisse. "Kids always do . . . despite . . . Well, I'm going to do my best for you. Come on, now. Come with me." She wasn't sure if it was her imagination, or if Celisse came more readily this time. Was her body less stiff? Her face less stern?

Marie-Thérèse carried her down the hall and into the bathroom. Celisse appeared abruptly terrified as she shut the door. Marie-Thérèse hugged her. "Celisse, nothing's going to hurt you. Don't worry, honey. I won't let anything happen to you. I promise."

Celisse said nothing, but clung to Marie-Thérèse stiffly.

Sitting on the edge of the bath with Celisse on her lap, Marie-Thérèse began filling the tub. It wasn't a large jetted tub like the one Josette had installed in her bathroom during her last pregnancy, but it had always served their family well, and it was especially great for small children. When Larissa and Brandon had been young, bathing together had been a highlight of their day . . . and hers.

When the tub was half filled, Marie-Thérèse stood Celisse on the floor and began slowly undressing her. This time she didn't resist, although her body remained rigid. Her underwear were stained with feces as though she didn't know how to wipe herself properly. Marie-Thérèse glanced at Celisse and saw that she was trembling, her eyes wide with fear.

"That's okay," Marie-Thérèse said. "We'll just teach you how to clean that next time. It's not important."

When Marie-Thérèse reached out to her to put her in the tub, Celisse began to cry and shake more violently. "What's wrong, honey? The water's warm, I promise. Look, feel it." Marie-Thérèse had heard of some parents washing their children with scalding or freezing water as a punishment for potty-training accidents. She herself had been tempted to do so with Larissa, but had never given in. Once or twice, though, she had lost control and spanked a three-year-old Larissa for messing in her pants and hiding behind the door. Marie-Thérèse had felt guilty for days afterward, and decided the Spirit was telling her that she needed to find a better way. The lesson was a difficult one to learn—nothing with Larissa had ever been easy.

Had any of this happened to Celisse, perhaps repeatedly? Maybe they would never know.

Gingerly she placed Celisse into the water. The child clung to her hands, tears falling from her eyes. "That's okay, honey, I'm not leaving. We're just going to wash some of this dirt off. Don't worry. It shouldn't hurt."

Pascale had told her that Celisse had been sexually abused and had become upset when the doctor tried to examine her, but Marie-Thérèse wasn't prepared for the marks and lesions she now saw on Celisse's thighs and all over her frail body. Who could do such a thing to a child? She wept with Celisse as she gently helped her sit.

"Does that sting?" she asked. As usual, there was no reply, but the water didn't seem to be causing the child additional pain. Abruptly, Celisse let go of Marie-Thérèse and folded her arms as if she were cold. Her tears stopped but her small frame still shook with occasional silent sobs.

"I know what you need. Some toys. I don't know what experience you've had with water, but here we have fun with it." Marie-Thérèse was reluctant to leave Celisse so she called out, "Larissa! Larissa. Come here, quickly!" Larissa's room was next to the bathroom and she should hear her plea, whereas Mattieu and Brandon wouldn't likely hear her over the television.

Larissa came into the bathroom as Marie-Thérèse was soaping a soft washcloth and carefully cleaning Celisse's back. "Did you call me?"

Marie-Thérèse glanced around. "Yes, could you get a few toys for her?"

"What ones?"

"It doesn't matter. Something that can go into the water. Just pick from the basket of toys your Uncle André brought."

"Okay."

Marie-Thérèse spied something on Celisse's hip that looked like a swollen purple pimple without a head, and was larger than an adult thumb. What could it be? She would have to ask Pascale what the doctor had said when he had examined her. Hopefully, it was only a bug bite of some kind and would go away. Celisse winced as she washed it, though Marie-Thérèse rubbed ever-so-softly. "Just getting clean," she murmured in a soothing voice. "I'm trying to be very careful to not make it hurt, but we must get clean."

Larissa returned to the bathroom with an armload of toys. "How about these?"

"Good. Let's just put them all in."

Celisse stared, her remaining sobs ceasing instantly.

"She thinks we're crazy," Larissa said.

"I know. I bet a lot of things we do seem odd to her."

They were silent for a long time, and then Larissa whispered, "I really am sorry about this morning. I didn't mean to hurt her." Her voice choked. "I just . . . it was a reaction. Mom, how could someone hurt her that way? She's so little."

Marie-Thérèse met her daughter's tearful eyes. "I don't know. I just don't know."

"She'll be okay—won't she?"

"I hope so."

Larissa stayed for a few moments and then left without a word. Marie-Thérèse began to wash Celisse again. When she was finished, she made funny voices and moved the toys around. Once, she even made Celisse smile.

At long last she drew Celisse from the bath, wrapped her in a fluffy towel, and picked her up. "See, that wasn't so bad, was it? And tomorrow we'll do it again, toys and all."

Celisse laid her head on Marie-Thérèse's shoulder. Placing her lips briefly on Celisse's fresh-smelling hair, Marie-Thérèse went to find her some clothes.

Chapter 5

Her baby was gone. Vanished. And Desirée Massoni had no clue where to begin looking. For all she knew Benny Tovik had put Nadia up for bidding on the black market.

Desirée wondered what she would do. She knew what she *should* do—inform her estranged husband Raoul Massoni about the baby's existence—though that wasn't necessarily what she would choose. It was much easier to walk away and pretend Nadia had never existed. Benny would gouge a lot of money out of someone, but that didn't concern her; she would eventually get her share from him. What's more, Nadia would have a good home—most likely with rich parents.

Of course, if Nadia's father ever found out, there would be big trouble.

Who's to tell him? I'm the only one who knows she's his.

Nadia should never have happened at all. Desirée knew she should have taken care of it when she had first discovered her pregnancy. But something had stopped her.

What?

Deny it as she might, she knew it was Raoul Massoni who had stopped her from getting an abortion—even if he didn't know it. Though they had been separated six times over the past three years, Raoul retained some hold on her. Maybe it was because he hadn't filed for divorce, and that he always was so ready to believe and forgive her when she needed somewhere to go.

The last time she had left him was seven months ago, when she had been four months pregnant. She had never told him about the baby. He would have made her stay, and she wasn't ready to be a prisoner, though she had every intention to give him the baby when it was born.

When they placed Nadia in her arms everything changed. For a month Desirée could do nothing more than stare at her baby and wonder at the miracle of life. Even now, the memory brought a warm feeling of longing.

Then the reality set in—the daily feedings, the crying, having to find a baby-sitter when she wanted to go out. The outrageous costs. Her parents had given her money, and she had been tempted to call Raoul, though she had already received a large sum from him the week before Nadia was born. She had suddenly realized that no amount would really help; the rest of her life no longer belonged to her.

But at twenty-five she wasn't willing to give it all up.

She should have called Raoul then, but she had been too stubborn. Something inside told her this would be the last straw with him. In her own way, she loved him—and especially the idea of him waiting, faithfully and patiently, for her to come home, while she experienced the best life had to offer.

Desirée loved Nadia, too. At least when she was happy and cooed, or when her friends told her how cute the baby was. So she had clung to Nadia for a while longer. Three days ago a caterer had offered her a temporary job in Paris and she had asked a friend to watch Nadia for the night. But the party was great and by the end, Desirée had met some nice people and had continued the party with them in another location. Only this morning had she remembered about her daughter and come home.

Too late. Nadia was gone, and so was the friend watching her.

Desirée debated silently. Pacing her small apartment, she spied the rattle she had bought for Nadia only last week. One end was a flower, the face of it a child-safe mirror. On the yellow and red handle were the words *Mommy loves me*. Nadia couldn't hold it up yet, but would be able to soon.

Desirée shook the rattle. It made a lovely sound that coaxed smiles from Nadia almost every time. Turning it, Desirée caught a glimpse of her face in the mirror. The heavy makeup around her brown eyes was smeared from her partying and her dark hair was mussed. But what called attention was the tiny shimmer of tears in her eyes.

Holding the rattle abruptly to her chest, Desirée stomped into the bathroom. She would go see Raoul and tell him about the baby so he could find her, but she would do it *after* she had fixed her face.

* * *

Desirée felt a little nervous as she let herself into the apartment she had shared with her husband on and off since their marriage three years ago. It was Saturday morning, and Raoul would likely be home, perhaps even still in bed as it was the only day he didn't have work or church obligations. Every time she returned home, the locks were unchanged and the apartment was always the same.

That's why she felt shocked as she saw the pile of boxes in the entryway. Moving boxes. Anger flared through her heart. *How can he do this to me?*

Raoul came from the hall, carrying another box. He looked the same—tall with broad shoulders, auburn hair short around the base of the hairline and slightly longer on top, and attractive gray eyes that widened as he saw her. "Desirée." With the word came the familiar emotions she saw in his face whenever she came home after a separation—hope, longing, desire. Maybe that was why she continued to come.

"Hello, Raoul." She waited until he set down the box before hugging him. Out of habit, she held onto him longer than she should have. He didn't push her away, and that took the edge off her irritation at the array of boxes. "Are you going somewhere?" she asked, drawing back, but not releasing him completely. She had forgotten how tall and handsome he was and how appealing his good-boy image.

He regarded her quietly a long time before replying. "I'm moving. I didn't think . . . I mean it's been seven months since you came around. And more than two since you called. I didn't know if . . ."

"If you would ever see me again?" Desirée frowned, mostly to see his reaction, but also because she didn't like to think of him not being here.

"Marc died," he said, as if that explained everything.

"Marc?"

The muscles in his jaw tightened and annoyance entered his voice. "One of my partners, my sister's husband—Rebekka's husband. You remember Rebekka, don't you?"

"Of course." Desirée didn't have anything against Raoul's sister, though they had never been friends. It all boiled down to religion, of course. Rebekka was as stuffy as Raoul in that regard. "And I know who Rebekka's husband is. That's too bad. He was a nice guy." Yes, a nice guy who had given her money on more than one occasion during her pregnancy when she hadn't dared to approach Raoul.

"She's taking it rather hard. She loved him so . . ." Raoul shook his head, searching for a word that fit. "Much. Anyway, I want to be there for her."

"As she always is for you," Desirée said tritely.

Her tone was lost on him. "Exactly. So what about you? Why are you here?"

She stepped closer to him. He watched her without speaking, as though waiting for the words he longed to hear. He wanted her back, she could tell that, but there was a difference this time. Normally when she appeared, he would beg her to return. The last time he had required her to make promises she hadn't kept, but he had still begged. This time he only waited.

Footsteps sounded in the hall, coming in their direction. Desiré heard snatches of a melody sung by a woman's voice. She came into view, a woman with straight, shiny black hair to her shoulders, and though her size and most of the rest of her features were average, she had a beautiful smile and hazel eyes that fairly leapt with vitality. Desirée didn't know her, but recognized her type immediately: wholesome and without guile, and likely a member of Raoul's church, or some similar religion.

Desirée felt helpless to look away. Anger and jealousy surged to life in her heart.

The wide smile on the woman's face faded into uncertainty. She held up hands clad in yellow rubber gloves. "Sorry if I'm interrupting." Her eyes scanned Desirée, obviously not happy to see her there. "I'm pretty much done with the kitchen, Raoul. Would you like me to start on the bathroom?"

Raoul smiled at her with an open, unguarded expression, one Desirée hadn't seen in a long time. "Thanks, Valerie. That'd be great. I don't know what I'd do without you."

"It's nothing." But the young woman didn't leave. Instead, she dipped her head toward Desirée.

"Oh, I haven't introduced you, have I?" Raoul said quickly. "Valerie, this is my, uh, wife, Desirée. And Desirée, this is Valerie Bernard. She's a secretary at work. Well, more than that, actually. I think her new title is office manager. She about runs the secretarial department now. Without her, we'd all be lost."

"Pleased to meet you," Valerie said. She sounded nice enough, but Desirée detected disappointment in her eyes.

Desirée gave her an insincere smile. "And you. But if you'll excuse us, my *husband* and I have private things to discuss."

Valerie's smile faltered. "Of course." She turned and disappeared down the hall.

"You didn't have to be so rude," Raoul said. "She's here to help me, you know."

"Yeah, right. Since when are you on a first-name basis with all the lowly secretaries? Face it, the only help she wants to give you is finding a replacement for me."

Raoul bristled. "She is not! There's no one more sweet and giving than Valerie. No one! And in all the years she's worked for the company, our relationship has never been anything but professional. Besides, what would you care? *You're* certainly not up for the job of being my wife." There was a tense silence as they stared as each other. Desirée wanted to slap his face, but she stifled the impulse when he added, "Are you?"

The temptation was there. She could promise to stay—promise him anything he wanted and they could have a few months together before he started talking religion and she got itchy feet. By then she would have all the funds she needed stored up for the future. She wouldn't even have to tell him about Nadia.

Desirée closed the space between them and kissed him. The passion was there as it always was—strong and lasting. Her arms crept around his neck. "We can make it work," he muttered. "We *will* make it work this time."

Sure, whatever he wanted to believe. Maybe she even believed it a little herself.

The kiss deepened, and Desirée was consumed with her feelings for her husband. She really did love him! She shook her purse from her arm and let it fall to the ground.

The rattle in the purse made its customary noise. She wanted to ignore it—she silently cursed herself for bringing it along. Without that reminder it would have been so easy to tell Raoul whatever he wanted to hear. Of course then she would never know what happened to her daughter.

She pushed away from him almost violently. "What?" he exclaimed.

"I'm not staying," she told him stonily. "I came only to tell you something."

Retrieving her purse from the floor, she dug into it and extracted the rattle and a bent photograph. "You have a daughter. I named her Nadia. She's two months old this week."

Raoul blinked at her in disbelief. Then the rush of questions began. "Where is she? How come you didn't tell me! But this is wonderful news! Oh, I can't believe it! Come on, take me to her!"

"I don't know where she is!" Desirée nearly screamed the words. "I went to work and left her with a friend in my apartment building. She wasn't there when I got back—I can't find Nadia or my friend." Tears built in Desirée's eyes, and for the first time since her daughter's disappearance she was close to losing control. "I think she might have been sold on the black market. My friend and I, we know some American guy named Benny Tovik. I trusted her, but she might have done it for enough money. She knew I planned to turn her over to you anyway."

"I can't believe you!" Raoul voice was full of hurt, and worse, anger. "How could you do this to me! To our baby! After how much I've loved you, and how hard I've tried to make you happy! All these years I've been hoping you would come back to stay, that we could make something of our relationship, have a family. But it's not going to happen, is it? You've used me all along!"

"We've used each other!"

"No!" He shook his head vehemently. "Don't even start that! It's not true! I'd give my life for you. But you . . . For heaven's sake, you hid my own child from me when you know how much I want a family." The way he said *hid* made it sound like a dirty word. "You never once had any intention of staying, did you? And now you've . . ." There seemed to be no words to fill his need and instead he grunted his disgust.

Desirée could bear it no longer. "I came, didn't I? I'm telling you! Now you can find her and . . . keep her." She backed away from him, swallowing hard against the sobs that came to her throat. "I could have gotten an abortion, you know. I would have if it had been any other man."

She had her hand on the doorknob. "A curse on you and your stupid values! If you could have just relaxed enough to see that my way of life isn't so terrible. We could have been happy! But no, you couldn't do that. Well, I'll tell you something: I'm finished with you so why don't you just marry your prissy little secretary in there and get out of my life?"

With a jerk, she yanked open the door and fled before he could begin preaching religious muck. She didn't need him to find happiness. What she needed was a double shot of whisky. That would put everything into perspective.

She was entering the bar when she realized that at least one good thing had come of the encounter with Raoul. If she knew him at all, he would find Nadia and give her a good home with all the love and material things she could ever need. Desirée would no longer have to feel guilty.

* * *

Raoul watched Desirée leave with disbelief. He had the too-familiar urge to run after her, but his knees had suddenly gone weak. He sank to one of his moving boxes, not caring that it sagged under his weight.

I have a child, he thought.

The circumstances were so utterly different from what he had dreamed of such a discovery that he could hardly decide how to act or what to feel.

I have a daughter.

He had longed for this day. For years he had waited for Desirée to come to her senses. He kept the promises he had made when they married, even knowing that she had not; and the hope that she would change had never left his heart, just as the pleas on her behalf had never left his prayers. He had dreamed of having a family with her.

But not like this.

I have a daughter!

Besides not telling him of their daughter's existence, Desirée had left the infant unprotected. In the past he had excused many things in her behavior but this was too much. A burst of pure knowledge radiated through his being, and all at once he *knew* he had been waiting in vain. *She's never going to change if becoming a mother didn't change her. She doesn't want to change, and until she does—if she ever does—there is nothing I can do.*

His hand still clutched the photograph and the rattle Desirée had given him. The black-and-white photo showed a dark-haired baby with a tiny, swollen face. Her eyes were open only a crack and her face wore a serious expression. He felt at once a kinship for the baby, though he knew that the ensuing months must have changed her features dramatically. Would he even know her if he passed her on the street? His heart said yes, but his mind understood the impossibility.

I must find her.

He would start with the police. If Nadia was being sold on the black market, they would know where to point him, perhaps they would even investigate on his behalf. A private investigator might help as well. His father would know a good one.

Tears came to his eyes when he thought of his parents, Danielle and Philippe Massoni. They had longed for a grandchild, and now they had one. If only he had known before! Already he had missed so many precious hours of his daughter's life. *I'll make it up to you,* he promised her silently. *No matter what, no matter how long it takes, I'll find you.*

The fear that he wouldn't be able to find her at all hovered over his shoulder. But he refused to give into despair. Desirée might be lost to him, but he wouldn't give up on their daughter.

"Raoul? Raoul? Raoul!" Valerie's voice came to him from far away. "Are you okay?" She still had her rubber gloves on, and was carrying a bottle of bathroom cleaner. "I was saying that we're out of sink cleanser and I'll need to go get some more. Raoul, what is it? Please, tell me!"

Raoul silently offered her the picture of Nadia. Valerie discarded her gloves and the bottle of cleaner and reached for it. "I have a daughter," he told her. "She's two months old. And my wife has left me for the last time." He didn't know why he added this last bit, but he felt relieved that he had voiced the thought aloud.

"She's adorable," Valerie murmured. "Where is she?"

Tears in Raoul's eyes nearly obliterated her features. "I don't know, but I'm going to find her." He outlined Desirée's story, and by the time he had finished, Valerie's eyes were also bright with tears.

"I'm so sorry." She put a comforting hand on his shoulder. "Look, you go on and get a search started. I'll take care of things here—that's what you're paying me time and a half for, remember? Don't worry about a thing. I can take care of it all."

Raoul leapt to his feet. "You're right! I have to get going. Thanks so much. I really don't know what I would do without you." He put his hands on her arms and squeezed briefly, then started for the door.

"Wait! You'll need the picture."

He actually laughed. "Oh yeah," he said sheepishly. "I forgot."

"Well, it's not every day you learn you're a father."

Raoul paused at the door. "Did I ever tell you that you're going to make someone a wonderful wife, Valerie? I only wished I—" He broke off, amazed at what he had been going to say—that he longed to go back to being the person he had been before making the horrible, youthful mistake of marrying Desirée. That he wished he had met Valerie before he had met his wife. But how could he say such things when he was still legally married? Besides, his marriage had given him little Nadia, and he would never give her up.

"You're great," he finished lamely.

"Yeah, yeah, yeah." Valerie shooed him away. "Now go!"

Raoul didn't need a second invitation. He grinned at Valerie and hurried from the apartment. As he drove toward the police station, he reached for his cell phone. "Hello, Mother?" he said. "You'd better sit down. I have something important to tell you."

Chapter 6

"Any luck at all?" Rebekka asked her brother on Saturday night when he arrived at her apartment.

Raoul shook his head. "Like an idiot, I got angry and ran Desirée out before I could get any real information. And despite all day banging our heads together, the police haven't been able to help me. All we have to go on is that Desirée gave Nadia to someone in her apartment building and they both know a black-market baby guy—someone called Benny. Problem is, the people who live in her building are not very stable. They're mostly druggies. They come and go for weeks at a time, and sometimes there's a whole bunch of people camping out for parties and the like. The police are interviewing the people they can find right now, and I went over and showed Nadia's picture to everyone I could find with no result. I don't know—it's discouraging." He slumped in his seat and laid his head on the backrest of the sofa.

Sitting on the sofa next to him, Rebekka reached out her hand to rest it on his arm. She toyed with the idea of telling him about her own baby, but couldn't find the words, not yet. Her dream for Marc's child was too personal to share with even her big brother. Besides, she didn't want to exult in her relative good fortune when he was in such turmoil. There would be plenty of time for that later.

"I know. It's so incredible! I have a child—a daughter! I've stared at her picture so long that I feel like I'd know her if I saw her. But then I think that's stupid. The photo is so worn and Mother says babies change a lot in the first little while."

"Still. It's possible."

"But I could just as well pass her on the street and not know her."

"We can't think about that."

"You're right. What I need is to concentrate on finding her." Raoul jumped to his feet and began pacing.

"What can you do? I'm willing to help, if I can."

"I don't want to burden you. You've had enough trials lately."

Rebekka swallowed a lump in her throat. "Marc's dead. There's nothing I can do about that. And though even saying it feels as if I'm tearing out my heart, I have to go on. Your little girl is my niece, and I would like to help. Isn't there something I can do? I can talk to Desirée once we find her."

Abruptly, Raoul sat in the stuffed chair opposite Rebekka. "Dad and I have an investigator out looking now, and he came up with an idea." He leaned forward eagerly, elbows on his knees, hands together. "He's thinking that maybe we could try to adopt through the black market. You now, pose as a couple who want a baby, and try to make our criteria for a baby closely match Nadia. We might find her that way."

"Sure. I'll do anything. But if this Benny guy is Desirée's friend, won't he know you? I mean, she must have a picture of you around somewhere."

"She left most of that stuff at our apartment. But you do have a point. We've gotten back together so many times, he might have seen me with her. Besides, I've been there asking questions—someone might remember."

"André would do it." Rebekka regretted the words the minute they came from her mouth. She needed to see less of André at this point, not more. She needed to depend on herself. "Or Zack or Mathieu," she added.

"Yeah, that would work. And it would be more realistic since you and I have a fairly strong family resemblance."

"You are very good looking," she said, keeping a straight face.

He caught her hand. "I think that's the first joke you've made since . . . Oh, Rebekka, sometimes this world is so much harder than I expected. But we'll get through, won't we? Together, I mean."

Rebekka blinked through her tears. "Yes, of course. And the sooner you move in, the better."

"But what about Nadia?"

"I'd love to have her here, too. I'd bet Mother would be willing to pitch in while we're working. You know how much she's wanted a grandchild. And one of Josette's boys or Brandon could watch her after school if needed. Since I'm working from home, I can supervise."

"What about when your translating job ends? I mean, you've been freelancing for them since you came back from America."

"I'm not worried about that; there will always be new manual editions. Or I can always find another company to work for. Besides, I inherited Marc's stock. I'm one-third owner in your company now, remember?"

There was a painful silence during which Raoul rubbed her hand. Then he said, "I can't tell you how much I appreciate your letting me come to stay here, Rebekka. I really can't be at my apartment anymore. I've realized in the past few days that I only stayed there out of hope. But I'm finally ready to move on—especially after learning about Nadia. Desirée and I are finished for good. I was a little worried, though, about coming here with a baby. I didn't know if you . . ." With his free hand he scratched his head in his customary stalling gesture. "Well, let's just say that today I've been considering going to Mom's instead."

Rebekka felt suddenly panicked. At times during the past month she had wanted desperately to be alone, but now she was afraid of that very thing. "I guess you could if you feel that's best."

"Not really. I just didn't want to make trouble for you. I'd rather come here since you're still willing."

Rebekka gave an internal sigh of relief. "It's decided then. You move in with me and we'll find Nadia together."

"I'll let you know about the fake adoption stuff, but right now I'd better get back to my apartment and see what's going on. I left poor Valerie—you remember Valerie, don't you?—cleaning and packing this morning when I went to the police station. Some of the other office personnel joined her this afternoon. They've probably gone home by now, but if they haven't, I'd like to take them to grab a bite to eat before I head back to meet the investigator. Want to come?"

"Thanks, but no. I'm really tired. Another time, okay? Besides, Mother said she was going to stop by tonight. You know, checking up on me."

"We'll do it another time then—a celebration dinner when we find Nadia." His face turned bleak. "Oh, Rebekka, where do you think she is now? Does she have enough to eat? Is someone holding her and taking care of her? When I think of her so helpless and tiny . . ." He moaned and raked his hands through his hair. "These are going to be the roughest days I've ever endured. I thought it was bad before with Desirée, but now—" He stood and swiftly bent to kiss her cheek. "I'd better get going."

She walked with him to the door. "We'll find her."

"I know." He gave her a smile that was only a hint of his usual self.

Shutting the door, she walked slowly, gingerly to the kitchen. She had begun to walk everywhere like that lately when she was alone, like a seasick sailor on a boat. Riffling through the cupboards, she found a banana and a pack of salted cashews. *It's probably not the best dinner, but it's what appeals to me. At least it should kill this craving for salt. I guess I need to buy some dried beef.*

She had just settled down on the sofa in her living room to eat and to do a little translating work on her laptop when the doorbell rang. Taking a handful of nuts, she went to answer the door. "André," she said, "what a surprise. What's up?" She didn't add how nice it was to see him. No, better to keep things more casual.

"I came to see how you were."

"I'm fine. Much better than yesterday."

"Well, it should get better from here on out. As long as you eat frequently."

"Shouldn't you be with Thierry? I know how you look forward to his time off."

"He's with the girls—took them to a film. I'm meeting up with them later."

"Oh . . . well . . . so, come in, I guess." She backed up and motioned with her hand. She stayed well away from him in case he decided to kiss her cheeks in greeting. At the thought, she felt her face burn.

"I just saw Raoul in the lobby. He told me what's going on."

"It's a shame about what happened with Nadia, but we'll find her."

"I said I'd help with the black market adoption thing. We figured it would require less work if you and I posed as the couple since we both have the same last name already."

"I didn't even think of that."

"Well, they'll probably want to see ID."

She took a breath. "I was just doing a little work in the living room."

"Have you eaten?"

"I'm working on it." She showed him the nuts. "They say nuts have the right kind of fat."

"You need it."

Silence fell as they stood in the entryway. Rebekka imagined huge walls between them, but for the life of her she didn't know what was causing the barriers. When André had called briefly the previous evening to check up on her, they had talked without reservation.

"So how's Marie-Thérèse doing with those children?" she asked.

"Good, I guess. It's a really sad situation. The older child will need a lot of love and care if she's ever to have a normal life. But then, kids do have a tendency to rebound quickly. Even those who are severely abused or neglected. Look at Thierry—he's a prime example."

"What about the baby?"

André lifted his right shoulder slightly. "Seems perfectly fine to me. Josette said she was too quiet. Doesn't let out a peep unless she's really hungry. She's a darling child, though. The girls went crazy over her." He hesitated. "Uh, Rebekka, I've been thinking."

She didn't like the seriousness of his voice. "Should we sit down?" She started forward, but he grabbed her hand, the one holding the oily cashews.

"You didn't tell anyone about your baby, did you?"

"No. And I can't now. Not with Raoul's daughter missing." She lifted her chin. "And it is my decision."

His brows drew in concern. "But they deserve to know—especially my parents. Marc's their son. It will mean a lot to them to know he left behind a child."

She tore away from him, leaving the cashews in his hand. "Don't you think I know that? But as you also pointed out yesterday, I could lose this child. I wouldn't want to get their hopes up for nothing." It was an excuse, and she knew he wasn't fooled. "André," she said more softly, "look, I'll tell them all soon. I just need a little more time alone for me and Marc's child, *my husband's child.* As soon as I tell everyone, it's going to be a shared thing, and rightly so, but I need this time between just me and the baby. You can understand that a little, can't you?"

He nodded, but reluctantly. "There is something else I've been wanting to talk to you about." He rolled the cashews around in his hand.

"What else could there possibly be?"

"I think we should get married."

Her heart slammed inside her chest. "Get—what? Of all the crazy things to say! André, what on earth are you thinking?" She gaped at him.

The muscles in his cheek rippled, as though he clenched his teeth while deciding what to say. "Marc wanted me to take care of you," he responded at last with a voice that was calm and reasonable. "And your baby needs a father. We get along, the girls love you—so why not? We can view it as a type of business relationship—for the good of all."

"André, we don't live in biblical times. A man just doesn't marry his brother's wife anymore and go on as though nothing ever happened!"

"Well, maybe they should! At least the woman would be cared for. Reminds me of the early times in the church where men would marry several widows to take care of them."

"I don't need a man to take care of me!" She walked away from him

and then back again, pacing like a caged animal. Her heart pounded furiously, and emotions welled up in her breast, although she could not
completely identify all of them. Outrage, most certainly, exasperation,
too. Frustration? Maybe. A wish that she could accept such a rash
proposal? No, never that. Or could . . . No! But there was a hint of tenderness in her heart, though decidedly overwhelmed by the immense
yearning for Marc.

She whirled on André, noticing how attractive he was, how thick his
hair, how broad his shoulders, how earnest his expression. "Why not?
Why not, you ask? Because it's *crazy*! People get married because they
love each other, not because of a dying wish! And not because of a baby.
Never for business!"

"But Marc—"

"Is dead!" She took a deep breath and forced a calmness she didn't
feel. "Look, André, I loved Marc—you know that. And I will *never* marry
again."

Now he stared at her. She could tell there was something he wanted
to say, and finally, it came, sounding forced: "You're right. Of course,
you're right. People should marry for love. I just didn't want you to have
to go through this alone."

"I'm not going to." Rebekka felt oddly deflated. The discussion was
too much, too unexpected. "I need to get some rest, so if you'll excuse me
. . ."

"Rebekka, wait!"

She stopped, gazing into his dark, kind eyes and terribly handsome
face, trying to hold back the tears that seemed to come of their own voli-
tion. "Yes?"

"Once before Marc . . . you and I . . . we cared for each other."

She swallowed hard. "You were mourning Claire. I was scared of
losing Marc during his kidney transplant. Remember? That's what we
decided."

"I don't know if I remember it that way."

"Oh? Then how *do* you remember it?"

His right shoulder rose in his unique half-shrug.

"Well, I married Marc," she said slowly and softly.

His face became abruptly rigid. "So you did." Without another word
he turned on his heel and strode for the door.

After it had shut behind him, Rebekka stared at it for long minutes.
What had he meant with his sterile proposal? For a brief flash she remem-

bered quite another André, a man who had stared at her with love and tenderness in his eyes.

It wasn't love, she thought. *He was missing his wife, that's all. And I had always loved him as a friend. That's all it was.*

What she couldn't reason out was why his suggestion of a marriage of convenience had made her feel so dreadful.

* * *

André stalked angrily from Rebekka's apartment. He was stupid to have thought she would accept his idea! Stupid to think that he could walk so easily into her life! As he waited for the elevator, he let off a few punches into the air, working off some of his hurt. Why hadn't he been patient as his mother had suggested? And why couldn't Rebekka care for him?

Once in the street, he got into his car and sat completely still. His emotions teetered inside, though, threatening to overwhelm him. A car passed and André scowled in the sudden bright lights. As the lights faded, his fury and hurt slowly dwindled.

Of course, she didn't accept me, he thought. *What was I thinking? That I could make up for Marc's death in just one sentence?*

Yet it hadn't been just one sentence; he was willing to commit the rest of his life. Still, Marc had been gone only two months, and he should have allowed her more time to heal. While he had been busy recognizing his love for her these past months, she had been struggling to survive her husband's passing. Yes, he missed Marc and mourned his death, but he had the girls and Thierry so the pain was not nearly as intense as what Rebekka endured.

I'm an idiot! If only my emotions didn't keep getting in the way!

But she did feel something for me once, I know she did, his thoughts continued. Had he done the right thing by stepping aside? The question tortured him for the past two days.

And what else could he have done? Rebekka had been torn in two by the decision forced so abruptly upon her, and Marc had been devastated by her withdrawal. *They belonged together*, André thought. *They were happy. I did the right thing.* For love of his brother and Rebekka, he had kept his peace and lived with his choice.

And now?

He wanted to be with Rebekka, to help her with her pregnancy and to be a father to her child and a husband to her. But he had seen the repugnance in her eyes, the impossibility of her letting him into her life. His dream would never come to fruition.

What should I do?

Marc had said to watch over her, and André was determined to do just that. One way or the other, he would see that she was happy—even if it meant losing her again.

At home he dialed his sister's number. "Hi Josette. Look I need your sister-in-law's number in America. Well, I actually need the number of Rebekka's boss from her. No, I can't ask Rebekka, and don't ask me any questions right now, okay? We'll talk about it later." He jotted down the number. "Oh, and please don't tell Rebekka. I don't want her to know— at least not yet. Thanks."

Feeling more unhappy than he had felt since Claire's death, André placed the first call to America. The second would be even harder.

Chapter 7

"You feel safe here, do you?" Marie-Thérèse sat on the floor Monday morning, peeking into the tent she had created under Brandon's desk for Celisse. The little girl lifted her eyes. She didn't smile, but seemed content. Cuddled in her arms was the doll André's daughters had brought her.

Marie-Thérèse wanted to prepare Celisse for Pascale's arrival, but was unsure how to go about it. She adjusted Raquel, as the baby was now called, on her lap and scooted closer. "Do you remember that nice lady, Celisse? The one who brought you here? Well she's coming back today."

No response, except from the baby who began rooting around for something to eat. "I'm going to get Raquel here a bottle and be right back." Marie-Thérèse rose and went into the kitchen. Raquel calmed with the motion.

"You are such a wonderful baby," she cooed. "Aren't you, Raquel, aren't you?" The baby's eyes lit up, and she flashed Marie-Thérèse one of the tiny grins that melted her heart. She felt a little guilty as she played with the baby. Was she ignoring Celisse? Would that happen in the next home they would go to? Would Celisse be left alone to cower under a table while adorable Raquel stole all the attention? And if so, what kind of a relationship could the sisters possibly hope to share later in life?

The phone rang and Marie-Thérèse scooped it up. "Hello?"

"Hi, Marie-Thérèse, it's Pascale. How are things?"

"We're doing fine. Well at least Raquel is. Celisse—"

"Raquel?"

"My son thought the baby should have a name. Anyway, she's adorable. And very good. Everyone loves her."

"Well, since I still don't have any records on the baby, Raquel will do nicely. How is Celisse?"

Marie-Thérèse sighed and sat down on a kitchen chair, holding the phone with her shoulder so she could feed the baby. "She's had a hard life, hasn't she? I never realized how hard. Pascale, how could someone do such cruel, evil things to an innocent child?"

There was a long pause. "I don't know. It's really something I can't get used to either."

"You shouldn't have to."

"I know. But it's out there. A lot more than we'd like to believe."

"About Celisse. I know you've been doing this for a long time and you probably have seen much worse than this, but I think she might need a lot of one-on-one attention. She could get lost in the shuffle—especially with Raquel around."

"I know that. But we have a policy. Families must be kept together if at all possible."

"Then—and I hope you won't mind me saying so—you must find someone who can help her, who will focus on her." Normally, Marie-Thérèse wouldn't have dreamed of telling Pascale how to do her job, but Celisse needed so much and had no one else to speak for her.

"I plan to. In fact, that's why I'm calling."

Marie-Thérèse swallowed the sudden lump in her throat. "You found someone?"

"No. I've got a couple who I believe will work, only I haven't approached them yet. Would you mind keeping the children another week? Two tops. You will be reimbursed for expenses, of course."

"I guess I could do that." Marie-Thérèse didn't stop to examine her emotions, but she smiled at Raquel lying in her arms.

"Oh, thank you. I really appreciate it. I'll be by later this evening with some forms for you and Mathieu to sign. Policy stuff mostly, some personal questions. Nothing major. I really can't thank you enough. "

"Any word from their mother?"

"Not yet. But the police have several leads."

"You'll let me know?"

"Of course."

Marie-Thérèse's neck was starting to ache because of the awkward position of the phone between her ear and shoulderblade, but there was more she had to say. "She can't go back there, you know."

"Don't worry, I'll make sure of it."

"There is something I've wanted to ask you. Celisse has a large purple mound on her hip. Looks oddly like a huge pimple. Didn't used to have a head, but it's changed quite a bit in the past few days. Now the whole top of it is sort of white. And very painful—she cringes if she bumps it or if the waistband of her pants scrapes it. Did the doctor say anything to you about what it might be?"

"No. He didn't. But then there were so many marks on her body and Celisse wasn't exactly happy about the examination. She fought every inch of the way—never seen a child so upset. Not something I want to repeat, but we'd better have her back there if you feel it's something to worry about."

"I think it is. But I don't want to cause her more—wait a minute. I know, my mother has an old friend who used to be a nurse. Retired now. Maybe I could have her come here and check it out. It might be less traumatic. Then if we need to do something more, we can pursue it from there."

"All right. Good." Pascale sounded relieved. "I'll be in touch, then. And call if you need anything. Or let me know when I stop by tonight."

Marie-Thérèse hung up the phone and sat with Raquel in her arms, her tiny gulps the only sounds breaking the peaceful silence. She kissed a soft cheek and breathed in the baby shampoo scent of her fine hair. "Larissa looked a lot like you do," she murmured. "How time passes."

* * *

"Another two weeks?" Larissa screeched. "Good grief, admit it! The woman wants you to adopt them, doesn't she?"

"Larissa!" Mattieu's voice was stern.

"Look what you did, idiot," Brandon put in. "You scared Celisse under the table again. And it took Mom and me forever to get her to sit on a chair! Sometimes you are so selfish!"

Larissa jumped to her feet, nose wrinkling in disgust. "It's not you who'll end up giving up your privacy, dummy."

"What do you mean? I already gave up my room."

Larissa ignored him. "That's it, isn't it, Mom? You'll have your precious new baby—" she motioned to Raquel "—and I'll be sharing a room with not one but two brats who will get into my stuff and mess it all up! Well, I won't have it. I'll run away first. Jolie's parents would let me live with them."

Mathieu stood to face his daughter, fists clenched, but still under control. Marie-Thérèse wanted to scream out at them to stop. Though these scenes were not anywhere near as frequent as they once were, she couldn't bear it when her daughter caused such havoc.

"You are *our* daughter," Mattieu said. "You will not go live with Jolie."

"I'm almost sixteen—not a baby anymore."

"Then please lower your voice. You'll scare the little girls."

"Fine. But I'm going to Jolie's."

Mathieu stepped in her way, just as Marie-Thérèse jumped up from her chair to do the same. "Tonight is family night," he said calmly. "However, we would be glad to have Jolie over for a lesson." Neither Mathieu nor Marie-Thérèse approved of Jolie or understood Larissa's continuing friendship with her. But they tried not to make a big deal out of it—especially as Larissa had finally made a few friends in the ward and with a nice girl who lived on the bottom floor of their building.

Larissa threw him a look of disgust. "No thanks. I'm going to my room." She stomped out.

Marie-Thérèse breathed a sigh of relief. She usually let Mathieu deal with Larissa's outbursts when he was home because he would always maintain his calm, whereas she was likely to become emotional and say things she would later regret. There was nothing more Marie-Thérèse hated than being out of control.

Mathieu put his arm around her. "It's okay, honey. Larissa's a good girl. She's just a little territorial. Once she knows her boundaries, she'll stay in them."

"I hope so."

"I think she was just testing us with that bit about Jolie," he said. "I know for a fact she hasn't spoken to her in weeks. I heard her say so to her friend at church last Sunday."

"That's something, but I just don't understand her. Most girls would love to mother a baby."

"Hadn't you better . . .?" Mathieu glanced toward the table, spread with baked fish and potatoes. But he wasn't looking at the food.

"Celisse." Marie-Thérèse rushed to the table and bent down, reaching for the little girl. For all that Celisse was small, Marie-Thérèse was out of breath when she finally accomplished the task of gathering the unwilling child into her arms. "Hey, don't mind Larissa. She's just a little loud. She's not mad at you, honest."

Brandon stuck his face in Celisse's. "She's mad as in crazy," he said, tapping his temple. "But she doesn't hurt anyone. She's okay, just noisy." He held out his arms. "Come to Brandon?"

Celisse studied him gravely. For the past three days, he had tried repeatedly to get her to come to him, but she had always refused. At least she had stopped cringing whenever he or Mathieu spoke to her. Yesterday, she had actually accepted several toys from Brandon and had allowed Mathieu to hold her hand at church.

Now, catching Marie-Thérèse by surprise, she leaned toward Brandon and nearly fell onto the floor. Brandon's hands shot and caught her. He held her to his chest. "See that's not so bad, is it? I told you—I'm very nice." Brandon grinned at Marie-Thérèse. "She likes me. Cool."

But almost immediately, Celisse pushed to get down. "That's right," Brandon said, unfazed. "Four years old is big to be carried. You can walk by yourself, can't you? Now let's go back to the table and eat. Fish is good. Let's eat it all so Larissa can't have any." He laughed and held out his hand. Celisse put her little one in his and they traversed the few steps to the table together. "There now, sit in my chair. I'll sit on the bucket. Don't worry, I don't mind. You don't have to go under the table."

Mathieu winked at Marie-Thérèse. "Now that's progress. He's really good with her—and determined." He paused a moment before adding, "You know, Larissa's right. If Celisse and Raquel were to stay, we'd really have to move to a bigger place. And buy a bigger table."

"Three bedrooms is plenty for a family. And they aren't—" Marie-Thérèse glanced at Celisse and broke off.

Mathieu took her arm. "Kids, go ahead without us. We'll be back in a minute."

Celisse reached out to Marie-Thérèse, casting a frightened look at Brandon. "Hey, I can watch you," he said. But the child would have none of it. She held her arms out to Marie-Thérèse, her fingers making grabbing motions. Brandon sighed. "You'd better stay, Mom."

So they sat down to dinner. After a while, the conversation began to flow again, as though there had never been any interruption. As usual, Celisse shoveled her food in almost without stopping. When they were halfway done, Larissa came from her bedroom and sat in the single empty chair. No one said anything, but Mathieu smiled at her and Marie-Thérèse passed the dish of potatoes. Celisse stopped eating for a moment to watch Larissa, but then continued without utterance.

The atmosphere became relaxed and Marie-Thérèse felt full of love and thankfulness. She didn't even mind when Celisse went to the bathroom and returned smelling like she had missed her destination altogether. She simply led her back to the bathroom, explained about using the toilet again, gave her a bath, and put her into her pajamas.

After a family night lesson, games, and a dessert, the older children retired to prepare for bed. As usual, Mathieu put Raquel down in their room, while Marie-Thérèse sat on Brandon's bed and read a story to Celisse. The little girl relaxed against her, eyes drooping.

When she finished reading, Marie-Thérèse took a peek at the sore on Celisse's hip, before tucking her in. "That doesn't look too good, Celisse. I wonder what it could be?" She touched it gingerly, and Celisse gave a small gasp and pulled away. "I'm sorry. I know it hurts. We'd better get this looked at, okay?"

"No." It was the first word Celisse had spoken since her arrival on Friday, and Marie-Thérèse felt a small measure of triumph despite its meaning.

"You don't need to be afraid." All at once, Marie-Thérèse felt she was lying. Celisse had a lot to be afraid of, and nothing could change that. "At least," she amended, "not about this sore. We'll get someone to come here and look at it. A nice woman. I'll stay with you every second."

Celisse turned her face to the wall. Sighing, Marie-Thérèse tucked the covers around her, kissed her forehead, and left the room.

The doorbell rang, but Mathieu, already finished with the baby, beat her to the door. "Hello, Pascale," he was saying as Marie-Thérèse came into the entryway. "Long time, no see."

"Yes, it has been awhile. You look well."

"Never better. Marie-Thérèse takes good care of me."

"Well, I won't be but a moment. I know you have a full house."

"We'll need to do this in the kitchen," Marie-Thérèse said. "Brandon's been sleeping in the sitting room so that Celisse can have his room."

Pascale smiled. "He's such a nice boy."

"Yeah. Well, having the television in there helped his decision," Mathieu said. "We have to keep reminding him to go to bed."

"I bet," Pascale said with a laugh as they went into the kitchen. "But that's good to hear. He's a normal boy, that's for sure."

"Would you like to see the girls?" Marie-Thérèse asked. "I mean, isn't that part of your job?"

"Yes, actually, I would like to see them."

"They're asleep, or at least they should be." Marie-Thérèse led Pascale to the bedrooms where both girls were sleeping peacefully.

"They look great," Pacsale said as they shut Celisse's door.

"We try. But Celisse—there's a lot of issues. She really needs some one-on-one."

"Has she responded to you?"

"Yes. But Raquel takes a lot of attention. I'm lucky I have Mathieu and Brandon to help with her while I'm occupied with Celisse."

They were quiet as they returned to the kitchen. Then Pascale asked, "So you really think they should be separated?"

"No. Well . . ." Marie-Thérèse hesitated. "I don't know. Today while my older children were in school, it was sometimes easy to ignore Celisse. She seems content just to hide under the desk all day. And Raquel—well, she used to be really quiet but she's growing more demanding as she realizes that we're here for her. I guess I just wouldn't want Celisse to be overlooked."

"I see." Pascale pulled a file from her bag.

"But then I do know how important it is to keep siblings together," Marie-Thérèse added. "Like you said on the phone today. My little sister and I were adopted by my aunt and uncle when my parents died. But I know I told you that before. I love all my adopted siblings, but Pauline was always something special. Up until the day she died, I considered her all mine. I don't know how to explain it, but having her live in the same house helped me immensely."

"You had a great adoptive family," Pascale commented. "There aren't many people—even relatives—willing to take on two extra children, especially when one has HIV like Pauline did."

"Yes, I did. And maybe if you could find such a situation for Celisse, she could have both the attention she needs *and* a special relationship with her sister."

Pascale nodded. "That's exactly what I'll try to do."

Shortly Marie-Thérèse and Mathieu were filling out more forms than Marie-Thérèse had imagined were necessary.

Pascale scanned the documents as they completed each one. "You know," she said, "it's too bad you couldn't be the foster parents. You really have the perfect profile."

Marie-Thérèse said nothing. She didn't even look at Pascale, though she felt the other woman's eyes digging into her.

"Someone will be by tomorrow for a brief look around, if you don't mind. It's really only a formality since you are doing me such a favor. But they just want to be sure, despite the fact that it's temporary. You know."

"Sure," Mathieu said. "We understand. In fact, we'd be concerned if you didn't send someone out."

When Pascale had finally shut her briefcase and left, Marie-Thérèse breathed a sigh of relief. But it was short-lived.

"You know, we really could move to a bigger place," Mathieu said without warning. "I know I still tend to handle money terribly, which is why you are in charge of our finances, but I think we have established ourselves enough to buy a bigger place. Don't you? I mean, I kind of like how your sister has a separate room for the TV and toys. It would be kind of nice not having that mess in the sitting room all the time. And we could do with a second bathroom. Larissa and Brandon spend way too much time in there. And if we had another bedroom—"

"Three is plenty. And we don't watch that much television."

"No. But—"

"Three bedrooms is bigger than many people have. A lot of people in the apartments around here have only two."

Mathieu pushed his chair closer to hers and took her rigid hand in his. "It's not what others have or don't have. It's a question of what we want and need. There aren't too many people in this country who have more than one or two children." He chuckled and added, "Unless they're members of our church, or maybe Catholic." His expression became earnest. "Moving's not really important to me, but I guess I thought if we did move, maybe we could be a part of these little girls' lives. Larissa might not mind so much if she knew she could keep her own room. I could talk to her."

Marie-Thérèse had known everything would boil down to this. She had felt it all along since the moment she had opened the door to Pascale and let the children into her home. "No."

Mathieu's brows rose in puzzlement. "What do you mean no? I've seen you with Celisse and Raquel. You really care about them."

"They are children of God. Of course I care about them." The pressure in Marie-Thérèse's head was building.

"Then I don't get it."

Marie-Thérèse fought to keep her voice steady. "Larissa. We prayed and we felt it was right not to adopt—for her sake."

"But we prayed before all that and we got the answer to adopt. So maybe it was just a temporary delay. We should ask again."

Marie-Thérèse felt a double agony within her heart. Yes! She cared about Celisse and the adorable Raquel, but . . . "Foster parenting is only temporary. Even if . . . we could lose them."

"We." Mathieu smiled but his voice wasn't triumphant. "You said we. That's a start. But I knew that was what was bothering you. You're afraid of losing them."

Marie-Thérèse blinked back tears. "It's not like adoption. Their mother could reform. She could take them back."

"Or they could die," he said gently. "Like your parents and your sister. Like Brandon almost did when he had that allergy attack."

In her mind Marie-Thérèse traversed the years and landed back at the terrible day by Brandon's bedside in the Intensive Care, not knowing whether he would make it, and wondering if she could endure another loss. Her testimony had wavered, but in the end she had offered him to God . . . and God had given him back to her whole and healthy. After that it didn't seem so hard to forget about the adoption and focus on Larissa and Brandon. In fact, it was easier. Fewer children meant fewer nights of worry . . . and fear.

But she was not ready to admit that aloud. Slowly she said, "We didn't adopt because we decided to focus on Larissa—to save her."

"Yes. Partly." Mathieu's voice was so tender, it made her heart burst with love for him. "But I know you've been afraid. I don't think you've ever really recovered from that scare. Have you? Isn't that part of the reason you didn't want to adopt?"

Marie-Thérèse stared at the tabletop and didn't reply. Mathieu was right; he was always more perceptive than she gave him credit for. Not adopting was her way of protecting herself from further pain—a selfish way, she saw now, given the need that little Celisse had for someone who could love her.

"The way I see it," Mathieu continued, "is that the Lord has given us a great opportunity. It's not something we searched out, but something He sent our way. We owe it to Him to at least pray about any decision we make."

Marie-Thérèse wasn't ready to believe it could be that easy. "Someone else might be better qualified."

"Or not. I think you underestimate yourself—and the rest of us as well. Even Larissa."

"And if we decide to try and then we lose them?" She dragged her eyes up to meet his.

"First things first. We'll pray, okay? I want you to feel as strongly about this as I do. And if I'm wrong, I would like to know. But whatever happens, we'll take things as they come—together."

"You already love Raquel."

He nodded. "Yes. And Celisse, too, though she'll need more time to trust me. But the point is that we have a lot to offer these children. It won't be easy, but the past few days have been really good, despite the confusion and work."

"I know," Marie-Thérèse had to agree. "I have enjoyed them. And Brandon seems to be in heaven having them around. But Larissa . . ."

Mathieu shrugged. "Honey, if it's right, we'll find someway to help Larissa understand. Prayer and fasting and talking things out worked before when she was having a hard time. It can work again. She's really come a long way these past few years." His hand tightened on hers. "I love you, Marie-Thérèse." He leaned forward to kiss her, and she let her arms curl around his neck.

Mathieu was right. She couldn't let her fears stand in the way of helping Celisse—or of following the Spirit. "Okay," she agreed. "I'll do it. Pray, I mean."

"So will I."

Chapter 8

By Monday evening Raoul had moved into Rebekka's apartment. Though he was morose about the lack of information the police had turned up about Nadia, just having him near made Rebekka feel happier. Without Marc the apartment was so lonely. Sometimes the silence was too much to bear—especially now that Marie-Thérèse was no longer making her daily visits. Or André. But she had better not go there.

"Raoul, you don't have to make me dinner," she said, coming into the kitchen.

"Why not? You spent the day working like I did—in between directing the movers with my stuff."

Actually, Rebekka had not worked that day. She had spent most of the time before and after the movers, lying on her bed and trying not to lose her meals. It had been all she could do to drag herself out of bed to tell them where to put Raoul's things. What did get done, she owed to Valerie and the four muscled men who came in the moving van, but she wasn't about to confess that either.

"I had Valerie send most of the furniture into storage," she said, sitting in her chair.

Raoul set a plate of an unidentifiable mixture in front of her. From past experience, Rebekka knew the mess contained baked rice and beans topped by tuna and cheese, though much of it looked as though it had been passed through a grinder. What's more, its pungent aroma immediately made her stomach queasy.

"The private investigator Dad hired has made contact over the Internet with that Benny character Desirée mentioned. At least we think it's him. It took some time to wade through all the agencies and people that seem legitimate, and then he found Benny's name—probably a pseudonym but at least it matches what Desirée said. The PI put in for a baby girl—under your name with a hefty rush bonus attached. We'll see what happens. If all goes well, we'll make an appointment with him this week."

"How will we know if the baby's Nadia?"

Raoul frowned. "That's the hard part. We'll have to get her prints and match those with the ones on Nadia's birth records. Once they're reasonably sure, they can detain the baby and Benny until they can do more tests. Even if it's not Nadia, the police will want to know where Benny got the baby."

"Sounds complicated." Rebekka moved her fork around on the plate, but didn't raise it to her mouth. She kept her face well back from the smell, knowing it said something about Raoul's state of mind that he didn't notice her reluctance.

"Well, if we find Desirée, she can identify Nadia. Or if we could find the friend who was baby-sitting. Only the police have no leads on that either. We don't even know the friend's name. Could be anyone." He took a bite of food but barely chewed before he jumped to his feet. "Look, I'm going to my room for a minute. I'm going to check my computer for messages. The private investigator promised to forward any e-mails he exchanged with Benny-the-baby-seller."

"The-baby-seller?"

"Yes, that what the PI and I've started calling him."

Rebekka waited until he was gone before scooping her mixture into the plastic-lined garbage can and covering it with a few crumpled napkins. No use in worrying Raoul. Then she broke off a thick piece of French bread, tore it open, and placed a slab of mild cheese inside. Taking a large bite, she sighed. Raoul had also brought home an assortment of her favorite cheeses, but she daren't eat them. She was having enough trouble keeping food down as it was.

Yesterday at church had been difficult. André's daughters had insisted she sit with them, and she had agreed, although it made her uncomfortable. Marc should have been at her side, not André and his children. As much as she loved the girls and his adopted son Thierry, thinking of all she had lost made her so angry. Not at God or even at the man who had caused Marc's death, but at André for not *being* Marc. It was stupid and senseless, but the emotions were very real. For the entire length of the meeting, she had avoided talking with André or even looking at him because seeing his face reminded her of Marc.

Oh Marc! The tears came and she discarded her half-eaten sandwich on the counter.

"Still hungry?" Raoul's voice said behind her. "There's a lot more. You don't have to eat a sandwich. Oh, the cheese. I knew you'd like that. Mild? That's not like you. But—" He broke off abruptly. "Are you okay?"

Rebekka bit back the tears. "I'm fine, really. Sometimes—I just miss him." She began to sob and he held her in his arms, much as she had held him the first time Desirée had left him.

After a while she pulled away. "Sorry. I can handle it—mostly. I know that we were married in the temple and that we'll be together forever. But sometimes . . . well, forever is a long time away."

Raoul looked miserable. "I'm so sorry, Rebekka. Is there anything I can do?"

"Just being here is enough. And don't mind me. I'm just emotional. But I can't fall apart so much—I've done nothing but cry the past few months. And it's not good for—for me."

"Marc would want you to be happy."

She wiped her cheeks with both hands. "I know that. Thank you. " She took a deep breath. "So did you find out anything?"

"Actually, yes. Benny-the-baby-seller says he's in town for the week—kind of funny since Desirée seems to think that he lives here in Paris—and that he'd like to meet with you and your husband. The PI suspects that he wants to check out the situation and make sure you're above level before he brings in the baby."

"So when do we meet?"

"On Wednesday. At a hotel downtown."

"I can do that. What time?" She was relieved it wasn't scheduled for tomorrow, which was when André had made her a doctor's appointment—though how he got her an appointment with such short notice, she didn't know. He could be insistent and she hoped he hadn't annoyed anyone. That could make the visit awkward for her. In fact, now she wished she had never agreed to the appointment at all. She didn't want to go alone.

"You'll meet with him at noon. The PI thought that would be the most likely time that André—posing as your husband—could get off work."

"Well, that does seem logical. Would you . . . uh, tell André? I don't know if I'm going to be seeing him before then."

"Sure." Raoul didn't seem to think her request odd.

"Well, I've got a news release to translate." Rebekka moved toward the hall. On second thought, she grabbed her sandwich from the counter.

"Are you sure you don't want a second helping of my tuna surprise?"

"No, actually, I really like this cheese you bought. And it's convenient for working. But thanks for dinner."

He nodded and turned back to the table. Rebekka escaped, wondering how much longer she could hide her pregnancy from him. At times she had an overwhelming urge to confide in him and her parents, but when she thought of the decisions and plans she would be required to make once she made the announcement, she became bitterly depressed. She didn't want to face reality; she wanted to dream about her baby, Marc's baby. About the life they would have had together.

The office was where she felt Marc more than in any other place in the house. Here they had passed many late hours working together, sitting on the couch, sipping hot cocoa, or simply lying lost in each other's arms. Oh, the dreams they had shared!

"Marc," she whispered into the empty room. "I miss you."

Over the long desk hung a large painting: a couple kissing by the Seine River. Every time Rebekka saw the painting, memories flooded her senses. She had just come from talking with André, and he had urged her to go to Marc. After a long search, the river was her last resort. Marc had been there waiting, and she had fallen into his arms. An artist on the parapets had taken their picture and begun to paint them, capturing the joy in her heart more fully than she could have believed possible. Later, they contracted with him to finish and deliver the painting. Next to Marc himself, it was Rebekka's greatest treasure.

Closing her eyes, Rebekka sank into her chair, letting the emotions wash over her. The cheese sandwich was forgotten in her hand. *Steady, steady. Not too much reaction. Remember the baby.* The desperation faded, but the loneliness remained. She switched on her computer, but stared blankly at the screen. Translating the news release from English to French seemed so inconsequential, so utterly purposeless.

After a time, she became aware of the sandwich still in her hand and ate it methodically without enjoyment. For the baby. She had barely finished when the shrillness of the phone rang loudly in the quiet. Deciding to let Raoul answer in the kitchen, Rebekka opened the news release file. She had translated the first sentence when a quiet tapping came at her door. "Come in."

"Uh, sorry to interrupt, but some guy's on the phone asking for you. An American by the sound of it. Can't understand a word he's saying. Except your name."

Rebekka smiled. "Probably Damon Wolfe, you know, my boss. But I told him the release wouldn't be done until tomorrow." She frowned, her hand on the office phone. "I hope he doesn't have more for me. I only just started working again, and I'm not sure how much I want to do."

"Well, good luck."

"Thanks." Rebekka lifted the receiver on her desk. "Hello, this is Rebekka."

"Rebekka, boy, it's good to hear your voice!"

Rebekka didn't speak. After a long moment, she said, "I'm sorry, but who is this?"

"It's Samuel, you know Samuel Bjornenburg from Cincinnati. Technically your supervisor, though we haven't spoken since you ran away to marry that Frenchman." His voice was light and teasing, and immediately an image of the tall, blonde, handsome owner and CEO of Corban International popped into her head.

"Of course, Samuel. Sorry! I didn't recognize your voice for a minute." When she lived in Utah before her marriage, they had dated and had become very close, despite the fact that Samuel wasn't a member of the Church. At one point, she had considered possibly pursuing a relationship with him, but that had only been fleeting, before she realized that her faith in God would not allow her to settle for "until death do you part." Still, she had liked him—a lot—and things might have ended differently if the Lord's inspiration hadn't led her in another direction.

"Rebekka, I know you requested that your assignments come through Damon, given the awkwardness between us since your marriage, but I had to call when I heard what happened. I'm so sorry about your husband. I know how much he meant to you."

Silent tears streamed down Rebekka's face, but she forced her voice not to show them. "Thank you, Samuel. I appreciate that."

"Can I see you?"

"You don't have to . . . America's a long way . . . I'm fine."

"I'm going there this weekend anyway for Damon. A big hospital shindig to promote our joint products. In fact, I'd like you to come, if you would. I think you would make a prettier dinner partner than our other translators, not to mention more intelligent."

Rebekka laughed through her tears; Samuel was nothing if not direct. "Thanks, but I don't know if I'm up to something like that."

"Then to heck with it. We won't go. It was only an excuse. And I'm coming to see you whether you want me to or not. I'll call you when I get in."

"But . . ."

"See you, Rebekka. And take care of yourself. I'm hanging up now before you can protest, so don't be offended."

The line went dead and Rebekka stared at it a full minute before placing the receiver in its cradle. She felt suddenly more tired than she had all day. "I wish you wouldn't come, Samuel," she whispered. "It won't make any difference."

Yet for a moment, she had felt a leap of joy at hearing his voice. What had he been up to in the past years? Why did he want to see her? Had he married? No, he wasn't the type to date while committed to another. But was his invitation a date or just work? *Work*, she decided. And they were friends, so maybe he was simply being kind.

Like André.

Or maybe not.

Rebekka turned back to the news release but couldn't focus on the words. She was so, so tired, though it wasn't late. Maybe she would rest on the couch for a few minutes. She made her way across the carpet and lay down, but a excruciating pain enveloped her entire being as she recalled how much time she had spent there with Marc—talking, laughing, dreaming. She couldn't see because of the pain and wondered if this was how a living death felt.

Oh, Marc, I can't do it without you! I just can't!

Then a warm cocoon spread slowly around her entire body, easing the terrible hurt. She imagined she could almost feel Marc's arms around her, his legs tucked next to hers.

Rebekka shut her eyes and slept.

Chapter 9

Early Tuesday morning, Marie-Thérèse fed Celisse and Raquel as the other children readied to leave for school. Mathieu squat down by Celisse's chair. "Look," he said. "There's a very nice lady coming to see you this morning. She's going to tell us why that bubble on your side hurts so much. She's going to help. Marie-Thérèse will be here the whole time. I know it won't be fun, but be brave, okay? Can you do that for me?"

Celisse nodded once, solemnly, and Mathieu grinned at Marie-Thérèse in triumph. "Let me know, okay? As soon as the nurse leaves."

Marie-Thérèse thought his worry was endearing, but Larissa rolled her eyes. "It's just a big pimple, Daddy. I get them all the time."

"Not this big," Marie-Thérèse said. "It's as big as your nose—just not so protruded. Hey," she added when Larissa punched her playfully on the arm, "I didn't mean your nose was big. I'm just comparing the size. Your nose is the perfect size for a *nose*."

Larissa felt her nose and sniffed. "Yeah, sure." But she was smiling and Marie-Thérèse was relieved. She never knew when Larissa might really take offense and go into a tirade.

"Kids, you'd better get going now. Hurry, or you'll miss your train." She looked at Mathieu. "You too, honey."

Mathieu gave her kiss and started for the door. Larissa and Brandon charged after him.

Marie-Thérèse began to clear the kitchen table. "Well, Celisse. Looks like it's just you and me . . . and Raquel, of course." Celisse made no response, but she picked up her cup and handed it to Marie-Thérèse. "Thank you, honey."

When the doorbell rang a short while later, Marie-Thérèse cast an apprehensive glance at Celisse. "That must be my mother's nurse friend. I'll bet she met Mathieu and the kids as they left the building; they must have let her in downstairs. She's really nice. I think you'll like her. Do you want to come with me to open the door?"

Celisse shook her head and stared at her fingers in her lap.

"Well, I'll be right back then." Marie-Thérèse picked up Raquel and left the kitchen.

She opened the door to an older lady with dark, graying hair, dressed in a casual pant outfit in a mute shade of yellow. Over her arm was a handbag of the same color. She was as tall as Marie-Thérèse, though rather decidedly round, and her face wrinkled when she smiled, as though she had done so often over the years. "Marie-Thérèse?" she asked.

"Yes. Are you Monique?"

The older lady nodded her gray head. "Monique Boucher. It's nice to see you again."

"Thank you so much for coming. I'm very grateful." Marie-Thérèse opened the door wider for her to enter. "I know we've met a few times, but it's been a long time."

"Yes, a pity, isn't it? I think the last time I saw you was at your wedding. I guess we all get busy with our lives. Ariana and I keep in touch, though. We go out to lunch at least once a month."

"My mother told me you were the one who converted her to the gospel."

Monique brought a hand to her ample chest. "Oh no, the Spirit did that. I was just the one who happened to be the vehicle."

"Well, we appreciate it all the same. Without the gospel . . . well, life just wouldn't be the same."

"I hear you." Monique held out her hand to Raquel who had fallen asleep in Marie-Thérèse's arms. "What an adorable child! About two months, yes?"

"We're not sure. They said she may be as young as two weeks, but I find that hard to believe. I think she's at least six, given where she's at developmentally. But she is rather small. As soon as they find the mother, they'll be able to pinpoint a date for her."

"Well, she looks healthy, at least. That's something." Monique looked around the narrow entryway. "So, where's my little patient?"

"In the kitchen—I hope." Marie-Thérèse led the way, noticing the tile in her narrow entryway was dirtier than she usually allowed and the carpet runner needed vacuuming. Maybe she could squeeze in the time to clean them today.

In the kitchen, Celisse was nowhere to be seen. Marie-Thérèse peeked under the table but the child wasn't there either. She grimaced. "Oh, no. I guess she's still scared. We tried to explain what was going on, but she's . . . well she's had a rather hard time of it."

"So I gathered from what your mother told me when she called last night. Poor child."

"Well, let's go to her bedroom. I bet that's where she's at. We made her a little tent there."

Sure enough, Celisse was under the desk, as close to the wall as she could get. The doll that had been in her arms so much in the past few days, lay discarded nearby. Marie-Thérèse placed Raquel in Brandon's bed, checked the bedrail to assure herself it was secure, and then knelt in front of the desk. "Celisse, my mother's friend is here to see you. Don't worry. I said I would stay with you the whole time." She reached for Celisse but the child cringed and let out a soft cry that tore at Marie-Thérèse's heart.

"Here, let me talk to her a minute." Monique sat on the brown carpet, folding her legs Indian style. Given her build, it couldn't be an easy position to maintain, but her happy face showed no discomfort.

Marie-Thérèse held up the sheet and watched doubtfully. She kept herself in Celisse's view so the child would know she hadn't been deserted—again.

"Celisse, I'm Monique. It's very nice to meet you."

Celisse said nothing.

"Do you know I've got a granddaughter just your age? She's really pretty, like you, except she doesn't have blue eyes. Boy, you have pretty eyes. And my granddaughter—her name is Olive—has a doll like that. She loves to take it everywhere with her and dress it in different clothes like a real baby. Sometimes she comes to my house and we make crepes together. Have you ever made crepes? I could show you how. I bet your doll would like to see . . ."

Marie-Thérèse listened as Monique rambled on, talking about her granddaughter, her dolls, and the crepes they made. She talked about other things too, like how she used to work as a nurse and about all the people she had made well. Marie-Thérèse's thoughts gradually wandered. This room, too, showed the lack of her attention in the past few days, though no one except her seemed to notice. She studied the shelves in the room, seeing how unorganized they were—everything jammed in wherever there was space. Unlike Larissa, Brandon never did seem to care for his possessions. *I should tell Larissa how much I appreciate her neatness*, she thought, vowing to do so that day.

Every now and then, Marie-Thérèse glanced back at Celisse, but she didn't see any change in the little girl's demeanor until abruptly she reached out for her doll and held it to her chest.

"There you go," encouraged Monique. "Your doll was missing you, sitting there all alone. I'm glad you decided to take care of her. She'll always be yours, you know. No one will take her away, no matter what you do or don't do."

Marie-Thérèse wondered where that idea came from. Had Celisse thought they would use the doll against her somehow? But Marie-Thérèse kept silent, deciding that Monique knew better than she did about talking with abused children. She must have seen it in her years of practice or studied it in nursing school.

"I bet your doll would love to make crepes," Monique began to unfold her legs. "Do you think you could help?" She climbed to her feet, straightening her shirt and adjusting the purse on her shoulder. "Is that okay, with you, Marie-Thérèse? Do you have flour? And what about jam or whipped cream? We can't have crepes without whipped cream. And chocolate. We'll melt it over the crepes."

"But . . ."

Monique winked at her. "Don't worry. I have plenty of time. And I really do have a hankering for crepes. Celisse, if you'll come into the kitchen, we'll let you put in the ingredients." Then without another word, she went from the room. Marie-Thérèse scooped up the sleeping baby and followed.

"I don't know if it'll work," Marie-Thérèse said in the kitchen, settling Raquel in her baby carrier.

Monique smiled. "Well, we'll have time to find out, I guess. Do you have an apron I could use?"

"Yes, but I don't have a crepe-maker."

"Oh, I never use one of those anyway. A simple skillet will do."

Marie-Thérèse prayed silently as she helped Monique set out the ingredients for the crepes—flour, milk, eggs, salt, as well as strawberry jam, chocolate bars left over from family night, whipped cream, and nuts for toppings. "I'll also need a little butter for the pan," Monique added. "Or margarine. Whatever you have." In went the eggs, milk, and flour, and Monique beat the mixture with a wire whisk. She hummed as she worked.

Marie-Thérèse continued to pray. From the corner of her eye, she saw Celisse slide into the kitchen on silent bare feet. Monique didn't act surprised. "You can put in the salt," she said, handing it to her. "Just a few shakes. And then stir it in with this."

Celisse shook the salt into the batter, looking at Monique for reassurance. "That's right, maybe one more shake. Good. Now stir. That's okay if you get a bit on the table. We all do it. Now come over to the pan. Marie-Thérèse, can she stand on that chair? Be careful, the pan is hot, Celisse. We just spoon the batter in like this. Then you take the pan and lift it like this and spread it all out evenly. Then we let it cook just a little, and flip it. There. The next time you can do it. I'll help. Or Marie-Thérèse can help you."

Before long they had a small mound of warm crepes, and they sat at the table slathering them with a mixture of interesting toppings. Celisse's favorite was whipped cream and melted chocolate, while Marie-Thérèse preferred the jam and Monique used only butter. They washed it all down with hot chocolate.

"Boy, I haven't had such a great snack since I made these with my granddaughter," exclaimed Monique. "I doubt I'll be able to waddle out the door any time soon, I ate so many. You'll have to roll me into the hall."

Celisse actually smiled.

Monique put her face next to Celisse's. "Remember how I said I'm a nurse? Or was for many, many years. I helped a lot of people get better before I got old and decided it was time for me to stay home and rest. You have a sore, don't you? And it hurts. I know it does. And we have to look at it. Whether it's me or somebody else, Marie-Thérèse has the responsibility to make sure you stay healthy. So what's it going to be? Are you going to let me look at it and tell you what it is, or do you want to go to someone else? Either way, Marie-Thérèse will stay with you."

Unwaveringly, Monique held Celisse's gaze. For a long moment there was utter silence in the kitchen and then Celisse held up a slender hand at pointed at Monique. Relief chased out the anxiety in Marie-Thérèse's heart. After seeing the pain Celisse had gone through already, she had not wanted to force anything else upon her.

"Good, honey," Marie-Thérèse said. "I'll help you." Before the child could change her mind, Marie-Thérèse stood her on the floor and pulled the elastic of her pants down to expose her hip and the sore. It was oozing now, a dark pus that smelled worse than anything Marie-Thérèse could remember smelling in a long time. A yellow stain was already spreading on Celisse's clothes.

Monique peered at the sore without touching it. "Yes, that's what I thought it might be from your description. Still, it's not very common. It's a boil."

"A boil?"

"Yes. Like the ones inflicted upon the people of Egypt during the time of Pharaoh and Moses. Terrible things. Painful, and sometimes not easy to get rid of."

Marie-Thérèse stared at the boil and at Celisse's blank face. "What causes them?"

"Well, there are a number of different reasons— including bacterial infection, illness, stress, food allergies. Sometimes, though, we just don't know the reason. Another cause in Celisse's case might be poor nutrition and poor hygiene—given the unsanitary conditions she was found in. We won't know for sure, but we do know her body has toxins and is getting rid of them. With a good diet and proper care of this boil to prevent it from recurring or spreading, she will likely never have another one."

"It can spread?" Marie-Thérèse asked.

"Yes, even to other people. But if we keep the area clean, use only clean towels on her—and no sharing towels—and wash our hands after we handle it, we shouldn't have any problem."

"So how do we get rid of it?"Marie-Thérèse looked uncertainly at the sore, feeling repulsed by the smell and the pus. Poor Celisse!

"Well . . ." Monique gingerly felt the puffy red skin surrounding the sore. Celisse's lips clamped together, but she didn't let out a sound. "With something this severe, I'd say we have three options. One would be for a doctor to simply cut it out." Immediately, Celisse stiffened. "Don't worry, hon," Monique reassured her, "there are still other ways we could try first. I only mentioned the cutting because that would really be the most simple. They would take it out, make a stitch or two and you wouldn't have to think about it again."

"What are the other options?" Marie-Thérèse slid her fingers along Celisse's arm in a soothing gesture.

"It's imperative that we keep it draining. Because once all this pus comes out, it will likely heal over and form again and repeat the entire process. A doctor could make an incision and an insert some gauze to keep it open. Or we could use a method that might take a lot longer, but that nearly always works with a minimal amount of pain."

Marie-Thérèse glanced at Celisse. "The minimal pain is probably our choice. What do we have to do?"

Monique stood and began rummaging through her bag on the counter. "I brought some comfrey that we can make a poultice from, and then you must change it—probably twice a day for three or four days and then once a day for another week or two or three after."

"That long?" Marie-Thérèse wondered if Celisse would still be with them by then. She had prayed about asking Pascale to allow them to continue to foster the girls, but did not feel she had received an answer. Inwardly, she sighed.

"Yes, this one could take up to a month to heal completely. But the poultice shouldn't hurt her—I mean, at least not anymore than it does already. In a few days even that pain will be gone. But don't let that fool you. You must keep the comfrey on until there is no more oozing at all. It won't be easy, but it usually works."

Marie-Thérèse smiled at Celisse. "Well, I'm up for that if you are. I'll change your bandage every day and get it better. Okay with you?" Celisse's head went up and down.

"Okay now," said Monique opening a bottle of a green powdered mixture. "This just mixes with water. I have some gauze here, but I need some tape and some plastic wrap if you have them. The poultice won't do any good if it dries out. And I'll need some wash cloths wet with hot soapy water."

Marie-Thérèse went to gather the items, while Monique helped Celisse lie on the kitchen table. "This might sting a bit," Monique was saying, "but just grit your teeth. I have a lollipop here to help you be brave."

Celisse put the lollipop in her mouth, her blue eyes round. She wasn't exactly smiling, but her expression was one of the most pleasant Marie-Thérèse had ever seen on her face.

Monique put one of the now-warm wash cloths over the sore and let it sit for a while. Then she removed it and placed her fingers on the skin on either side of the sore, pushing down slightly. "There's so much pus in here that we don't want it to leak out of our bandage. Bacteria—usually staphylococcus is in the pus of a boil, and that's what can make them spread. So we'll just get as much out without actually squeezing—we don't want it to spread internally. See, I'm not even touching the sore, just on the skin around it. Very softly because it's really painful."

Abruptly, the dark pus piled out of the sore. Monique's sturdy hands were very gentle as they massaged—if it could be called that, but even so Celisse whimpered. She didn't cry. Marie-Thérèse wiped up the pus gently with another washcloth and was amazed at the amount that emerged. Again and again, she wiped it away. After a while, the pus was a lighter color and Monique lifted her hands. The middle of the sore was now a small crater. "I know that hurt, Celisse," Monique said. "You are a brave girl. And now it won't hurt hardly at all when the elastic on your pants hit it or if someone bumps you. The reason it was hurting so much before was because of the pressure of all that stuff inside. But now most of it is out. And now all Marie-Thérèse has to do each day is to take off the poultice, wipe away any pus, and put on a new one. In a month, you'll have only a scar to remind you that it ever hurt at all."

Marie-Thérèse looked at the stains on Celisse's clothing. "After we get the poultice on, we'll need to get you changed. That way you won't have to worry about it spreading."

"We really should wash the whole area before we put on the poultice," Monique said. "And our hands as well."

Within fifteen minutes, Celisse was washed, had the poultice on her hip, and was wearing a new set of clothes.

"Thank you so much," Marie-Thérèse told Monique. "I don't know what I'd have done without your help."

"It's no problem at all. I'm glad to help. And I'm glad Celisse has someone like you. It's not everyone who would open their home to two needy children."

Marie-Thérèse wanted to object, wanted to say that she hadn't volunteered for the children, but that they had been thrust upon her. She'd had no choice. That in fact, she was afraid to have them there at all. Not because of the work involved, but because of the fear of losing them. But it all sounded too stupid for words, too selfish, and so she chose to remain silent, though she felt guilty at the praise.

"Let me know if you have any questions or need any more help," Monique said as she headed for the door. "The only thing I would watch for is if Celisse develops a fever or chills, or if the boil suddenly develops one or more red streaks going away from the sore. Those could be signs of something more serious and you would want her to see a doctor immediately. But I really think you won't have any problems."

Marie-Thérèse thanked her again and walked her to the door. Before she left, Monique bent down and gave Celisse another lollipop. "Because you were so brave," she said. "But save it for after lunch, okay?" At Celisse's grave nod, Monique arose, patted Celisse's head, and left.

The baby awoke then and began to cry. Taking Celisse's hand, Marie-Thérèse returned to the kitchen where the baby was still in her carrier, trying to suck on her fist. "Looks like we'd better get Raquel something to eat," she said to Celisse. She scooped the baby into her arms and immediately, Raquel began sucking on her sleeve. "There, there. Patience, little one." It took only minutes to prepare a bottle and to watch the infant sucking greedily and with such innocent abandon that Marie-Thérèse couldn't help but love her.

The bottle was only half gone when a putrid smell wafted up from Celisse. Marie-Thérèse looked at the child, who stood by the chair, staring at her feet. Under Marie-Thérèse gaze she began to inch toward the table. "Oh, no you don't," Marie-Thérèse grabbed her arm before she could slide under. "Did you go potty in your pants?" Celisse didn't answer, but Marie-Thérèse knew the answer. The past few days she had spent a lot of time with Celisse, teaching her to wipe properly, but she had begun to suspect that Celisse's problem went beyond learning to wipe. And what appeared in Celisse's underwear three times a days was blacker and more odorous than even human waste had a right to be.

Marie-Thérèse took a deep breath. "Celisse," she said, striving to hide all signs of anger, "you know you're not supposed to go in your pants. That's what the potty is for. You're a big girl and you need to go there. You don't wet your pants, do you? Of course not. And you shouldn't mess them either."

Other words raged in Marie-Thérèse's mind, but she bit them back, reminding herself that this child had never been taught the most basic things. Hadn't Pascale said the apartment had been full of feces, and that Celisse's clothes had been unsalvageable? Celisse had even come dressed in castoffs kept by the agency. Marie-Thérèse sighed and let go of Celisse's arm. "Don't go under the table. We have to go clean you up. Just a minute, though, while I finish feeding Raquel her bottle."

An hour later Marie-Thérèse was sitting on Brandon's bed with her back against the wall reading a picture book. Raquel lay along the length of her knees, wide awake, but Celisse had fallen asleep at her side. Marie-Thérèse shut the book and for a blessed minute listened to the silence. The wood wall clock on Brandon's bed ticked softly and steadily toward one o'clock. Where had the morning gone? She had laundry to do, seemingly double now with the girls here, and the bathroom was worse than it had been for a long time. She would have to get a freshener in there to rid it of the smell of Celisse's dirty underwear.

A rush of thoughts assaulted her: *What am I thinking, telling Mathieu I will pray to see if these girls should be in my life? They wouldn't be in my life, they would be my life. I wanted a baby, a baby like Raquel, not a problem that would take away all my control. What was I thinking? What was Mathieu thinking? Oh, dear Father in Heaven, can I do this? Can I really be a mother to these little girls—to Celisse? She needs so much, she takes so much . . . and then what if . . . what if . . .*

Marie-Thérèse couldn't complete the idea. Celisse couldn't be returned to her mother, could she? And what about Raquel? For a brief, bitter moment Marie-Thérèse wished she had never seen the children, that she hadn't opened the door to Pascale or let her inside—anything to save herself more heartache. She only stopped short of wishing the police hadn't found the girls in the first place, although the appalling thought did cross her mind.

I can't do this! I don't want to! I won't! she silently cried.

Trembling, Marie-Thérèse gently laid Raquel on the bed next to her sleeping sister before falling to her knees. *Dear Father, help me! I feel so inadequate . . . so frightened. But then when I think of what Celisse has been through, I feel so guilty and horrible inside. Why shouldn't I be able to help her? Who else can love her and take care of her like I do? Can I even love her? I do want what's best for her. But she's so . . . needy. And I . . .*

Marie-Thérèse trailed off, thinking of her neat cupboards and her alphabetized system of organizing her canned and boxed goods. She thought of the last Friday of the month where she always sat down and made plans for the next month's meals—even to making up each week's shopping list. She would also make at least four meals to freeze and eat during the month when she wouldn't have time to cook a proper meal. Then there were the crocheted bedspreads she was working on for Josette and her mother. How would she ever have time to finish them for Christmas if she had to worry about Celisse? And of course there was Larissa. How could she make sure her daughter didn't do something drastic if she was always cleaning out dirty underwear and coaxing Celisse from under the table? In fact, when was the last time she'd carried on a decent conversation with either of her children? And when would she ever sleep?

Am I so selfish? she thought. *This is all about me, isn't it? And Mathieu thought it was only because of fear that I hesitated. But I don't want to do something so hard, something that will cause me to lose control of my life.*

A gurgling sound disturbed her self-examination, and Marie-Thérèse opened her eyes. Raquel lay on the bed, watching her silently with wise brown eyes, and a rush of sweet love filled Marie-Thérèse's heart. Then her gaze wandered to Celisse. Even in sleep, her small face did not relax completely, as though she waited instinctively for something terrible to happen.

As it has in the past, Marie-Thérèse thought.

She swallowed hard. All at once the uncertainty and fear vanished like mist in the afternoon sun. *Nothing like that will ever happen to her again! Not if I have anything to say about it. I will make Celisse happy! It won't be easy, and some days I will probably want to quit or run away, but I will make it! The Lord has always given me the strength I need. He will not fail me . . . or Celisse.*

The change in Marie-Thérèse's heart didn't come with bursting fire-works, a notable vision, or even with a burning in her chest; rather it was a quiet knowledge that entered her heart suddenly and with such profoundness that she felt forever changed. There was work to be done and she was the one to do it. It was as simple as that. And yes, she would also be the one to receive the subsequent joy. Whatever self-pitying had come before was erased as though it had never been. In the eternal scheme, her concerns were nothing in the face of this child's tremendous need. Thankfully, she closed her eyes and finished her prayer

She had her answer.

Chapter 10

Rebekka awoke early on Tuesday, and after a breakfast of dry toast and chocolate milk, she finished translating the newspaper release and sent it to her boss in America. She knew he would send it to Samuel and that he would be the one to get it to the papers. Maybe it was time she did work more with Samuel. After all, it wasn't like he was still holding a torch for her, or anything. Even if he was, there was no danger in her returning the feeling. Her heart would forever be with Marc.

In her room, she readied for her doctor's appointment with heavy heart. How different today was from the last appointment, when she had been bursting with anticipation. The only difficulty had been keeping the suspicion of her pregnancy from Marc that morning as they readied for the day.

"What is it about you this morning?" he had asked, kissing her and holding her close.

"I'm just so happy," she replied. "I love you so much."

"You are my life, you know that?" He'd told her a hundred times, but she never tired of hearing the words. The love in her heart threatened to overflow and drown them both.

If only she'd known.

At the restaurant where she waited to meet Marc, she had told the maître d' that day was the happiest of her life. Why didn't she know better? Why hadn't she gone to Marc's office when she was early instead of to the restaurant? She could have told him there. They would have been delayed, celebrating their joy. They would have reached the intersection long after the purse-snatcher and his victim were gone. There would have been no tragedy.

Better yet, she could have asked him to go to the doctor with her. Either way, he would be alive today.

Rebekka sank to her bed, silent tears cascading down her face. She knew it wasn't really her fault, but that didn't make her miss him any less. She wrapped her arms around her waist and stared into nothingness.

* * *

André reached Rebekka's apartment at nine-thirty, in plenty of time to get her to the doctor's appointment at ten o'clock. He had put in three hours at the office already that morning, to take care of pressing work. Raoul had come in early, too. With Marc gone, work was piling up and they needed to figure out what direction they should take for the company. Nine months ago André's younger brother, Louis-Géralde, had come home from his mission to the Ukraine. He had begun working for the company, and was doing quite well, but far from able to fill his older brother's shoes. After a few more years of education and training, maybe, but for now they were still short-handed.

During the last month André and Raoul had discussed taking on another partner, and had even gone so far as to hear a few offers. But that left opening the company to someone who wasn't family, and neither of them liked that idea. So today they had finally agreed to hire a chief operating officer to handle the day-to-day operations. Once arrangements were made, André and Raoul would still own the company and be involved in all the important decisions, but they would be relieved from much of the daily pressure. They both needed that now.

As he drove up at Rebekka's apartment building, there was a flower delivery man pushing on an intercom button, obviously waiting to be let inside the building. There was no answer to his ringing. The man gave his watch a frustrated glare and punched the button again. André saw that it was Rebekka he was trying to reach.

Where was she? He hadn't even imagined that she might not be home. She was still feeling ill in the mornings, and besides, Raoul mentioned that she had a lot of translating to do. Why wasn't she answering? An uneasy feeling settled in his gut.

"That's my sister-in law's apartment," he told the man, taking out his keys. "I'm going up if you want to come. Or I can take the flowers for you."

"Her name Rebekka Perrault?"

"Yes."

"Sign here please."

André scribbled his name and the man thrust the heavy vase of flowers toward him and was gone. "Good thing I'm not a flower thief," André mumbled. He balanced the vase carefully as he opened the door to the lobby. Even if Rebekka wasn't home, he could put them on her counter and meet her at the doctor's.

Not until he was leaving the elevator on the fourth floor did he wonder who the flowers were from. They were of varied kinds and colors, interspersed with green ferns and bunches of baby's breath. The only flowers he recognized were the white-petaled daisies. The aroma reminded him of a spring day in a flower garden.

Who had sent them? He fingered the card, but it was sealed and he felt he had no business opening it. He only hoped it wasn't something that would cause Rebekka more pain. Surely most of the funeral flowers would have been long delivered. Perhaps one of his sisters was trying to cheer Rebekka up.

Shaking his head resolutely, André walked to Rebekka's door. When no one answered his ring, he let himself in. The apartment was absolutely silent. "Rebekka?" he called. No answer. He set the flowers on the table, his mind racing ahead. *She must have had an errand to run before the appointment. I can still meet her there.*

The dying plant by the kitchen window called his attention. Already he had replaced the plant twice, knowing Rebekka must love it because it had been Marc's. Rebekka had never seemed to notice the difference in the plants, though they were of slightly differing sizes, but she had thanked him several times for remembering to give it water.

The soil around the plant was still moist, so André turned to leave. Something stopped him—almost as though he had hit an invisible barrier. *Stupid*, he thought and moved toward the door. *See, no invisible wall. Only your own strange thoughts.*

He paused. *Or maybe not.*

Quickly he swivelled on his heel and walked the other way, down the hall toward the bedrooms and Rebekka's office. The office door was open and no one was inside, Raoul's door was closed, but in the other bedroom Rebekka was sitting on the neatly made bed, fully dressed in a smart long-sleeved pantsuit that set off her still-slender figure. Her dark auburn hair was in place, her high cheek bones and wide-set eyes accentuated with exactly the right amount of makeup, but her oval face was utterly blank as if Rebekka herself were not inside the beautiful shell. Her arms were wrapped around her middle, their support seemingly the only thing keeping her erect.

"Rebekka?" he asked, feeling he had intruded upon an agony too private to share. And yet he couldn't leave her this way. That wasn't even an option.

As he approached, he could see a trail of drying tears on her smooth cheeks, and more tears shimmering on her eyelashes. She blinked but didn't appear to notice his presence.

"Rebekka." His voice came hoarsely, full of the love he felt for her in his heart. Her face turned in his direction, but her dark, cloud-gray eyes held no recognition. He pulled her unresisting body into his arms, holding her tightly.

For a moment she lay limp in his grasp, and then her arms went around his chest and she laid her cheek on the stark white of his dress shirt. Her body began to quake with soft sobs that seemed to be coming from somewhere deep within her soul. He continued to hold her, fighting the feelings in his own heart. There was pity, yes, and a deep mourning for the brother he had lost. But there was also more—a longing to have Rebekka hold onto him for reasons that had nothing to do with Marc. He took a deep breath and pushed the emotions aside. He gently massaged the back of her head, smoothed the already soft hair. "It's okay, Rebekka," he murmured. "Everything's going to be okay."

She didn't appear to hear him, but she didn't let go, and after a while the sobs stopped and she drew in a shuddering breath, pulling back from him. "I'm sorry . . . I shouldn't cry."

"You have every right to cry." Despite himself, he put a gentle hand on the back of her neck and wiped the tears from her face with his fingertips.

"No, I . . . because of the baby."

"A little release won't hurt the baby, and it'll do you a world of good."

"Why are you here?"

"I came to take you to the doctor."

Her eyes looked beyond him to the door. "I don't want to go . . . alone."

"I know. That's why I came. Come on." He took her hand and led her to the door.

"But my face . . . I've been crying."

"You look beautiful."

For the first time since he'd entered the room, she looked at him and really saw him. She smiled. He held her hand all the way down to the car, completely forgetting about the vase of flowers.

* * *

As André went around the car to open her door, Rebekka dabbed at her face with her compact and spread on a little lipstick. She grimaced at the wan face in the mirror. She didn't look beautiful as André had said—

not even close. Crying made her few freckles stand out like flies on top of a fresh bucket of milk. She'd seen that very thing once on a field trip as a child and it had always stayed with her. *Oh well. Nothing I can do about it now.*

André opened the door, smiling gently at her as if she were made of glass. No wonder, with the way she had let him see her back at the apartment. Then there had been that terrible and wonderful moment when he had held her. For an instant, she could almost believe it was Marc holding her, and she wanted it never to end. *Crazy. I'm crazy*, she thought. But no. It was just a mistake. A mistake made by a lonely, pregnant woman.

She had been feeling well this morning, but now she was sick again. *A good sign. That means I'm not losing the baby.*

The reassurance was nice, but she wanted to actually hear the heartbeat. She craved to know with absolute certainty that the baby was all right. Maybe she would even buy one of those fetoscopes she had read about so that she could listen for the heartbeat whenever she became worried.

The nurse called her in to give a urine sample. Within minutes, she was back in the waiting room with André. Her eyes wandered over the large area, furnished with oversized sofas and chairs, tall fake plants, and tables with magazines geared for new parents. She picked one up and thumbed through it, seeing nothing. "I should really buy a book or two," she said aloud for something to say. "I hardly know what to expect."

"I have a few you can have. They were Claire's. Well, we both read them, but she . . ." André trailed off. He sighed loudly and let his gaze swing the length of the room, resting for a brief second on the occupants—mostly women in differing stages of pregnancy.

"You don't have to stay."

"Yes, I do."

Your duty, she thought with more than a little bitterness.

"I mean," he added, "that I'd really like to stay. If that's all right with you."

"What about work?"

"It'll keep. Your brother's there. And we've decided to hire a COO."

"Do you need me to sell my stocks?"

"No. Unless you need the money."

"I don't need the money. The apartment's paid for and the stock dividends are more than enough for the rest of my needs. But you know all that."

He nodded absently. "Marc made sure you would be well-taken care of. Just in case."

Rebekka tried not to feel anything at the words, but they made her furious. Marc had always believed he would die before her. Had his premonition of doom actually led to his accident? But no, she couldn't believe that. Marc loved her and he would have fought to stay with her.

"Rebekka Perrault?" came a friendly voice. A nurse near the examination room doors waved to her. "You can come too, Mr. Perrault."

Rebekka had taken several steps in the nurse's direction, but at those last words she paused and looked back at her brother-in-law. He was standing and looking after her with a question in his eyes.

All at once Rebekka wanted him to come with her. She didn't want to explain about her husband's death or feel the nurse's pity. She didn't want to be the only woman there who didn't have a man interested in her unborn child. Since she had only seen the doctor once—after a recommendation from Josette—he didn't know her well enough to recognize André or realize he was an imposter. He was acquainted with the family—in fact, his own father had delivered Marc and Josette—but he didn't know each personally.

"Do you want to come with me?" she asked. "I mean, it's not like it's going to be anything big. They'll just take my blood pressure and listen to the heartbeat—stuff like that. They did all the other tests the last time."

André nodded, apparently relieved that he wouldn't be required to see her in an embarrassing situation, and for one irrational minute she regretted inviting him inside. But her regret vanished as he took her arm and led her past the nurse. Her legs suddenly felt so wobbly that without his support, she doubted she would have made it to the examination room.

After having the nurse take her blood pressure, Dr. Samain asked Rebekka questions about how she was feeling, and then without even lifting her shirt, he felt her abdomen to assess the size of the baby. Lying on the examination table, Rebekka watched him, his face seeming too thin to support his heavy jowls that bulged at his jaw line.

"It looks like the baby is growing—despite your own weight loss." The doctor's muddy brown eyes looked at her more kindly than sternly.

Rebekka struggled to a sitting position to defend herself, but before she could utter a word the doctor continued, "I bet you've been sick and you might be for a few more weeks—or even longer. But no matter what, you must eat. The baby will be growing at a tremendous rate in the second trimester and he or she will need the nutrition."

"Okay," Rebekka managed past the tumult of other responses in her head: *Excuse me, but my husband's dead.* Or, *it's hard to eat when your life is gone.*

The doctor met André's gaze. "I do have a few patients who don't gain much during the first trimester, but losing weight is a serious no-no. If she doesn't start gaining weight or if she's so ill that she can't eat, we may need to try vitamin B shots or another alternative. But don't let her skip meals no matter how sick she may be."

"I won't," André promised with such seriousness that Rebekka felt a sudden crazy urge to laugh and to yell, *He's not my husband. Ha! I fooled you!*

"I'm feeling better in the mornings now," she said instead.

Dr. Samain nodded, making the overhead light dance across his shiny dark hair. Rebekka wondered if he used an oil to achieve such luster. "Nevertheless," Dr. Samain continued, "I'd like you to come in next week or at least call to let me know how you're doing. There's no reason not to help you through the sickness part." He paused. "If that's indeed what's causing the weight loss."

"Well, I haven't felt much like eating," she admitted. "But I'm really trying now."

The doctor cocked his head, eyes seeming to delve into things she'd rather keep hidden. Rebekka felt her breath come more rapidly, and the familiar pain leap to her throat. If she didn't leave the room soon she would burst into tears.

André stepped closer and put a casual arm around her shoulder. From her seated position on the examination table, Rebekka came to his chest. She was glad she didn't have to look into his eyes, but could simply absorb his strength.

"We've had a recent tragedy in our family," André explained. "I think that, more than anything, is what has been responsible for Rebekka's weight loss. But she's doing all right. We all are. And I tell you, we are very excited about this baby. Is it possible to hear the heartbeat?"

"Oh, of course! That's next." Dr. Samain pulled out a device from the wall as Rebekka lay back down on the table. "We usually go right to that after checking the size of the uterus, but I needed to stress the gravity of the weight loss. Hmm, let's see. In just a minute we should . . . Maybe a little further over here. There! Do you hear it?"

Rebekka did. The sound reverberated from hidden speakers in the walls. Thump, thump, thump. She closed her eyes and let the sound flood through her. *My baby! . . . Marc, do you hear that? It's our baby!* Thump, thump, thump. Her own heart still raced, seeming to beat in tune with the rapid beat of her baby's heart. An unidentifiable emotion surged into Rebekka's heart, like nothing she had ever experienced. *It's my baby! Mine! Oh, I love him so much already.* Then she smiled. *Or her.*

She opened her eyes and found André watching her. He smiled without speaking and she felt he understood exactly what she was feeling. He reached out a hand and caught a tear as it fell from the corner of her eye. But they were happy tears, this time. She grabbed his hand and squeezed a thank-you for his presence.

The doctor let them listen for another moment before withdrawing the wand. "Well," he said, "that's a pretty strong beat. And slower than some, though much more rapid than an adult. Might be a boy. But an ultrasound will tell for sure. After we talk next week we can schedule one. Would you like that?

Rebekka nodded. "I'd like to know if it's a boy or girl."

"And we'll be able to check out a lot of his other systems that way— heart, lungs, the works. If nothing else, it gives peace of mind."

Rebekka accepted André's help from the table, though she scarcely needed it now. Her soul still sang to the beat of her baby's life. Thump, thump, thump. How wonderful the sound! How utterly mundane, yet how unique!

In the car, Rebekka watched André's profile as he negotiated the narrow, crowded streets. He really didn't look all that much like Marc when she thought about it. Sure, there was a family resemblance, and both were good-looking, but Marc had been thinner, more rugged, and André was broader, stronger-looking, and more . . . determined? There was something in the set of his jaw that told her he would do the right thing no matter the cost to himself. For some reason this almost made Rebekka angry. André was a wonderful man—he deserved to be happy. He certainly shouldn't be wasting his life watching over his brother's widow.

"André," she began, "thanks. I mean, for coming. It helped. But I don't want you to feel you have to come next time or anything. I'll be able to handle it. Or I could bring someone from my family."

He was silent for such a long moment that Rebekka wondered if he'd heard. And then he said, "Rebekka, I *wanted* to be here today. If you don't want me to come in the future, just say so. I won't stick my nose in where

I'm not wanted." His eyes turned toward her briefly, their expression hidden by his sunglasses.

"It's not that! Boy, you are just so exasperating!"

He gave a dry chuckle. "Nice to see the color come back into your face. But hey, keep in mind that if you decided to bring your brother or your parents with you to the doctor, you're going to have to tell them about the baby first."

He was right. And for now that wasn't an option. Soon, but not yet.

"Now where are we going to eat lunch?" André asked.

His tone dared her to refuse him, but she just smiled. "Somewhere very expensive. I'm in the mood to be pampered."

In the end he did take her to an expensive restaurant, but the smell of the gourmet food made her stomach queasy. Instead, they opted for take-out sandwiches from the small café next door. Rebekka savored the delicious fresh bread.

"I think I practically live on bread and milk, you know," she said with a sigh. "But not rye anymore. I hope I still like it when I'm no longer pregnant."

"You will," André assured her, managing his sandwich and the steering wheel with ease.

When they arrived at her building, André didn't come up to her apartment, which Rebekka supposed was just as well. They both had to get back to work. But Rebekka found she dreaded being alone, and she almost asked him to stay. Almost. Then she remembered the way he'd held her that morning and how comforting it had been.

No. Better to be alone. She had to depend on herself now.

In the kitchen, she found a surprise: a huge vase of mixed flowers. *André!* she thought. *How thoughtful.* She picked up the phone to call him. He hadn't arrived at work yet and she didn't have his cell number memorized. She left a message instead. "Thanks for the flowers," she said. "They're beautiful."

After she hung up, she spied a card, tucked way down among the flowers. Eagerly, she opened it. André had never written her a note before.

> *Hi Rebekka!*
> *Looking forward to seeing you this weekend.*
> *Love, Samuel*

So it hadn't been André at all, but Samuel! He must have called this morning from America to have the flowers delivered. Rebekka didn't know what was more embarrassing, her message to André or that she had really believed he had brought them. Why would he be bringing her flowers anyway? It wasn't as though he felt romantically toward her. And did that mean Samuel *did* have romantic intentions?

I hope not, she thought. *It'll be one more thing to deal with.*

Shaking her head, Rebekka headed for the bedroom. She was too tired to dwell on her volatile feelings a minute longer. *Whoever said that being a teenager was like being on an emotional rollercoaster has never been pregnant*, she thought. *This is much worse!*

"Come on, baby," she whispered. "Let's take a nap." With a hand on her stomach, Rebekka lay on her side and slept.

Chapter 11

On Wednesday morning Rebekka felt better than she had in months. For breakfast she was even able to take a few bites of the exotic cheeses Raoul had bought her.

"Good," he said, downing the contents of his glass in one long drink. "I was beginning to think you were sick."

"Actually, I'm feeling really good today."

"All ready to meet Benny-the-baby-seller?"

"Sure." Rebekka felt herself flush. André would be at the hotel that afternoon, posing as her husband. By now he would have received her message thanking him for the flowers that he hadn't sent. Normally, she would have laughed such awkwardness away. Why couldn't she now? *Another thing to blame on pregnancy hormones*, she thought. Still, a little emotional discomfort was nothing compared to finding baby Nadia. She would do her part, André or no André.

"Noon, sharp. You won't forget?"

Rebekka set her cheese on the counter near where she was standing and placed her hands on her brother's shoulders, staring into his anxious face. "Of course I won't forget. This is my niece we're talking about. Besides you, I want her back more than anyone."

"A baby in the family—can you imagine that?"

"Yes." Rebekka's voice was soft.

"Mom's already started buying outfits." Raoul sighed. "Anyway, I don't think it'll be dangerous today, but you never know. If you see a weapon of any kind, get out of there."

"What about the police?"

"They have the room bugged and have installed hidden cameras. You don't have to worry about any of that. Just try to get him to show you the baby. Or at least commit to it. The police don't really believe he'll have her there today."

Rebekka took a photograph of baby Nadia from the pile of copies Raoul had laid on the table. "What does the PI say? Does he think she'll be there? Do you?"

Raoul's face became bleak. "I hope so because every day that passes is one more day we're apart. One more day that she grows up without me."

Neither voiced the fact that even if Benny had a baby to sell, it might not be Nadia.

"I'll do my best, Raoul," Rebekka told him.

"I know. And I'll be with the police in their van outside."

Rebekka waited until Raoul left for work before leaving the apartment on her own. She didn't want to be questioned about what she planned to do this morning. Putting on a scarf over her auburn hair, dark sunglasses, and her long coat and gloves, she felt relatively unrecognizable. The October air was brisk and the light bright, so her attire wouldn't attract attention, but it could serve as a form of disguise for any unwanted eyes. Which might prove important later. Or not. It was too soon to tell.

When she arrived in the run-down neighborhood, she checked the paper twice to make sure she had the right address. According to Raoul, this was the apartment building Desirée had lived in until she disappeared after telling him about Nadia. It was no a pretty sight. Trash littered the streets and gathered in gaping holes in the cobblestone walk. Rebekka saw a diaper among the debris and a sanitary pad and other unmentionable and unrecognizable items. The surrounding buildings were covered with graffiti and nearly every window was broken. She shivered, though not from the cold. She was intensely glad for the light and that she hadn't been foolish enough to come here after dark. How had Desirée kept Nadia safe in such a place?

"Hey, baby," crowed a young boy from his seat on the broken cement steps leading into Desirée's apartment building. Rebekka thought he couldn't be more than about twelve. As he spoke, he stopped bouncing a small rubber ball against the cement in front of him and gave her a deliberate once-over, winking in a way that far belied his age.

Rebekka bit back the retort on the edge of her tongue. *This might look like a little boy bouncing a rubber ball but what do you bet he's got a knife in his pocket?*

"Hello," Rebekka replied, deliberately making her voice flat and expressionless. "I'm looking for Desirée. You know where she's at?"

"What's it worth to you?" He held out his hand and rubbed his fingers together.

Rebekka played out several scenarios in her mind before answering. If she offered him money, how could she guarantee that he would answer? He might take her money and run. Or he might just call in a gang of his little friends and take all her money.

She sat by him on the steps, carefully staying at arms' length. He had started bouncing his ball again, but she could tell he was waiting for her reply. "What's it worth to me?" she repeated with a sigh. "Nothing, really. I just . . ." *What the heck, this works with men my own age . . .* She removed her glasses and used the open, earnest look Marc had always been unable to refuse. "You see, she's a friend of mine, and I really, *really*, need to see her. But I don't have any money." She smiled at him and waited.

He stared at her, blinking in surprise. "Well, I . . ." He missed his ball but she leaned forward and caught it in her fist. "I don't know where she's at. I . . . wish I did."

"Well, another friend of ours is the person I'm really looking for." Rebekka bounced the ball to him across the step.

He nodded knowingly. "The blonde, I bet. Lana. They were always hanging out together."

"Did Lana watch the baby?"

"Don't know. The baby was kind of cute, though. I watched her once or twice myself. Desirée paid me pretty good too."

"Did you tell the police that?" she asked.

The boy's eyes narrowed suspiciously. "Hey, I don't talk to no cops. You ain't a cop are you?" He tensed his hand around the ball, perhaps getting ready to throw it at her.

"No. No. Just interested. There's a big market for babies—if you get what *I* mean."

"Yeah, yeah." He nodded and bounced the ball back to her. She caught it and rolled it around her palms a few times while she thought up the next question.

"Lana around? I mean, I could talk to her."

"Naaaa. Ain't seen her for at least a week. Cops might 'ave picked her up, though. She drinks a lot."

Rebekka sighed. For all she knew, Lana might not even be the friend who had watched Nadia. If she was, she certainly wouldn't be hanging around waiting to get caught for selling someone's baby. But at least Rebekka had a name to go on.

"Maybe someone else has seen her," Rebekka said. "Is there an apartment manager?"

The boy snorted. "Nope. Nobody cares about these places, so long's the rent's paid. Last time the water went out, took 'em five days to get it on again. And we're lucky when we have hot water."

Rebekka threw him the ball and stood, replacing her dark glasses again. "Thanks," she said. She paused, thinking that he suddenly looked so young and defenseless sitting there. "Where's your mom?" she asked.

He shrugged. "Workin'."

"Don't you go to school?"

He made a face at her and jumped to his feet. "You better not be a cop. We don't need no one poking their nose in 'round here. Leave if you know what's good for you." With those final words, he ran down the street and disappeared into one of the numerous doorways.

Rebekka forced herself to turn back to Desirée's building. Nadia was what mattered now, and the most important thing was for Rebekka to find out everything she could and get out of here.

She walked up the crumbling steps and through the broken outside door. The lobby was a mess. There was a layer of grit over the marble floor and an old tire stood against the wall beneath the rusty mailboxes. A battered bike lay beside it and an old broom teetered atop, as though someone had once toyed with the notion of sweeping the place. Cigarette butts sprinkled here and there, but Rebekka was relieved to see no used needles or other drug paraphernalia. Nor did the place smell like urine, though it was far from the flower freshener smell of her own lobby.

She studied the mailboxes. There were names there, some unreadable. And none of them looked familiar. Well, fortunately it was a small building—less than a third the size of hers—and there was nothing for it but to knock on all eight apartments. Given the dread these people had of the police, maybe she could find out something the authorities had overlooked. Raoul had obviously believed the same thing, which was why he had come here, and she wasn't going to be discouraged by his failure. On her mission she had learned that the sister missionaries were able to get into many places that were locked to the elders. Of course she wasn't a sister anymore, and she was quite alone. Maybe coming here wasn't such a good idea.

She climbed the steps to the top floor. Another thing she had learned on her mission was that it was always easier to start at the top and go down each flight as she finished knocking the entire floor. As if gravity was in their favor, or something. Of course, most of the buildings in the areas where she had served had elevators, and this building didn't sport even a broken one.

There wasn't a light in the stairway either, but large windows on each landing gave her plenty of light. All the windows were broken and taped or missing the glass entirely, and she glimpsed out at the neighborhood each time she passed, hoping to catch some sight of Desirée.

There was no answer in the first apartment. In the second an unshaven, barrel-chested man in boxers and a tank top answered, his eyes heavy with sleep—or perhaps hung over from a night of drinking. "What'dya want?" he asked. Then he seemed to become aware that she was not just a stranger, but a young one of the female variety, and he straightened up, smiling at her. Rebekka wished she wasn't so frightened.

"I'm looking for Lana," she said. "Or Desirée. Do you know where I can find them?"

He rubbed the graying whiskers on his cheeks. "No. No. Don't know either of them. But I've only been here a couple days. This here place belongs to buddy of mine, who's out of town working. Might be home today or tomorrow. You could wait." He opened the door wider.

Rebekka shook her head and stepped back.

"It's okay," the man said. "A lot of people crash here. Come on in. Don't cost a thing."

"Uh, is anyone else there now? Maybe they've heard of Lana?"

"Nope. Just me. They might come wandering in, here and there, though. I have some coffee . . . or a little whisky if you like."

"No, I'm fine. But thank you. Have you see anyone here with a baby?"

He laughed coarsely. "Nope. You want a baby?"

"Uh, thank you. I have to get on my way."

He shook his head, mumbling something under his breath. Rebekka half expected him to lunge at her, but he simply shut the door. Breathing a sigh of relief, she went to the next door, praying to find someone who knew Lana.

No such luck. At the next apartment, she found several very young, droopy-eyed girls who were likely runaways. One of them told her Lana often stayed at the apartment, but that she might have moved on by now. She didn't know Desirée.

At the next three apartments there was no answer.

Rebekka went down the last flight of stairs and was confronted with the grimy lobby again. She knocked at one of the remaining two doors. An older, heavyset lady opened it. Her silver hair was drawn tightly back from her face, making the distrustful expression on her haggard face more pronounced.

"Yes?" she asked, wiping her big red hands on her white apron. Underneath the apron, she wore a blue and white flowered dress, cheerful despite its owners demeanor.

"I'm looking for Lana."

"Don't know her."

"No? She's a blonde, and she's friends with a really pretty woman with dark hair . . . Desirée Perrault. Wears a lot of makeup, tight clothes . . ."

"Humph, you're talking about most of the women in the building 'cept me, of course. I'm here not because I'm trash, but because I don't have any money. Can't work cuz I got a bad back, and my husband died and left a bunch of bills."

"I'm sorry. I know it must be hard."

The woman looked over Rebekka's long wool coat. "You don't know the life I've led." She went down the few steps from her apartment to the lobby and grabbed the old broom. "I'm not a junkie or a partier like the rest of 'em here. Neither is my neighbor." She pointed her chin in the direction of the only door Rebekka had not yet tried. "She takes care of her invalid husband. They ain't there now. Went to the hospital. If he dies, she's going to move in with me to save rent. We might even be able to go somewhere else." With short, angry strokes, she began sweeping the lobby floor. "Thought I'd make it look nice for them when they return. Not that it does much good with that riffraff upstairs. They'll just scum it up again." Hefting the tire, she threw it outside and watched it roll down the broken steps.

Rebekka's heart did go out to the woman, but she had a job to do. "Well, there was also a baby."

The woman stopped sweeping and stared at her. "The baby. Yes, I do remember the baby. A darked-haired woman's baby, I think. But like I told the police, I don't know anything about what happened to it. Is it dead, do you think?"

Rebekka blinked back the tears that rushed to her eyes. "I hope not. We're looking for her."

"I knew that woman had no right to that baby. She was always one of the worst. And that blonde she was with—hmm, mostly so drunk the cops kept having to lock her up."

"Is that all you know?"

She laid the broom against the wall. "Yes. I wish I could help you more. Of course, there might be someone up there who could help better." She waved her hand at the ceiling. "Though most of them don't remember yesterday, much less last week."

Rebekka thanked the woman and left the building, once again slipping on her sunglasses. Apparently, the police were right; there was nothing to learn here. Of course, there had been four apartments she had not been able to try, plus the woman and her sick husband on the lobby floor. Maybe she could return another day.

But not alone.

Rebekka felt eyes on her as she slipped behind the wheel of her car and drove away. She didn't even mind her missing hubcaps and hoped the boy on the steps would use the money from their sale to buy something useful.

Chapter 12

Rebekka was two minutes late meeting André in the lobby of the chosen hotel because she had to stop and get something to eat, knowing if she didn't, she would become so sick that she wouldn't be able to get through the meeting with Benny-the-baby-seller.

"Are you all right?" André asked, coming toward her and taking her hands. He bent toward her and Rebekka expected him to kiss her cheeks, but instead his lips brushed hers, sending an electric shock throughout her body. "Hello, honey," he said loudly. "I was worried you couldn't find the place."

"Oh, I did have a little trouble with traffic," she said, catching on. They weren't in the room with Benny yet, but they were already in their role as husband and wife. Of course André wouldn't have kissed her cheeks!

André's eyes wandered over her face, and he gave her a sympathetic grin, squeezing her hands. "Well, let's go on up, then." He kept hold of her hand as they headed toward the elevator, and Rebekka was intensely aware of his presence.

Rebekka's eyes noted the atmosphere of the hotel—the crystal chandeliers, the leather furniture, live plants in ceramic containers, and gold trim on the walls and ceilings. This was not the nicest hotel in town but obviously a very good one. The surrounding comfort, however, dimmed in comparison with her nervousness. *It's because of Benny*, she told herself. *It has nothing to do with André holding my hand.*

Once the doors of the elevators closed and they were alone, Rebekka shook her hand free on the pretense of checking her makeup in her compact.

"You look great," he said. "A little pale, maybe. Have you been sick this morning?"

"No. Actually, I'm fine." Then she rushed on, "About the flowers . . . I didn't look at the card . . . uh, before I called."

An unidentifiable look passed like a shadow over his face. "I figured that much."

"Well, thanks for bringing them in and setting them on the table. How did you get in my apartment yesterday anyway?"

The bell chimed and the doors slowly swung open. André reached for her hand again. "So . . . who sent them?" he asked, ignoring her question.

"A guy I work with—Samuel."

There was a tightening in his cheek and jaw muscles. "Isn't he the guy you nearly married when you lived in Utah?"

"I didn't nearly marry him. I was just thinking about seriously dating him."

"Sounds like the same thing to me."

She was about to reply when he added in a whisper, "We'd better talk later. It's show time."

She nodded and let him lead her down the hall. Her heart thundered in her chest as they stood before room 410 and knocked. What if Benny wasn't there? What if he didn't have Nadia? The tumult of question made it difficult to think clearly.

A short balding man answered the door. "Hello, I'm Benny Tovik," he said. He was big without being grossly fat, and his clothes were dated—at least ten years out of style. The gold ring on his finger and the thick gold chain around his neck looked real, but Rebekka couldn't be certain.

Benny-the-big-bald-baby-seller, she thought fleetingly. *This is all just too unreal.* She took a deep breath and pushed the unwanted thoughts to the back of her mind. A mistake now could cost them Nadia.

"Hello, we're the Perraults," André said, pumping the man's hand. "André and Rebekka."

"Come in, come in."

Then Benny was shaking Rebekka's hand, vigorously up and down. He was shorter than she was by at least a head, and she had a great view of the thinning hair surrounding the shining circle on the top of his head. She had to gently tug her hand from his, hoping her fake smile hadn't slipped. His touch was like grease that seem to cling to her hand long after he'd let go.

Desirée had told Raoul that Benny was American, but he didn't look like any of the Americans Rebekka knew. In fact in his coloring and facial structure, he looked typically French to her, though shorter than the average.

"Please have a seat," he said, indicating chairs next to a round table.

No American accent, she thought, forgetting for a moment that the hidden microphones would record that fact.

When they were seated, Benny leaned forward in his chair. "Well, I trust you and all, but could it be possible to see some ID?"

They had planned for this. Reaching across the table, they showed the identity cards they'd had made with the same address for the occasion, and André also took out his driver's license. Rebekka murmured something about neglecting to bring her license so Benny wouldn't realize that her address wasn't the same as her "husband's."

As he studied the cards, Rebekka looked around the average-sized room, noting the double bed, the TV set on a sturdy coffee table, the framed painting of the Eiffel Tower, and the gold-and-white wall paper. Set in an alcove, there was also a microwave on a counter next to a small sink and refrigerator. A large window with heavy tapestry shades completed the layout. Not deluxe accommodations by any means, but decidedly better than most rooms she had seen in her travels.

"Very good," Benny said, handing back the cards.

"Uh . . ." André cleared his throat. "We'd like to see ID, too, if you don't mind."

Rebekka didn't think Benny would like that, but he whipped out a blue passport from his shirt pocket. "Sure thing. I'm American, you see. That's how I can get around so well to find children who need to be adopted. With an American passport, the world is completely open."

Rebekka nodded in agreement, though she suspected the passport was a fake. If he was American, wouldn't he have at least a slight accent?

"So you want a girl baby, do you?" Benny asked.

They nodded. "Between about two and three months old," André said. "We've heard that most infant deaths occur before two months, so we want to make sure the baby's healthy." This was something Raoul had come up with last night to make sure the baby would be around Nadia's age.

Benny picked up a briefcase under the table and withdrew a notepad from it and jotted something down. "Anything else?"

"Yes, well, it may sound stupid . . ." Rebekka began.

"Go on. I assure you, I have heard it all."

"Well, we wanted the baby to look like us. You know, dark hair, dark eyes—either gray or brown—and white skin."

Benny frowned. "How white are we talking—Norwegian white?"

"No," Rebekka said. "My husband's family does have a bit of olive tones, so that would be okay. But we'd like her to look French. I know that may sound silly, but I don't want people guessing she's adopted. We plan to keep it a secret."

Benny consulted his list. "Would red hair be an option? You have red."

"Well, my wife's hair is really a very dark auburn," André broke in. "Almost brown. So if it were really dark, that'd be fine, but not bright red, or red-blonde. That would be too much of a difference."

"I see." Benny tapped the end of the pen on his wide chin. Rebekka was sure he had seen right through their charade and would call them on it, but instead he said. "I think I might be able to help you, but it—" he cleared his throat "—will require a fee above the amount we already discussed. I actually do have such a baby available, but I was going to give her to another couple who have been waiting a lot longer than you. To bump you ahead will require a rush fee."

"How much?" they said in unison.

Benny lifted the page he was writing on, wrote something on the paper beneath, then ripped it off, folded it and passed it to André. When he unfolded it, Rebekka caught sight of a lot of zeros. But it really didn't make a difference. They would agree to pay anything if it helped them find Nadia.

"It'll take me a while to get this money," André said hesitantly. "A few days . . . maybe a week."

"I'll need half in three days and another half when we sign the contract. And we must sign the contract before I turn over the baby."

"Could I see her?" Rebekka asked. She didn't have to fake the eagerness in her voice. "I mean, when we pay the first half? We'll want to see that she's . . ."

"What I promised, eh?" Benny chuckled. "I'll do you one better." He reached into his briefcase and withdrew a cell phone. "You can see her right now."

Rebekka exchanged a surprised glance with André. This was more than either had hoped for!

Minutes later a nondescript woman with dark hair and swarthy skin knocked on the door. Benny didn't greet her, but snatched the small bundle she carried and settled it in Rebekka's startled grasp.

"Oh!" she exclaimed. Then she murmured, "She's adorable!"

André put his arm around her and touched the baby's soft cheeks. "Beautiful," he murmured in agreement.

The baby was so tiny that Rebekka felt awkward holding her, fearing she might somehow damage the infant. At the same time the baby seemed to belong in her arms. Dark hair framed the small, perfectly proportioned face, blemished only by a minuscule flurry of rashes on her forehead; and the eyes staring up at them were dark, though the exact color was difficult to determine. She had two miniature arms and legs and every finger was accounted for. She was absolutely perfect, and Rebekka loved her immediately.

Except for one thing: she wasn't Nadia. Her eyes were wider set, the shape of her face more round; and her skin was a shade too dark to be Desirée and Raoul's daughter. Tears leaked from Rebekka's eyes. She so wanted this to be Nadia!

Lifting her face to André's, she saw that he also knew the child wasn't the one they were searching for. "Isn't she a little young?" he asked.

"Oh, no. Certainly not," Benny assured them with emphatic waving of his hand. "She's two months old. Born a week premature, but in perfect health." He reached for the baby, but Rebekka stepped away.

"Just a minute more . . . please?"

Benny nodded, and she sat on the edge of the double bed with the baby while the men talked. The woman who had brought the baby stood placidly by the door, her fleshy face showing no emotion. Rebekka bet she wasn't the baby's mother. No mother would be able to stand by so stoically and watch another woman buy her child. No, the woman was likely someone who was paid to watch the baby while Benny did business.

Big business, Rebekka thought, remembering the zeros. *Enough to buy several nice apartments.*

So who loved this baby? There had to be someone. Benny was obviously doing everything he could to profit from the child's existence. Rebekka could only hope the mother of the baby had given her daughter up willingly. *I wouldn't be able to do so*, Rebekka thought. *She's too precious.*

Was that why Desirée had kept Nadia so long without telling Raoul? Had she felt a connection to Nadia?

At least Nadia has us searching for her. I wonder if anyone cares where this child ends up.

An idea formed in her mind. "Ah, Benny?" she said. "The baby—I think she needs a diaper change. Could I . . .?"

Benny laughed, and for a moment Rebekka imagined seeing dollars signs in his eyes. He motioned to the woman who fished into her bag and brought out a diaper and a small tub of wipes. She put them on the bed and then returned to her post by the door.

André came to stand by the bed, but Rebekka flashed him an intent stare, willing him to keep Benny occupied. "I can do this, honey," she said. "Why don't you work out the final details with Benny?" Then for a drama's sake, she added, "We will be able to get the money, won't we? She's so perfect!"

André blinked at her once and Rebekka wondered if she'd overacted. Role-playing had never been her strong suit. But he smiled and turned back to Benny.

Rebekka laid the baby on the bed next to the diaper. She put her own purse nearby, purposefully spilling the contents. "Oops," she said, laughing as self-consciously as she knew how. "Oh well, I can pick it up in a minute," she cooed to the baby. "You come first."

She knelt next to the bed, unsnapped the baby's one-piece outfit, and pulled out her legs. She wore yellow and pink striped socks underneath. "Oh, we'd better take off those socks so I don't accidentally get them dirty." Her feet were tiny and perfect, except for the skin that was flaking off.

Wasn't flaking skin the sign of a much younger infant? Rebekka wished she knew more about babies. "My goodness, little one, you are so tiny and look at those little feet. They look good enough to eat!" The baby smiled briefly. Rebekka knew that probably said something about her age as did the completely healed belly-button, but wasn't sure what.

She had changed enough diapers to know how it was done, but never on such a small baby. Her problem was getting the tapes tight enough. "There, I think that's it," she said, rolling the old diaper tightly so Benny and the woman wouldn't know it hadn't been messy after all. "We'd better get your socks back on."

Using her spilled purse as a shield, she wiped her compact off on the bed before taking the baby's foot and planting it on top. Then she quickly redressed the baby. "There, all done," she said a minute later. It nearly broke her heart to give the baby back to Benny, but the infant didn't seem to mind.

"In two days we'll meet again," Benny said. "I'll e-mail you to tell you the place and time, okay?"

"Take good care of her," Rebekka told him.

He grinned. "Oh, we will. We always do. And soon she'll be with you forever."

Benny motioned to the door, but Rebekka said, "My purse. It spilled on the bed."

"Well, we'll just go ahead of you," Benny said. "See you in two days." He pumped Rebekka's hand and then André's and started for the door. The woman, once again holding the baby, followed.

Rebekka's hand felt greasy from Benny's touch, and crossing to the bed, she wiped her hand on a tissue from her purse. "Does the man ever wash his hands?" she wondered aloud. She gathered up her things and put them into her purse—except for the compact which she cradled carefully in her hand.

"What's that for?" André asked.

"I got the baby's footprint."

"She wasn't Nadia. I'd bet that baby's at least a month too young."

"I know, but maybe someone's looking for her as well."

He sighed. "Or maybe the mother just needs money."

André was right, but she shrugged. "It was something I had to do. If anything, it will prove to Raoul that she wasn't Nadia."

They drove separately to the police station where shortly afterward Raoul and two officers appeared. Raoul hugged Rebekka. "It wasn't Nadia," she whispered. "I'm so sorry. But I got her footprint to be sure." She handed the compact to the older of the two officers. He passed it to his partner, who immediately left the room to get it analyzed.

"Come on," the older officer said. "Let's go into our detective's office. We have more information we'd like to share with you."

Another officer with a square face and dark hair sprinkled occasionally with fine strands of silver hair met them at the door to an office. He was as tall as André, but even more broad across the shoulders, reminding Rebekka of a boxer or a weight-lifter. "Hello, I'm Detective Francom," he said, "and I'm in charge of this case." He didn't invite them to sit in the few hardback chairs in front of the desk, and they didn't ask.

"I'm Rebekka Perrault, Raoul's sister."

"I'm André Perrault."

Detective Francom shook their hands with a firm grip that rivaled any LDS missionary's. His blue eyes gave Rebekka the impression of missing nothing. "This won't take long and I'm sure you have places to go."

"We have time," André said.

"First we need to let you know that while we do appreciate your willingness to help, as you did today, the new information gathered only makes us feel it's probably too dangerous to stage another meeting."

Rebekka swallowed hard. "But we told Benny we'd see him in two days. Do we tell him we backed out?"

"What about the baby?" André added.

"Well, let me explain a bit first," the detective said, shuffling a stack of reports on his desk. "I've been working with not only our police officers, but with the private investigator your family hired as well. We've found out quite a bit about our friend Benny. In fact, before he met with you, he came from meeting another couple who also want to adopt the same baby."

"Were they posing like us?" Rebekka asked.

"No. They really are looking to adopt. Up until we talked to them today, they had no idea that Benny's setup is illegal. They've already given him a lot of money—nearly their entire life savings. I don't know if they'll get it back, but we'll try."

"You mean Benny was going to sell the baby to several different families?"

"Yes. In fact, your PI set up another meeting tomorrow for our police decoys, and Benny has promised them that he has a baby girl for them. Eventually, we're going to get this guy. Only problem is, we don't know if he'll have the baby with him. And even if we do get him, we may not be able to find who the child belongs to."

"I got her footprint," Rebekka said.

"That will help if she was born in a hospital and a record was taken, but she might have been born on the streets. It may be impossible to find her parents."

Rebekka sighed. "I had no idea it'd be that hard." She glanced longingly at the hard chairs, feeling suddenly ill.

"And if he suspects anything, he'll bolt for sure."

"Where does this leave us with Nadia?" Raoul asked.

The detective shook his head. "I don't think Benny has her. He used the same baby with both meetings. I don't think he'd do that if he had another baby girl."

Raoul frowned. "Then we're back to square one."

Rebekka put a hand on Raoul's shoulder to comfort him. Then she snapped her fingers. "Wait a minute. Do you have anything on a woman named Lana? She lives in Desirée's apartment building and a boy there said they were friends. Said she drinks a lot, too. That the police had picked her up a few times. You would have a record of that, wouldn't you?"

The reactions around her were vastly different: Raoul immediately looked more hopeful, the detective thoughtful, and André angry. André spoke first, his eyebrows furrowed so tightly that they stretched into one hairy line. "You went there. Alone?" He turned to Raoul. "You know what kind of a neighborhood that is, and you let her go? In her condition?"

"I didn't let her go." Raoul blinked in puzzlement. "And what do you mean 'in her condition'? You make it sound like she's . . . " He stared at Rebekka. "Are you *pregnant*?"

With a dark look at André, Rebekka nodded. "I was going to tell you, but I . . . well, I wanted to make sure I wouldn't lose the baby," she finished lamely.

Raoul's expression became thunderous. "I would never have let you meet with Benny if I'd known. Never! What if there'd been a problem and your baby was hurt?"

"Goodness, what was he going to do, throw me on the ground and jump on me?" she retorted. "Besides André was there."

"Not this morning, I wasn't," André nearly yelled. "You could have asked me. I'd have gone with you."

She clenched her fists at her side. "Then I probably wouldn't have learned anything! People talked to me. They might not have to you."

André opened his mouth to say something further when the detective raised his hand. "Since your wife is all right," he said to André, "I think that perhaps we should concentrate on what she learned. I'm sure she'll promise not to go back there again."

Rebekka glared at him. "I will promise no such thing! I'll do everything I can to get my niece home. Anything! I wouldn't have to go there if you'd done your job in the first place. And I am not this man's wife!" She pointed a finger at André. "I am married to his brother."

Raoul took her hand and eased it down from its accusatory position. "The detective has been very helpful, Rebekka. He's doing his best."

"I really am," Detective Francom said. "Now how about you begin at the top and tell us what you found out?"

So Rebekka began with the young boy bouncing the ball on the steps. She left out her feelings of fear and her repulsion at the run-down apartment building. Most everyone had already been there and knew what the place was like; they didn't need a reminder. When she was finished, Detective Francom sent the remaining officer to run a check on the name Lana.

André shook his head. "So that's what happened to your hubcaps. I wondered. And in broad daylight. If you had gone at night . . ."

Her anger flared again. "I *didn't*. That would be stupid. And as you can see, I'm fine."

"That's why you didn't eat the cheeses," Raoul said suddenly. "It is Marc's. I mean, of course it's Marc's. Mom and Dad and the Perrault's—they're going to be so happy."

"But *I'm* going to tell them." Rebekka scowled at André. "And only when I feel like it."

André didn't look repentant. "Raoul at least should know since he's living with you."

The detective went to answer a knock on the door, gliding like a boxer with a minimum of wasted movement. He was shaking his head at their conversation. Did he wonder where her husband was, why she lived with her brother, and why André was so obsessed with her safety? *Let him wonder*, Rebekka thought.

The detective spoke to the officer quietly, before returning to the others. "Bingo! We picked up a woman named Lana last Friday. She was wasted, but not just on booze, and it's taken her several days to come down. She hasn't made bail yet, so we're holding her for trial. They're questioning her about Nadia now."

"Could I see her?" Raoul asked nearly tripping on his feet as he stepped forward.

The detective frowned. "Hmm, let's see what we get first and then we'll see."

"I can wait." Raoul folded his arms across his chest.

"So can I," André added.

Rebekka glanced back and forth between the two men. André returned her gaze with a glare. "I hope someone is running our company," she said pointedly. She turned to the detective. "Now do you have a bathroom, because I'm just about to be very sick." She ran from his office in the direction he indicated, barely reaching the room in time.

When she emerged much later, André was waiting outside with a cup of water and half a loaf of french bread. "Peace offering?" he said, extending the bread.

Rebekka accepted them gratefully and let him lead her to a chair in the hall. Taking a bite of bread, she sighed heavily. "A little too much excitement, I think."

He looked as though he was going to say something, but decided against it. "Raoul is with that Lana character now."

"He is? Already?" Rebekka shoved a large chunk of bread into her mouth. "I want to see her too. Where are they?" She looked up and down the deserted hall.

"Not so fast! You'll get sick again."

"André," she moaned.

"Okay, come on. Eat as you walk."

There was a momentary delay before they were allowed into the room with Lana, and Rebekka took the opportunity to eat most of the bread and drink all of the water. At last, they were allowed in the questioning room where Detective Francom, Raoul, and a woman were sitting at a table. They looked up as Rebekka and André entered.

"Hi," Rebekka ventured.

"She insisted on coming in," André said by way of apology.

"That's okay." Detective Francom motioned them into chairs next to Raoul. "It can't hurt. Please, have a seat."

But Rebekka walked over to stand near the woman. "I'm Rebekka, Raoul's sister. You must be Lana, Desirée's friend."

"How did you hear about me?" Lana said in a weary voice. Everything about her was weary and sagging, from her bleached blonde hair to the skin on her too-thin body. Her watery brown eyes were bloodshot and devoid of hope. She had the look of one who had grown prematurely old from a life of drinking and drugs.

"Didn't they tell you? I talked to a boy in front of your apartment building. He was about twelve, had a bouncing ball. He told me you were Desirée's friend and that he sometimes watched Nadia."

"Oh. Must be Henri. He's always hanging 'round. But I don't know where the baby is. I told them that. And I ain't got to say more."

Rebekka's legs threatened to collapse. She eased herself into the chair next to Lana.

"Are you okay?" Raoul asked quickly.

"It's the pregnancy," André offered.

Rebekka ignored them and concentrated on Lana. "Look, Raoul didn't even know that Nadia existed before last Saturday. Desirée didn't tell him until she was missing. Desirée said she entrusted Nadia to her friend and I think that friend was you."

Lana's only reply was shrug.

"She was informed of all that before your brother was allowed in," the detective said, briefly flexing his powerful-looking shoulders. "She said she didn't know anything about the baby. She appears unwilling to help us. I hoped that seeing your brother would convince her otherwise."

"Did you ask her about Benny-the-baby-seller?"

The detective gave a slight grimace. "I was just about to." He focused his attention on Lana, and she met his intent stare with one of her own. "Monsieur Massoni's wife not only said she left the baby with a friend, but that the friend might have given her to a mutual friend, a Benny Tovik. Come on, Lana, what do you say to that?" He smiled at her invitingly.

Lana's lean chin jutted out an inch further, increasing her defensive posture. "I'd say that I didn't have to answer you without a lawyer present. I know that much. I don't care how strong you look or handsome you are, Monsieur Detective, your charm don't work with me. So lay off!"

Rebekka saw Raoul's emotions simmering and knew he was about ready to explode. "Look Lana," she said, leaning toward the other woman. "You know what kind of a life Desirée lives. A baby needs more stability than that. We can give her that. We *want* to give her that . . . and more. My brother is a wonderful man and a steady provider. You know that if you know anything about his relationship with Desirée. And my parents and I will be right there along with him to give Nadia everything she needs, including boundaries and limits. I will raise my own child right along side her. We will love them together. Raoul has a right to know his daughter, and she has a right to know her father. Please help us!"

Lana didn't reply, but her hard gaze swung back and forth between Raoul and Rebekka.

"Please," Raoul implored. "I need my little girl. And she needs me. Please. For Nadia's sake."

Lana's lips pinched together tightly as she considered. Finally, she spoke, "No way would I give Nadia to Benny, no matter what Desirée said. I knew she loved that kid. I loved that kid. I wouldn't do nothing to hurt her. No way. I even urged Desirée to give her to you at least a dozen times, but she wanted to keep her—even though she hated the crying. Of course, Nadia doesn't cry much . . . anymore. She was a good kid."

"But what happened to her?" Rebekka asked. "You did have her, didn't you? Or did Desirée lie to us?"

They were silent as they waited for the reply. Lana's eyes dropped to the table, and Rebekka saw a tear emerge from beneath her thin lashes. "I—I had her. I remember Desirée asked me to watch her on

Wednesday—she was working a catering job and wouldn't be able to make it home that night." Lana paused and swallowed noisily before continuing. "But she didn't come home on Thursday either and I was getting worried 'cause I had to work on Friday. I couldn't just leave Nadia alone. I drink when I get worried and I drank a lot that night. And took a little something else. I don't remember what happened after that."

"What do you mean, you don't remember?" asked Detective Francom.

"What about Nadia?" Rebekka put a pleading note into the question.

Lana's eyes met Rebekka's. "What I mean is the next thing I knew, I woke up here. I don't know what happened to Nadia."

Raoul abruptly slammed his fist on the table and rose to his feet, leaning toward Lana menacingly. "What do you mean, you don't know what happened to Nadia? You don't get drunk or take drugs when you're watching an infant! No one in their right mind would do that! You can't just lose a baby! What kind of a monster are you?"

"Monsieur Massoni," the detective said without a trace of warmth in his blue eyes. "Please contain yourself or I will ask you to leave."

The veins in Raoul's neck stood out as he fought for control. Rebekka knew him well enough to know that he wasn't going to succeed without some time away from the situation. "André, take my brother on a walk, please."

"But—" began Raoul.

"Now." Rebekka stood and pushed her brother toward the door. "You're not helping anything," she told Raoul. "Go get some fresh air."

André put an arm around Raoul and half-dragged him across the room. "Rebekka's right," he said. "Let's go."

When the door shut behind them, Rebekka turned back to Lana, determined to undo the damage caused by Raoul's outburst. "Lana, you must understand why he's upset. Nadia is his daughter and he's never even seen her, thanks to Desirée. He's lost a lot of time with Nadia, and the realization that he may never have a chance to make up that time is a very heavy burden to bear. You understand that, don't you? He's got every right to be angry over this situation. He means no offense to you personally. He just wants his daughter."

Lana glared at her. "Oh, I can see that. I ain't stupid. But he's right, I shouldn't have started drinking or doing anything else. For what it's worth, I'm glad Nadia has a father who cares so much." She raised her chin and her jaw worked briefly before she continued. "But I do know that I *never* would have hurt Nadia on purpose—sober or drunk or drugged." Her brown eyes were abruptly more watery than before. "I took care of Nadia. I know I figured out what to do and took her some- where. I just don't remember where." With that announce- ment, she put her head in her hands and began to sob.

Rebekka was touched, and she reached out to Lana's arm. "I believe you, Lana. I believe you tried to take care of Nadia. So now all you've got to do is to remember where you left her. Will you try? Her life might depend upon it."

Lana nodded and wiped at her face. "I'll try," she said. "I loved her, too. I really did."

"I know."

Rebekka left Lana with the detective and went to find André and Raoul. Both looked up at her expectantly from the chairs outside the questioning room. Rebekka quickly outlined what more she had learned. "Lana just doesn't remember where she left Nadia. But she believes that she left her somewhere safe. We have to believe her."

"She's a drunk and a druggy," Raoul said, his face despondent. "Oh, how did I risk my child to such a woman?"

Rebekka knew he was referring to Desirée, not Lana, and she had no answer. She couldn't understand her own heart, much less Raoul's.

Her brother continued mournfully, "And what does she mean when she said Nadia doesn't cry much anymore? What did Desirée do to her so that she wouldn't cry?"

No one had an answer.

"We have to keep believing," André said. "She's out there somewhere and we are going to find her."

Rebekka took hold of her brother's hand. "Come on, Raoul. I'll drive us home."

Chapter 13

Four times Celisse messed in her pants that day. By the time her husband came home on Wednesday evening, Marie-Thérèse was exhausted and more than a little angry. Mathieu took one look at her stirring dinner on the stove with more than needed force and put his warm arms around her.

"Tough day, I see," he said.

She let out a long frustrated sigh. "It's just that I feel like I'm on an emotional rollercoaster. One minute I feel so happy to be helping Celisse, to be doing something that will make a difference in her life. And then, suddenly, I'm furious. She keeps messing her pants more and more, no matter what I do or how kind I am to her. I know she can use the bathroom. I know she understands—not once has she wet her pants. Just poop. And it's the stinkiest poop I've ever cleaned up. Sometimes I feel like she does it to spite me."

To her relief, Mathieu didn't laugh, or tell her she needed to pray for strength, as he may have earlier in their marriage. Heaven knew she had already been doing more than overtime on her knees. She had felt the presence of the Lord and was thankful, but today she needed a break. The best thing Mathieu could do for her was not to find an easy solution to her problems, but to hold her silently while she drank in his presence and support.

"I've only had the children since Friday," she continued, laying her head on his lean shoulder. "And I don't know if I'm up to it. The house is a mess and I . . ." She trailed off, not wanting to admit how out of control she felt.

"Do you think we should discuss this as a family?" Mathieu asked. "Perhaps if we enlist the children, let them know how you feel. I know I could certainly do more to help out. I'm sorry it's been so hard."

Marie-Thérèse's frustrations began to ease with his understanding. "You do a lot. You practically take care of Raquel every minute you're home."

"But Raquel is easy." He waved to the baby who watched them from the baby swing Josette had lent them. She smiled and Marie-Thérèse felt an urge to pick her up. Raquel was easily satisfied and even more easy to love. Marie-Thérèse could spend hours simply watching her—if she weren't so busy with Celisse.

She lowered her voice and said, "I don't want to give Raquel up. But sometimes—a lot of times—I don't feel that way about Celisse. Isn't that awful?"

"No. It's understandable. But does this mean . . .?"

"I'm not giving up—yet. I felt the Spirit the other day. I know I'm supposed to help Celisse."

"Have you called Pascale yet and told her we'd like to keep them?"

Marie-Thérèse felt her eyes widen. "Oh, no! I forgot! There was just so much going on. I never seem to have a free minute. And I've wanted to talk first with Larissa and Brandon about our decision . . . Oh, Mathieu, what if she's found a home for the girls? I know I've been sitting here complaining about Celisse but what if . . .?" Marie-Thérèse was amazed at her own emotions. How could her attitude change so drastically in less than a minute? *I want to get off this rollercoaster!* she screamed silently. But she knew she couldn't—or wouldn't. They were the same thing.

"Let's call her now." Releasing her, Mathieu went to the phone, while she quickly looked up Pascale's number. The agency was closed, but he left a message, saying it was urgent. "I'm sure she'll call back when she can."

Marie-Thérèse let herself be reassured by his confidence. "I guess I'd better go find Celisse. I put her in her room after the last potty accident. I know logically that this whole mess is really not her fault—that it somehow stems from the abuse and neglect she's gone through—but I needed to calm down before I lost my temper. She doesn't deserve that."

"No, though I do understand the frustration. Anyway, a little time in her room won't hurt her." Mathieu looked around. "Where are the kids, anyway?"

"Larissa's in her room—actually doing homework, I think. And Brandon's in the sitting room watching a video he borrowed from a friend."

"Brandon!" Mathieu called. A minute later he appeared and father and son shared a hearty hug. "Would you watch Raquel for a minute while we go talk to Celisse?"

"Sure," Brandon said. "Can I take her out of the swing, though? I want to watch my show."

"Of course." Marie-Thérèse watched as Brandon removed Raquel from the swing.

"I've got a great video for you to watch," he said. "Don't worry, I'll cover your eyes during the scary parts." Raquel smiled at him and tried to put her hand in his mouth. Brandon pretended to nibble it.

Mathieu took Marie-Thérèse's hand as they walked down the hall. "I've been thinking," he said. "What if Celisse's problem isn't just your normal potty-training accidents?"

"It's not—that's what I've been trying to tell you. I know I've only trained two children, but it doesn't seem normal. Even Josette says that and she's got five boys."

"Well, maybe we ought to take her to the doctor. Or if you think that might be too traumatic, we could call up that nurse friend of your mother's. She might have an idea."

Marie-Thérèse felt her burden lighten. "Maybe you're right. I wanted to talk to her about finding a good pediatrician, anyway. Our doctor is good, but I think Celisse has problems trusting men. Besides, we need a doctor who specializes in sexual abuse."

"That's probably a good idea," Mathieu said solemnly. Then he sighed. "Oh, Marie-Thérèse, what have we gotten ourselves into?"

Marie-Thérèse actually managed a chuckle. "I don't know, but I'm glad we're in it together."

* * *

An hour after dinner they put Celisse and Raquel to bed and called Larissa and Brandon back to the kitchen table. There was one chair empty: the new one Grandma Ariana had brought over for Celisse.

Larissa looked at them warily, while Brandon's stare was curious. Mathieu cleared his throat. "Look children," he began, "your mother and I have been talking seriously about the future of Celisse and Raquel. We know their being here has not been easy for any of us—especially for your mother. But since the day I met those little girls . . ." He paused, suddenly overcome with what he wanted to say. Marie-Thérèse reached for his hand, touched by the open display of his emotions.

Swallowing twice, rather noisily, he continued, his black eyes glinting with moisture. "Since the day they came into our home I felt they belonged here and that we had a chance to make a real difference in their lives." Larissa began to speak, but Mathieu held up his hand. "Wait. I know you'll all want to speak but I need to finish first." He took a deep breath. "I knew your mother would be the one who would be primarily responsible for their care, should they stay with us, and I didn't want to force her into any decision she would regret. She was reluctant." Mathieu's eyes met Marie-Thérèse's briefly. She could almost feel a smile in the glance.

"Her reluctance stemmed from a lot of areas—many of which I don't think either of you could begin to understand. But she was certainly worried about our relationship with each of you . . . as well as Larissa's continuing objections to us adopting."

"And I was afraid of losing them," Marie-Thérèse interrupted. "The girls, I mean. I think you kids can understand that. I was afraid of losing them like I lost my parents, and my sister, and almost lost Brandon that time in the hospital. I mean, after all, the girls aren't ours. They could be taken away and put in a more suitable home at any time . . . or even with their mother."

"Even after what she did to them?" Brandon blurted.

"We don't know she did it," Larissa said.

Brandon rolled his eyes. "She allowed it to happen—it's the same thing. She didn't fight to help her kids. She let people do horrible things to Celisse. She doesn't deserve to have them back. I think they should stay here!"

"I won't share my room!" Larissa's face began to grow red. "That's what'll happen eventually. Me and them in one room. They'll be all over my stuff—touching it, using it, messing it up. I don't want them here!"

Mathieu calmly took his hand from Marie-Thérèse's and reached for the portable phone sitting on its charger. He offered it to Larissa. "Okay, why don't you call their mother and ask her to pick them up? Will you be responsible for what will happen to Celisse?"

Marie-Thérèse held her breath. They didn't know Celisse's mother's number, nor had the police even found her yet, so there was no way they could call her. *What are you doing, Mathieu?* she asked silently.

Larissa didn't take the phone. "Well, there has to be another place for them to go. Mom can't handle this anyway. She was crying when we got home from school today." The words came placidly, but her chin quivered slightly. She wrinkled her freckled nose. "I want things to go back the way they were."

Mathieu replaced the phone and stared at her silently for a few minutes. "I'm trying to understand how you feel, Larissa, and I want you to know that I'm in total agreement about you having your own room. You are a teenager now and these girls are small. You sleep at different times, your needs are different. I am in no way suggesting that you give up your privacy."

Marie-Thérèse touched her husband's arm to let him know she had something to add. Mathieu stopped talking and everyone looked at her expectantly. "I just wanted to add here how proud I am of you, Larissa for keeping your room so nice and clean and orderly. I think I've begun to understand your concern about your room in the past few days since my own order has been so undone. It's really frustrating and I wouldn't want you to face that if you didn't want to. Your dad's right. You're old enough to need your own space separate from any little kids." Marie-Thérèse was gratified to see a small smile on her daughter's face.

"Actually," Mathieu said to Larissa, "you and Brandon would be more suitable roommates." He held up a hand to prevent another onslaught of protests, "But I know that since you aren't the same sex, that isn't really reasonable. What I'd like to do tonight is discuss our options. But first I want your mother to tell you what happened when she prayed about Celisse and Raquel."

All eyes turned to her, and Marie-Thérèse smiled, trying to recapture the spiritual feelings that had so overwhelmed her the day before. "As your father suggested, I was really reluctant about doing anything permanent in respects to the girls, though I could see that he wanted to. Every day I saw him growing closer to them, and finally, we talked and we both agreed to pray about any decision we would make. Dad continued to feel like we should try to become their foster family—with the possibility of adoption later on. But I kept worrying about my orderly life, my fears, and"—her eyes met her daughter's—"about Larissa's reaction. I realized that if they stayed the girls wouldn't just be a part of my life, but they would take up almost *all* my life. I didn't know if I was willing to sacrifice that much time, to lose that much control. And I didn't know if that would be fair to you two." She heard the embarrassment creep into her voice. "Had it just been Raquel, the decision would have been much easier. Raquel is . . . well, she is so precious." Tears sprang to her eyes. "But so is Celisse, and she needs us even more than Raquel. I told God I didn't want to do it, and I felt so guilty for admitting it. And then it came, this . . . this feeling."

She sat up straighter in her chair, looking directly at Larissa, silently pleading for her to understand. "And that's when I knew I had to try. I couldn't just stand by and let Celisse drop through the cracks. She had come to us for a reason, and suddenly my concerns didn't mean anything if we could make an eternal difference in her life. I know it won't be easy, but if we all help, we can do it *and* be happy."

Brandon was nodding, but Larissa's face showed no expression. Mathieu's brow furrowed in frustration. "Larissa," he said gently. "If your mother and I had been able, we would have had more children. We've always wanted more children. We have the chance here to not only achieve our dream, but to do something that can make a difference in the world. Celisse needs us, don't you see that? But helping her doesn't have to mean our good times are over, or that our feelings for you and Brandon will change. Please, tell us how you feel. Let's talk about it."

Larissa's gaze dropped to her hands, tightly gripping one another atop the table. Her short, spiky black hair shone under the lights. "I think you've already decided."

"We still want to know how you feel," Marie-Thérèse said. "You and Brandon have always been our chief concern."

"Maybe until now," Larissa mumbled, not bothering to hide the bitterness in the words.

"We love you." Mathieu's voice was calm. "And if you can give us a good reason for not helping the girls, we will certainly take it into consideration."

Larissa wrinkled her nose again, several times as though she needed to blow it. "I don't think you would, not really," she said waveringly. "Because we're not enough. You still want more." Her brown eyes rose to meet her father's black ones, and Marie-Thérèse saw tears in them. "You want more daughters, at least."

Mathieu scooted his chair closer to Larissa. He placed his hand next to hers but she moved hers away. "Look, honey," he said. "No matter what, you will always be my little girl, my firstborn daughter—flesh of my flesh. You are the first baby I ever walked the halls with all night. The first child I ever took to the zoo or had smear ice cream down my shirt." Mathieu smiled at that, and even Larissa's lips twitched. "No one could ever take your place in my heart. But you see, Larissa, love isn't one of those finite things like cookies or chocolate that we have to gobble up quickly to get our share. Love is something that increases with the giving. The more you give, the more you *have* to give. There is room in my heart for the girls, just as there was for you and Brandon when you were each born. It doesn't mean I love you or Brandon any less. This I promise you with my whole heart. That's why we're sitting around this table right now. Your mother and I want your support—and Brandon's. We need to do this as a family." He took her hand now, and Larissa let him.

"I really won't have to share my room?"

"No. In fact, your mother and I talked briefly about moving into another apartment. With the sound investments your mother has been making over the years, not to mention the trust fund her parents set up for her as a child, I think we'll be able to swing it. We'll even get a place with two bathrooms."

Larissa's tight frown faded. "That would be nice." She waited a minute before asking, "And I won't have to baby-sit?"

Marie-Thérèse was disappointed by the question, but she understood Larissa's concern. "No," she said. "We won't make you baby-sit. However, I hope after a time you'll want to."

"Then I guess I don't really mind too much." Larissa inclined her head toward Mathieu's. He followed the gesture and as their heads touched, Marie-Thérèse read contentment on their faces.

"I'll baby-sit any time you want," Brandon said into the silence. "But what if you have to take me to the doctor? Won't she even have to watch them then?"

"Yeah, right. That'd be like every day practically," Larissa sneered, pulling first her head and then her hand from her father. "You're always sick."

"It's not my fault I have allergies to a few things."

"To almost everything, you mean," she shot back.

"Children, Brandon's allergies are not at issue here," Mathieu said with a warning glance. "We promise we won't make Larissa baby-sit unless she wants to and that's that." He rubbed his hands together. "Well then, it's decided. We'll become the girls' foster family, if they let us, and maybe more down the road. Meanwhile, we'll look for a four-room apartment with two bathrooms."

"It won't be easy to find," Marie-Thérèse said.

Mathieu smiled. "Maybe easier than you think. I know just the real estate agent."

"Uncle Zack!" Brandon shouted.

"Have you already talked to him?" Marie-Thérèse's words came more sharply than intended. She hated the idea of Mathieu going behind her back.

"Of course not, but he'll find a place. The Lord wants us to help these girls and I'm sure He'll help Zack find us the perfect home."

Larissa rolled her eyes at her father's comment, but didn't look too unhappy.

"Until then, we'll make do here," Mathieu said. "Brandon's doesn't mind sleeping in the TV room and Celisse—and eventually Raquel—will share his room."

Marie-Thérèse stood and pushed in her chair. "Well, I guess it's time for bed."

"Of course, we'll have to do something about Larissa's hair first," Mathieu teased. "With those sharp spikes she just might make her pillow pop. She just about brought blood when her head touched mine a minute ago."

Brandon sniggered, but Larissa stuck her nose in the air. "I *like* my hair."

"So do I," Mathieu quipped. "Just don't poke me when you hug me goodnight. Come here now, o thou daughter of mine, and give me a big hug and kiss."

Marie-Thérèse thought it was a good sign that Larissa laughed with them and didn't stomp off to her room at the teasing. Beside, while her daughter's hair was much too short and spiky for Marie-Thérèse's tastes, at least it wasn't green or orange.

"Goodnight," Marie-Thérèse said, kissing and hugging Brandon before he went to the sitting room to sleep. As usual, she placed her head against his chest to make sure he was breathing without effort. The last time they had seen the doctor, she had learned that not only had he developed allergies to several more foods, but he was also borderline asthmatic, and the doctor asked her to monitor his breathing. Unbeknownst to Brandon, she often checked on him in the middle of the night.

"I'm fine, Mom," Brandon whispered.

"Good."

Marie-Thérèse followed her daughter down the hall. At her room she opened her arms for a hug. To her gratification, Larissa actually hugged her back. "I love you, Larissa. More than you will ever know until you are a mother yourself. And you may not believe me now, but Celisse and Raquel have love to give too—to you. Think of how close I am to your Aunt Josette, of how often I call her on the phone to talk or how often we visit one another. Next to your father she is my very best friend. It always made me so sad to think you could never share that closeness with another woman. And now maybe you will. Years down the road, you might just find that these new little sisters—should we be fortunate enough to keep them—could be the best gift you have ever been given."

"But what about all the extra work?" Larissa asked hesitantly. "You were crying today."

"It wasn't the first time—you should have seen me when you and Brandon were little! But I'll be all right. Really."

"I wish she'd just stop pooping in her pants. That's so gross. And it makes the bathroom stink all the time."

"Maybe nobody ever taught her differently."

Larissa brows drew in thought. "That's so sad."

"I know. That's why we want to help. That's why we *have* to help."

Larissa drew away and looked at her steadily. "You know, Mom. I don't really want them here, but I suppose if they have to be here then it's good they have you. I think you're a really good mom."

Marie-Thérèse blinked back her tears and tried not to act surprised at the compliment. "Thank you, Larissa. I really appreciate it. You don't know how much I needed to hear that today."

"Maybe I did." Larissa smiled almost shyly. "G'night, Mom."

"Goodnight."

Larissa shut the door and Marie-Thérèse stared at it for a long time. She couldn't decide if this was the first of many blessings or the calm before the storm.

Chapter 14

Rebekka was weary when she finally arrived at her apartment with Raoul. He had been upset after the incident at the police station and she worried he might do something desperate. He was just so angry . . . and desolate. André had promised to see to Raoul's car—left back at the hotel—and to take care of work.

Rebekka was feeling completely sick when she and Raoul arrived at their apartment, and it was all she could do to get herself a large glass of milk and a croissant for dinner. Raoul came out of his depression long enough to ask her how she was feeling.

"I've been worse," she told him.

He sat in the kitchen chair opposite her, elbows on the table and head in his hands. "I wonder if I will ever know if Desirée was sick while she was pregnant with Nadia," he said morosely. "I'll never have the experience of seeing my first child born, of dressing her to take her home from the hospital. Of watching her eat her first meal. Desirée took all that away from me in the same selfish way she did everything else. I wonder if she ever loved me at all."

"Hey, what's not to love?" Rebekka said, trying to cheer him.

He stared at his fingers. "Me, apparently."

Rebekka sighed. "Look Raoul, the problem is hers. It always was. Yes, there were signs before you got married, but you're not the only one who's made a mistake in life. Desirée would have burned anyone she married. You loved her, you forgave her repeatedly, you did your best. She didn't deserve you. It was her fault, not yours."

"She told me she would have aborted the baby if it had been any other man's." He gave a self-deprecating laugh. "I know it's strange, but I do find some comfort in that. At least I meant something . . . or enough to save Nadia."

"When Desirée walked out on you, she walked out on the best thing in her life," Rebekka said, willing her brother to see her sincerity. "You are a wonderful person—and don't you forget it."

Raoul managed a weak smile. "Thanks, Rebekka. It was a good idea, moving in with you. I don't know what I'd have done these past few days without your support."

"It's been mutual." Despite her determination to be strong for him, her voice wavered.

"Oh, Rebekka. I'm sorry. You miss him, don't you?"

She nodded. "Yes." She let a comfortable silence fill the room and then said, "Though today was easier. I was so caught up in trying to help find Nadia that I hardly had time to think about him. I mean, he's never far from my thoughts, but today, I didn't feel that desperate feeling that seems to twist my insides. Does that make sense?"

"Yes." He laid his hand over hers where it lay on the table. "I think I know that desperation very well." He snorted. "It's different, of course. My situation."

And it was. Rebekka believed his situation was much worse. At least she had the hope of eternity with Marc, whereas Raoul has only betrayal and broken dreams. "I'm sorry, Raoul."

"Thank you." He stood, squeezing her hand one last time. "I don't feel like eating so I'm going to turn in. I'm exhausted. Didn't sleep much last night thinking about Nadia. And I want to go in to work early— maybe five. I won't wake you when I leave."

"Sounds good. I—I'll let you know if I hear anything. It's early. There's still time for something to happen tonight."

He nodded and walked slowly toward the hall. In the doorway, he paused. "Uh, Rebekka, I'm very happy about your baby. I really am." He blinked hard and she could see tears glinting in his eyes and on his cheeks. "I know how much having Marc's child means to you. And if you need anything—even someone to help get your frustrations out—let me know. We have to stick together."

"I will." She wanted to thank him, but her throat was too tight. Another word and she would cry.

"Oh, and you know how much André cares about you, don't you?" Raoul continued. "He's a great guy."

Rebekka blankly watched her brother leave the kitchen. *Where did that come from?* she wondered. *Of course André's a sweet guy. But doesn't Raoul realize that André is only fulfilling what he perceives as his duty?* Rebekka took another sip of cold milk, wishing now that she had taken the time to heat it in the microwave.

This has to stop, she thought. *I can't have André hovering over me because Marc asked him to. Somehow, there has to be a way to get him to back off. Some way that won't hurt him.*

But what? She'd have to prove to him that she was happy for one thing.

Even if she wasn't? Rebekka sighed. Solving her dilemma might take more time than she was willing to invest.

As she pondered her options, the buzzer near the door sounded, signaling that someone wanted into the apartment building. She sauntered into the entryway, marveling at how much better she felt since she had eaten again. Though she had never been fond of milk, it was now quickly becoming her best friend.

"Who is it?" she asked.

"Flower delivery."

Flower delivery, she repeated silently. *But Samuel already sent me flowers yesterday. Who would have sent more?*

Yet it would be like Samuel to send another bouquet. He was the sort of man who knew how to woo a woman properly. "Though I am not available for wooing," she said aloud.

"What?" asked the man over the intercom.

"Uh, nothing. Come on up." She pressed the release button and heard the door click open.

A few minutes later, the doorbell rang and she looked through the peephole to be sure the man had flowers. Sure enough, a young boy barely out of his teens staggered under the weight of a large vase of red and white roses. Rebekka shook her head in amazement.

"They're really heavy," he grunted as she opened the door. "Do you have somewhere you want me to put them?"

"In the sitting room would be fine," Rebekka said. "It's only a few steps. This way, please. Wow, they are certainly gorgeous!"

"Yep," he grunted. After he set them down and she had signed the delivery form, the young man hurried out of the apartment. Rebekka barely saw him go. She touched first a red rose, so dark it was nearly black, and then one as white as her wedding dress. There were also several varieties of roses that were a beautiful mixture of red and white.

She reached for the small dark green envelope. It resisted her first tug and she pulled again, scraping her middle finger on a thorn. "Drat!" she exclaimed, as the blood started to leak from the small gash.

Sitting on the sofa, she pulled a white card with an embossed green border from the envelope. Without reading it, she blotted her bloody finger on the envelope. Marc would have sucked his cut, she mused. No matter how many times she had told him it was unsanitary, he had always insisted that he needed all the blood he had and wouldn't waste a drop.

When the flow had ebbed to nothing, Rebekka glanced at the card, ready to savor the words which were scribbled with green lettering:

> *I would have liked the other flowers to have been from me, too.*
>
>   *Love, André*

Rebekka didn't know what to make of his offering. Had he felt so bad about her mistaken assumption that he had to remedy it by actually sending flowers? But why? Since he was the only one who had been in the apartment, it was only natural she would have assumed he had brought them. And even if he had, the act wouldn't have meant anything other than a celebration of her pregnancy. But now. . .

The fragrance of the roses demanded her attention. She let her thoughts slide as she leaned forward to breathe in the heady aroma. André's face came into her mind—so much like his brother, and yet . . . so unlike him. A tenderness she had not believed herself capable of feeling ever again since Marc's death seeped slowly in her heart, seemingly out of nowhere. And with it came the music.

She hadn't touched a piano for over two months, but now she felt the urge to play. Her eyes flew to the small upright piano against the sitting room wall. She noticed that someone—she didn't know who—had kept its cherry wood exterior polished to a brilliant glow. Memories rushed out at her.

Once she had thought she might pursue music as a career and in her years of study had won many awards. But her love of languages had been stronger and in college she had double-majored in French and English. For a while she had worked at the American Embassy in Paris, but now she did only translating. She loved her job, but music—that was her release, one she had forgotten about since Marc's death, as she had so many other things that had been important to her. She stared at the piano now, unable to move or to comprehend the feelings in her heart. How could there ever be music again without her husband? And yet the desire to play was there, beckoning.

The ringing of the phone called to her from far away. Over and over it sounded, until Rebekka finally shook her head, clearing away the tender feelings in her heart. The ringing was instantly louder. She dived for the phone, praying the caller would not hang up. *I promised Raoul I would let him know if the police called*, she thought.

"Hello?" she asked quickly.

"Rebekka?"

"Yes. Who's this?"

"It's Desirée."

Rebekka's heart seemed to skip a beat. "Desirée! Where are you? We've been looking everywhere!"

"Look, I'm not staying on the phone long and I'm not telling you where I am. I just need to know . . . did you find Nadia?"

Rebekka gripped the phone more tightly. "No. Not yet. We did find your friend Lana, though. In jail. She said she didn't give Nadia to Benny."

"She's a good friend."

There was a sniff on the other end on the line, but Rebekka couldn't tell if Desirée was crying or if she had a cold. "A good friend? How do you figure that? She *lost* Nadia, for crying out loud. She can't remember where she put her. And there's always the possibility she gave Nadia to Benny and doesn't remember. Maybe that's how she got the money to buy the drugs and alcohol she was using."

"Drugs? She doesn't normally . . . Well, if she said she didn't sell Nadia, she didn't. Lana wouldn't lie. At least not about this."

"Hey, you're the one who suggested she might go to Benny. Don't be so defensive. I'm just worried about Nadia."

"She'll be okay." Desirée's voice sounded sure. "Lana's trustworthy. Even drunk she's responsible."

Rebekka wanted to remind Desirée that there were also drugs involved, but felt it would get her nowhere. "Look, isn't there anyplace you know of that Lana might take her? Did she have a family somewhere? Another friend? A co-worker?"

"No. I don't know who she might go to. But I'll think about it and let you know."

"Why don't you go into the police? They could use your help."

"No! I won't. I can't."

Rebekka's anger was steadily increasing. "Desirée, this is your baby we're talking about!"

"No. She's Raoul's now."

Rebekka wished she could hit Desirée over the head with the phone. "At least you should talk to Raoul."

"No. I won't do that, either. But I'll call you back if I remember anything."

"Nadia could need you *right now*," Rebekka said quietly.

There was a long silence. At last Desirée said. "No, she needs you and Raoul." Then she hung up the phone. Rebekka waited until the dial tone came back to be sure. With a sigh, she placed the receiver on its cradle, feeling a deep sadness. How far gone Desirée must be to abandon her baby!

Yet she *had* called. There *had* been concern in her voice. That must mean something. Rebekka would simply have to pray for her to call back with some information. Or that Lana remember where she had left Nadia.

As if driven by her desire, the telephone rang again. "Hello?" Rebekka asked eagerly.

"She has a birthmark," Desirée said without preamble. "On the right side of her bottom. You can only see it when you change her diaper."

"On her right side," Rebekka repeated.

"Yeah. Looks like a heart—an upside down heart. Actually, it's two brown freckles kinda overlapping. Dark brown. Sticks out a bit." She cleared her throat. "It's really cute."

The phone went dead again in Rebekka's hand. She took a few seconds to digest the information and then began searching in her purse for the card Detective Francom had given her.

"Hello, Detective," she said when he answered. "I'm glad I caught you before you left for the day."

He chuckled. "I often work late. I don't have anyone waiting up for me, and I enjoy my work, so this is mostly where I am."

"That's good, I guess," Rebekka mumbled, feeling distinctly sorry for him. "I wanted to let you know that I heard from my sister-in-law."

"You did? Did you get her location?"

"No. But she didn't know much anyway. The only information she had was that Nadia has a birthmark on her right buttock, normally covered by her diaper. It's two overlapping freckles that sort of make a heart—upside down. I'm not sure exactly where it is, but that should help, right?"

"Any information is important."

Rebekka thought he sounded bored. "I tried to get her to come in to talk to you, but she wouldn't."

"I'm not surprised. She wouldn't like what would happen."

His comment rankled. "Well, I don't believe Desirée was acting responsibly," Rebekka said, "but I don't think you can charge her with leaving Nadia in the care of her friend. If anything, it's Lana who could be charged—right?"

"I wasn't talking about her role in the child's disappearance."

"Then what? What else has Desirée done?"

"Well, I suppose since she's your sister-in-law, and since you'd eventually hear it from your brother anyway, I wouldn't be overstepping my bounds to tell you that she's been driving a little too fast. She's been ticketed."

"A traffic ticket? She doesn't want to help us find her baby because of a lousy traffic ticket?"

"Well, it's not just a single traffic ticket. Like I told your brother today, she has more than a dozen. Suffice it to say that if we found Desirée Massoni, we would be detaining her for quite some time."

Rebekka sighed and rubbed her temple with her fingers. "At least that explains why she vanished."

"Yes, and if we thought she had a more prominent role in your niece's disappearance, we'd tap your phone to find her. As it is, I wouldn't be able to get a court order for that."

Rebekka was silent. Her heart ached to think that because of Desirée's lifestyle, she was unable—no, unwilling—to help her baby. *How does that make her feel if it makes me want to cry?*

"Uh, Madame Perrault?"

"Oh, excuse me, Detective. Did you say something?"

"I was saying that we found a connection to Benny Tovik that you might want to know about."

"Oh?"

"Yesterday evening we found a sixteen-year-old woman dead of a drug overdose. In a subsequent search of the apartment, we found a thousand dollars in cash, an address to a rather seedy motel, and a few pictures of a baby that remarkably resemble the infant you and your husband described seeing with Tovik. I—"

"Detective Francom, he's not my husband," Rebekka interrupted. "André Perrault is my brother-in-law."

"I'm sorry. I remember you saying that today." He paused, for the first time sounding uncertain. "In fact, it made quiet an impression. Your, uh, brother-in-law didn't looked pleased at all when you pointed it out."

"My husband's dead," Rebekka said bluntly. "He was killed in a car accident over two months ago. He didn't know that I was expecting.

André and his brother were very close. It's been hard for all of us."

"I'm sorry. Again, I apologize for the mistake."

"It's all right. We probably should have mentioned it. Now, as you were saying—about the girl?"

"Yes. I had her parents in just now and apparently the daughter was pregnant and they had a big fight and she left. Been gone about six months. They don't know where she's been since. She was due about three weeks ago."

"That might fit the baby's age—especially if she was born a week or so early. She didn't look two months old to me. How can you be sure?"

"The baby wasn't born in the hospital—as we suspected, but we are dusting the apartment and its contents now. If we find a match to the print you took today, we'll have enough to arrest and convict Benny. There is no way he could convince the court that he legally obtained the baby from a minor child. And the parents are pretty desperate to find their grandchild. The baby is all they have left now."

"How sad," Rebekka said. "Let me know, will you? I really hope that baby belongs to them. I feel better knowing someone wants her."

"There are thousands of couples who want her."

"I meant that . . ." Rebekka trailed off. She was so tired she didn't know what she meant anymore. "Anyway, thank you."

"You're welcome. Please feel free to call me again if you have any more information."

"I will."

"And don't worry," he added. "We'll do our best."

She sighed. "And if that's not good enough?"

"I don't know. I can only do my best."

"I know. I really do appreciate that. Thank you."

"Goodbye, Madame Perrault."

"Goodbye, Detective."

Rebekka no longer felt like playing the piano. She set the phone on the table and wandered down the hall. It had grown dark in the past hour, reminding her that winter was well on its way. She didn't turn on the lights, but felt her way in the dimness. Without knowing why, she found herself in the office, staring up at the portrait of her and Marc by the Seine River. Guilt overcame her as she remembered how Marc had not been her constant unseen companion today as he usually was. She hadn't even once talked to him.

I'm sorry, honey, she thought. *I do love you. It's just . . . when I think about you, it hurts so much. And today was so busy. I actually felt I was making a difference, that I was helping Raoul. You understand, don't you?*

There was no answer, but Rebekka knew him well enough to know that wherever he was he did understand. But would there ever come a time when she would think about him and their life together without the feeling of great loss? A time when she could remember the joy without also experiencing the pain?

She simply didn't know.

What she did know was that she had to distance herself from André. His very presence was disconcerting and confusing. Though why that was she couldn't explain. She did know that for some foolish, absurd, illogical reason, she kept replaying in her mind his ridiculous proposal of marriage.

Chapter 15

"Marie-Thérèse, that's wonderful!" Josette exclaimed, her face flushed with animation. "We'll have a family party to celebrate." She grabbed Marie-Thérèse in a tight squeeze before dropping into a kitchen chair.

"Aren't we getting together on Sunday for dinner anyway?" Marie-Thérèse asked. She was still in her robe after seeing the children off to school. For once Celisse and the baby had slept late, and she had been enjoying her moment of free time when her sister arrived unexpectedly. Josette's visit was welcome, but she wondered if her sister noticed the mess in the kitchen and the worse one in the sitting room where Brandon's belongings were strewn about in his usual haphazard way.

"Yes, but your news can't wait until Sunday! It deserves it's own announcement. Oh, I can't believe it! I'm so excited for you!"

Marie-Thérèse sat across from her sister, amazed at her energy. How did she keep it up with five little boys to take care of? "Well, I'm still waiting for Pascale's approval. She hasn't called me back yet. Mathieu and I only told the children last night."

"What about Mom and Dad?"

"You're the first one I've told."

Josette leaned forward, and a lock of her long dark hair fell in a dark puddle onto the table. "Good. Don't tell anyone else. You can make an announcement tomorrow night."

"It's Friday—everyone may have plans."

"Then they can change them!" Josette laughed. "Don't worry, I'll make sure they do. Anyway, the only one who really might be planning something is Louis-Géralde, and he can just bring that cute little girl he's dating over to the party. They've been going out two months now—I wouldn't be surprised if he had an announcement of his own very soon."

The idea that their youngest brother might soon be getting married felt odd to Marie-Thérèse. Louis Géralde had been home from his mission in the Ukraine nine months already, but it seemed like only yesterday he had left.

A silence had pervaded the kitchen and Marie-Thérèse looked closely at her sister's beautiful face. There was a sadness there beneath the vivaciousness, one that bit into Marie-Thérèse's heart.

"You're thinking of Marc," she said.

Josette closed her eyes without speaking, her dark lashes contrasting sharply with the white of her skin. For a moment, Marie-Thérèse saw their mother Ariana in her features. When Josette's eyes opened, they held tears. "I knew the moment he was gone," she said. "I was sitting at home reading to David and suddenly the tears just started to come. It was . . ." She struggled to speak through her emotion. "It was some silly, happy story, you know, with the children dancing around counting things, and there I was crying. It was like a part of me had died. At first I thought something was wrong with Zack or one of the children, but then Dad called to tell me about Marc."

"He was your twin," Marie-Thérèse said gently. "You were very close."

"I remember Mom said she felt the same way when her twin died. I'm glad I had Marc longer than she had her brother and that he was able to have some years married to Rebekka." Tears leaked from the corners of Josette's eyes and made steady rivulets down her cheeks. "But I miss him. Not every day—with five boys I'm mostly too tired to do any thinking at all, but whenever I have a minute . . . I just miss him so much. The idea of a family party without him . . ." She sighed. "I think it would be easier if he had left something behind. You know, a child. Something we could love as much as we loved him. I've even thought of having another baby myself and naming him Marc—of course he'd be a boy, that's all I know how to make—but then that really wouldn't be the same thing, would it? And I don't think either Zack or I would live through another pregnancy." She impatiently dabbed at her wet cheeks. "I can't stop wondering how Rebekka even makes it through each day. If I didn't have Zack and the kids, I'd be lost."

"Me too," Marie-Thérèse agreed. "Rebekka has no one really—except Raoul and her parents. That's really not the same thing. And now suddenly I'm feeling guilty because I haven't been to see her as much as I should this past week. These girls keep me rather busy."

"I know what you mean. Even though I have only David at home during the day, I'm always busy. That's why I dropped him off this morning at Mom's. Thought maybe I could get some grocery shopping done without the hassle today. Do you need anything while I'm there?"

Josette's tears were drying now, and Marie-Thérèse knew from the determination in her voice that she was purposefully focusing on something other than Marc. They had both learned that doing so was the cure to a broken heart.

"I need an entire list of things," Marie-Thérèse said. "Too much to ask you to get. I need to go myself, but I haven't dared taking the girls out. I'm afraid Celisse will mess her pants."

"You could use a diaper."

Marie-Thérèse stared. "I never even thought of that! I mean, she's four years old!"

"I know, but sometimes an hour of relief can buy you a world of patience. Believe me, Anton taught me that. I thought he'd never potty-train in time to go to school."

"Then get me some diapers, okay? Big enough to fit Celisse."

Josette stood. "Okay. I'll be back in an hour or so."

"Thanks."

Marie-Thérèse walked her sister to the door, thinking how much less burdened she felt with the short exchange. Even the prospect of grocery shopping seemed exciting after being practically imprisoned in the apartment since last Friday.

Almost a week, she thought. *How much my life has changed in that short time.*

Marie-Thérèse went to check on the girls and found Raquel lying awake in her bassinet. She dimpled when Marie-Thérèse walked into the room, and began moving her arms and legs in excitement. A rush of love filled Marie-Thérèse's heart to bursting. She picked up Raquel and cuddled her carefully. "I love you so much baby. You are so precious. You know that? Yes, you are. I love you so much." Tears sprouted unbidden. What if Raquel couldn't be hers? With each day that passed Marie-Thérèse loved her more, and Celisse, too, despite her problems. Marie-Thérèse hugged the infant to her chest tightly. *I won't allow either of you go back to your mother. I'll protect you.*

"Come on," she said aloud. "Let's go check on your sister and then get you dressed.

Celisse was awake and Marie-Thérèse had just finished bathing and dressing the girls when Pascale finally called. "Hello?" Marie-Thérèse answered a bit breathlessly.

"Marie-Thérèse? It's Pascale."

"You got our message."

"Yes. And actually, I just got off the phone with your husband. He called me again this morning."

"And?" Marie-Thérèse tried not to hold her breath, but she was afraid Pascale would hear her nervousness in the shallow breathing.

"And I would be delighted to put in your request. Of course, there'll be more paperwork and some classes you'll have to take, but the girls can remain in your care."

Marie-Thérèse took a slow and easy breath. "What about adoption?"

"Given Celisse's condition, I think it would be a miracle if the mother was ever awarded custody again, though stranger things have happened. Some mothers actually straighten up when faced with losing their children, but I really doubt that will happen in this case. Celisse has not only been neglected, but seriously abused. And the fact that we haven't been able to find the mother is also very much on our side."

"Maybe she's dead. I mean she always came back before, right?"

"She may be afraid of being caught. I believe we'll find her—hopefully soon. We won't be able to move toward adoption until we do find her."

"And if we never do?"

"Well, there is a time limitation. But let's discuss this when you come in, okay? I'll give you all the information you need to know. And meanwhile, you'll be receiving money for their care. That's how fostering works. It's not much, but it'll pay their food and basic expenses."

"What about that other family you had lined up? Aren't they going to be disappointed? Especially about Raquel?" Marie-Thérèse had to know.

Pascale was quiet a long moment. "There never was another family, Marie-Thérèse," she said. "Oh, I was trying to find one, but I was praying that you and Mathieu . . . I knew how much you two wanted a child before. No matter how many other families I thought about, you kept coming to my mind. And frankly, I hoped you'd grow attached to them and want to keep them. Can you forgive me?"

"Yes." Marie-Thérèse smiled through her tears. "Oh yes. They *were* meant to be here. That much is true. I just hope . . ."

"That everything works out," Pascale finished.

"Exactly."

"It will. Now, let me tell you what we need to do next."

* * *

Later Thursday afternoon, Marie-Thérèse felt nervous as she approached the physician's office carrying Celisse. That morning after she had talked to Pascale, Monique had not only called with the name of a female pediatrician who specialized in working with abused children, but had also succeeded in wheedling a brief appointment for that very day. Feeling confident after an uneventful trip to the grocery store with a newly diapered Celisse, she had left Raquel with Josette and jumped at the opportunity. She wanted to begin helping Celisse deal with what she had been through—emotionally and physically—and find out if there was a reason for her bowel problems.

Dr. Veronique Lerat was a tall, thin woman with black, shoulder-length hair and a round face. She looked young and pleasant, though a little sterile in her white lab jacket. Celisse hid her face as she entered the room, but when the doctor didn't touch or threaten her during Marie-Thérèse's long explanation of the circumstances, Celisse relaxed. She even began playing with the dolls on the nearby table. After a while, she let Dr. Lerat feel her stomach over her clothes, but protested when she tried to examine her further. Dr. Lerat did not push the matter.

"From what you describe and from what I feel when I touch her lower stomach area," Dr. Lerat said, "I believe Celisse has an impacted bowel. Basically that means she's been holding in her bowel movements over a long period of time until her bowel stretched much larger than normal, perhaps even to the size of an adult's. Usually this begins because a child doesn't want to eliminate because its painful—either because of constipation or a tear in the skin. What is coming into her underwear each day is slippage from around the impacted poop. Little if any of the old stuff is being eliminated. New waste slips around, becoming very odorous on its way down."

"The bathroom does smell for hours after we wash the underwear," Marie-Thérèse commented. "But what can I do?"

"The cure is rather simple: we have to eliminate the cause—most likely poor nutrition. But it will still take time for the bowel to resume and maintain its normal size—often up to a year. I will give you a prescription for a laxative that is safe for her size and for an extended period of time. Whatever you do—don't stop the treatment until I tell you to, even though you'll see a noticeable improvement right away. If you stop even six months into the program it will likely come back. In severe cases such as hers, I've seen that happen too many times to count. It's very important that we fix this now. An impacted bowel can lead to many other problems—the least of which are tiredness, headache, listlessness, general feeling of unwellness."

"Could this be in anyway related to her . . . her abuse?"

"I'm sure it is, though it certainly can happen to children who aren't neglected and abused. Sometimes children aren't really neglected, but the parents are so busy, they forget how vital nutrition is for young children—for everyone really—and they feed them convenient or fast foods with no vegetables. Since Celisse is no longer in her former situation, and it sounds like you've put her on a proper diet, I think she's well on her way to full health. Meanwhile, the laxatives will force her to eliminate so that the bowel won't remain distended. Over time it will shrink and she won't need the help. The only suggestion I would have is that you remove refined foods such as white flour and sugar for a month or so and then use sparingly afterward. And instead of apple juice, give her an apple so that she can get more fiber. Same with other fruits. She should have at least one vegetable at every meal."

"I can do that." Marie-Thérèse always served a lot of vegetables, and she knew a place that sold whole wheat bread. "Of course, there's a lot more here that we're dealing with—the other doctor she saw seemed to think she might need some surgeries related to the abuse."

"That's not unlikely. What we really need to do is schedule a time to talk to Celisse together with my partner who actually deals more with the emotional side of abuse while I deal with the physical side. Together we'll gain her confidence and explain to her why she needs an examination and what will happen. Then we'll see where we need to go from there. Without a thorough physical examination, I can't tell you anything more about her condition. And I don't want to traumatize her by forcing that exam. It's not advisable unless there's an urgent physical problem that needs to be taken care of."

"How long do you think it'll take? I mean to explain it so she understands and feels comfortable?"

"It varies. Some children are fine after one visit, others need five or six or ten. Some need more. But I'd say there's no hurry. The other doctor who examined her would have noted any overt problems that needed immediate attention. But I'll call him just to be sure."

"Well, he missed the boil."

Dr. Lerat smiled. "Given the scarring you describe, I'm not surprised. But Monique did just right on that. It'll be fine. However, I'll take a look at it while you're here, if you like."

"I would."

The doctor arose from her chair and crossed to the one next to Marie-

Thérèse where Celisse stood by the dolls. She reached to expose the area, talking to Celisse softly, but Celisse immediately recoiled from her touch.

"Come on, Celisse," Marie-Thérèse cajoled. "Look, what if *I* take off the bandage and the doctor just peeks at it?" That was acceptable to her, so Marie-Thérèse eased down the side of her pants and removed the bandage.

"Excellent," the doctor said after a few moments. "It's still draining. I see no reason not to continue with Monique's recommendation. It might take a month, but it'll heal."

"Thank you."

"Very good." Dr. Lerat held out her hand to Celisse, flat with the palm up. "I bet Monique taught you how to make crepes, but did she teach you how to give five? Go on, slap my hand. Come on, just hit it like that."

Celisse stared for a second before tentatively placing her hand on the doctor's.

"Great!" encouraged Dr. Lerat. "Now do it a little harder."

Celisse obeyed, and then smiled hesitantly. The smile lit up her face and Marie-Thérèse felt a lump come to her throat. "Thanks, doctor," she said softly.

"You are welcome, Madame Portier." Dr. Lerat regarded Celisse in silence for a while. "Does she ever talk?" she asked.

"She's said only a few words. But she understands, I know she does."

"We'll work with her. Children are more resilient than we realize."

"I hope so. Thanks again."

Marie-Thérèse made another appointment and left the office. On the way to the car, Celisse walked beside her, every so often giving a little bounce to her step. "So, did you like that doctor?" Marie-Thérèse asked.

Celisse nodded. "She nice."

Marie-Thérèse's heart jumped inside her chest. She squeezed Celisse's hand. "That's right, Celisse. She's very nice. Now let's go get your little sister, okay? Larissa and Brandon will be home soon."

* * *

On Friday morning, Marie-Thérèse surveyed the disarray in the kitchen. She couldn't believe the utter disaster. She had stayed up late cleaning after the children had gone to bed. Mathieu had started to help her, but Raquel had awakened and he had to rock her back to sleep. Marie-Thérèse had finally given up after loading the dishwasher and sweeping the floor. But after breakfast this morning, it looked just as bad as it had the night before.

Marie-Thérèse sat down and sighed. It wasn't that her family wasn't helping out—they were doing their chores and mostly remembering to take their dishes to the sink—but she was so occupied with all the new needs that she didn't have the time to do much cleaning—especially the deep cleaning.

At her place on the table, Celisse stopped eating and stared at Marie-Thérèse, her blue eyes large and worried. "Don't worry, Celisse. I'm not going to lose it—yet." With a sigh, she arose and half-heartedly began to clear the table.

She was jolted from her attempt by the doorbell. "Hmm, wonder who it could be." Likely, it was one of the neighbors since the outside buzzer hadn't sounded first. But when she peeped out the spy hole, she saw a short, heavyset woman with long black hair pulled into a bun. In one hand she carried a plastic tote filled with various bottles.

Marie-Thérèse opened the door warily. "May I help you?" she asked, searching for a kind way to tell this woman she was not interested in buying anything.

"I'm Ireline," she said. "I'm here to clean. Tell me what you want done."

For a second, Marie-Thérèse was tempted. But with the new apartment in the works, she needed to save every penny. Besides, she would have to learn to cope on her own eventually. "You must have the wrong house. I didn't ask for a cleaning lady."

"Yes, it's all right here." The lady pulled out a folded sheet of paper. It said:

Surprise! Here's your baby shower present for your new additions. Years ago I said I'd pay for cleaning when you got a new baby and here it is. Ireline will come twice a week and stay for as long as it takes for the first month, and then once a week for the next two months. She's a wonder! I don't know what I would do without her coming each week (except move every few months to get away from the mess—we all know what a horrible housekeeper I am). Enjoy!

Love, Josette
P.S. See you tonight at the family party!

So Josette *had* noticed the condition of her house! *And knowing me like she does, I'm sure she knew how crazy it was making me.* Marie-Thérèse nearly laughed.

"Well?" asked Ireline, shifting her tote to rest on her wide hip.

"Come in, come in." Marie-Thérèse opened the door wide. "I am only too glad to let you come in. Believe me, though, it's mess. Especially in the kitchen."

Ireline took one look around and shook her head. "This is nothing compared to your sister's place. Those five boys . . ." She shrugged and began to remove her supplies from the tote.

Chapter 16

Josette was glad Zack took the afternoon off to help her wrap things up for the family party that evening. She hated driving in Paris, while her American husband had seemed to take to it instantly. On his mission he had driven while serving as assistant to the president, and after that he had never looked back.

Today he was her chauffeur as she visited the bakery, the butcher's, and a half-dozen other small stores to find exactly what she wanted to serve at the party. She wouldn't make any of the dishes as there was no time, except for her special yogurt cake that Zack so loved.

The party would be held at her parents' double apartment, of course, since theirs was the only place large enough to hold the entire clan, but she was taking care of all the food. Marie-Thérèse had her hands full and Josette hadn't wanted to burden Rebekka with requests, and neither of her brothers were very good at organizing foodstuffs. Her mother would have helped, but Josette knew she had enough to do with the decorating, table organization, and set up.

"Everyone is coming, aren't they?" Zack asked.

Josette thought about it as she strapped David into his car seat. "Oh, no!" she said. "I didn't talk to André! He wasn't home last night—must have taken the girls somewhere, and then I forgot to call back."

"Let's just swing over to his work." Zack ran his hand through his blonde hair, and tossed her the endearing grin that always made her feel a rush of love that had never dimmed through fifteen years of marriage. "If he's not there, the receptionist will be able to let us know where he's at. It'll only take a few minutes and this food isn't in any dire need of a refrigerator."

"Good idea."

Inside, they were met by Valerie Bernard, the office manager, looking very professional in a suitdress and with her shoulder-length black hair swept into a loose bun. "Hi Josette, Zack," she said, waving at them with the manila folder she carried. "Are you here to see André?"

"Yeah, we're having a family party tonight, and believe it or not, I forgot to tell him."

"He's in his office," Valerie said. "And if I know him, he doesn't have plans."

Zack hefted David in his arms. "Why don't you go ahead, Jose. This little boy of ours wants a drink."

"Okay, I'll meet you back here in about two minutes." Josette turned back to Valerie. "Thanks. It was nice seeing you again."

"You, too." Valerie started to walk away, but then hesitated. "Uh, Josette. I was wondering, did you invite Raoul?"

"Yes. We always invite him and Rebekka to all our family gatherings. Even before Rebekka married Marc, she and Raoul have been as close as family."

"Yes, I know. Ever since Raoul was seven and Rebekka five, right?" Valerie blushed and her beautiful hazel eyes glistened brightly. "And isn't Marie-Thérèse married to Rebekka's mother's cousin?"

Josette laughed. "Oh yeah, I always forget about that. We met Mathieu because we were so close to the family. Funny how things work out."

"Yes, it is. Raoul talks a lot about you guys." Valerie shrugged. "We spend a lot of time together here at work."

"I'm glad you and Raoul are close. He needs support right now."

"I like to think I'm here for him. I mean if it weren't for him and for Marc, I wouldn't have this job or joined the Church last year. I feel I owe them a lot." She looked down at the papers in her hand, flushing again slightly.

"Nonsense. From what I see, you earned this job, and everybody knew the only thing preventing you from being a Mormon was your baptism. If anyone was born to be a Mormon, you were."

Valerie laughed, and her plain face came alive with her smile. "Well, what can I say? It was as though I was waiting for it all my life—no matter how corny that sounds." She took a backward step. "Well, thanks. I just wanted to make sure Raoul wasn't going to be alone tonight. He's been pretty restless since this stuff with his daughter. It's eating him up not being able to find her."

Josette felt her mouth round to an *O*. "I didn't even consider how this might affect him! Oh, I can't believe I've been so insensitive! Here I am planning a party and he's . . . Do you think I should cancel?" She lowered her voice. "It's just that my sister has begun fostering two little girls with the intent to adopt them—if possible. And with Marc gone and all, we need . . ." To Josette's frustration, tears crept from the corner of her eyes.

Valerie put a hand on her arm. "Oh, no. I think this will be good for him. It'll do him good to talk it all out. And Rebekka will be there, won't she? She'll keep an eye on him."

"Actually, Rebekka is coming, but she says she's leaving early. Apparently a friend of hers is coming in from America." Josette frowned. "Something about her work, I think." At Valerie's frown, an idea flashed through Josette's head. "Hey, I know. You should come. That way you can keep an eye on him."

"Well, I'm hardly family."

Josette slapped her forehead in the way her father had always done. "There I go again. Of course you don't want to come, and it's not as if Raoul needs baby-sitting. I'll keep a watch on him myself rather than impose on you. I'm sure you have other plans—it being a Friday night and all."

"No, it's not that. It's just . . ." Valerie's brow wrinkled in consternation. "Well, he's not divorced yet, though I know he's seen his lawyers about it. But it's going to take awhile. I just don't want anyone to think that I have other . . . you know, interests. Because I don't. We're just friends."

Josette hadn't seen that coming. And why hadn't she? Of course! Valerie was obviously in love with Raoul, though she didn't seem ready to admit it to herself. Wheels began to churn in Josette's head. "Then come as a family friend," she urged. No, she wasn't trying to set Raoul up, but if his marriage with Desirée was truly over, he would eventually need to find a good spouse. And friends often made the best kind.

"Well . . ." Valerie smiled. "Okay, I guess. If you're sure it's okay."

"I'm sure. And it's not as if you're a stranger. Everyone knows you. You'll fit right in." Josette began to back away, happy to have appeased her guilt about Raoul.

"See you tonight then." Valerie took her leave and Josette continued to her brother's office.

She knocked once and was immediately bid to enter. "André," she said, as he met her halfway across the room.

"Josette. You look great!" he said, kissing her cheek. "Hey, you're not pregnant again, are you?"

She laughed. "Not on your life. I have my hands full, thank you very much. And I don't look great when I'm pregnant—more like a round blob with long hair." With a hand she tossed her dark hair over her shoulder.

"Says you. We think you're lovely. And you and Zack have such beautiful children. I don't know if it's right for you to stop at only five."

Josette lifted her chin. "Right? Ha! When you have as many children as I do, then you talk about what's right."

"Well, I still lack two, if I include Thierry, so I guess I'll shut up." He indicated a seat. "So what brings you here?"

"Oh, I can't stay but a minute. I just came to tell you we're having a get-together tonight at Mom and Dad's."

His eyebrows rose. "Any particular reason?"

"Well, actually, yes. But it's a surprise." She held up a finger at his tale-tell grin. "And no, I'm really *not* pregnant. What's with you and babies lately? If you were a woman, I'd swear you're baby hungry."

"Hey, this time I didn't say anything."

"Yeah, but I saw you with Marie-Thérèse's little Raquel and then with Sister Janis's baby on Sunday."

He lifted one shoulder. "They're cute."

Josette felt there was more he wasn't saying, but she could never read him as well as she had Marc. She had been able to look at her twin and know what he was feeling every time.

"Josette? Are you listening?"

She shook her head. "What?"

"I just asked if you would mind giving me some advice—just between the two of us. You know, as my older sister and as Marc's twin. He was always my guide, you know, but now . . ."

She shivered and glanced toward the door, almost expecting Marc to walk through it. "Sure," she said. "But I warn you, I've got groceries in the car and Zack's out there waiting somewhere with David."

"It won't take a minute." He crossed the few steps to the two chairs in front of his desk and sat down. She followed suit. "When Marc died," he began, "he asked me to look after Rebekka."

"Yes, you told us that."

"Well, I think looking after her means making her happy, and I'm not sure how I can do that."

This was easy. "Just be her friend," Josette said, leaning back in her chair. "Listen to her. Help her with her car, home repairs, or whatever."

"What about a husband?"

Josette blinked. "What are you saying?"

"Rebekka is very young. To think that she will go her whole life without getting married again is pretty ridiculous."

"Yes. But it's much too early for her to even think about—"

"There's more," he interrupted. "Things you don't know. Things I can't tell you."

"Then how do you expect me to give you any advice?"

He took a deep breath. "Fair enough. Okay, here it is: I asked Rebekka to marry me."

"You what?" Josette sat up straight. "Are you saying—you what?"

"I made her a business proposition. We'd get married and that way I'd be able to take care of her. You know how fond I am of Rebekka. And she loves my daughters. I think it'd work out great."

"B—but," Josette spluttered, waving her hands in exasperation. "You can't get married under those conditions. Marriage isn't a business deal."

André frowned. "That's what she said."

Josette began to relax. The idea of his marrying Rebekka to take care of her was ludicrous and she was glad Rebekka at least understood that. "I think you can take care of her without marrying her. I don't think Marc ever meant for you to do such a thing."

He opened his mouth to speak and then shut it again. Finally, he said. "But that's where you're wrong, Josette. I think Marc did mean just that."

"But why on earth would he mean that unless . . ." She leaned forward, gazing at him intently. "Oh André, is there something you're not telling me?"

His gaze fell to the carpet. "There's a lot I haven't told you or anyone. Mom and Dad know part of it."

She waited in silence, fearing that if she spoke, he wouldn't continue.

"Do you remember when Marc got out of the hospital after his last transplant? And Rebekka broke off their engagement?"

"Oh, yeah. I remember only too well. I thought Marc would die from a broken heart." She wasn't exaggerating.

"I know. That's why I stepped aside."

"You stepped aside? What's that's supposed to mean?"

"Rebekka helped me through Claire's death, and during Marc's illness we became very close. I—I realized I really cared for her. Of course, I was still deep in mourning, and she was in love with Marc. There was something between us, but it wasn't the right time. Eventually, I realized there never would be a right time, and I was content to see them happy together."

Josette was slowly beginning to understand, and her heart burst with tenderness toward both her brothers. "Oh, André. Did Marc ever know?"

André pulled at his eyelashes, removing a stray lash or perhaps a tear.

Then he rested his elbows on the armrests, hand steepled over his chest. "He guessed much later. He said he never blamed me. Then he told me to watch after Rebekka."

"Then, you're right. He *did* want you to marry her."

André glanced at her in surprise. "You understand."

"Yes. That is just like Marc. I know how he thinks." Josette jumped to her feet. "And I tell you that for the first time since his death, I'm furious at him! How dare he try to manipulate you like that! You deserve to marry a woman you love, a woman you can have a true relationship with. And so does Rebekka! You both can't be forced into a business relationship because Marc wants you to guard his claim!"

André had risen with her, and he put his hands on her shoulders. "But I don't think that's why he did it," he said calmly. "I think he wants us to be happy."

Josette brought her fingers to her mouth. "Happy? Oh André, are you saying you still love Rebekka?" If that was the case, then he was right— right about everything. Marc *would* have wanted them to be happy. The decision wouldn't have been a simple one for him, but he would have made it with enough time.

"Yes." André's jaw tightened and his voice came hoarsely. "I fought against it at first, but since Marc's death my love for her has grown so much it hurts when I think about us not being together. I want to take her into my arms every time I see her. And believe it or not, my love for her has made it easier for me to cope with Marc's death. Not easy, mind you, but *easier*. As though I know I have his blessing, that he's closer somehow. Problem is, I don't believe Rebekka cares for me now and even if she did, I think there's so much guilt and loss around our relationship and Marc's death that she will never see beyond it. So how can I make her happy? Oh, Josette, what am I going to do?"

Josette hugged André. "I don't know," she said. "But we'll find a way. Let more time go by. Maybe that will help."

"That's what Mom told me," he said with a sound that was half laugh and half cry. "But then why do I feel I need to act quickly? Like she's slipping farther away each day?"

"Don't worry," Josette said. "I'll think of something."

He drew away. "I already did."

"What?"

"I called up her old boyfriend, the one she almost married when she lived in Utah. He's coming to visit. Maybe he can make her happy since she won't let me."

Josette stared at her brother, barely recognizing him. "You what? Okay, now I'm mad! Of all the stupid, idiotic things to do! She's in mourning, for crying out loud! She's vulnerable! She needs time to settle her emotions! And here you have forced the issue. Did you even stop to think that she might feel so guilty over her feelings for you—if she still has any for someone so stupid—that she might actually fall into this guy's arms just to get away? Then he'll whisk her away to America and that'll be that. He may be an okay guy, but if you and she are meant to be together, then she may *never* find happiness again." Josette punched André on the arm. "What were you thinking? Stop being a martyr and go after the woman you love! Marc's gone, you have his approval. There's no need to sacrifice your feelings anymore!"

André looked stricken. "I was just . . . I was giving her a choice."

"You are not giving her a choice. You are forcing the issue. You are pushing her away. Did you even tell her you loved her? No, I thought not. You just offered her a *business* partnership. As if any woman would ever agree to that. We want love, romance, passion! Ooo! You make me so mad." Josette clenched her fists and glared at him. "That doesn't mean I won't think of something to help you," she added, "but . . . Oooo!"

"I know it probably wasn't the right thing to do," André said into the silence. "I see that now. But at the time she had just rejected my proposal very abruptly. I was hurt and also desperate to do something to help her. And I guess deep down I was still unsure that Marc really did mean what I thought he did. I mean, giving me his blessing to pursue Rebekka? It's crazy! But you just said yourself that it *was* likely, and you knew him better than anyone."

Josette had never seen him more miserable. "I wish you would have come to me sooner."

"Believe me, so do I. But where Rebekka's concerned, I never seem to know which way is up."

There was a tap on the door. "Josette?" came Zack's voice.

"Come on in, honey." Josette tried to obliterate all traces of exasperation from her face as Zack entered carrying David. André had shared his feelings with her in confidence and she wouldn't make him tell Zack now. There would be plenty of time for her to let her husband know what was going on later. She felt no guilt at planning to tell him; in the Perrault family spouses were always included in the "between you and me" request. In fact, André might fare better if she told everyone.

"I think we'd better get that food to your mom's," Zack said.

"I'm ready."

Zack nodded toward André. "So we'll see you tonight?"

"I don't know." André rubbed the dark shadow on his chin. "Will I need to shave?"

"Of course not," Josette replied. She smiled at him, trying to make up a little for her outburst. He had been asking advice, after all, and she shouldn't have become so angry—wouldn't have if she didn't care so much for him. "But please come." Then she couldn't help adding, "If you stay long enough, you might be able to meet Rebekka's friend from America. I believe he's flying in tonight." She began to close the door.

"Uh, Josette," André called.

"Yes?"

"Thanks for listening. I'll take what you said to heart."

"You'd better." She shut the door and walked away. *Oh, Marc*, she thought. *You did want them to marry! You must have been thinking about it for a long time.*

Despite the arrogance of the idea, Josette felt a new admiration for her twin. No matter how long she had to think about dying and leaving Zack, she could have never planned a new wife for him. She simply wouldn't want to share him. Still, for all Marc's planning, she didn't know how this was going to work out. *You can't control another's emotion so easily, Marc. You just can't.*

* * *

André felt like the utter idiot Josette had accused him of being. Why had he called Samuel Bjornenburg? Had Rebekka's refusal of his proposal made him so embittered that he would throw her into another's arms? No, rather it had been the look in her eyes. The look that said she would never allow herself to love him. *I just want her to be happy.*

According to Josette, he should declare himself to Rebekka. But that would leave him open to rejection—again.

You never fought for her, his heart accused. *You let her go.*

"What else could I do?" he whispered. "I couldn't hurt Marc. It would have killed him. I would have lost them both."

André sat behind his desk, pondering what he should do next. The very first thing would try to repair the damage he had done by calling Samuel in America. Josette was right. It was too soon for Rebekka to think of a relationship with anyone—much less a man who did not share her religious beliefs.

Marc's child needs a father, he thought, *and Rebekka needs someone to look after her.*

André wanted to be the one to do both those things. His mother and his sister had counseled him to give her time, but the urgency never left his heart. Were his emotions driving him on, or something unseen? Marc? The Spirit?

He tried to think how he would have felt if he had died instead of Claire. Would he have wanted Marc to take care of his wife? Perhaps marry her if Rebekka did not exist? The idea of Claire in even his dear brother's arms was not easy to stomach. And yet . . . worse was the idea of her enduring alone.

All at once he *knew* Marc must have gone over this very thing in his mind. And had come to the same conclusion. A scene that had happened at Christmastime almost a year ago flashed into memory. Marc had come into his office to show him a book of rare piano music he had bought for Rebekka. "I can't wait to see her face when she opens this," he said.

André could imagine it too, but he forced himself not to think of her face lighting up, of the kiss she would give Marc. It was none of his business. He would go home to the girls and Thierry and be content.

Marc didn't leave, but leaned against the edge of André's desk. His smile left and his face, staring at the music, became solemn. "You remember when I was in the hospital?" he asked, "and I told you about that feeling I had while visiting Rebekka in America? The feeling that I would not have long to be with her?"

"Yeah, I remember. That was when you said you wouldn't marry Rebekka unless you knew you were going to live. She wanted to have a civil wedding in the hospital so she could later seal herself to you if . . ."

"If I died." Marc set the music on the desk and met his eyes. "You agreed that I shouldn't marry her and bind her to me if I didn't plan to be around. That some day she might find someone else and want to be sealed to him instead."

"Hey, I only agreed. You came up with the idea. You made the decision. I don't think I could have been so strong."

"I spent a lot of hours lying in that hospital bed thinking about it."

André watched Marc curiously, wondering where he was going with all of this. "But you didn't die and you and Rebekka *are* married. Are you saying you wished you hadn't married her?" The idea made André's gut wrench with his loneliness.

"Of course not. Rebekka's my life." There was no mistaking Marc's sincerity. "And every day I thank the Lord for the time I have with her. It's just . . ." He frowned and began to pace the room. "Some day it will still happen. She'll be alone. This kidney won't last forever, and I'll have to have a new one. The transplant might not go well. And there's that fact that I'm ten years older . . . Well, lately I'm having trouble sleeping. I keep worrying about this for some reason. I keep thinking how stubbornly loyal Rebekka is and how if something were to happen to me how she might pine away—and be miserable for the rest of her life. I don't want that for her. That's not living. And since I can't figure out what to do on my own, I was thinking—just thinking mind you—that maybe I should ask the advice of my wise little brother."

André wished he had his sunglasses on, afraid Marc might detect the envy in his eyes for the life he shared with Rebekka. He stared at the desk for a long minute, composing himself and his thoughts. Then slowly André arose and went to stand by his brother. "If you did ask me, Marc, I would say that you don't really need to worry because the Lord knows what he's doing. I would remind you that He loves Rebekka even more than you do. I'd tell you we'd all take care of her. But I know you know all that, so you probably don't have to ask."

"Maybe I just need to hear someone else say it."

André put his hand on his brother's shoulder, staring deeply into his eyes. "I would do anything for you and Rebekka. Anything. That's a promise. I love you both very much." He swallowed hard. "Very much. But I think . . . why don't you tell Rebekka how you feel?"

"I've thought of that, but I don't want to scare her again. I tried several times before we were married; she didn't seem to want to hear."

"Well, that was then. You aren't on the brink of death now. Tell her. She's a strong woman. And then just love her and make every moment count. Make every day better than the last. Never go to bed fighting. Isn't that all you can do?"

Marc nodded. "Right. I've been doing that."

"Then if something were to happen, you'd have no regrets."

"Do you have regrets with Claire?" Marc asked.

André shook his head, blinking back sudden tears. "Not the day-to-day stuff. It was hard taking care of her when she was so sick during the first years of our marriage, but love makes up for a lot. And it's comforting to know she's happy in heaven." He put his arms around his brother. "For what it's worth I think you'll be around for a long time. I think you worry too much."

Marc returned his hug. "Thanks, André. Thanks a lot. It's just that life is so *good* right now, and I wonder what could possibly top it. I'm a partner in a flourishing business, I have a supportive family, I have the gospel of Jesus Christ, I have the world's most beautiful woman as my wife, and I'm sure that soon we'll have a child. I am perfectly content."

André drew away. "I'm glad, Marc." He meant every word. He didn't even mind that his brother's happiness made his own life seem stark by contrast. In reality, he had also enjoyed all the blessings Marc named, except the current companionship of a special woman. He vowed not to allow that one lack to make him ungrateful.

Now, almost a year later, André understood that Marc's searching for answers that day was what had led him to discover how André had felt about Rebekka before their marriage. He must have also realized that she had once shared those feelings—however slightly or briefly—and this knowledge was obviously why Marc believed Rebekka might be happy with André . . . eventually. Yet Marc certainly hadn't calculated how much his death would have affected Rebekka, or that she would be carrying his child. Or that her feelings for André had long died.

Then again, a flame once living could return to life. Couldn't it?

André sighed and glanced toward the large family portrait he kept on the wall. It was the last one he and Claire had taken with the girls before she had died. He still talked to her, but today her smile seemed more enigmatic than usual. No help there. So he wondered silently how Marc had really felt when he learned that André had harbored undeclared feelings for Rebekka before their marriage. Had he been angry? Had he been shocked? Had he wanted to punch him?

Probably all of the above.

But he also trusted me, André thought. *He knew I would never do anything untoward or try to come between them. He knew that whatever I felt was in the past. And he must also have known that Rebekka loved him more deeply than she had ever cared for me.*

Then another sobering thought came to André's mind: *Marc also knew that I would never let Rebekka face life alone if he should die.*

There was no resentment in the thought, only a knowledge that his brother trusted him with the thing that meant the most to him. It was a huge confidence to place in anyone.

I love her too, Marc, he thought. But could he tell her? If he did, what would she say?

André rang his secretary. "Would you reschedule my appointment with the architectural crew? I have somewhere to go tonight and I need time to shave and get ready." If Rebekka's American friend was going to be there tonight, he had better look his best.

Chapter 17

Rebekka was surprised to find Detective Francom walking up to her apartment building Friday afternoon as she arrived from the corner bakery with a fresh loaf of bread for lunch. "Hello, Detective," she called.

He turned around, smiling, the silver in his hair accentuated by the weak sunlight overhead. "Ah, Madame Perrault, I was in the neighborhood so to speak, and thought I'd drop by to see you. I have some news for you and your brother."

"My brother isn't home."

"He's not available at work, either. I called."

"Would you like to come up?"

"Thank you. It will take only a few minutes."

"Well, I'm about to eat—in my condition it's about all I do. I'm forced to eat, or I get sick. Will you join me?"

"Perhaps something to drink—nothing alcoholic as I'm on duty."

"We don't have anything alcoholic. Religious reasons."

"Oh?" He held the building door open for her.

"Yeah, I'm a member of the Church of Jesus Christ of Latter-day Saints."

"You mean the Mormons? Those American missionaries with the white shirts and ties?"

She punched the elevator button. "Yes, actually. Though they aren't all American. I served as a missionary for two years. So did my husband, my brother, three brothers-in-law, a sister-in-law, and my husband's parents. Of all of them only one brother-in-law is an American. He lives here now with my sister-in-law—the one that served a mission."

"Sounds like a big family," he said as the elevator arrived on her floor.

"They are. Mine isn't. I have only one brother. My parents are members of the Church, though."

He nodded politely and followed her into the apartment. Rebekka wondered if she'd been babbling. Probably. She was doing a lot of things she would normally never do. *Blame it on hormones again.*

She made the detective some hot chocolate before settling at the table with her own bland sandwich and mug of warm milk. He seemed lost in his thoughts and she waited impatiently. She had plenty to do that afternoon. "You said you had news?" she prompted.

"Yes. We caught Benny Tovik yesterday and he is now behind bars waiting to talk with his slick lawyer. But even he can't get him off this time. Just before the meeting with our fake couple, the baby you saw was positively identified as being the child of that deceased girl—thanks in part to those prints you got us."

"That's great."

"Yes, the grandparents were glad to have the baby, though it certainly won't bring their daughter back."

"Did Benny have anything to do with the girl's death?"

"Nope. Drug overdose, plain and simple. But she was underaged and he knew it. He was selling her baby illegally."

"Do you think she purposely did it because of the baby?"

He set his mug on the table. "You mean, take too many drugs?" he asked flatly.

"Yes. Because she felt guilty at giving her up. Or having her in the first place."

"Probably. Or maybe it was an accident. We'll never know. At least the baby will be all right. I think they're good parents. Some kids, no matter how much you teach them, don't listen."

Rebekka thought of Desirée. Her parents weren't members of the Church, but for all Rebekka knew they could be decent people—despite their disapproval of Desirée's marriage to Raoul.

Her hand went to her stomach where her own baby grew. How grateful she was for the gospel to help raise her baby. But would it be enough? How could she do it without Marc's strong guidance? *Does André ever feel this inadequacy without Claire?* she wondered. Maybe she should ask.

The room had gone too silent, and Rebekka forced herself to remember the detective's presence. "So, have you heard anything about Nadia?" she asked.

His hand cupped his mug and lifted it again. "No," he said before taking a swallow. "Actually that's what I came to tell you. This morning Lana remembered possibly dropping Nadia off at a friend's. She thought that since the woman already had a child—or children, we're not sure—she would be a good choice as a sitter."

Rebekka leaned forward eagerly, her meal forgotten. "Was she there?"

Detective Francom frowned. "Well, that's the thing. Lana still doesn't remember which friend she dropped her off with. She began making a list of people she knows who have children—the list is surprisingly long—but then she experienced some pretty strong withdrawal symptoms and we had to hospitalize her. It's anybody's guess as to if she'll remember the right person."

"Oh." Rebekka felt her hopes dwindle again. "But it's good news that the woman had children, right?"

He grimaced. "One would think so, but when you're in that kind of lifestyle—I don't know. We're checking out a few leads and we'll let you know the minute we find out anything."

"I wonder when this will all end." Rebekka propped her elbows on the counter and let her chin drop to her hands.

"Shouldn't be long now."

She wished he would leave so that she could lie down. Her head had begun pounding already and there was still that family party to get through tonight. Should she tell them about Marc's baby? She wasn't sure she was ready to share the news just yet.

"We've put the bit about the baby's birthmark on the wire," the detective said. "It might just be the link we need."

She managed a smile. "I thought you weren't really interested in that," she confessed.

"I'm sorry if it came out that way." His forefinger traced the lip of his empty mug. "Sometimes I come across a bit brusque. I was grateful you called with the information."

Rebekka pushed back her chair. "And I appreciate you coming by, but I'm sure you have more important things to do."

He stood up at the same time she did. "Thanks for the hot chocolate, Madame Perrault."

She walked him to the door. "Goodbye, Detective."

"You have a good day. If you hear from your sister-in-law, give me a call."

* * *

The ringing phone pulled Rebekka from a deep sleep where Benny-the-baby-seller ran after her waving his fake American passport and trying to kidnap her baby. She awoke with a start, her heart pounding furiously in her ears.

"Oh," she moaned, grabbing for the portable phone which was ringing somewhere on the floor. "Hello?"

"Hi beautiful!" came a cheerful voice

"Huh?" Rebekka lay back on the bed and tried to shake the fog from her brain. "André?"

"Wrong—it's Samuel. Don't tell me you forgot I was coming in tonight."

She sat up. "Oh, Samuel. Hello! No, I didn't forget. And thank you for the flowers. I meant to call, but I just . . . life's been pretty hectic lately."

"That's okay. You can make it up to me my letting me take you to dinner. Your choice of restaurants."

"Are you in town already? I thought you weren't coming in until later this evening."

"I'm here. Just arrived at my hotel, in fact. So what will it be, black tie or casual?"

"Anything would be—oh, wait! They're having a family party tonight and I'm invited." She raked her hair back from her face. "Since I thought you were coming in later, I'd planned to leave the party early. I wouldn't have agreed to go at all, but . . . well, Marc's family has been so good to me over the years. We're really close."

"Well, I can't pretend I'm not disappointed, but there's always tomorrow."

"No! You can come with me—if you don't mind. I'm sure they won't. And my brother-in- law, Zack will be glad to see an American, especially someone who's taller than he is."

"Yeah, that gets noticed here a lot."

"Then you'll come?"

"You sure they won't throw me out?" His voice was only half-teasing. "I mean that's your husband's family were talking about. Won't they see me as the enemy?"

"Of course not!" *Except maybe André*, she added silently. "They will be very gracious, I promise. And we'll leave early. The food is likely to be wonderful—free, too."

"Hey, I'm there. What time shall I pick you up? I've rented a car."

"Oh, no. I'll pick you up. I've seen you Americans drive here, and it's not a pretty sight. Except for Zack. Now he could give us lessons."

"If I weren't so manly, I'd take offense at that," Samuel said, laughing.

"Or if you weren't so accustomed to chauffeurs, you mean."

"That too." He was silent a moment before adding, "Ah, Rebekka, I've missed you. I really have."

Rebekka couldn't say the same thing and remain truthful, but despite her determination not to feel anything, she realized she was looking forward to seeing Samuel very much. "I'll see you tonight, Samuel."

"What time?"

She looked at the clock on the wall opposite the bed, the elaborately carved one Marc had given her for their first anniversary. He had wanted her to put it in the sitting room, but she had preferred keeping it where she could lie in bed and watch the black hands tick out each second. Not that she'd had much free time back then to watch. Now with her morning sickness, she had been spending way too much time staring at that clock.

"Rebekka? Are you there?"

"Sorry. I was checking the time. I didn't realize it was so late. I'll pick you up at six-thirty, okay? That'll give me an hour and a half to get ready and find your hotel."

"I'll meet you in the lobby," he said. "But make it a little earlier if you can and we'll share a drink there first, to catch up on old times before we go to your family get-together."

Rebekka said goodbye and hung up, already wondering what she was going to wear. While she hadn't gained back all the weight she had lost, she had gained two pounds since her doctor's appointment—a large amount for three days—and it all seemed to have gone right to her abdomen. When she examined herself in the mirror, she couldn't see any difference in her stomach, but with her hand she felt a rounded lump there and it was beginning to bother her to wear anything remotely snug— especially if it had an elastic waist.

She tried on several outfits just to be sure, but every time she put on something that even remotely emphasized her figure, she kept imagining it squishing the baby. She knew the idea was illogical, but couldn't put it out of her head. Most of the outfits that fit her fine in the waist were now uncomfortable because the changes in her body had made the shirts marginally too tight. *I don't want to look like . . . Desirée.* The thought was unkind, but Rebekka didn't repent for it. Nadia's life was in danger because of Desirée. She sighed. *I guess it's high time to buy some maternity clothes.*

Finally, she settled on a brown dress with gold buttons down the front and gentle princess seams on the side. A gold jacket embroidered with brown thread completed the ensemble. Not only was brown her best color, but she was comfortable, and no one would ever be able to guess her secret. She brushed her dark auburn hair until it shined and then sprayed it to keep it straight. While her hair wasn't curly, it did have a tendency to wave and tonight she wanted to look her best. Too long she had let herself wallow in despair; it was far time she took control. Feeling confident, Rebekka grabbed her purse and headed for the car.

Samuel was waiting in the lobby as promised, looking very tanned and tall. His sandy blonde hair was longer than she remembered and his eyes more green. He crossed the room and kissed her cheeks before enveloping her in a hug that took her breath away. "You look exactly the same," she said, "except your hair is longer on top, isn't it?"

He chuckled. "It's the latest style from Paris, haven't you heard?" He held her back and studied her for a long moment. "You on the other hand look nothing like I remember. You were always beautiful, but now . . ." He shook his head. "Wow!"

"Oh, you old flatterer." She punched his arm and laughed.

"Come on. Let's go to the bar and catch up. Don't worry, I already made sure they serve things without alcohol. What'll you have?"

Usually, she ordered lemonade, but now it gave her heartburn. What she wanted was milk, but he might ask questions if he remembered that she had never been fond of milk, and she didn't think she could drink soda. "Orange juice," she said. That was something she could still enjoy in small amounts.

They sat on the swivel stools, laughing and joking, bringing back vividly the months Rebekka had lived in America. They chatted about everything, and Rebekka discovered how much she'd missed conversing so thoroughly in English. She often practiced with Zack and with the American missionaries at church, but this was different. More than a few times she found herself fumbling for words.

When it was time to leave for the family party, Rebekka was reluctant, but she stood and accepted his proffered arm. "Oh, Samuel, so much has happened since we met. You don't hold it against me, do you? My marrying Marc?"

He was silent a lengthy moment, as though thinking deeply about her words. "I believe you have to follow your heart. And no, I don't hold it against you any much as you would hold it against me if our positions were reversed. But I am curious—now that your husband has been . . . uh, taken from you so unexpectedly, do you regret your choice? Even just a little bit?" His green eyes watched her intently.

"No."

"Just no. No explanation?"

How could she explain the trauma of Marc's transplant, of André's sweet wife dying and Rebekka's ultimate choice between the brothers? No, he didn't need to know any of that. What was important was that she wouldn't change her decision for all the time in the world with *any* other man. Marc was and continued to be her soul mate. Samuel by comparison had been only a friend, one that she had considered marrying only because he was a nice guy and she had wanted to be married.

She gave him a small smile. "I love Marc," she said simply.

"I see." Was that disappointment in his eyes? Did it matter? He slung his arm over her shoulder. "So, are you going to show me how a native Frenchie drives?" His manner was teasing again, and she felt a rush of gratitude toward him.

The drive through Paris was uneventful, and they arrived at the Perrault's apartment building only fifteen minutes late. Rebekka took her time parking and when she turned off the engine, she made no attempt to open the car door. This would be the first time she had faced the entire Perrault clan at one time since Marc's funeral. She half-wondered if André had set this up to force her to tell his family about the baby. But she knew him too well. *No, there is some other announcement to be made.*

"What's wrong?" Samuel asked. "Are you all right? Can I do something for you?"

She smiled faintly. "No. Actually, I'm feeling pretty good—better than I have in months. But . . ." She glanced at the building looming overhead. "There's something I need to tell them, and I don't know if I'm ready."

His eyebrows rose. "Oh? Anything I should know about? A move back to the states, perhaps?"

"No, nothing like that, though it's just as drastic." She let her gaze drop to the steering wheel. "I don't want to talk about this now, okay? If you don't mind. But I'll tell you later."

He reached over and touched her cheek, coming away with damp fingers. "I don't mind, Rebekka."

They waited in silence for about five minutes, and then Rebekka checked her face in the mirror, did minor repairs, and said, "Okay, I'm ready."

"Hey, you're not facing the enemy, are you? I thought I was the one doing that. Or is there something else you're not telling me?"

To her surprise, she laughed. "Oh, no. You're going to love these people. I guarantee it."

* * *

André wondered why Rebekka was late. Was she sick? Was she staring off into the distance with tears running down her face? After not-so-subtle encouragement, Raoul had called their apartment, but there was no answer.

"She's probably on her way," Raoul said from his chair at the long table. The kitchen was large—twice the size of a normal one since the apartment was actually made from two apartments years ago when Jean-Marc and Ariana Perrault had all their children at home.

Josette pushed her six-year-old son's hand away from a plate of sweet bread. "Maybe she went to have her hair done since her friend is coming in from America."

André knew the comment was directed toward him, but he ignored it.

"By the way, you look nice tonight, André," Josette said, batting her eyes at him. "I see you decided to shave after all."

André again didn't take the bait—how could he with all the family listening? "You look particularly radiant yourself, Josette." He turned to Zack. "Are you sure you're not having another baby?" *There, that'll change the conversation.*

"I wouldn't mind, but . . ." Zack trailed off when he saw his wife's thunderous face. "But we really have all we can handle right now. Five boys . . . maybe someday."

"But you have to have a girl," Marée said. "Don't they, Daddy?"

André stifled the urge to pick up his youngest daughter and hold her tight. The eight-year-old was bursting with the excitement of being with her cousins and wouldn't appreciate being confined. Maybe later as the party wound down she would deign to remember her father. Likely she would want him to carry her to the car. Her sister Ana, only a year older, would also beg for the ride, reverting for a few moments to the little toddlers he remembered so well. Thank heaven they were both petite like their mother had been, or he wouldn't be able to lift them both at the same time.

"Isn't Thierry coming home this weekend?" asked Louis-Géralde who had brought his date, Sophia. She was a very cute, shy blonde girl with pale blue eyes, whose facial features clearly showed her family's

Nordic heritage. She didn't say much, but everyone liked her.

"No. He has some studying he needs to do for a big test on Monday," André replied. "He thought he'd better stay at school."

The buzzer in the entryway rang, startling André. *Thank you, Father*, he thought. Aloud he said, "It must be Rebekka downstairs."

Marée was already running to the door, racing with several other Perrault children. There were only eleven children in all, including Marie-Thérèse's two extra, but André thought they always seemed to have the energy of twice that many. He wanted to go answer the door himself, but resisted the urge.

"It's Valerie!" shouted Marée after talking into the intercom.

"Oh, yes. I invited her," Josette said.

Ariana came into the kitchen. "Invited whom?" She wore a flowing green dress that immediately brightened the room.

"Valerie, the office manager at André's office."

"Hey, it's my office too," Raoul joked, coming to his feet and extending a hand to Ariana. "And thank you for coming to the party, Sister Perrault."

Ariana laughed, her brown eyes sparkling. "Raoul, it's good to have you. Jean-Marc will be out in a minute. He's on the phone with some church business, but he's hurrying."

"Stake business, eh?" André put in, though he really wasn't listening. His ears still strained to hear another ring from the lobby.

Ariana began setting out the best silverware, which she did at every family party. "Actually, being a counselor in the stake presidency has been easier than being a bishop. There are fewer meetings to attend and we even get to have him in church with us every now and then."

"She's here!" a child screamed. André tensed, but they were just talking about Valerie who had arrived in the elevator.

Everyone greeted Valerie, and Raoul changed chairs to sit by her. Talk moved to work and then to Raoul's missing daughter. Rebekka had still not arrived.

André was about to go look for her, when the doorbell rang. This time he did go answer it, flanked by children. To his relief it was Rebekka, looking beautiful in a gold and brown outfit with flat dress loafers. She looked happy, as though she had been laughing. He drank in her face, her smooth hair, and her gray eyes.

"Rebekka!" yelled Marée, throwing herself at her aunt. "We've been waiting sooooo long for you! Where have you been? Hurry and come in.

We're hungry, and Aunt Josette won't let us have any treats until we have dinner!"

"Well, we'd better hurry right in," Rebekka said with a laugh.

She gave André an uneasy smile and moved past him. It was then André noticed the person with her, though how he could have overlooked such a tall man was unexplainable. "Oh, André, this is Samuel," Rebekka said. "You remember me telling you about him? His plane came in early and I asked him to come along. You don't mind, do you?"

"Of course not. Welcome, Samuel." André offered his hand to the stranger when what he really wanted to do was to shut the door in the man's face.

Samuel gave him a smile and a nod that acknowledged André's part in his being there—but to André's relief he didn't saying anything about the phone call. Samuel was lean, tan, and his sandy-blonde hair was cut longer on top in the latest mode. He was also the CEO of his own company—just the type of man Rebekka was likely to be attracted to. André wished again that he had not acted so impulsively.

He followed them into the kitchen where everyone had gathered. Even the old grandparents were there, except Grandma Louise—his father's mother—who had died peacefully in her bed last summer. His eyes drifted to Rebekka's face. There was tenseness there now as the introductions were being made, but she was still smiling.

She had even been laughing.

Maybe he *hadn't* been wrong to call Samuel, after all. But his heart rebelled at the thought. *I love her,* he thought. And Marc wanted me to tell her.

Ariana and the others welcomed Samuel with good grace. Apparently, he didn't speak French, though he understood some of what was said. When Zack discovered Samuel was from Cincinnati, he immediately involved Samuel in a conversation about the Cincinnati Bengals. They spoke in English, and Samuel appeared more at ease. Rebekka's worried expression gradually faded, but André's heart continued to ache—at what he wasn't sure—and he was grateful when Marée came to sit on his knee.

Jean-Marc Perrault, head of the family, came into the room, looking every day more distinguished as silver strands took their place in the once-dark head of hair. He grinned at the gathering, reminding André of Marc, though he knew he himself resembled his father even more than his brother had. Except for the grin—that only Marc had shared with his father.

"Welcome everyone," Jean-Marc said. "I'm glad you've all been able to come tonight. I don't know exactly why this party was called, but I'm glad it was and that I didn't have to do anything in the planning." Amid the ensuing laughter he continued. "The balloons and streamers and the table set up was taken care of by my beautiful wife, and Josette, my equally lovely daughter took care of all the food."

"Even the cake?" asked Marée.

"Even the cake," her grandfather confirmed solemnly. He held up a hand to avert further questioning. "Now I know there is an introduction that needs to be made, at least to me, but since I also know how hard it is to wait for cake, I suggest we go right to the prayer and begin our meal. We can find out all about our visitor as we eat. All right?" A chorus of cheers from both children and adults alike met his suggestion. "As the patriarch of this wonderful clan, it is my privilege to choose someone to say the prayer. And this time I choose myself since I would like to contribute in at least some way." He took Ariana's hand and bowed his head.

André watched everyone else do the same. But for an instant, Rebekka's eyes met his and they seemed to communicate—something. What? The prayer began and they both quickly lowered their heads. When the prayer was over, André tried to catch her eye, but she didn't look his way again. Had she felt the bond between them, or was it only in his imagination?

Chapter 18

Rebekka felt as if she were under a microscope. Did the Perrault family think she was dating Samuel? Did they wonder if she planned to move to America again? Maybe she should. Not with Samuel, of course, but on her own.

But she knew she couldn't. Not with Marc's child anyway. He deserved to know both sets of grandparents and the aunts, uncles, and cousins, and she wasn't about to sever that link. Besides, she didn't know if she could survive without their support. Her mother would especially be devastated to have her grandchild so far away, whether or not they ever found Nadia. No, running away wasn't an option.

André was the worst of all—she felt his eyes on her each second, perhaps judging her every action. Did he think her unfaithful to his brother's memory? Or was he trying to silently convince her to tell his family about the baby? Or was he jealous?

Jealous? Where did that come from? Rebekka studied him from underneath lowered eyelashes, but he was talking to Josette. Had she only imagined his stare? She looked away before he caught her watching him.

When dinner was over, the children pounced on the treats, devouring them. Celisse seemed particularly hungry; she sat on Marie-Thérèse's lap eating anything within reach. Afterward, the older children started to leave the room to play games.

"Wait." Marie-Thérèse stood, still holding Celisse. "I have an announcement to make. That is, Mathieu and I have an announcement." Mathieu, with Raquel cradled in his arms, came to stand by his wife.

"Ah, I knew there was a reason for this gathering," Jean-Marc said, smiling gently at his adopted daughter.

Celisse buried her head in Marie-Thérèse's neck at the sudden attention, half of a sweet roll still clutched in her hand. "Well, Josette thought we ought to let you know that Mathieu and I have decided to become foster parents for Celisse and Raquel. And if we are allowed, we are eventually going to try to adopt them."

Amid the chorus of cheers, André asked, "Hey, Celisse, what do you think about that?"

When Celisse didn't answer, Marie-Thérèse said, "We tried to explain last night, but I don't now how much she understands. She does seem a little more relaxed."

"She sure eats a lot," said Anton, Josette's second son. At nine he was the family self-appointed tattle-teller. "I don't see how she fits it all in."

Josette clamped her hand over her son's mouth. "Well, there are a lot of issues Celisse has to deal with. What's important is that she will always have enough food now—as much as she wants." She stared hard at Anton.

"Well, the medicine the doctor gave her is really working," said Marie-Thérèse. "We had a rough evening last night as the laxatives began working, but today she's been perfectly clean." She tickled Celisse. "Haven't you, Celisse?"

To everyone's surprise, Celisse lifted her head and nodded at Marie-Thérèse. Then she buried her face again. Marie-Thérèse patted her back and gave her a hug.

"We're moving," Larissa said to no one in particular. "And I'm getting my own room—I don't have to share at all."

"We all have to share," said Emery, Josette's oldest boy. "I'm turning fourteen this month and I still have to share with Preston. And Anton and Stephen and David share their room, too."

"I'm almost sixteen," Larissa said loftily.

"Not for four months!" muttered Brandon.

Larissa ignored him. "I *need* my own space."

"So you can stay up all night, I bet," Anton said.

Six-year-old Stephen pounded on his mom's arm. "Hey, I want my own room."

"No way," Josette said. "Marie-Thérèse and I shared all our lives and you can too. It'll make better friends of you . . . I hope." She sighed. "If only bedtime weren't so noisy!"

Everyone laughed except Rebekka. If Marc hadn't died, she would have laughed right along with everyone as she planned the sleeping arrangements of her unborn children. But there would be no children now, only one child who would never have siblings.

When we find Nadia maybe we can raise them as . . . But, no, Raoul wouldn't likely remain single. Rebekka's eyes drifted toward Valerie and Raoul. It was plain to her that Valerie was in love with Raoul. He obviously cared for her, too, even if he didn't know it yet. His divorce would soon be final and then Rebekka bet Raoul would move forward.

Ariana raised her wine glass, full of red punch, and clinked on it with a spoon. "I'd like to say something." Everyone quieted. "I'm so very happy for you, Marie-Thérèse and Mathieu. It's been a long time coming, and I know it won't be easy, but you will do a great job. And I want you to know that I'm here for you to watch these girls at least once a week during the day so that you can get out and do what you need to do."

"Thanks, Mom." Marie-Thérèse had tears in her eyes. "But you don't have to—"

"Of course I do. Whether or not you succeed in the adoption, they're my grandchildren while you have them."

Jean-Marc stood up and clinked his glass. "What Marie-Thérèse was going to say, honey, was that you don't have to limit yourself to one day a week to baby-sit." He grinned at all the laughter which Rebekka joined in spite of herself.

Ariana kissed Jean-Marc in front of everyone. Their children made catcalls while the teenagers groaned and shut their eyes. "This is good," Ariana said softly. "We need more children in this family. More laughter. Especially now."

In her mother-in-law's eyes, Rebekka saw the same longing she felt in her own heart for something of Marc's to love. She had kept this baby secret for more than two months after Marc's death—how could she keep his child from them any longer?

She arose and clinked her own glass in her trembling hand, nearly sploshing the red liquid over the rim. "I—I also want to add my congratulations. And I need . . . well, I need to make an announcement myself. I hope Marie-Thérèse will forgive me for stealing a bit of her show here."

The family waited in a sudden anxious silence, their eyes sliding between Samuel and Rebekka, making obvious assumptions. Only Raoul and André, both of whom knew the truth, smiled at her encouragingly. Rebekka's throat was suddenly dry. From across the table where he sat with Marée on his lap, André had stopped spreading purple onions over his second helping of salad and nodded. His eyes told her that he would speak for her if she wanted, and that offer gave her strength.

"I—I also hope that you will understand why I haven't spoken before now," she continued, setting her cup on the table. "But I—it was something I needed to keep to myself for a while. I—I'm expecting Marc's child. I'm more than three months along now. The baby is due the third week in April."

The expressions on their faces made Rebekka happy she had made the announcement. Ariana immediately rushed up to her and hugged her tightly, followed by nearly everyone else.

Marie-Thérèse cried, "I'm so glad, Rebekka. I'm so *so* glad."

Josette was wiping her own tears as she hugged Rebekka. "If you need anything, you tell me, okay? Have you been sick? What did the doctor say?"

Rebekka answered the questions as best she could, but as she caught sight of Samuel watching her, she grew self-conscious. She shouldn't have invited him here after all. He would likely be feeling awkward with her now. Why hadn't she waited until she was alone with Marc's family? Of course, he should know about the baby, and this was better than telling him alone. Or did it concern him at all?

At least it was easier than I thought it was going to be, she thought. No one had berated her for not telling them sooner, but instead had lifted their voices in celebration. Ariana especially looked happy, and Rebekka was fiercely glad. Over her lifetime, her mother-in-law had lost her brother and three children, and she deserved to feel joy. Rebekka wondered how Ariana had dealt with the loss of her children. If something happened to this life inside her . . . Rebekka shivered and vowed not to think about it.

Soon the congratulations and questions died down. The children slipped away to play their games and the adults settled down for a talk. Rebekka pushed back her chair and stood. "I'd better get going," she said. "I . . . Samuel has just come in from the states and he's got to be pretty tired."

Josette grinned. "I'm sure you two have a lot to catch up on." There was a note in her voice that Rebekka couldn't place, almost . . . teasing? Rebekka brushed the idea aside.

"Actually, we do," she said edging her way toward the door. She was relieved when Samuel understood and followed her.

"Goodbye, Samuel," Zack said in English. "It was good talking with you."

"Look me up if you're ever in Cincinnati," Samuel replied. "I'll make you the best five-way chili you've ever had."

Rebekka made a face. "That wouldn't be hard since I doubt he's ever had the dubious privilege of eating such . . . such . . ." Words failed her.

"Slop?" supplied Samuel with a wicked grin.

She shrugged. "Your words, not mine." They all laughed—at least those who understood English.

"Uh, Rebekka." André appeared at her side. "Can I talk with you a minute?"

"Sure." She followed him into the hall.

"You did the right thing, telling Mom and Dad and the others. You made them happy."

"I hope Marie-Thérèse doesn't feel that I was stealing the show."

"Oh no, you just added to it. This is a night we'll remember for a long time."

She smiled at him. "Thanks for saying so." Assuming their conversation was over, she started around him to tell Samuel she was ready.

"Wait," his hand fell on her arm with a gentle but electrifying pressure. "I need to talk to you . . . alone."

Her heart started pounding furiously in her chest. Why? What could he possibly say that would frighten her? After that crazy marriage proposal, what could be worse? "I've got to get back to Samuel," she protested. "I shouldn't leave him alone. He doesn't know anyone here."

"Later then?" He was so close to her that she could smell the aftershave on his face—a face she noticed was smooth with recent shaving.

"Okay . . . whatever." She forced her reply to sound offhand, and willed the pounding in her chest to stop. "But no preaching, huh? I'm not running away with Samuel. We're just friends."

The muscles in his jaw clenched. "Are you sure? I don't know many people who would travel overseas to comfort a *friend*."

"You'd come." Rebekka didn't know what made her say the words.

He nodded without hesitation. "Of course."

"Because of Marc," she continued, tasting gall. Everything always boiled down to André's promise.

His hand on her arm tightened. "That," he said slowly, "is where you are wrong. I wouldn't come because of Marc. I would come because of *you*."

His face came closer to hers and she found it difficult to breathe. "He's here on business," she managed. "That's all."

"I don't think so."

They were silent a moment, standing so close that Rebekka had the sudden urge to feel his lips against hers.

What! What crazy mixed-up pregnancy emotions were these?

She stepped back quickly. "I'll see you later. I have to go." She turned from him and fled, not understanding any of the emotions tumbling in her heart or why the image of André staring at her seemed burned into her heart.

* * *

Watching Samuel put a hand on the small of Rebekka's back as they exited the apartment, André fought helpless fury.

"Now I understand the hurry," a voice said behind him. "You knew all along she was pregnant—I was watching you as she told us."

"So?" He turned to face Josette, and her taunting smile vanished.

"Oh, André, I'm sorry! I wasn't thinking. That's got to hurt seeing her leave with Samuel and knowing it's your fault he's here."

"I'm going over there later." André said. "I'm talking to her tonight. Without Mr. What's-his-face around."

"That's good. But isn't it such a wonderful miracle—Rebekka being pregnant! I'm so happy about it, and I haven't seen Mom so happy since Marc . . . But tell me, does the baby have anything to do with why you want to marry her?"

"No. It's *not* the baby. I *love* her. Yes, the urgency is because of the baby, but it's for her sake. She needs someone to be there for her. To help her through."

"I'm not the one you should be telling this to. You know that, don't you?"

André lifted a shoulder in frustration. "What irks me the most is that he seems to be a nice guy."

"Yeah, a really nice guy. Would Rebekka like any other kind?"

He glared at her. "You're a lot of help."

"I'll stay at your place and watch the girls until you get home tonight," she offered. "Consider it a peace offering."

"They're staying here tonight. Mom volunteered to have them."

"Does Mom know?"

He shrugged again. "Not from me."

Without warning Josette hugged him. "It's going to be okay, André. I just know it."

"Thanks," he whispered.

* * *

Samuel and Rebekka went to a movie. Rebekka was glad the theater was dark and that she didn't have to make idle conversation. They hadn't talked about her revelation, but she sensed a subtle difference in his attitude toward her; he seemed to treat her with even more care.

After the movie, he insisted on accompanying Rebekka to her apartment. "I'll take a taxi back to my hotel," he said. "I want to make sure you get home all right."

She was going to make some retort, but decided it felt good to have him worry about her. "Then come up for a drink, okay?"

He smiled. "Hot chocolate?"

"Plain milk for me—warm." She knew he would likely prefer something with alcohol, but she didn't offer an apology. He was already familiar with her peculiarities.

They took their drink into the sitting room, where her piano seemed to mock her from the corner. "Will you play?" he asked.

She shook her head. "Not now." Hoping he didn't ask why, she hurriedly changed the subject. "So why are you really here?"

Samuel's green eyes showed no surprise at her question. He gave a laugh and shook his head. "I should have known you would see right through me."

When she didn't reply, he continued. "I'm supposed to be getting married next month, and everything was going according to plan until I received a call about what happened to your husband. And, well, I won't lie to you—it hit me really hard that suddenly you were free."

"Who called you?"

He smiled gently. "Don't you know?"

"No. Or I wouldn't have asked."

"Then before we get to that, let me tell the entire story first." He set his cup and its plate on the coffee table and leaned toward her, elbows on his knees. "My fiancée was aware of my feelings for you. I told her long before we became serious that I had wanted to marry you when you lived in America, but that you had chosen another man and was happy. I was going on with my life." He gave a wry smile. "It was much harder than I expected, considering we hadn't known each other long, that we had never committed. But I did go on. I found love and was satisfied—until recently when I found out your husband was gone and you were alone." He rubbed his left thumb absently over his right wrist. "Suddenly I wondered if it wasn't our second chance. Polly saw right through me and made me come. She said she didn't want to wonder if I had married her out of obligation or as a second choice."

"Wow, that's some lady you have there," Rebekka said. "To let you go like that when you might not come back."

Samuel settled back against the couch abruptly. "Was there any real chance of that Rebekka? Ever? I mean since that day when you didn't come to Cincinnati on the plane? I waited for you, you know."

"I know," she whispered.

"Well?" His voice was gentle, but demanded an answer.

"I just don't know," she said. He sighed and she hurried to add, "Samuel, you don't know what it's meant to me to see you. To forget my troubles for a while. To know that you still care for me. But there's the baby and . . . and Marc's family."

He nodded. "Ah, there's the catch. And also the answer to my question. You were right, they're a wonderful bunch of people—people I would love to know better—and I understand that you would never leave them. I don't know how you did in the first place when you came to America to work."

"It was hard," she admitted. "Leaving the Perraults was as difficult as leaving my own family. They've been a big part of my life since I was five."

"And now you're back for good. You will never leave France again."

She nodded slowly. "Not for an extended time. They have a right to see Marc's child grow up. And I—I need them too."

"They're members of your religion?"

Again she nodded.

"You believe you'll be with your husband again, don't you?"

"With my whole heart." Her voice shook as she spoke.

In a swift move he leaned forward again, taking her hand. "The crazy thing is Rebekka that I have begun to believe it too. And I wouldn't want to share you with him. I was born Catholic, my parents are Catholic, and I am a moral person, but you know I have never given much stock in the trappings of religion. Now suddenly I wish to have the assurance you do—that there is life after death. Not as a drop in the cup of water that is God, or in some other general way, but as His children." He stopped, shaking his head. "I shouldn't have come, should I?"

Tears had filled her eyes as she spoke. "Yes," she whispered, "because now you can go home and marry your Polly—and eventually you will understand what it's like to love someone for eternity."

He stood slowly. "I should go. If I work all night, I can take an early flight home tomorrow. I need to call Polly."

"I understand." Rebekka arose and walked with him to the door.

He stopped as she opened it, looking down at her with an unreadable expression that would be forever captured in her memory. He took a deep breath and reached for her hand. His touch was tender and loving. "Thank you, Rebekka. For everything. It has been a pleasure knowing you."

"And you, Samuel. Goodbye."

He didn't seem to register the finality. Instead, he continued to hold her hand. "Rebekka," he said softly, "it *is* possible to love two people."

Unreasoning fear swept through her, as though the weight of eternity hung on that moment. "What do you mean?" She had the distinct feeling that if she were to throw her arms around him he would stay. She purposely pulled her hand from his.

"André cares for you, you know," Samuel continued. "I'm thinking perhaps you married the wrong brother."

"Go home to Polly," she replied. "Send me an invitation."

She watched him leave, remembering too late that he hadn't called a taxi. No matter, Samuel could take care of himself; he knew enough French to get back to his hotel.

Back in the sitting room she found herself trembling. Over and over she replayed the scene in her mind, but the ending was always the same. Samuel was right; she had made her choice on the day she had not flown to him in Cincinnati.

"He never told me who . . ." In a moment she ran to her bedroom and through the French doors to her balcony. Below, Samuel was emerging from the building onto the cobblestone sidewalk, lit only by the streets lights on their tall poles. "Wait!" she called.

He looked up the four storeys and waved.

"Who called you?"

"What?" He put a hand to his ear.

"I want to know how you knew about my husband. Who called you?"

She thought he smiled, though because of the distance and the darkness, she couldn't be sure. "You still don't know?" he asked.

Rebekka felt the urge to strangle him. "Who?"

"André."

With another cheerful wave, he stepped to the curb, just as a taxi drove up. *He must have used a cell phone*, she thought.

She watched Samuel drive away, but her thoughts couldn't be farther from him. Why had André called Samuel? Had he wanted to pawn her off on him? Was he that desperate to fulfill his promise to Marc?

"I'm going to *kill* him," she muttered. But another thought was forming in her mind, one that might just fit into her own agenda. If André wanted her happy with Samuel, well, she *would* be happy with Samuel— if only in pretense.

And André would be freed from his promise.

Chapter 19

"Mom, are you okay?" Rebekka asked.

There was a sniff on the other end of the line. "I'm just so happy. I can't believe this! I know how much you and Marc wanted a baby. Should I come over?"

"Goodness no, Mom. It's after eleven. I only called because I couldn't wait anymore to tell you." *And because I didn't want you to hear it tomorrow from anyone else.* "I'm sorry if I got you up."

"I wasn't sleeping anyway. Your dad and I just got home from our date. We were getting ready for bed when the phone—" Her mother broke off.

"Hey, it's Dad," came her father's voice. "Your mom's rather choked up a bit right now. Congratulations, honey. We had no grandchildren and now we have two. This is great!"

"If only we could find Nadia."

"We will. We won't rest until we do." The confidence in her father's voice made her feel they really would find Nadia. Never mind that it had been a week since her disappearance or that the chances of her recovery significantly diminished with each passing day.

"Well, I'm going to turn in now," she said.

"Goodnight then, honey. We'll see you tomorrow."

There was a rustling noise and her mother's voice came back on the phone. "Thanks for calling. I love you."

"I love you too." Rebekka hung up the phone and yawned. She was stumbling to her bedroom as the buzzer in the hall rang. "Oh, Raoul, I bet you forgot your keys."

"Yes?" she asked.

"Hi," said the voice on the intercom. "It's me."

Rebekka's desire to sleep completely vanished.

* * *

André arrived in the street by Rebekka's apartment building at eleven and was relieved to see lights. Then he had tortured himself with visions of Samuel and Rebekka alone in the apartment. But there was no trace of Samuel when Rebekka let him into her apartment.

Still he asked, "Are you alone?"

"Well, Raoul's not back yet, but then he doesn't turn into a pumpkin before twelve. Not like a pregnant woman who begins to wilt on the vine after nine." She smiled but he noticed she didn't invite him past the entryway.

"You don't look wilted," he said, glancing into the sitting room. "Ah, I see you received the flowers. They look nice there on the coffee table."

"Yes, I—" Her cheeks flamed. "I didn't call to thank you, did I? I'm sorry, I've been . . . I love them. They're lovely."

"You thanked me before, remember? Besides, I didn't send them for the thanks."

"Then why did you?" Rebekka looked immediately sorry for the words. "Forget that," she muttered. "I don't know why I always lose it when you're— Never mind. Tell me, why are you here? Do you know how late it is?"

"You'd said we'd talk later. It's later." André was distinctly aware of her closeness, the smoothness of her hair, the fourteen freckles on her face, the smell of her perfume—of everything about her. Of the fact they were alone.

"I didn't mean tonight."

What should he do? Should he kneel on the floor and confess his love? Should he take her in his arms and kiss her? The urge to do that very thing was so strong, he almost couldn't stop himself. "Rebekka . . ." Tthe sound came out strangled.

"What?" There was a wariness in her eyes now, or had it been there all along?

He took a step toward her. She didn't back away, but stared at him. He forced himself to continue, his heart bursting with emotion. "Rebekka, I asked you to marry me before, but what I didn't tell you was that I—I love you. I have loved you for a very long time."

Her mouth dropped open slightly, and he could see the pearl-white of her teeth. With one movement he pulled her into his arms, pressed his lips against hers. There was a startled look in her eyes, but she responded. The kiss was sweet—everything he had imagined.

"I've waited so long," he murmured against her cheek. "Marry me. I need you. You need me. Tell me you love me just a little?"

Then the moment was abruptly over. "I—I . . ." Her hand went to her mouth. Tears welled in her gray eyes, threatening to storm over.

His hands were still touching her arms. "What is it, Rebekka? What is it? I know it's soon. *Too* soon. But I want to be your husband and a father to your baby. I'll wait as long as you need. Just tell me I have a chance. Tell me you still feel a little of what you felt in your heart before you married Marc. Please."

She backed away from him, eyes wide and luminous, her lips parted. "I—André . . . I . . ." Her head shook back and forth ever so slowly.

A sinking feeling formed in the pit of André's stomach. "Rebekka, I should have told you sooner that I loved you. But how could I with Marc . . . gone. Please don't look at me like that. I would never hurt you or take advantage of you."

At that she straightened and took a deep breath. "André, I care about you very much. And I appreciate all the help you've given me. But I—I don't love you. Not in that way. It would never work between us."

"What do you mean it won't work? I felt your response just now! You kissed me back! Please, at least give me a chance. Let me show you how good our life could be."

"No," her voice was stronger now. "I can't. I promised Samuel. We're dating now."

He shut his eyes, and willed himself to be calm, to not feel the old pain, now renewed to a tortuous high.

"Don't you see? I'll be happy now," she said, placing a hand on his arm. "You will have kept your promise to Marc."

"Dang it! This isn't about Marc! This is about *us*. I don't care about my promise to Marc except that it gave me the permission to follow my heart. I love you, Rebekka. *I love you*."

Her hand fell to her side. "I'm sorry. I wish I could tell you any different." She paused and added, "You called Samuel. I should thank you for that. But if you lo—why? Why did you call him?"

There was a bitter taste in his mouth. "Because I made a mistake. I was discouraged about the chances of you letting me into your life, and . . ." He paused to try and steady his voice before he lost his composure completely. "And I guess I'd rather lose you than hurt you."

She had no answer to that, but it didn't matter because he wasn't finished. He had come to long and too far to give up now. "Years ago I made a similar choice—because I knew Marc loved you more than life, and because I knew you loved him. But I won't let you go again." He pointed at her chest. "I am going to fight. And make no mistake, this time I'm going to win."

Then because he couldn't bear to leave her without touching her at least once more he closed the few steps between them and kissed her cheek. "I love you, Rebekka. Don't forget that."

He turned on his heel and strode from the apartment.

* * *

For the second time that evening, Rebekka watched a man leave her apartment. But this time her pulses raced and every fiber of her being demanded that she run after him and beg him to stay. But she couldn't. Now that André had told her the truth, she was separated from him by an even a larger gulf than before. Not because she didn't care for him—she was beginning to very much—but because in that timeless moment when he kissed her she had forgotten Marc. In that singular, exciting, thrilling, special moment, she had forgotten the years she had loved her husband, had forgotten even that she carried his baby.

If she allowed herself to love André, she might lose Marc. And that to her was the ultimate unfaithfulness.

She didn't cry. She forced herself not to cry. There had already been too many tears, and she had the baby to think of now. Slowly, she went down the hall.

Rebekka had changed into her warm thermal nightgown—nights were becoming increasingly cold now—and was sliding beneath the covers when she heard the key in the lock. *André?* her heart asked, but that was ridiculous. He didn't have a key? Or did he? She remembered the morning of her doctor's appointment. How had he gotten in? She would have to remember to ask.

The door to her bedroom slowly opened and Rebekka saw her brother framed in the light of the hall. "Are you awake?" he asked, blinking blindly in the dark.

"Yeah, I'm awake."

He moved forward soundlessly on the carpet and sat down on the foot of her bed as she rose to a sitting position. "I just needed to talk to you for a minute."

"That's fine." She pushed her hair back from her face. "I don't know if I could sleep anyway."

"Oh, why? Something happen with Samuel?"

"No, not really." Then she remembered her plan. Now it was more important than ever that she pretended to be involved with Samuel. "Well, that is, yes. He's really a great guy. I'll be seeing more of him." She felt guilty at the lie, but what else could she do? Raoul and André worked together every day and Raoul would likely slip if she were to let him in on her secret.

He was silent a long moment and even in the dim light, she could see the consternation on his face. "That's great, I guess. But . . . hey, Rebekka, he's not even a member. I don't want to put a damper on things, but look what happened with Desirée and me."

"Samuel is not Desirée. He's a faithful, wonderful man."

"Still, do you want him raising your child?—Marc's child?"

"We had a good talk tonight. I think he's going to see the missionaries. But member or not, Samuel really is a good person. You can trust me on this."

"Oh." His voice sounded defeated, but she ignored the implication.

"So what happened after I left?"

"What?"

"The party. Did they talk about me?"

He grinned. "No, Rebekka, they didn't talk about you. At least not until I left. Well, Josette did talk about how handsome Samuel was and that seemed to irritate a few people. Or at least one."

"Oh? Who?"

He scratched his head. "Hmm, can't remember exactly."

Rebekka knew very well he was baiting her so she let it go. What did it matter what André said after she left? She didn't care—or at least she had to pretend she didn't.

"So did Valerie enjoy herself?"

"Yes, I think so. We, uh, we left a little early." He wasn't looking at her now, but at the wall.

"What happened?" Pushing her blankets aside, she scooted closer to him. "Tell me."

"Uh, nothing. I found out she had come on the bus and I didn't want her to go home that way. She would have asked André to take her, but he was rather preoccupied with something. I volunteered."

"And?"

"And nothing. I let her off at her apartment building, made sure she got in okay and drove off."

"I hear a but coming."

He shook his head. "Not a but exactly." He rubbed his forehead with his fingertips. "I can't believe it! I've been so worried about finding Nadia and having my divorce finalized that I haven't been thinking about anything else. But suddenly watching Valerie walk away from the car, I realized I didn't want her to go." He let his hand fall and looked at

Rebekka. "I—I'm still a married man! I shouldn't be having these feelings."

Rebekka stifled the urge to laugh. He had been repeatedly wronged by Desirée, yet in spite of the impending divorce, it seemed he had never considered a future without her. What would he say if he knew she had let André kiss her tonight? *Talk about unfaithfulness.* "Your divorce will be final soon," she said, placing her hand over his. "And then you can worry about your feelings for Valerie. Has your lawyer found any trace of Desirée?"

"Not yet. The papers are all drawn up, though. All she has to do is sign when we find her. We've left messages with her parents, her last job, and at the bars she's been known to frequent—just about anywhere we can think of."

"You don't think she'll fight the custody, do you?"

His laugh was bitter. "No, I think she'll be glad to be free—especially when she sees the endowment I'm setting up for her monthly expenses. She can't touch the principal but even without that she'll have enough to get by nicely if she doesn't spend it on drugs or alcohol. After her death, the endowment reverts to my children to be split equally, or to you and your descendants if mine can't . . . be found." He swallowed hard. "It doesn't matter if she objects or not. I'd fight her to the death on this. I can't let Nadia grow up with her as a role model."

"Valerie on the other hand would be a good one," Rebekka pointed out. "I know she loves children. The Primary has never run so well as it has with her as the first counselor."

Her brother sighed. "Do you think she would ever look at me twice? I mean, after the divorce and all?"

Rebekka was tempted to tell him Valerie already loved him, but it was too soon. The woman didn't even know it herself. "I think," she said slowly, "that she'd be crazy not to. And if there's one thing Valerie isn't, it's crazy."

"She is pretty great." He slapped both hand on his thighs as he arose from the bed. "Well, I guess I'd better get some sleep. Tomorrow I'm going searching for Nadia again in Desirée's neighborhood. I keep thinking I'll find some clue there."

"I'll come with you," she offered.

He leaned down and gave her a hug. "Thanks, Sis. I don't know what I'd do without you.

Chapter 20

November, one month later

Rebekka tried to pull herself out of bed, but for the past month, she was having a recurring pain in her side that defied all her efforts to ignore. With a long sigh, she lay back down on the bed and tried to breath evenly, willing the pain to go away. She kneaded her ever-growing stomach with her fingers. *Is this normal?* she wondered. Josette had assured her that the baby didn't feel any of the aches and pains of pregnancy, but still Rebekka wondered if this torture she felt could be good for her child.

She couldn't believe how big she was already. While at first she had measured smaller than normal, now her once-flat stomach seemed to stretch as she watched, and she had gained another eight pounds. "That should make the doctor happy at my next visit," she mumbled, taking another breath before she tried again to rise from the bed. This time she succeeded.

At least her morning sickness seemed to be completely gone—despite Josette's warnings that it could last more than five months. There had been other changes in her life as well. Her eyes no longer slid to the other side of the bed to where Marc used to lie. The pain of his death was at last dimming, and she found that as she concentrated her love on their child, she could even laugh again without feeling the heartbreak. She still missed him, but figured she always would.

"Well, you've got to get up," she told herself aloud. "It's Wednesday already and you promised Damon you'd have the chapter five manual updates done by Friday." Steeling herself against the onslaught of pain, she forced herself from the bed. To her relief the pain diminished significantly once she was on her feet.

After another of her frequent visits to the bathroom, she wandered into the kitchen, thinking of the work she would do that morning. She found Raoul at the breakfast table with Detective Francom, looking happier than he had all month.

Raoul sprang to his feet. "Oh, Rebekka, it's good news. Desirée's friend has had a breakthrough after her last drug treatments. She thinks she knows were she left Nadia! Detective Francom drove right over there, but no one's at the apartment. He's having all the neighbors questioned, and they're tracking down the building owner to see what records he has on the tenant."

"That's wonderful! I'm so happy!" Rebekka hugged him.

"Well, don't celebrate yet," the detective reminded them, also arising. His eyes seemed to take in every detail of Rebekka's thick flannel nightgown and white velour robe. Though very modest, she knew she must look like a sight. "I hate to put a damper on things," Detective Francom continued, "but this woman, whoever she is, has had Nadia for over five weeks and hasn't reported her abandoned. That's not a good situation. Not at all. And from the one neighbor I did talk to, we suspect she hasn't been around for a long time."

"You think she kidnapped Nadia?" Rebekka asked.

"I'm not jumping to any conclusions. I'm just saying that we still need to be careful."

Raoul's worried look returned. "There are other baby brokers."

"Exactly," said Detective Francom. "But this is a solid lead and we are going to do everything in our power to get your baby in your arms where she should be."

"Thank you." Raoul's voice was filled with emotion.

Detective Francom nodded and then looked at Rebekka. "And how are you feeling lately?"

She managed a smile. "A little fat. But actually very well, thank you."

"That doesn't stop her from dating a very wealthy and important American business man," Raoul said. "Well, mostly it's on the phone, now. But they're serious. And he's not even the one sending all the flowers you see around here. That's someone else entirely, but Rebekka's completely involved with her American."

Rebekka wanted to hit Raoul and deny his words, but that meant she would have to explain the truth about Samuel and André. She wasn't prepared to do that—yet. Not until she had convinced André to stop his pursuit of her. So far he showed no signs of desisting. Each and every day since his proposal, he had sent her flowers or potted plants by way of a local florist. She tried to be annoyed when she talked to him, but mostly he made her laugh. He hadn't tried to kiss her again, however, for which she told herself she was grateful. Never once had he asked about Samuel, and feeling guilty, she didn't volunteer any information.

The detective smiled. "Good," he said. "A beautiful woman like you needs to go on with her life. He's a lucky man."

Rebekka was touched by his kindness. "Thank you."

He nodded. "I guess I'll be on my way."

"I'll walk you out," Raoul said. "I need to be going too. I'm visiting my lawyer this morning and it's expensive to keep him waiting."

"I hear you."

The men left and Rebekka eased herself into one of the vacant chairs, pondering over the idea of finally having Nadia with them. The infant would be three months old now. Would she be upset to leave her care-giver? *Please let it be someone loving who has been taking care of her*, she prayed.

Her hand massaged her distended stomach. If she was separated from her own baby, she couldn't imagine what she would do. Next week at her doctor's appointment, she would have an ultrasound and find out what she was having. It didn't matter, really, but she wanted a son to carry on the Perrault name. So far, only Josette had boys, and they carried their American father's last name—Fields—and André's adopted son had kept his original family name out of respect for his natural aunt, André's deceased wife.

Rebekka was about to get dressed when the buzzer rang. At first she expected André's usual flower delivery, but was surprised to hear Desirée's voice over the intercom. "Sure, come on up!" she called. A million questions filled her head, not the least of which was whether or not she should call Detective Francom.

No, I'll wait and see what she has to say.

While she waited for her sister-in-law to ride up the elevator, Rebekka hurriedly changed into a rib-knit sweater and skirt set—an outfit from her new maternity wardrobe— and ran a brush through her tangled hair. She reached the door just as the bell rang.

"Come on in," she invited, taking in Desirée's appearance. The woman looked cold, as though she had been outside a long time. Rebekka could feel the chill radiating from her as she passed. Desirée wore jeans that were at least two sizes too tight and her white T-shirt showed every one of her ample curves. She had always worn overly snug clothing, but this was worse than Rebekka remembered; Desirée had obviously gained weight since they'd last met. Instead of being carefully made up, though, her pale face was devoid of makeup and her long dark hair hung limply around her shoulders. She looked ten years older than the twenty-five she could claim.

"I know, I look a mess," Desirée said.

"No, I just . . . you look different."

"I can't seem to care about my appearance anymore. I just sit around and eat and feel miserable."

"Have a seat." Rebekka indicated a chair and Desirée complied.

"I saw Raoul leave. I've been waiting out there an hour. I forgot a jacket and it was freezing. But I had to see you."

Rebekka arose and poured milk in a mug and slipped it into the microwave. "Why?"

"Partly because I wondered about Nadia."

"They haven't found her yet."

"I know."

Rebekka didn't ask how she had found out. "They did find a lead today, though. Your friend is still undergoing treatment for drug and alcohol addiction and she apparently remembered where she left Nadia— or thinks she does."

Desirée sat up straighter. "Where?"

"I don't know her name—the detective didn't say. But I know she has at least one child of her own."

"That's good, then."

Rebekka sighed. "Yeah, except the lady's missing."

"Oh." Desirée's expression became even more glum.

Rebekka offered her the warm milk, and when she accepted it, began making another for herself. The familiar weakness she always felt after not eating for an extended period of time had come upon her and she needed something in her stomach quickly. "Here's chocolate if you'd like," she added, handing Desirée the carton.

"I talked to my parents," Desirée said into the silence that followed. "They told me about the terms of the divorce, and I want to sign."

"Raoul went to his lawyer's this morning. You could go over there now and get it over with."

"Well . . ." Desirée sipped her milk and looked uncertain. Rebekka could never remember seeing her this way. Desirée had always selfishly done exactly what she wanted with no regard to anyone who stood in her way. This uncertainty was out of character—at least for the Desirée Rebekka thought she knew.

"We know about the tickets," Rebekka told her. "He won't turn you in."

Desirée looked momentarily startled. "My parents are going to help me with that," she said.

"Did you tell them about Nadia?"

She nodded and there was a shimmer of tears in her eyes. "Yes. And now they're upset that I want to give up custody to Raoul. They'd rather have me come home and keep her. But I can't live with them again, and I'm sure as—" She broke off obviously embarrassed to swear in front of Rebekka. "I'm sure not going to let them raise her. I know Raoul will give her the love and . . . the discipline that she needs. It's the right thing to do."

Rebekka watched her silently for a moment, her hand going again to her own unborn child. Did Desirée really know that giving up her daughter was right, or was she doing it because she couldn't be bothered? Had she really begun to understand the importance of setting limits? Given Desirée's history, Rebekka couldn't be sure if she was acting or being truthful.

"You're having a baby," Desirée said.

Rebekka forced her hand away from her stomach. She had thought the habit odd and embarrassing in other pregnant women, but now she couldn't help herself. "Yes. I'm almost four and a half months."

"Do you know what it is?"

"No. Not yet. I'm having an ultrasound soon."

"That'll be fun." Desirée's attention wandered.

"I'll go with you if you like," Rebekka said.

"Where? Oh." Desirée's brown eyes focused again on her face. "Well, that's sort of why I came. My parents, they gave me money. Told me to get a new outfit—to face the judge about the tickets. If I pay them all, I may get off with only community service, or probation. I hope."

"It's possible."

"And I want to go to sign the divorce papers. But I don't want to go looking like this."

At least you're not wearing your leather mini-skirt, Rebekka thought. "What do you mean?" she asked carefully. "Aren't these the clothes you always wear?"

Desirée rubbed her face. "I've gained so much weight, but it's not just that. I don't know how to dress. Where to go. I—everything I like makes me look . . ." She gave a little sob. "I want to look nice. Professional. Like you. That's why I'm here."

Rebekka was shocked. She and Desirée had never been friends, and in fact she had suspected that Desirée hated her. She had certainly mocked Rebekka enough over the past years. *Like a playground bully*, she thought. *An insecure, playground bully*. But she couldn't hold the past over her sister-in-law—not when she looked so earnest and so lost. Was this what Raoul had seen in his wife? Was this why he had tried so long and so hard?

"Okay, I'll go," Rebekka said, coming to her feet. "But only if you'll sign the divorce papers afterward. Raoul needs to go on with his life. Deal?"

Desirée nodded, a tear escaping from her eye. "I should have let him go a long time ago." She lowered her face to stare at the table. "A part of me thought that if I held on, he could make me good. But all I did was cause him pain. Him and Nadia."

Rebekka sat back down in her chair. "Oh Desirée, women can't depend on others for happiness or for their choices! No one can make us be good or be something we don't really want to be. We have to do it ourselves. *We* are responsible for our lives, not anyone else. The change has to begin inside us."

"It's not easy, is it?" Desirée asked, meeting Rebekka's gaze.

"No." Rebekka's voice came out a whisper. "But it's like learning to walk. We put one foot in front of the other and sometimes we fall down. So we have to get back up."

"I feel like I fell off a cliff."

Rebekka smiled. "Oh, yes, I know that feeling."

There was a stark, uncomfortable silence and then Desirée spoke. "I'm sorry about your husband. I really am. He was a good man. He was always nice to me. He gave me money sometimes, you know. Especially when I was pregnant." She started to cry. "He didn't know about the baby, of course. I wore clothes to hide it. I couldn't tell him because I knew he'd tell Raoul. But sometimes—at least before I got too big—I would wait outside work when I knew he'd come by. He always had a kind word for me and would slip me something."

Rebekka felt her tears spill over onto her cheeks. "That sounds like Marc. Thank you for telling me."

Desirée let her face fall into her hands, and then down onto the table as her fingers raked through her hair. "Oh, how can this all be happening? How?"

"We make our choices and the consequences happen," Rebekka said. "If we repent and remain faithful, the Lord can lighten our burden considerably, but there is still a consequence—good or bad."

Her head whipped up. "Nadia didn't make any choice! Your husband didn't make a choice!"

"I believe Nadia did. I believe we all know before we're born about the circumstances we'll be born into and we agree to them."

"You think Marc agreed to die?" she asked incredulously. "To leave you alone with his baby?"

Rebekka had never thought of it in those terms before, but her answer came with sureness. "I think he knew, yes and agreed. In fact, I'm sure of it." Her tears came in earnest now because Rebekka realized that she, too, must also have agreed in the premortal life to face the test of losing her husband. But had she then any idea what that would entail? Had she really been so strong? "All of us have trials," she continued, becoming aware that Desirée was waiting for more. "And some are harder than others. But one thing I've always believed is that God loves us and if we do our best, He will help us not only endure, but to be happy."

"I wish I believed that."

It was an echo of the words Samuel had spoken to her the last time she had seen him. Was he married now? Had he looked up the missionaries? Or at least become active in his own religion? "You can Desirée." Rebekka told her. "You have lived with my brother long enough to know how. The next step is up to you."

Desirée nodded silently. Again Rebekka wondered if her attitude were an act or the beginning of real repentance. She prayed that it was, as Raoul had done for so long. *But it's too bad she didn't see the light sooner*, Rebekka thought. *Before she lost Nadia.*

"I need to put on a little make-up," she told Desirée. "And use the bathroom—I spend half my life in the bathroom now. Wait a minute, okay?"

Rebekka hurried, fearing that when she returned Desirée would be gone. But when she finished, Desirée was still waiting at the kitchen table, staring into nothingness.

"I'd better take a few snacks," said Rebekka, stuffing a bite of croissant into her mouth. "Want one?"

Desirée accepted the croissant listlessly and watched without speaking as Rebekka packed her purse with rolls, fruit, and a small carton of milk that didn't require refrigeration. Thus armed, she grabbed her keys and headed for the door.

"We'll use the subway so we won't have to find a parking place," she told Desirée. They would likely end up walking even more if they took her car to the shopping district.

Desirée was not herself. Usually bright and vivacious, today she was morose and quiet. But as they emerged from the subway, she slowly loosened up and began to smile and speak with more hope. Rebekka learned that Desirée's car had been repossessed, that she was working at a bar and renting a room from a friend on the other side of Paris.

Rebekka chose one of her favorite stores and went inside. Desirée immediately looked uncomfortable, which made her only stick out more. With confidence, Rebekka plucked a few outfits from the racks, held them up to Desirée, discarded some, and replaced them with others. "These'll be great," she said.

Desirée looked doubtful. "They looked rather . . . well, dull. Boring. And they're much too big. I don't wear that size."

"Humor me," Rebekka replied, pushing her toward the dressing room. First Desirée tried on a double-breasted black pantsuit that emphasized her curves, but wasn't tight. The color slimmed her figure and made her eyes look large in her pale face. "Excellent," Rebekka said.

"I look like I'm going to a funeral," moaned Desirée.

"No, you look powerful. This is a power suit. I know you might feel a little awkward in it right now, but if you wear it for a bit, you'll see what I mean. It'll become the most comfortable thing you own."

"It does feel good not to have it tight. But I do plan to lose these extra pounds."

"No problem. Look, elastic waist. And you can have the waistline taken in a bit on the jacket. Or you might find it looks even better looser. The one I have I can still fit into and I'm pregnant."

"You're not that big."

"I'm getting there."

Next Desirée tried on a knit sweater and skirt set like the one Rebekka was wearing. Desirée complained again about the size, but when Rebekka pointed out how much more comfortable it was, she consented. Then Desirée tried on a few pair of pants, a column dress with detailed embroidery, three blazers, and a sweater. Several of the choices were definitely not right, and Rebekka had to exchange a few of the sizes, but most of the clothes made Desirée look like a new woman.

"My parents didn't give me enough money for all this," Desirée said. "But I really want it all." She frowned. "Story of my life."

"You have enough for the black suit and the knit sweater set," Rebekka said. "And I'll buy a blazer, the sweater, and the brown dress pants, and the black pumps. Because the colors are right you can mix and match."

Desirée took her hand. "Thank you, Rebekka."

Rebekka could feel her sincerity. "Look, Desirée. After we pay, you change into the black suit, okay? Then we'll go somewhere else and find the accessories."

At first Desirée walked clumsily and awkwardly in her new outfit, but soon she began to move with greater confidence. Her speech was less coarse as well. Rebekka almost couldn't believe the difference in both her attitude and demeanor.

They found a pair of inexpensive gold-colored earrings at the next store and a matching necklace. "They will do for jewelry until you can afford real," Rebekka said. "And do you like this purse? Will it hold everything you need?"

When they finished shopping, they stopped at a café for a snack. A group of men dressed in suits nodded to them as they waited at the counter to place their order. As Rebekka ordered a pastry filled with cooked turkey, Desirée whispered, "Are men always so polite to you?"

"Well, occasionally there's a bad apple, but mostly, yes. I ignore any who aren't polite."

Desirée chewed on this for a while and as they walked to a table she said, "You know, I bet I could find a better job if I wore this suit."

"I bet you could." Rebekka pulled her milk from her purse and opened the lid.

Desirée was silent a long time before speaking again. "I've been going to a support group that helps people stop drinking. They tell me I need to quit working at the bar. And that I need new friends."

"They're right."

She sighed. "I know that now. What I don't know is if I'm strong enough."

"You will be," Rebekka said, drinking her milk. "Come on, hurry up and finish. I know just the thing to put you in a good mood."

They walked a short distance along the cobbled walk near the Seine River. The Eiffel Tower rose in the background and every so often they saw tourists snapping pictures. This had been one of Rebekka and Marc's favorite places to haunt since childhood. She always loved the vitality here, and was grateful the memories didn't bring her pain today. Instead, peace filled her soul.

"Where are we going?" Desirée also seemed more relaxed.

"Let me surprise you."

Rebekka took Desirée to a hair salon. It wasn't the place she normally had her hair done since she knew they booked days in advance, but she had heard many recommendations for this salon. The lady at the front desk was able to work Desirée in for a cut and a facial. "Go easy on the hairspray," Rebekka told the stylist. "And the makeup—we're trying for a professional look here."

"Of course," the man said. "She is no barmaid, eh? You can tell by her clothes."

Rebekka stifled a smile. "Exactly."

"And for the Madame?"

"Another day perhaps. We have an appointment soon."

While they worked on Desirée, Rebekka looked up Raoul's lawyer in the phone book and called him. "I'm bringing Desirée down to sign the papers in about an hour," she told him. "We may not have another chance, so I hope that's okay."

"We'll work it in. Should I call Raoul? He doesn't really need to be here, but maybe he'll want to be."

Rebekka hesitated. If Raoul saw the change in Desirée would if make a difference? Or was this change a pretense? Desirée had fooled them all before—and her brother repeatedly. And if a real change was beginning, what did it mean for Nadia? Raoul said it was over between him and Desirée, that there had been too much hurt and deception between them. "No," she said slowly. "I'll call him myself and see what he wants to do."

She dialed Raoul's direct line, and Valerie's face kept coming to mind. What had Raoul even seen in Desirée? Yes, she had an undeniable appeal to men, that was true, but in everything else she came up short. Unless Raoul had glimpsed the Desirée she had seen today. *I still don't know if this is the real woman. Then again, maybe losing Nadia has helped her . . . I hope.*

"Hello?"

"Hi, it's Rebekka."

"Did Detective Francom call?" Raoul asked eagerly.

"No. Something else. Look, I'm with Desirée."

"You are? Where? Will she sign the papers?"

"Slow down. Let me explain. She came to the apartment this morning and we've been talking a lot. We're about to go see your lawyer. She wants to sign."

"Does she realized that custody of Nadia goes to me?"

"Yes. Her parents want Nadia, but she knows she belongs with you."

"Thank heaven!" He heaved a great sigh.

"Raoul?"

"What? What's wrong?"

Rebekka bit the inside of her bottom lip, wondering how she could pose the question. "About Desirée. Are you sure it's over? What if she were to change tomorrow?"

There was such a long silence that Rebekka wondered if he'd hung up. "Raoul?" she asked.

"I've tried for almost three years," he said. "I've prayed every night. I've given her every leeway—even when she was immoral. Over and over, I've forgiven her and reconciled with her, and every time she has laughed in my face as she goes back to her . . . ways. It wasn't until this situation with Nadia that I realized I can't do it again. I forgive her for cheating on me, I even forgive her for hiding Nadia, but the love I had for her in my heart is gone. There's simply nothing—nothing that isn't tainted by her unfaithfulness. We have no spiritual experiences to bind us, we have no temple marriage—or marriage of any sort. What little of her heart she gave to me, she also gave to a hundred other guys. She refused to meet me even partway. And now I must do what I feel is best for myself and my children—present and future—and Desirée isn't a part of that. I wish it had ended differently. I wish her well. I hope she changes, but I can't wait for it to happen. I can't be a part of it. I pray that if she does change, she will find someone who cares for her as much as I once did. I should never have married her, Rebekka. All the signs were there, but I was too caught up in my so-called love to see it. So the answer is no. It would make no difference if Desirée changed, even if we could prove it was for real, which I don't believe for a second."

"Okay. I wanted to make sure. I'll take her now. You don't need to be there. In fact, feeling the way you do, it's probably better that you aren't."

"I think that's wise. Call me when it's over, okay? I mean, it'll still have to go to the court, but once she signs, it won't take long."

"I will. Goodbye."

"Thanks, Sis."

Rebekka hung up the phone, thinking of Samuel the Lamanite as he preached to the Nephites in the Book of Mormon. Feeling for the copy she always carried, Rebekka thumbed through Helaman until she found the verse she was looking for:

> *"But behold, your days of probation are past; ye have procrastinated the day of your salvation until it is everlastingly too late and your destruction is made sure . . . ye have sought for happiness in doing iniquity . . ."* (13:38)

Raoul felt that his relationship with Desirée had reached this point, and she had to agree that he had given her every opportunity. He deserved a faithful companion and helpmeet. Yet was it too late for Desirée in relation to the Lord? Rebekka didn't think so, and the next verse gave her hope:

> *"O . . . that ye would hear my words! And I pray that the anger of the Lord be turned away from you, and that ye would repent and be saved."*

Rebekka had never liked Desirée; in fact, she had detested her at times for the pain she caused Raoul. But she sensed a real change this time—one she felt wasn't full of the manipulation that had permeated Desirée's other attempts at "repentance." *I will try to help you, Desirée, if you'll let me. I'll be your friend.*

The haircut and wash did wonders for Desirée. Rebekka was surprised to see she had chosen a short sleek look which suited her well. "I told him to do what he thought best," Desirée said.

"Do you like it?"

She glanced in one of the huge mirrors by the cash register. "Yes. I do. I really do."

Because the shooting pain in her side had returned and walking was painful, Rebekka hailed a cab to drive them to the lawyer's office. She shrugged off Desirée's concerns. "Just pregnancy related. Probably because of the extra weight I'm carrying."

At the lawyer's office, Desirée seemed nervous again. "Are you sure about this?" Rebekka felt forced to say, despite her loyalty to Raoul.

Desirée nodded. "More than I've been about anything. My marriage is over. I knew it the month after we were married. I was no good for him."

"You are a daughter of God," Rebekka said quietly, "every bit as much as he is a son of God. You also deserve happiness."

"But I didn't *choose* it, did I?" There was obvious bitterness in Desirée's voice. "I appreciate what you're saying, Rebekka. I really do. But you and I both know Raoul is out of my life forever. I blew it. And now I finally do want to change, but I don't trust myself enough to believe I'll really do it."

"Then trust in God. You need to believe it's possible. He made you and you can do it."

Desirée's eyes filled with tears. "I hope you are right." She signed the documents in all the right places as the lawyer looked dispassionately on. When she was done, he told her when she would have to appear before the judge for the final decree.

In the lobby of the building, Desirée kissed Rebekka's cheek, whispered another thank-you, and headed for the door. "Wait, how can I reach you?" Rebekka asked.

"I'll call," Desirée promised. "Or you can leave a message with my parents if you find Nadia. As soon as I clear up the ticket mess, I'll go in and see the police. I don't know what I can do to help, but I'll try."

Rebekka watched her go, feeling suddenly melancholy. Would Desirée make any progress? Or would she continue to drown herself in alcohol and her addictive lifestyle in order to block out the reality of her failed marriage and her daughter's disappearance?

Exhaustion and frustration fell over Rebekka, but she didn't begrudge the money she had spent on Desirée; Marc had left her plenty and her own parents were well-off. Plus she was still working.

I would trade it all for another year with Marc, she thought.

To her surprise no anger or resentment came with the thought. *Thank you, Desirée, for reminding me that I have a choice. I chose to come down to this earth and marry Marc, knowing we would have trials, and now, like you, I must choose how to live the rest of my life—and whether or not I will be happy.*

She signaled another a taxi, digging her hand into her side. Next week at her appointment she would ask the doctor about this pain.

Chapter 21

It was Wednesday, three days since André had seen Rebekka. The last time had been on Sunday at church. He knew she had a doctor's appointment the following week and he planned to be there. The doctor thought he was the husband and until Rebekka told him differently, he was going to be there to play the part. But he couldn't wait that long to see her or talk to her alone. Every minute together meant another building block to their relationship—one her boyfriend Samuel couldn't hope to match while he continued living in America.

André felt good about confessing his feelings to her. At least he didn't have to hide them anymore, and though her revelation about Samuel was disturbing, he wasn't giving up. He hadn't yet publicly announced his intentions to the family, but since he had talked to Josette, most likely Zack, Marie-Thérèse, and Mathieu knew. He felt sure his mother, always sensitive to her children and their feelings, would have figured it out as well—and that meant his father also knew. And Raoul had to suspect something with the continuous shower of plant life in their apartment. André felt sure everyone was rooting for him.

Rebekka herself was an enigma. She talked with him, laughed with him, and even seemed happy to hear from him when he called, but the moment he broached anything serious—like her relationship with Samuel or his feelings for her, she would close up like the prayer plant he had bought her last week. He always backed off, determined to win her, but not wanting to hurt her in the process.

Today he *had* to see her. He longed to feast his eyes on her beauty and to assure himself she was still here. Often in his dreams, she would run away with Samuel to America and he was left standing at the airport alone. He couldn't let that happen. Yet ultimately, it would be her choice and hers alone.

As it had been to marry Marc. He tried not to feel unhappy at the thought. *I have a second chance.*

André swung by his daughters' school and picked them up. They loved to see Rebekka, and if he took them along, he would be able to keep things more casual, and he might be able to talk her into going out for dinner later.

Ana and Marée were excited. "I love going to Rebekka's," Ana said. "She lets me feel the baby. It kicked. At least I think it was a kick. It's kinda hard to tell."

"It'll be easier as it gets bigger," André assured them. He felt an unreasoning jealousy that the girls had been permitted to feel the baby when he had to stay at arm's length. *Get a grip*, he told himself. Doing so was hard when he was sure Rebekka only needed time to see what a wonderful husband he would be to her.

"Why are we stopping here?" asked Marée. "I thought we were going to Rebekka's."

"I just want to dash in this shop for a moment and buy some flowers for Rebekka," André said. "It won't take a minute." The flowers would be his excuse to visit.

"Oh." There was just a little too much knowing in Marée's reply.

The girls accompanied him into the shop. "Those!" begged Ana. "The big yellow ones. Those are so beautiful."

"Those are sunflowers," said the shopkeeper. "Very popular these days. I can make them into a beautiful arrangement."

André inclined his head. "Okay. Please do. With a vase."

"Oh, but Daddy, look at this basket!" Marée was fingering the edge. "It has one, two, three, four, five different plants inside! One with purple flowers. And they're growing right out of the dirt, but it's in a basket. Let's buy this for her. Please. She'll love it!"

André knew Rebekka often forgot to water plants, but she must enjoy them since she and Marc always had a few around the house. "Yes," he said. "We'll take that, too. Both." The girls squealed their contentedness and André felt like a hero. The shopkeeper also looked pleased. *Well, why wouldn't he? I've become his best customer this past month.*

In a way he knew it was childish to keep on sending plants and flowers, but he would do so until the moment she agreed to marry him. At least she wouldn't be able to forget him easily. Smiling to himself, he carried the vase of sunflowers out to the car, while the girls trailed after him, swinging the basket between them.

They arrived at Rebekka's before four o'clock. She buzzed them into the building lobby immediately, and André felt uncharacteristically nervous as they rode up the four floors to her apartment. Part of him squirmed in anticipation, and the other part worried about what to say.

The door was ajar when the elevator opened, but Rebekka wasn't at the door waiting. "I guess we just go in," he said to the girls. They found Rebekka in the sitting room on the couch, legs supported by the coffee table, arms outspread.

She was staring in the direction of her piano, but she turned as they entered. "Sorry, I was feeling too tired to get up again to answer the door. Thought you could find your own way in."

"We brought you something, Aunt Rebekka!" Ana exclaimed. The girls presented the basket and André placed the sunflowers on the coffee table.

Rebekka accept the girls' offering. "How lovely. Did you girls pick this out? You didn't have to bring me a present."

"I picked it out for the baby," Marée said, her turquoise eyes serious. She patted Rebekka's stomach."Do you think he'll like them?

"I picked out the sunflowers," Ana put in. "They're for you. But they were Daddy's idea. He wanted to buy flowers for you."

"Thank you all. I love them. They're beautiful."

André was staring at Marée's hand, still patting Rebekka's stomach, which was larger than he remembered from three days ago. He felt a loss, thinking of how he had talked to his daughters while they were in the womb, of how he and Claire had lain awake nights planning the coming birth and their hopes for each baby.

Rebekka swung her legs down from the coffee table and leaned over to finger a sunflower. "These look bright and happy, just perfect after the day I've been through."

"Oh, what happened?" Without waiting for an invitation, he sat beside her. Marée climbed on his lap, while Ana began exploring the room.

"Desirée. She came over this morning, and we went shopping for some presentable clothing for a court date she has pending about her driving tickets. She looks great cleaned up. I think she's serious about changing."

"We've thought that before."

Rebekka sighed and he noticed how tired she looked. "I know," she said. "But the point is moot anyway. She signed the divorce papers today and now all that's left is the final court appearance. She and Raoul are as good as divorced. I'm glad for him—he deserved better treatment—but I feel sorry for her. She has such a long way to go." She leaned back against the couch and tried to raise her feet again to the coffee table, wincing with pain at the attempt.

André quickly scooped up her feet and set them on the table.

"Thanks," she said.

"Your ankles are swollen."

"Yeah, I did too much walking today, and I'm retaining water like crazy. But worse is the pain in my side."

André was immediately concerned. "Pain in your side. Retaining water? Could be serious, either problem."

"I know. I'm going to ask the doctor about it next week. The appointment really should have been this week, but I had a deadline I wanted to make. And besides, I've been feeling well."

André didn't tell her he planned to be at the appointment. No use in giving her a chance to say no.

"You sure do have a lot of flowers," Ana commented. "And plants." Marée jumped off André's lap to follow her sister around the room, counting the containers.

Rebekka smiled mischievously. "Someone's been sending a lot of them lately. Must think I'm sick or something."

"There are a lot of different illnesses," André commented. He leaned forward and with the tips of his fingers and massaged one of her ankles gently. "I could rub them for you."

"Oh, you don't have to do—oooo." She leaned her head back and shut her eyes. "That does feel good."

André pulled her feet onto the couch and began to massage her ankles. Marée appeared at his side and began rubbing the other foot. "Aunt Rebekka's going to sleep," she said with a laugh.

"Mmmm," was Rebekka's only reply. Her dark auburn hair splayed out about her over the couch cushion, making her seem pale and fragile and small—except for the roundness of her belly. André worked his way up to her calves and down again, feeling the tension ease from her muscles. Marée soon returned to counting flowers and plants in the sitting room and eventually followed her sister from the room to search for more. André passed to Rebekka's other leg, quitting only when he felt her completely relax.

"Thanks," Rebekka murmured, opening her eyes. "I guess I needed that."

"Probably shouldn't wear high heels right now," he commented.

She grimaced, and her hand went to her side. "Actually, I didn't. Oh, this pain—what could it be?"

André shrugged, wishing he could help. But he couldn't very well offer to massage her side. If they were married, of course, it would be a completely different situation.

Her next abrupt question drove all other thoughts from his mind. "Do you think Marc knew he was going to die?" Her gray eyes were serious, holding his.

"I think he had a premonition, yes. But I don't think he *knew* exactly."

"I mean before he came to earth."

He thought about it for a moment. "I guess he probably did."

"Then I would have agreed as well." Her teeth bit the soft flesh of her inner bottom lip, bringing to mind her softness on the day he had kissed her.

"Possibly. What do *you* believe?"

She frowned, rubbing half-consciously again at her side. "I think I was much braver in heaven than I am here." There were tears in her eyes, threatening to fall.

"Nonsense. You have been nothing but brave."

"I miss him so much," she said. "And yet I'm mad at him too, and I keep wishing—"

A loud splintering crash came from the kitchen and they both jumped at the sound. "Uh-oh. They've broken something," he said, helping Rebekka stand.

They hurried into the kitchen and found the girls staring at the shards of a green ceramic pot lying on the floor mixed with a pile of potting soil. A scraggly, almost dead plant topped the messy heap. "I didn't mean to!" Marée launched herself into his arms. "I was just going to water it and it slipped."

"You shouldn't have been trying to carry it," Ana said. "I told her to use a cup."

"I can carry it! It just slipped."

"Girls! Stop fighting!"André scolded. "And how many times do I have to tell you not to take chances with other people's belongings. You must ask permission first."

Marée began to cry. "But Daddy, I was helping. I didn't mean to!"

"That's enough," Rebekka said. "No use in crying over a dead plant, right? I should have thrown it out already." She looked at André point-edly. "Besides, Marée, you are much more important to me than any plant—even if your daddy gave it to me." She shrugged and began walking toward the closet where she kept the broom.

André studied the plant. He didn't recognize it, but then he hadn't always picked out his offerings himself. Several times he had purchased over the phone and once he'd asked Valerie to order. In fact, the ceramic pot, obviously a beautiful piece, looked more like Valerie's style. "Rebekka's right," he said. "What's important is that you're not hurt, Marée. However, I would like you to be more careful in the future."

Rebekka returned with the broom and the trash bucket. André took them from her and began cleaning up the mess himself. "I remember once as a child I went through a phase where I was dropping a lot of things," Rebekka said. "My father—you remember how he was back then, André—well, he always was angry and yelled at me. I felt so bad, like I couldn't do anything right. But my mom, with her it was always my safety that came first. I knew she loved some of the things I broke, but not one of them was more important than me. With my dad, I was never sure. I know now as an adult that he loved me, but then it was hard for me to tell."

André remembered only too well the anger always burning inside Rebekka's father. *But he changed when he accepted the gospel*, André thought. *It didn't seem possible, but eventually, he changed.*

Still, he didn't miss the point of Rebekka's story. He hugged Marée. "I love you, honey," he murmured.

Marée's arms went around his neck. "I know, Daddy. And I can buy her another one."

"No need, really," Rebekka insisted. "Your dad has brought enough already."

"That's because he likes you," Ana said. Marée giggled.

André lifted one shoulder in a shrug. "Well, this is clean. I was worried it might have broken one of your floor tiles, but it doesn't look like it."

"Thank you." Rebekka accepted the broom from him and smiled awkwardly.

"So would you like to go out and eat with us later?" he asked, hoping he sounded casual. "I could go home and help the girls get their homework done and then we could swing by and get you on our way out."

"Yeah! Come, Aunt Rebekka!" shouted Ana and Marée. They put their hands together in a beseeching gesture and batted their eyelids.

Rebekka laughed, and the color seemed to return to her cheeks. "You girls are so funny—dinner's hours away yet. And the fact is I already ate out today at lunch, and I don't think I can face it again. I'm just not feeling well. My side hurts every time I move."

"Ohhh!" the girls chorused their dismay.

"Then can we stay and play at least?" asked Marée. "You can paint our nails like last time and then we can do our hair."

"Well," Rebekka vacillated.

André could tell she really didn't feel up to having the girls stay, but that she didn't want to disappoint them. "How about tomorrow?" he asked. "They could come after school." The girls usually went to daycare for a few hours until he was off, or occasionally to his parents. Before Marc's death they had also come to Rebekka's at least once a week. They missed those visits more than he would ever admit to Rebekka. Since she didn't have children of her own, and they hadn't a mother, the girls had considered Rebekka all theirs.

"That would be good," she said. "I should be feeling better. I'll even come and get you. Deal?"

"Well . . . okay," Ana agreed.

"That way we can bring our new polish," Marée added, face brightening. "Great-grandma bought us it for our birthdays."

"I remember." The color had again abruptly faded from Rebekka's face. "You know what? I'm glad you came over, but I think I'd better lie down now."

André took a step toward her. "Do you really think you should be alone?"

"I'll be fine. Don't worry." She laughed. "It was just all that exercise today. I'm getting old and fat, I guess."

"You are not!" said Marée.

Ana nodded solemnly. "You are the prettiest person we know."

Rebekka placed a hand on their shoulders. "Thanks, girls. You know, I do believe I've really missed our days together. You'll have to start coming over again."

"Yay!"

André met Rebekka's eyes over the heads of his enthusiastic daughters. "That would be nice," he said. *And one more day for me to show you how we belong together.*

As if reading his mind, she shook her head. For a long moment they stood locked together, as though neither could look away.

At last, André roused himself. "Come on, girls. Let's go home."

"Can we still go out to eat after homework?" Ana asked.

"If you beat me to the door." They were gone in a flash.

André followed more sedately with Rebekka. He could tell she was still hurting and matched his pace with hers. Then without warning, she clutched at her side and leaned against the wall. She slowly sank to the floor.

André knelt on the floor beside her, gathering her into his arms. "Are you okay? Rebekka?"

There was no answer.

* * *

Dr. Samain's round face was expressionless as he listened to the baby's heartbeat. Rebekka clung to André's hand, fearing the worst. His face was drawn and anxious. Standing beside him, his mother Ariana waited, her face calm. *She has already been through so many trials*, Rebekka thought. *But I'm not like her. I can't bear to lose my baby. Not after losing Marc. Please, Father!*

The doctor cleared his throat. "The baby's heartbeat is very strong," he said. "But right here," he kneaded Rebekka's left side, "is your intestine and I believe that's what's giving you the sharp pains. Constipation is common in pregnant women. And I think you passed out from normal symptoms of pregnancy. With the shopping trip today, you obviously overdid things."

"Then there's nothing wrong with me?" Rebekka asked. *Constipation?* she thought. *How embarrassing!*

"Well, I don't *think* so." Dr. Samain's hesitancy rekindle her fear. "I'd like to do an ultrasound to be sure."

"Why? What else is wrong?" Ariana met the doctor's eyes. "Come on, we've known each other a long time—your father delivered all but my first child and you've delivered several of my daughter Josette's. What aren't you telling us?" Rebekka was glad her mother-in-law was there to ask the questions because she felt too close to tears to say anymore.

Dr. Samain shifted under the fluorescent light. A small smile played on his lips briefly, making his hanging jowls more prominent. "Well, Rebekka is only a week over four months along, and I'm sure she told you that at her last appointment, I was very worried about her weight loss. But now, though she hasn't gained a lot, she's actually measuring *larger* than she should be at this point. That could be from a number of different factors, some threatening, some not. For instance, a non-threatening example might be that she is be farther along than she calculated, or that perhaps there's more than one baby."

André's eyes opened wide. "You think she's having twins? They do run in our family, you know."

"Fraternal twins run in the family," Ariana corrected.

"That's right," Dr. Samain said, "and fraternal twins run in the female line because it happens when a woman releases more than one egg at a time, usually two, and they both become fertilized, producing two babies. If Rebekka were a Perrault by birth—or rather a Merson since the twins connection comes through your line, Madame Perrault—I wouldn't be concerned at all until we've done more tests. And there's also the fact that I can't find two distinct heartbeats, though that certainly doesn't rule out twins. With an ultrasound, I can see what's going on for sure. At this point, we only know that Rebekka is measuring larger than most women at four months, and we need to check into it."

Rebekka was suddenly excited. She had never considered having twins. She turned to André. "Wouldn't that be something?"

He smiled warmly and pressed her hand. "So when can we find out?"

"Well, we have that appointment next week, and since the baby's heartbeat is strong and there are no signs of fetal stress, we could do the ultrasound then," Dr. Samain said. "We have a pretty heavy load today and it would be impossible to squeeze you in for an ultrasound. And I really don't feel it's anything we need to get done urgently. Especially if the pain goes away after taking the medication I'm going to give you."

"Thank you," Rebekka said. "And I really appreciate you seeing me so quickly like this today." To her relief her words sounded calm; she wasn't about to admit that she would give almost anything to know what was going on inside her stomach.

The doctor chuckled, showing deep laugh lines in his sagging cheeks. "Well, I'm always here if you need me."

"Thank you, doctor." Rebekka smiled as she accepted his help to slide off the examining table.

Dr. Samain looked at André. "You take good care of your wife, hear? No more long shopping expeditions."

Rebekka blinked in surprise, having forgotten she had let the doctor believe André was her husband at the last visit. She opened her mouth to speak, when André beat her to it. "Oh, I'll take good care of her, you can be sure. Don't worry about that. Thank you, doctor."

Ariana looked amused. "Yes, thank you," she repeated dryly, looking back and forth between them. Rebekka felt her face redden. Ariana was one of the few people who had known she harbored feelings for André before her marriage to Marc, but what would she say if she knew of his proposal?

André helped Rebekka out to the car where Ariana bid farewell. "I'm not even going to ask what that was about," Ariana said, a bemused smile on her face. She hugged Rebekka. "Keep in touch."

"We should have told the doctor," Rebekka said as Ariana drove away.

"Told him what?" André asked maddeningly.

"You know very well what."

He took his hand from the ignition where he had been about to start the car. His eyes met into hers. "Look, Rebekka. I love you and I want to marry you. Any time I can pretend to be your husband, I'm going to do it. Unless—" his brown eyes glinted "—you want me to call up Samuel boy to play the part."

Rebekka looked away, afraid he would read the lie in her eyes. "I'll call him myself."

"Good." His reply was terse, and Rebekka regretted starting the discussion at all.

They drove home in tense silence, stopping only to pick up the prescription the doctor had given her. When they drove up at Rebekka's apartment, she hopped out quickly before he could come around. "Don't bother coming up. I'll be okay. Thanks."

"I left the girls with your neighbor when you passed out," he said. "I have to get them."

"Oh."

They went together to collect the girls, thanking the neighbor profusely. Then André insisted upon returning to Rebekka's apartment to make sure she was all right. There, he explained the situation to the girls.

"You might be having twins?" Ana said with a little squeal. "I've always wanted to have twins. Grandma says I might. That practically all the women in her family do. Wow, I can't believe it! You're so lucky!"

Marée and André seemed equally excited, but Rebekka couldn't shake the odd feeling that had come over her since entering the apartment. Something that whispered all was not right with her baby.

"It's going to be okay," André said to her in a quiet undertone.

Already the sharp pains seemed to be easing because of the doctor's medication. Things *were* okay—or seemed to be. Rebekka squeezed André's hand. He always seemed to know exactly what to say when she really needed him.

* * *

When Rebekka had collapsed, André felt he was reliving a nightmare—the one where he had come home to find Claire deathly ill. The emotions were the same—guilt, fear, love, need, and anger. Only it was worse than the first time because he knew intimately the agony of loss that lurked just around the corner.

A wet rag had brought Rebekka back to consciousness, but she had been in such obvious pain that he had carried her to the car as he had his wife that fateful night. He was heading for the emergency room, when Rebekka roused enough to direct him instead to the doctor's office. André had called his mother on the way there and she agreed to meet them.

Because of the emergency, the doctor made room in his packed schedule to see Rebekka, and André waited with dread to hear the verdict. He had taken Claire to the doctor, too, and she had died.

Rebekka lived, and at Dr. Samain's reassurances, André's terror subsided. He even began feeling sheepish at his violent reaction. But he didn't want to feel that emotion ever again. The idea of losing Rebekka was not something he could endure. No one should have to experience that pain twice in a lifetime.

Back at her apartment, Rebekka acted restless and uncertain. She clung to his hand, yet refused his repeated offers to stay. Concerned about her being alone, André stalled long enough for Raoul to arrive from the office. Then he kissed Rebekka's cheek as he left, trying not to show his hurt when she flinched slightly as though his touch burned her flesh.

"See you later," he said.

"Thank you." She looked in his direction, but her gaze didn't quite focus. There was a lost air about her that ate into his heart. He wanted to hold her, to comfort her, to assure her Marc's baby would be all right. But she wouldn't permit it. He hated knowing that if he reached out to her, she would gently but firmly push him away. Yet there *was* something between them and he was determined to wake those emotions within her, to cause them to burn with the same intensity he felt. Maybe then she wouldn't be able to deny them. Maybe then she could allow herself to feel love again.

Raoul walked with André to the door. "I'll take care of her," Raoul said. "Thanks for being there today." His expression was compassionate, and André knew he understood at least some of how he felt.

"Samuel, does he call much?" André asked, not knowing why he tortured himself.

Raoul thought about it. "Actually, no. I've never seen her talk to him since he came to visit. But the time difference—they may talk during the day while I'm at work."

"What about the phone bill? A lot of long distance calls?"

Raoul shrugged. "I don't know. She takes care of the bills and just lets me know how much is my share. I tried to pay her rent, too, but she won't let me because the apartment is paid for." He hesitated. "I'm sorry, André. I wish things could be different."

"Me, too. Call me if you need me, okay?"

"I will."

André hated leaving Rebekka that way, but she didn't seem to want him to stay—or perhaps she didn't know what she wanted. He held on to that hope.

One thing for sure, he was going to be at her doctor's appointment next week, invitation or no.

Chapter 22

On Wednesday afternoon Marie-Thérèse sat in her new rocking chair in her new apartment, holding a sleeping Raquel against her chest, hearing her delicate breath, and smelling her fresh baby scent. The baby had gained six pounds over the last month and was outgrowing many of her clothes.

No longer the undernourished child that had come into their home, Celisse had also gained weight, and her cheeks were filling out. Her bowel problem was well under control and the few accidents she did have didn't bother Marie-Thérèse. There were lingering health and emotional problems, of course, and many visits to the doctor, but Celisse was settling in remarkably well. She still went under the table occasionally during the day, or under the crib in the room she now shared with Raquel, but she hid less frequently.

Though having the girls live with them had been every bit as hard as Marie-Thérèse had expected—or worse—she didn't regret the decision. For the love and the rewards had been returned more than tenfold. In fact, each day she thanked the Lord for the girls and prayed they would become available for adoption. She couldn't imagine life without them—long days filled with boring order and no little arms around her neck. Mathieu had been right: the love had stretched and grown to include these new additions to their family.

The recent move to the new apartment had helped family relations considerably—especially where Larissa was concerned. While she still didn't make any overtures toward Celisse or the baby, she seemed content with her new room and the bathroom she only had to share with Brandon. She hadn't complained in days and her grades, if not exceptional, had held steady.

As always, Brandon adored the little girls, and they loved him right back. If he was home, he was playing with them. Marie-Thérèse knew he liked them more than his blood sister.

Marie-Thérèse laid Raquel in her crib and headed into the kitchen where she had left Celisse to finish her late afternoon snack. "Raquel sleep?" Celisse asked.

"Yes. Sound asleep. It was way past her nap time, but we had fun at the park, didn't we?"

Celisse nodded. "Fun. I love park." While Celisse's speech improved daily, she still had a tendency to leave a few words out.

"We'll go again soon. How about after we go see the doctor on Friday? That's only two days away."

"Doctor?" asked Celisse.

"You know that lady doctor you really like, the one we've been going to each week."

"She nice," Celisse said solemnly.

"Yes, she is," Marie-Thérèse agreed. This visit would be pivotal, the doctor believed, because Celisse seemed to be able to trust them more each session, and finally they had scheduled several tests that would determine whether Celisse would need surgery to fix the physical damage inflicted on her. The tests would be uncomfortable and personal, but they felt Celisse understood the necessity and would not feel threatened. Marie-Thérèse prayed for everything to go well.

She set out two additional plates and glasses on the table. Larissa and Brandon would be home soon and they would enjoy a piece of the banana bread she had made this morning. Between the two of them they usually finished off an entire loaf.

The slamming of the apartment door showed she had timed her actions perfectly. She went to meet them—Brandon with his typical full body hug, and Larissa with her more reserved shoulder squeeze and peck on the cheek.

"I have bread for you," she said, pointing to the slices on the table.

"Yippee!" Brandon lunged forward and grabbed three pieces and put them on his plate. Then he filled up his glass to the brim—with juice since he was allergic to milk.

Larissa rolled her eyes. "Keep eating like that and you'll get fat."

"No, I won't," Brandon said through a mouthful of bread. "I burn off a lot. Besides, I'm a guy. We like to be a little big." He made a face for Celisse and she giggled.

Larissa slid a small slice of banana bread onto her plate. "Don't blame me—I warned you. I know some girls who used to not worry about it and now it's costing them to get rid of it."

Marie-Thérèse put her hands on her hips. "Since when did you begin to worry about your weight? It seems that's all you've talked about in the past few weeks—since we moved here, in fact. But you're tall and thin—exactly like I was at your age, and I don't have a problem."

Larissa sniffed. "I know. But a girl has to be careful." She stood and went to the refrigerator, pulling out a jug of cold water and pouring herself a glass.

Marie-Thérèse followed her daughter. "You're beautiful exactly as you are," she said, suspicions beginning to form. This new preoccupation of Larissa's with her weight, along with a few other comments she had made, were beginning to add up. "And if you *were* overweight, we'd talk about it. I'd plan special dinners to help you, and we'd exercise. Whatever, I'm sure you know that making yourself throw up is not healthy, and using those diet pills you can get at the pharmacy is just as bad. Either of those options are *very* dangerous with serious side-effects. You do know that, don't you?"

Her daughter held up her free hand. "Okay, okay. I was thinking about using the pills. A few of my friends do, but I didn't know they were dangerous. I haven't used any—I promise."

Marie-Thérèse sighed with relief. "Thank heaven! If you ever do have a weight problem, we'll tackle it together, even go to the doctor to see where you should be and what you should eat, but taking drugs is *out* of the question. There's no easy fix for weight loss—or anything else. You know my birth mother died because she contracted HIV while doing drugs and that because of her my father and sister died, too."

Larissa's face instantly lost its aggrieved expression. "Okay, Mom. I understand."

Marie-Thérèse believed her, but made a vow to search her room later just in case. Her daughter's privacy had limits, and drugs—including over the counter diet pills—were one of those limits.

"Brandon, Brandon, Brandon!" Celisse yelled, bursting in on their conversation. "Brandon!"

Marie-Thérèse heard the stress in her voice and glanced at the child, whose blue eyes were wide with fear. "What's wrong, honey?" Celisse pointed, and Marie-Thérèse followed the motion. To her horror, Brandon was lying face-down on the table, his face red as he struggled for breath.

She leapt to the cupboard where she kept the medicine the doctor had given her for such occurrences, though he had not had such a severe allergic reaction since the strawberry incident which had almost taken his life three years ago.

"Steady, Brandon," she said, after administering the spray into his mouth. "I'm here. Don't worry. Just breathe slowly. Nothing's going to happen. Just take it easy. The medicine will work very soon."

But it didn't. He lay in her arms struggling for each breath and becoming more agitated with every moment.

"Larissa, call the ambulance," Marie-Thérèse directed. "Hurry!"

With fumbling fingers Larissa dialed the number, while Celisse watched anxiously. The fear in the room was so palpable, Marie-Thérèse could feel it like a weight upon her shoulders.

"Just tell them Brandon's having an allergic reaction and that I need help," Marie-Thérèse directed.

Larissa followed her instructions, voice shaking, but clear. "They're coming, Mom. They said they'll be here in a minute. They want to know what you gave him."

Marie-Thérèse tossed her the spray, and Larissa spelled the name of the drug. Then she said, "They say it's okay to give him another dose. But no more."

Marie-Thérèse shot more spray into Brandon's mouth. He still struggled for breath, but he didn't swell further. "I'm here," Marie-Thérèse said over and over. "Everything is going to be fine." In her heart she sent up a plea to her Heavenly Father.

At last the ambulance arrived and Larissa let them into the apartment. They lowered Brandon onto a stretcher, strapped oxygen over his mouth, and took his vital signs. Almost immediately, they were ready to transport.

Marie-Thérèse was not about to let him out of her sight. "I'm going with them," she told Larissa. "Call your dad at work and let him know what's going on. Tell him to call our doctor. He'll know best how to treat Brandon when we get to the hospital, or at least tell the emergency room doctor his history."

"Okay," Larissa agreed. Her gaze swung to Celisse. "What about her and Raquel?"

Fury rose in Marie-Thérèse's heart. "Stop being so selfish! They are *your* sisters and you're going to stay with them while I take care of Brandon. And don't you dare do anything less than your best! If I learn you've been rude or unkind . . ." She left off talking to Larissa and turned to Celisse. "Don't worry, sweetie. I'll be back very soon. Everything will be just fine. The doctors will take care of Brandon and Larissa will take care of you." With a last warning glance at Larissa, Marie-Thérèse followed the ambulance workers from the apartment.

* * *

Larissa blankly watched her mother leave, wondering if her brother would be all right or if this time he would die. *No*, she thought. *That couldn't happen! Mom won't let it. Besides, they can always put a tube down his throat, can't they?*

But Brandon had almost died once before. It had been a very scary time, but one Larissa now thought of with fondness, because that was when she had realized how much her mother really did love her, not just Brandon. It was also the first time her prayers had been answered.

Larissa stood by the kitchen door for a long time before she remembered to call her dad. Her voice wasn't even shaking when she told him what happened. "He'll be fine, Dad," she said. "He has to be."

"I know, baby, but I'm going down there anyway. I'll call you the minute I know anything."

"Thanks."

Larissa sat down at the table and tried to eat her banana bread. But the mouthful wouldn't go down—not because she was worried about getting fat, but because she had started thinking about Brandon again. What if this time things didn't work out? With Celisse and Raquel around Mom didn't need Brandon like she used to. Maybe now that her mother was content, Brandon wouldn't be missed so much. Maybe that meant God would allow him to die. Sudden anger burned in the pit of her stomach. *If only those stupid little girls hadn't come! I hate them both! But Mom doesn't. She loves them—as much as she loves me.*

With growing resentment, she recalled her mother's stern face as she told her to watch Celisse and Raquel. *But they promised they wouldn't make me baby-sit. I knew it! It was only a matter of time until they forced me to tend those brats.*

Well, Brandon is sick, her more reasonable side told her. But she didn't want to consider excuses. Better to focus on the anger she felt toward her mother for going back on her promise. For making her watch that annoying little food vacuum who consumed everything in sight.

Speaking of which . . . Larissa looked around but Celisse was nowhere. Where could she be? Had she gone after their mother?

I don't care, she thought. But visions filled her mind—of Celisse alone in the street. Or Celisse stuck in the elevator or in the stairwell. Would she be crying?

Larissa flew to the apartment door and swung it wide open before her common sense kicked in. *Wait a minute. Mom left with the ambulance workers and she would have made sure the door was shut tight behind them. Celisse can't open it alone. Besides, she was at the table eating banana bread. I would have noticed if she went past me . . .*

Larissa retraced her steps to the kitchen. Celisse wasn't at the table but she was huddled under it—a place Larissa hadn't seen her go for at least two weeks. Her arms were wrapped around her knees which were drawn to her chest, and her head was hunched over them, as she tried to make herself into the smallest ball possible.

Like she doesn't want to be seen, Larissa thought. *Like she's trying to hide.*

Aloud she said, "Come out of there, Celisse. Brandon's going to be fine. Come on."

Celisse didn't move.

"Come on out right now and finish your bread," Larissa said in the same loud, firm voice her mother used when she expected to be obeyed.

Celisse didn't lift her head, but her shoulders began to shake and a quiet sob escape from somewhere under the mass of brown hair.

"Oh, come on," Larissa coaxed, dropping the pretense of maintaining control. "Stop that crying for heaven's sake!" *You brat,* she added silently. Then she felt guilty because Celisse's sobs grew louder and she curled herself even tighter than before.

Larissa watched her for a minute, wondering what to do. She could just walk away, but leaving Celisse alone crying under the table brought back the images of her outside in the street or in the elevator. Or in her birth mother's house, hiding from a would-be abuser.

An unfamiliar feeling came into Larissa's heart, evoking a profound emotion toward Celisse. What must Celisse be feeling? Was she scared? Was she afraid for Brandon, afraid she was being abandoned . . . or was she afraid *of* Larissa?

Larissa knelt on the hard ceramic tile and inched her way under the table. "It's okay, Celisse. Really. I promise. I wouldn't lie to you. I wouldn't. I'm your—" Larissa swallowed hard "—sister and I wouldn't lie to you." She reached out to Celisse, who kept herself tightly curled in her protective ball. Larissa picked her up and held her on her lap. Celisse was surprisingly light. "There, there, Celisse," she murmured, stroking her sweet-smelling hair. "It's going to be okay. I promise."

Celisse made no reply, but her sobs ceased. Larissa kept smoothing her hair and murmuring reassurances. After a few minutes, Celisse became pliant in her arms as she relaxed her hold on her knees. But she began to cry again softly. "Brandon, Brandon, Brandon," she said in a voice that held terrible pain.

"I know," Larissa's own tears spilled over. "I'm scared too, but we have to believe everything's okay. Any minute now, Mom's going to call and tell us. Those people will help Brandon—that's their job." Larissa held Celisse even tighter, rocking her small body back and forth.

"Brandon, Brandon, Brandon," moaned Celisse.

Larissa sniffed and one of her tears dropped into Celisse's hair. "Shhhh. It's okay. I'm here. Larissa's here."

Celisse gradually stopped crying, but she clung to Larissa like they had seen the baby monkeys do to their mothers at the zoo last week. Larissa's heart was full of emotions she could not name. She remembered her father telling her that love was not like a chocolate they had to share, but something that increased even as they gave it away. He had promised there would be enough to go around. Larissa hadn't believed him. She had *known* that everything they gave to Celisse and Raquel would mean less for her. But now all at once she understood what her father was saying. They loved her every bit as much as they ever had—it was only part of their time that was focused elsewhere. And Larissa had overlooked one important fact: the additional love Celisse would bring into her life.

It's love, she thought. *This feeling is love! I love Celisse! And I don't want to ever see her hurting.*

Suddenly Larissa's tears weren't for Brandon or for her own frustrations, but for Celisse and the relationship they had almost missed. She held onto Celisse as tightly as the small girl clung to her. "I'm here, Celisse," she whispered. "I know I've been mean and rude and stuff. I'm sorry. I'm going to be better from now on, I promise. I'm going to be the big sister you deserve. And nobody's going to hurt you again—especially not me."

How much of her words Celisse understood didn't really matter. Larissa felt her hug and it was enough. *How did my parents know?* she wondered. *They were right all along.* She made a vow to listen more to them—particularly to throw away the diet drugs Jolie had stuffed into her backpack at school. She wouldn't be needing those anyway. Her mother was right; if she ever did want to lose weight she'd do it the responsible way.

"Look," she said to Celisse. "I know a way we can feel better and help Brandon. Let's pray, okay? I'll say the words, you just think about them in your head. Picture Heavenly Father in your mind—you know like

Mom taught us the other night at family night. Pretend like we're speaking with Him. He'll help Brandon."

Celisse nodded and drew back a little to fold her arms and bow her head. Larissa marveled at her faith. Five weeks ago Celisse had never heard of God or Jesus Christ, but now she knew exactly what to do.

* * *

The EMT's gave Brandon a shot of medicine, and by the time the ambulance arrived at the hospital, his breathing was already less forced. "Looks like it's working," an attendant said as they rolled him into the emergency entrance.

"Good stuff," agreed another.

Marie-Thérèse felt her fear ebb away, taking with it her energy. She stumbled after the men and gratefully sank into a chair next to Brandon's bed. *Thank you, Father*, she prayed silently. Aloud, she said, "So he's all right?"

"Yes. Or will be soon." The young emergency room doctor was taking Brandon's pulse. "But I think we'll keep the oxygen on for just a bit more. Oh yeah, your doctor called. He's on his way. Likely he'll want to admit him for observation and full-scale allergy testing. Not very fun, but it'll help us identify what happened."

She sighed. "Yes, we've been through it before. It's probably flour. Or bananas. Or both. He was eating banana bread when it happened."

"A lot of children have wheat intolerance," the doctor said.

"That was about the only thing Brandon *wasn't* allergic to."

"Well, I'm sure you know that extra caution now and special foods can eliminate a lot of childhood allergies. When he's an adult, he should have a better time of it."

Marie-Thérèse took Brandon's hand. "Yes. Thank you. That's something. For now, we'll just keep plugging away."

"I hear they make some pretty good flour substitutes." The doctor smiled and put his hand on Brandon's shoulder. "I'll be checking in on you in a few minutes. Let us know if there's any change."

"Okay."

When the doctor left, Brandon tried to say something. Marie-Thérèse was relieved he was awake and that he had never completely lost consciousness. That alone had been a great reassurance.

"Aree," he said.

"I can't hear you. They want us to keep the oxygen on."

Brandon pulled the piece up slightly. "Sorry."

Marie-Thérèse shook her head. "You don't have to be. It's not your fault. And I know it was pretty scary for you."

He tugged at the oxygen again. "It was scary, but I wasn't afraid—not of dying anyway."

"Well, it's all over now," she said, smoothing his brown hair. "I know you must be tired. Go ahead and rest. I'll stay right here."

Mathieu arrived a few minutes later, and Marie-Thérèse went to call Larissa. "Everything is fine," she told her. "They gave him a shot and it started working almost immediately. I'm going to ask the doctor about getting a kit to keep with Brandon. It's stronger than the spray."

"I knew he'd be okay. I knew it!" But there was a tremor in Larissa's voice. Her voice became faint as though she took the phone from her ear. "See, Celisse. I told you he'd be all right. Brandon is fine. They fixed him and he'll be coming home soon."

Marie-Thérèse was amazed at the kindness in her daughter's voice. "Is everything, uh . . . all right there?" she asked.

"Yes, Raquel just woke up though. I think she's hungry."

"I keep a bottle in the fridge. You'll have to heat it up in the bottle warmer. Check it on your wrist to make sure it's not too hot."

"I know how."

Marie-Thérèse had been expecting more complaints, but Larissa and the girls seemed to be handling things without her. "Remember not to shake her to stop her from crying," she warned. "If you can't get her to stop, don't get upset. Just put her in the swing or in her bed and leave the room."

"I know, Mom. I won't shake her. She'll be fine. Don't worry. She hardly ever cries anyway."

"I'll be home as soon as I can."

"Oh, Mom, Aunt Josette called and she wants you to call her. She's worried. But she has some news. Rebekka fainted just a little while ago and André rushed her to the doctor. Turns out she's measuring bigger than she is supposed to. It might be a problem. Or it might mean twins."

"That would be great!"

Larissa laughed. "I know. Aunt Josette sounded a little jealous though. She said fraternal twins were supposed to run through her, not Uncle Marc."

"Could just be a fluke. And they might be identical."

"Whatever. Don't know why she'd want more children—she already has five."

"I think she'd like a daughter."

Larissa was silent for a long time. "Mom, maybe I do know why she likes having so many kids. There's a lot of . . . love in that family."

Marie-Thérèse smiled at those words coming from her tough, spiky-haired daughter. "And in ours too," she said softly.

"I know. I guess I'd better feed Raquel now. I love you, Mom."

"I love you too." Marie-Thérèse hung up the phone wondering what had happened. The defiant, selfish daughter she had left hours ago seemed to have evolved into a new person. She smiled. Well, this was one gift that wouldn't go unappreciated.

Wiping her tears, Marie-Thérèse dialed Josette's number.

Chapter 23

Rebekka was relieved when she woke Thursday morning without too much pain. But the torture began the moment she tried to get out of bed. She groaned softly as she kneaded her left side, trying to obtain relief. Her bowels were certainly clear now. Why hadn't the pain subsided completely?

A tap at the door startled her. She had thought she was in the apartment alone—Raoul should have been gone to work by now. "Come in."

Her brother stuck his head in the door. "How're you feeling?"

She grimaced. "Not good. But I assume it'll take a few days." She hoped he couldn't feel the fear in her voice. "Any news about Nadia?"

"Not yet." He sighed and took a few steps into the room.

"Something has to break soon. I'm certain of it."

Raoul brightened. "When you say it like that, I believe you. But you just need to worry about yourself right now. I know I haven't been much help lately, but that's going to change."

"You didn't tell Mom, did you?" she asked. "I mean about me fainting yesterday."

"No. You know how she is. She'd be up all night worrying about you."

"Good. I'd rather wait to see if it's anything we should even worry about before telling her."

"I do have some good news," he said. "Brandon's still doing fine this morning. According to André, they gave him a blessing last night and this morning he'll be let go after a few tests."

"Poor boy." Brandon's attack had been unexpected and unwanted, but his condition had at least had taken her mind temporarily from the problem with her baby. Or was it babies? She placed a hand over her stomach. *Don't worry, I'll take care of you—however many you are.*

"Aw, Brandon's a strong kid. He'll be fine." Raoul thumbed toward the hall. "I guess I'd better get going."

"Yeah, why aren't you at work?" she asked. "That's not like you."

He looked chagrined. "Well, actually, I couldn't sleep last night. Now that I'll be officially divorced next week—something I can hardly believe though goodness knows I've paid a small fortune to have my lawyer push it all through. Anyway, now that I'll be officially single, I . . . well, I was kind of thinking about Valerie and I didn't get to sleep until pretty late. I didn't hear my alarm. I was thinking about Nadia, too, of course."

"Of course." Rebekka laughed and was pleased to see him smile.

"Do you think I'm horrible?" he asked, picking up a sleek black statue of a ballerina that was on her dresser. "Thinking about asking Valerie out when I'm not even divorced? And when my daughter is still missing?"

"Actually, I'm glad to see you're going on with your life. You've done everything you can do about Nadia—hired the private investigator, walked the streets yourself, talked to everyone we meet. We've done everything we can, including that TV ad you and dad are planning. There's nothing more you can do. As for Desirée, you haven't lived with her for over eight months now, and heaven knows she never really considered herself married."

His smile vanished and he set the ballerina down. "There was goodness in her when I met her. She seemed to have a desire to do right. It just didn't last. I—I think alcohol addiction had a lot to do with it. She didn't mean a lot of what she did."

"Does this mean you've changed your mind?" Rebekka asked, swinging her legs out of bed. She gritted her teeth against the pain.

"No, but I think it means I might be able to forgive her someday."

"That's a pretty good beginning. Especially since you share a child. There may come a time when Desirée wants to see Nadia, or vice-versa."

Now it was his turn to grimace. "I'm sure there will. But according to our divorce agreement, she doesn't have unsupervised visiting rights. I insisted on that. If she wants to come and see Nadia, I'll let her, but she's not taking her anywhere."

"I think that's certainly best—for now. But some day that might change."

He sighed. "I know. And I guess I'll cross that bridge when I come to it." He shook his head. "There are certainly a lot of complications in marrying people without the same values—things you never even think of when you're young and in love."

"Oh, Raoul, don't talk that way! Yes, it was a dumb thing you did marrying Desirée, but break-ups happen even in marriages where both partners are members. Don't beat yourself up about it anymore. Go on from here and do your best. Don't think about yesterday."

Their eyes locked. "Is that how you get along?" he asked.

Rebekka shook her head. "Not yet," she whisper, feeling an abrupt and profound sadness. "Sometimes I think that I live only through the past."

"You can't live that way any more than I can."

"I know."

"I love you, Rebekka." Raoul hugged her briefly before retracing his steps to the door. He paused there. "There is a reason for all this, I believe there is. I just wish I knew what it was."

"Me too."

As he left, his words haunted her. They seemed familiar somehow, but Rebekka couldn't place them. Who had said something similar to her once before? And when?

She shrugged and pulled herself to her feet. Her belly seemed to have grown another inch during the night, though she knew it was only her imagination.

After dressing, Rebekka returned to her bed with her laptop. She worked for several hours translating, and then decided to design a flyer to pass around, describing Nadia, her suspected whereabouts, and her description, including the information about the heart-shaped birthmark. At least this way she felt she was doing something to help Raoul. Despite the encouragement, she had given him, she was beginning to lose hope herself. She only prayed that even if they didn't find Nadia, she would have a good home with two loving parents to raise her.

Satisfied with the flyer, she forced herself out of bed again and down to the copy shop where she ran off a thousand flyers and placed an order for five thousand more. "That should be enough to begin with," she told the clerk.

On the way home, she stopped at Josette's and gave her a third of the flyers.

"What a great idea!" Josette said. "We'll blanket the area with these and soon every single person in Paris will have heard about Nadia."

"I thought we'd start near Desirée's old apartment building," Rebekka said, supporting herself against the doorframe. "And spread out from there. Here's the map I copied with the section you and the kids can do. You'll need more flyers, but they should be ready by tomorrow. I paid extra for a rush job. If we work hard, we can have most of them done by Saturday."

"Come in and sit down, Rebekka," Josette said. "You look like you're going to pass out."

Rebekka complied, feeling ready to do exactly that. "I'm still feeling pain," she admitted.

"Look, give me all those flyers," Josette said. "And the receipt for the others. I'll take care of it all. I'll call the young people in the stake and organize an army." Her smile grew wider. "I bet the mission president would even let the elders pass out some. I'll spend today planning and calling and then tomorrow and Saturday we'll mobilize. This is great! Why didn't we think of this before?"

"We were supposed to have found her by now," Rebekka said, only too relieved to turn the project over to Josette. The pain in her left side was fading now, but she was suddenly exhausted.

"Well, this'll help. If she's still in Paris, we'll find her within the week," Josette predicted.

"And if she's not?"

Josette shook her head fiercely. "She is. She *has* to be."

Rebekka was too tired to argue. Besides, she wanted to believe Nadia was in Paris and would soon be with Raoul. "I'd better get home," she said, standing.

Josette's fierceness faded. "You need to get some rest. A lot of it. Don't take on too much, Rebekka. Being pregnant with one baby is hard enough, but if you really have two . . ."

Rebekka felt resentment—not at her advice, but at the worry that returned. "I just wish I knew what was going on—it's hard."

"I'll bet." Josette smiled in sympathy. "But if you do have twins— imagine! Marc's never going to let me forget that when we see him again. All my life I told him I'd have twins before he would! You have to admit, it's ironic."

Rebekka could imagine very well how her husband would have made quite a joke out of the situation. "It is funny," she said, laughing softly. "Thanks for reminding me."

Sudden tears glistened in Josette's eyes. "I was closer to Marc than I was to any human being other than my husband. We were together our entire life, from the moment of conception, separated only on our missions and then later when we married. Not a day goes by that I don't think about him." Josette reached for Rebekka's hand. "Despite all that, I can only imagine what you felt when he died. But I hope you know how much we love you and want to help."

"I do feel that—thank you."

Josette smiled and let go of her hand. "Especially André," she said. "He wants to be there for you."

"He told you?"

"Yes. And I think it's wonderful."

Rebekka said stiffly, "I don't love him."

Josette looked at her for a long time. "Yes, you do," she said finally. "The question is, do you love him enough?" She turned from Rebekka and picked up the phone. "I guess I'd better start calling."

Rebekka nodded. "I'll see myself out."

She was glad Josette lived on the bottom floor and that she didn't have to wait for the elevator or have many steps to negotiate. Once in her car, she rested again until she felt strong enough to drive home. Thoughts of André came to mind, and Rebekka didn't know which part of her body gave her more pain—her abdomen, her mind, or her heart.

Chapter 24

Marie-Thérèse came from the girls' bedroom where she had just put Raquel down for a nap. Rebekka had watched the baby for her that morning while she had taken Celisse to the doctor for their usual Friday visit. Celisse had done very well throughout the tests and afterward Marie-Thérèse had taken her to the park. Marie-Thérèse was glad she had left Raquel with Rebekka so that she could spend some time alone with Celisse. Rebekka had also seemed to enjoy watching Raquel.

"I know lunch is late today," Marie-Thérèse told Celisse as she returned to the kitchen. "But we had to get Raquel to bed. She was cranky."

"I not cranky," offered Celisse.

"Nope, Celisse is being a good girl."

Celisse beamed. "I went potty."

"Did you go to the bathroom while I was feeding Raquel?"

Celisse nodded.

"Good girl. Now how about some chicken and rice—how does that sound for lunch?"

"Mmm," said Celisse. She gave the same recommendation to any food Marie-Thérèse suggested, but the response always made Marie-Thérèse smile.

As they were finishing lunch, the phone rang. Marie-Thérèse stood up from the table and crossed to the phone on the counter. "Hello?"

"Marie-Thérèse, it's Pascale."

"Hi. What's up? Any news?" Marie-Thérèse prayed silently for good news, though it was likely too soon for the abandonment case she had filed against Celisse's mother to have achieved anything. She had hoped filing the case would speed up the adoption, but the wheels of the court moved slowly—especially where social services was concerned.

"Well . . . there is news. But not all good."

Marie-Thérèse tucked her hair behind her free ear and swallowed hard. "Tell me."

"Celisse's mother finally showed up today. Apparently she saw the ad we placed about putting Celisse up for adoption."

"And she's protesting?" Marie-Thérèse held her breath.

"No. Actually, she came by to give her consent. She understands that after all the evidence we have against her, there's no way we're handing Celisse over. She still faces charges, of course, but if she gives Celisse up for adoption, proving that she is trying to do what's right for her daughter, they will decrease significantly."

"But that's good. Unless . . . she doesn't want to give Celisse to someone else, does she?" Marie-Thérèse's heart began beating more rapidly.

"No. I told her all about you and your family, and she seemed satisfied that Celisse was in good hands. I said I could arrange a meeting, but she didn't seem to need that. Frankly, I don't think she really cares. It's sad but true. She's just doing what she can to get herself out of as much trouble as she can."

Marie-Thérèse abruptly realized what Pascale hadn't been saying. "Oh, Pascale, it's Raquel, isn't it?"

"Yes." Pascale's voice was gentle. "Madame Despain says Raquel isn't hers, that she was baby-sitting. We're not sure she's telling the truth, so we've got DNA testing scheduled for this afternoon—if you can make it. If it turns out she's telling the truth—that's she's not Raquel's mother—we'll have to turn the case back to the police to find out who Raquel really is."

Marie-Thérèse started to cry softly, placing her hand over the receiver so that Pascale wouldn't hear.

"Marie-Thérèse, are you there?"

"Yes," she managed.

"The test is at two if you can make it."

"Will it hurt them?" Marie-Thérèse didn't want either of the girls to face more needles.

"Just a swab in the mouth to get the skin cells. They won't need blood."

"Give me the address. I'll be there."

"I'm so sorry, Marie-Thérèse. I really am. But this could all still work out. It could."

Marie-Thérèse had to believe her; letting go of Raquel was simply not an option. "I love her so much," she whispered.

"I know."

Marie-Thérèse hung up the phone and found Celisse staring at her.

Marie-Thérèse wiped at her tears, but more took their place. "Mommy sad?" Celisse asked.

Marie-Thérèse thought how fitting it was for her to finally use the word "Mommy" since it seemed that Celisse really would be theirs forever. Before this moment she had customarily addressed Marie-Thérèse by "you" or used her first name.

Marie-Thérèse knelt down and held out her arms. Celisse flew into them. "I love you, Celisse," Marie-Thérèse told her. "I love you so much. And you really are going to be my baby! You're going to stay with me forever." She didn't say anymore, but cradled Celisse for a long time until the child fell asleep in her arms, worn out from her outing at the park.

Marie-Thérèse carried her to bed and then watched Raquel as she lay sleeping in her crib so innocently. "Who are you?" Marie-Thérèse asked. She wanted desperately to believe that Celisse's mother was lying, or that perhaps Raquel's real mother had died, but neither was likely.

Unable to bear her thoughts any longer, Marie-Thérèse returned to the kitchen and began to rapidly organize the cans she had bought the evening before at the grocery store—beans with the b's, pears with the p's, all in perfect alphabetical order. There were more cans than usual since she didn't seem to have the time to make as many foods from scratch. *Besides, there are more mouths to feed,* she thought as she organized the row of formula cans.

She stopped working abruptly as her tears made it impossible to see the labels. Sinking to the floor, she sobbed until there seemed to be no more tears left. Then she reached for the portable phone on the counter and dialed Mathieu's work number. She tried to be calm as she passed on Pascale's news, but her emotions took over.

"Oh, Mathieu, we're going to lose Raquel!" she sobbed. "I don't know how I can do that. I just—I love her so much! I'm so scared!"

"What time do you have to be at the hospital for the tests?"

"Two o'clock. I should leave now. The girls are sleeping. I gave them lunch and . . . Oh, Mathieu, what if it's the last time they sleep in there together?"

"We'll fight for her," he said.

Marie-Thérèse blinked hard, sending more tears cascading down her cheeks. "But what if she has a family who loves her? What if Celisse's mother is even a kidnapper?"

"Don't think that way," he pleaded. "Please. We knew it was right to take the girls—the Lord confirmed that. And whatever happens, it'll be for the best."

Marie-Thérèse knew he was right, but it seemed that no matter the choices she made, it always came down to losing someone she loved. With a deep breath, she pulled herself together for Mathieu's sake. "You'll meet me there then?"

"Yes. Since I'll be coming on the train, I might be a little late, but I'll be there."

"Thank you."

She hung up the phone, washed her face, and went to wake the girls.

* * *

"The test results will be in Monday," Marie-Thérèse told Mathieu. He had arrived just as they were finishing extracting a sample of Celisse's cheek cells. As Pascale had promised, the tests didn't hurt the girls, though neither were thrilled with the swabs in their mouths.

"They also gave me copies of the records of the doctor who saw them before Pascale brought them over," she continued. "He took their blood, and they aren't the same type. Raquel's is A, and Celisse's is O. That doesn't mean they can't be siblings—especially if they have different fathers, but . . ." She hugged Raquel more tightly. "It's not a great beginning. Anyway, they have the mother's sample and will be able to compare it."

"Come on, let's get out of here." Mathieu picked up Celisse and followed Marie-Thérèse to the car. They didn't speak most of the way, but having him there was comfort enough. Celisse, feeling the tension, stared at them with large eyes, but tiny Raquel promptly fell asleep.

When they arrived home, Larissa and Brandon—who had returned to school after missing one day—were already there.

"Mom, Aunt Josette came by with these flyers," Larissa said. "We're supposed to pass them out or something. Here's the map that says where."

Marie-Thérèse nodded absently as she set Raquel's carrier on the table. "Oh yes, Josette called me last night and said she'd be dropping them off. I forgot about it until now. And then . . ." To her chagrin she began to cry. Mathieu held her, whispering comforting words, while the children gaped.

"What's wrong, Mom?" Brandon asked.

"Is it Brandon?" ventured Larissa, looking at Brandon as though he hid some mysterious illness.

Marie-Thérèse shook her head. "No. It's Raquel."

They listened as Mathieu took over the explanation. Larissa grew red with anger, but Brandon kept shaking his head. "It's going to be fine," he said. "We've had her five weeks now. They just can't take her back."

"They can if they find she has a family," Mathieu said. "But we don't know yet if that's the case."

"Celisse's mother could be lying." Larissa said. Abruptly, she picked up Celisse and hugged her. "We aren't letting them go—either one!"

Marie-Thérèse blinked in amazement. Somewhere in the weeks of struggle it seemed they had somehow become a real family. Turning her head, she met Mathieu's equally surprised gaze. "We're not giving up yet, Larissa," she said softly.

It wasn't until after dinner that she took time to read the flyer Rebekka had made. "We'll have to pass these out in the morning," she said sitting down at the table where the children had laid out a board game. "It's nearly dark now and I don't think we should be in those neighborhoods after dark. Good thing it's the weekend. We'll go at—" She gasped as something on the flyer caught her attention. Holding her breath, she quickly reread the information.

"What's wrong, honey?" Mathieu said, looking up from the newspaper. "You're suddenly pale. Are you feeling well?"

Trembling, Marie-Thérèse passed him the flyer, pointing to a phrase. "Nadia is three and a half months old now," he read aloud, "and has a birthmark on her right buttocks that stands out slightly and looks like an upside down heart." He stopped reading and Marie-Thérèse watched as the color drained from his face.

"What is it?" Larissa demanded. "We've heard that Nadia has a birthmark before—at least I did. I didn't know it was on her bottom, though. But still, what's the big deal?"

Brandon's gaze went to Raquel, who was sitting in her chair on the floor, sucking on the toys Celisse had put into her hands. He picked Raquel up and laid her on the table. Slowly, he unfastened her diaper. "You never changed her," Brandon told Larissa, "so I guess you haven't seen."

For a long time no one spoke. Thoughts moved like fire through Marie-Thérèse's brain, traveling down to her heart where she wondered if she could stand the agony.

Then Larissa shook her head, tears falling. "No, no," she moaned.

"It might not be the same baby," Mathieu said in a near whisper.

"There are a hundred different types of birthmarks."

Larissa nodded violently. "Yeah, this doesn't even really look like a heart. Raquel can't be Nadia."

But Marie-Thérèse knew she was Raoul's daughter. "Raquel is the same age as Nadia," she said, trying to remain calm, "she appeared at the same time Nadia disappeared, Celisse's mother said she was only baby-sitting, and the woman who had Nadia said she dropped her off to be baby-sat. Raquel *must* be Nadia. I just don't know why it never crossed my mind before. I've been so busy . . . Raquel was supposed to be Celisse's sister."

Mathieu's face crumpled, and for a moment, Marie-Thérèse remembered all the nights he had rocked Raquel to sleep and all the time they had spent together staring at the miracle of her. "It might not be," he choked out. "The tests—we'll know on Monday."

She shook her head and said the words only she seemed strong enough to utter. "We have to tell him tonight."

Larissa glared at her. "No, Mom! No! You can't give her up! You can't!"

Marie-Thérèse felt her daughter's pain, knew it intimately. Hadn't she been the one to care for Raquel every day? Hadn't she fed her, changed her, bathed her, rocked her, and loved her? In all but name, Raquel *was* her daughter, and Marie-Thérèse couldn't have loved her any more than she did now.

"You can't do this!" Larissa shouted. She backed away from the table, shaking her head. "How can you do this?"

Marie-Thérèse stood and refastened Raquel's diaper and cradled her gently against her chest, feeling their hearts beat together. "Because I love her," she said. Tears seeped from her eyes and began a path down her cheeks. "And because I know the pain Raoul has been going through these past weeks. Don't you all see? If we can do anything to alleviate his pain, so that he won't have to go through one more night wondering if his daughter is dead or suffering . . . What other choice do we have? If Raquel is Nadia—and I think we all know she is—how can we not tell Raoul? How can we be responsible for letting him suffer one more night of not knowing!" Her voice broke with her own hurt. "Put yourself in his place. How would you feel if someone stole Raquel from us and we didn't know where she was or if someone was loving her . . . or hurting her? We must tell Raoul." Marie-Thérèse stood in front of her family, her eyes begging them to understand—and silently praying she would be strong enough go through with what she would have to do.

Mathieu clenched his jaw and nodded. "Of course. You're right." He laid his hand over hers where she gripped Nadia's small body tightly against her chest. "It's just so hard."

Larissa's face was wet with tears, but she too nodded. "Can I come with you? I want to say goodbye." She touched Raquel's cheek—no, Nadia's—and said, "I wish I had known all this before. I wish I hadn't started to love h—" Her fingers dropped onto her parents' joined hands.

Brandon picked up Celisse, not bothering to wipe away his tears. "We'll see her lots. Raoul works, and so does Rebekka. She's having a baby soon, and she's been sick. So we can watch her probably a little every day or a least . . ." His voice trailed off and he began to sob.

Marie-Thérèse hugged her gentle son, whose kind heart was hurting perhaps more than any of them with this revelation. "Yes," she said. "We'll watch her. And we'll love her just as we do right now. It's much better than giving her up to someone we don't know. We have to count that as a blessing."

They all hugged each other, even Larissa and Brandon, who hadn't shown any physical affection toward one another in years. Afterward, they packed Raquel's things in several large duffle bags and left the house.

Chapter 25

On Friday Raoul came home from work whistling. Rebekka looked up from the late dinner she was preparing and smiled. "What is it . . ." Then her mouth opened wide. "There's news—about Nadia, isn't there!"

Raoul threw back his head and laughed. Then he picked her up and swung her around, as Rebekka gritted her teeth against the pain. "Ow."

He set her down gently. "Sorry. It's just that Detective Francom called just before I left work. He said they believe they've located the woman Lana left Nadia with! He is going to question her and Lana and call me back tonight. Oh, Rebekka, I can't wait to see her! To hold her, though that's not likely tonight. But just to know that she's all right will be enough. I hope they can tell me at least that much." All at once his grin vanished and he started to cry.

Rebekka hugged her brother, ignoring the pain in her abdomen, feeling her own tears beginning to fall. Soon they would face the moment of truth. Was Nadia all right? Was she really all right? Or had their search been in vain?

"Josette collected the flyers I ordered," she said. "She already passed out all those I copied yesterday and is having the youth pass out the other five thousand tonight and tomorrow. Although maybe now they won't be needed."

There was gratitude in Raoul's eyes. "Thank you, Rebekka. Anything will help. This woman may not know herself where Nadia is. We can't stop looking until we find her."

"Okay, let's not get depressed again," said Rebekka, drying her face with the overlong sleeve of her shirt. "Let's eat instead. I'm craving salt, though, so the meat may be a little salty."

During dinner, the conversation carefully skirted any important subjects. Rebekka was glad because she was hungry. She helped herself to twice as much roast and rice as Raoul, though she could only finish half before she had to run to the bathroom and relieve her bladder.

Periodically, they would fall into silence and Rebekka realized they were both listening for the phone. When the sound of the intercom from below buzzed, it was almost a surprise.

"I'll get it," Raoul said. "Maybe it's him." He nearly ran to the entryway.

Rebekka hoped it was Detective Francom. *Please let him have good news*, she thought. Of course it could be someone else all together. Was André perhaps checking up on her? Her heart began to thud erratically at the thought. He had called four times during the day yesterday and had called her this morning while she was baby-sitting Raquel for Marie-Thérèse. "It better *not* be him," she muttered. But she smoothed her hair and made sure there was no food in her teeth just in case.

Raoul returned to the kitchen, a puzzled look on his face. "It's Marie-Thérèse."

"Hmm. Wonder what she wants? Maybe it's about the flyers. Josette probably dropped some off for them. Or maybe she left something of Raquel's when she was over today. I watched her this morning for a bit. She sure is a doll. I mostly just sat in my bed and held her. I didn't get any work done, but it was worth every minute."

"She is cute," Raoul agreed. "Hmm, I wonder if I could help pass out the flyers. You could call me on my cell if you hear anything from the detective."

Rebekka smiled. "Maybe we'd better see what they want first. Hey, I know—maybe they want us to watch Raquel and Celisse while they go. I would love that! Celisse doesn't like me much yet, but I'm sure she'll get used to me."

Raoul snorted. "She doesn't even want me to look at her. I doubt Marie-Thérèse would leave her here. You know how protective she is. She'd never leave Celisse crying."

"Well then she could at least leave Raquel. We'll need to practice for when Nadia comes home."

With a finger, Raoul rubbed a tear from his eye. "I don't know," he said softly. "Seeing her . . . it just hurts."

"I know. Maybe you should go pass out the flyers with them and I'll stay with Raquel."

The doorbell rang and together they went to open the door. Mathieu was in the forefront with Marie-Thérèse carrying Raquel slightly behind him. Larissa with Celisse in her arms was behind her father, and they could see Brandon still lingering by the elevator as if he wanted to escape.

"Come in," Rebekka said, looking at the gloomy faces. "Is something wrong?"

They didn't speak, but filed into the apartment, one by one. A closer look at their faces revealed they'd all been crying. "Is there something we should know?" Rebekka asked, searching Marie-Thérèse's face. She glanced at Brandon. "He's okay, isn't he?"

Marie-Thérèse tried to speak, but her tears choked off the words. Rebekka sent a helpless glance toward her brother, who shrugged back at her. He shut the apartment door behind them.

Finally, Marie-Thérèse turned to Raoul and pushed Raquel at him. "I read the flyer . . . the heart-shaped birthmark. Raquel has it. I think *she's* Nadia."

Raoul's eyes widened in disbelief. "Raquel . . . Nadia? That's impossible! You've had her for . . . I'm sure you would have heard about the birthmark . . . it can't . . ." His eyes went to the baby in his arms, searching her face with a stunned expression. Then he hugged her to him gently, tears sliding down his cheeks. "Nadia, Nadia, Nadia," he murmured against her dark hair. "Could it be? Could it be? Oh, please let it be!"

Rebekka began crying too. She didn't know what touched her more— her brother's amazed worship of his daughter, or the tears of the family who loved her as much as he did. Marie-Thérèse now clung to Mathieu, apparently no longer able to support herself. Larissa had buried her face in Celisse's neck, rocking her without seeing anyone. Celisse watched them all with a confused and scared expression. Worst of all, huge, silent tears wet Brandon's face as he stared at Raoul and Nadia.

"How?" Rebekka asked.

"We found out today that Celisse's mother claimed she wasn't Raquel's mother," Mathieu said. His chin quivered and she could tell that he was working to maintain control. "They had a DNA test today to see if she was telling the truth, but we were still hoping . . . Well, then we saw the flyer. I don't know how we hadn't connected the bit about the birthmark until today. We're sorry. We've just been so occupied with the girls and moving. If we had known . . ."

"I heard about it," Larissa said, lifting her tear-stained face from Celisse's body. "But I didn't know it was on Nadia's bottom. And I'd never changed Raquel's diaper anyway, so I never saw it."

"We came right over to tell you," Marie-Thérèse said in a whisper. "I'm sure the police would have tracked her down in the next day or two, but we didn't want you to go one more night wondering."

For the first time Rebekka noticed that both Brandon and Mathieu were carrying large duffle bags, stuffed near to overflowing. Apparently they had not only brought Nadia home, but also all the things they had bought for the baby they wanted to adopt.

"Oh, Marie-Thérèse!" Rebekka hugged her sister-in-law, wishing there was some way to take away her pain.

Marie-Thérèse's tears began afresh. "Can I just stay awhile to make sure she's all right?"

Raoul put a hand on her shoulder. "You stay as long as you need. I can never repay you for this. Never. Thank you so much for being the ones to take care of my daughter. You can't know how much that means to me. To know that she wasn't crying somewhere . . . neglected." His voice broke repeatedly as he spoke, but they all understood his meaning.

"Come," Rebekka told them. "Let's go into the living room and sort this out." There was still a deep fear in her that somehow they had made a mistake, that Raquel really wasn't Nadia.

Raoul sat with Nadia in the chair, holding her gingerly as if she might break. "Can I see the birthmark?" he asked.

"I'd like to see it, too," Rebekka said.

Marie-Thérèse nodded. When Raoul didn't seem to know how to begin, she took the baby from him and, after Mathieu moved several vases of André's flowers and spread a baby blanket, laid her carefully on the coffee table. "She probably needs to be changed anyway," she said.

"Will you show me how?" asked Raoul. He paid close attention as Marie-Thérèse showed him how to position the diaper, remove the old one, and clean her up.

"There's the birthmark," Marie-Thérèse said. It really was a heart—albeit a little lopsided—and Rebekka had never seen anything so beautiful.

"Now fasten the tabs like this," Marie-Thérèse said. "You do the other one." She smiled her approval as Raoul completed the job. Rebekka could sense that Marie-Thérèse was relieved to be there, to make sure Nadia would be all right without her.

"Tell me the whole story," he said, cuddling Nadia to his chest once again.

The Portiers began the story from the first and then together they pieced what had likely occurred in the days after Desirée had left Nadia. "So when Lana didn't come back for Nadia, Celisse's mother must have just gone out like she always did," Raoul said. "And Nadia's cries alerted the neighbors."

"Apparently the woman left Celisse alone a lot," Marie-Thérèse agreed. "She wasn't a very good mother."

They all looked at Celisse who had lost her frightened look as she cuddled in Marie-Thérèse's lap. Celisse stared nervously at their attention, but didn't appear overly concerned. Rebekka wondered if she would feel the same way when they left without Nadia.

Marie-Thérèse sighed. "In a way, I feel we owe Nadia a great deal—and more indirectly, Desirée. If it hadn't been for Nadia's cries, Celisse might still be in that hole with that . . . that woman." She held Celisse to her and the little girl smiled. The smile changed her entire face, making the blue eyes stand out and causing her cheeks to dimple. Could this be the same serious, solemn-faced child that had first come to the Portiers?

"She's a beautiful little girl," Rebekka said impulsively.

Marie-Thérèse inclined her head. "Thank you. We think so." She hugged Celisse again before her gaze slid to Nadia. Her smile faltered briefly and Rebekka saw the shadow of pain cross her features. Apparently it would be some time before Marie-Thérèse would be able to let Nadia go.

"I think we should call Detective Francom," Rebekka said. "He might be able to verify all of this. We don't want to make any mistakes."

At that subtle warning, Raoul's smile faded, and Rebekka thought she saw a glimmer of hope in Larissa's eyes. But not the others. They knew.

"You call him, okay?" Raoul asked. He seemed unable to tear his eyes from Nadia. Like any new parent, he was busy counting toes and fingers, discovering how to hold his daughter, and breathing in her scent.

Rebekka was put through to Detective Francom's office almost immediately. She plunged into the story and when she finished was out of breath. "You have the baby there right now?" Detective Francom asked.

"Yes. She was placed with my sister-in-law through social services. She thought the little girls were sisters, but apparently the mother showed up today and denied being the baby's mother."

"I have Madame Despain in my office right now," he said. "We were planning on taking her to see Lana, but maybe now that's not necessary."

"I wish you would," Rebekka said quickly. "We'd like to be sure."

"Well, we'll be able to match the baby with the records at the hospital where Desirée delivered, but I'll see what I can do."

"If Lana sees her and confirms that she's the woman. That's enough—at least for right now. The baby has a heart birthmark."

"I'll do what I can."

"Thank you."

They waited an hour in the living room before the detective returned her call, talking about feeding and nap times and silently staring at each other during the gaps in the conversation. "Lana has positively identified Madame Despain," he said. "And I've talked to the lady in charge of the case at social services. We'll have to verify everything medically, of course. But I for one am positive that we've found little Nadia."

Rebekka began to weep softly at the miracle. "Thank you," she whispered. "Thank you so much!"

"Normally social services would have to release her into your care, but since the family taking care of her is willing to let you watch her until she is officially released from social services, she can stay with you. They'll be in touch tomorrow to get it all straightened out. Or maybe on Monday. So for now, enjoy your niece. Hold on tight."

"We will."

Rebekka hung up the phone, aware of the intent eyes upon her. "Lana verified that she left Nadia with Celisse's mother. They still want to do tests but . . ."

Marie-Thérèse nodded. "I knew it. We all did. That birthmark is pretty unusual." She stood up quickly, losing her balance momentarily. Her husband jumped to steady her. "We'd better get home. I need to get Celisse to bed." Marie-Thérèse's eyes went to Nadia, and then away again.

Raoul saw the look and held Nadia out to her. "You can hold her if you want. And any time you'd like to see her, please come over."

Marie-Thérèse let Celisse slip down to the floor before she hugged and kissed Nadia. "We love you, honey," she murmured. "You'll be happy here." Her voice rose at the end, and Rebekka thought she was going to cry, but she didn't. Resolutely, she handed Nadia to her husband and bent down to pick up Celisse.

Each of the family in turn said goodbye to the baby. Larissa's tears seemed unending, causing Rebekka to want to comfort her. "Please," Larissa said to Raoul, "let us watch her sometimes. Brandon said you have to work and Rebekka's not feeling well."

"How about on Monday?" Raoul said immediately. "I have my divorce hearing with the judge and then I have to go to work. I don't want to, but I have so much to catch up on. And I know Rebekka has a deadline. Will you watch her that day?"

Larissa looked toward her mother, who nodded.

"Maybe, if you want, we could work something out more permanently," Raoul suggested. "I mean, Rebekka works too, and when her new baby comes . . . well, it would be a relief to have someone we can trust."

"We'll talk about it later then," Marie-Thérèse said, sounding strained. Rebekka wondered how many hours she would cry that night after she was home.

Brandon, who now held Nadia, kissed her soft cheek and returned her to Raoul. The family walked slowly to the door. In the hall, Celisse pointed to the baby. "My sister come, too," she said.

Marie-Thérèse pushed her hair behind her ear. "Celisse, I know we thought Raque—the baby was your sister, but she's really Raoul's daughter. We didn't know that. So they're going to watch her now. And we'll see her all we want, okay?"

Celisse glared distrustfully at Raoul. "Raquel come home."

"Sure, she's coming back on Monday. They're going to watch her. Remember when we went to the doctor this morning and Raquel stayed here with Aunt Rebekka? Remember how we went to get her later? Well, we'll come here to see Nadia. And Uncle Raoul will bring her to us to play with. How does that sound? We still have her swing and bed for her to use. Come on, now. Let's leave Raquel—Nadia to play. Her name's really Nadia, you know."

Celisse nodded and laid her head trustfully against Marie-Thérèse's shoulder. "Bye, Raquel," she said. "We come back. Be good."

Without another glance at Nadia, Marie-Thérèse opened the door and walked firmly to the elevator, pushing the button firmly. The rest of the family followed. Only Brandon looked back, and the tears in his eyes would stay with Rebekka for a long time.

Raoul shut the door. He moved as though to return to the living room or go into the kitchen, but then remained in the entryway staring at Nadia. "Are they going to be all right?" he asked. His eyes rose to meet Rebekka's. "It seems wrong for me to be so happy when they're in such pain. I know what this baby means to them."

Rebekka sighed. "There's nothing we can do about that. Nadia is your daughter and she belongs with you. But we can certainly make the transition easier. It was kind of you to ask them to watch her on Monday."

"Was it? Or are we only prolonging their pain?"

"Raoul, we've been a part of the Perrault family way before I married Marc. I was five and you were seven when we first met. We grew up with

Marie-Thérèse, Josette, Marc, and André. Even with Marc gone, they'll continue to be a major part of our lives. You work closely with André, I'm having a Perrault baby, we go to their family parties, and we see half of them each week in church. We can't avoid them—I won't avoid them. We need them and they need us. Besides, they love Nadia, and I think that letting them have a part of her will help them get over her loss. It certainly won't harm her."

"You're right." Raoul lifted Nadia and kissed her repeatedly. "I can't believe this . . . this feeling. It's unlike anything I've ever felt. She's *mine*. She's part of *me*."

"And Desirée."

"And Desirée. The good part of her anyway. Something I can keep." He smiled at Rebekka. "Hey, it was your flyer all along. If not for you, I wouldn't have Nadia with me right now. It could have taken days to make the connection. Thank you, Sis."

"You're welcome."

Still cradling his daughter, Raoul walked toward the living room. Rebekka let them go. There would be plenty of time later for her to bond with her niece, but for now, she would let Raoul start learning to become a father.

Her hands went to her swollen stomach, rubbing slightly to ease the itching sensation. The pain that had been constant during the past weeks still ached, but dully now, and she ignored it.

Feeling the sudden urge to talk to someone, she picked up the phone to call her parents. They would want to know about Nadia. They would want to rush right over and shower their granddaughter with love and the presents she knew her mother had been collecting over the past month.

But her fingers didn't dial that number. "Hello?" said a familiar voice—a voice that sent her pulse racing and seemed to weave cotton over her tongue.

"It's me," she managed.

"Rebekka!" He sounded so glad to hear her voice.

"I hope I'm not disturbing anything."

"No, I just got the girls to bed. They needed about ten stories tonight for some reason."

Rebekka tried to laugh, but it came out a sob.

"What's wrong?" he asked quickly. "Is it the baby?"

"No, no. It's—we've found Nadia!"

"That's wonderful! I can't imagine how Raoul must be feeling."

"He just stares at her. She's so perfect. But—" Rebekka swallowed hard "—it's not all happy news. You see, it turns out that Nadia was Marie-Thérèse's little Raquel. I know it all sounds confusing, but that's the way it turned out. I believe the Lord had a hand in protecting her, but I feel so bad for Marie-Thérèse right now. She wanted that baby so much. They all did. Even Larissa. You should have seen them tonight."

"I'm coming right over," André said.

"You can't—the girls."

"Thierry's here for the weekend. He'll watch them."

"I didn't mean to interrupt your evening." Rebekka began.

"I know. It's my choice. Hang tight, I'll be there in ten minutes."

Rebekka replaced the receiver, deciding to let Raoul break the happy news to their parents himself. In a few moments, she was sure he would remember them and call. She found herself in her bedroom, changing into a ribbed cotton maroon dress with long sleeves. The loose outfit reached her ankles and did better to conceal her growing stomach than most of her maternity outfits. Then she brushed her teeth and combed her hair. She didn't stop to think about why she cared about the way she looked or to examine her feelings more closely. All she knew was that she needed to talk and André was coming over.

* * *

André didn't have to wait long for Rebekka to open the door. "Hello," she said, her voice as smooth as satin sheets against his skin—only warmer. She looked beautiful to him as always, but her face was troubled. "Let's go for a walk," she suggested.

He noticed her forehead was drawn as though fighting a headache, or perhaps some other affliction. "Are you sure you feel up to it?"

She shrugged. "A drive then."

"What about Raoul?"

"I looked in on him a moment ago. He was calling my parents. I think they'll be here soon even though it's late."

"Come on, then. But grab a jacket first—it's cold outside."

Once in the car, André drove while Rebekka talked, detailing the night's events and how each person had reacted. From her description, André felt he had been there himself. "That was a courageous thing for Marie-Thérèse and Mathieu to do," he said. "They've got to be hurting. But I called Josette on the way over. She and Marie-Thérèse are close, and she'll be able to help her if anyone can."

Rebekka bit the inside of her bottom lip. "I think she'll need time."

She heaved a sigh. "At least Celisse's mother isn't going to fight for her."

"That's something. Celisse deserves a good family."

"That's exactly what's so hard about this whole thing," Rebekka said. "They're a great family. They would raise Nadia well and teach her proper values. Two stable parents, siblings—it's perfect. And then there's Raoul. He loves her. He's a good man, but he'll be divorced soon and life as a single father won't be easy. And what if he does marry? Will his wife love Nadia as he does? What about Desirée? Will she be in and out of Nadia's life? I feel really confused about the whole situation. I love my brother so much, and I've done everything I can to support him, but I admit that a part of me wonders if it would have been better for Nadia to have stayed with Marie-Thérèse as Raquel." She brought her hand to her forehead and rubbed the temples. "Oh, forgive me Raoul," she whispered. "I would never tell him that. Never."

André pulled over and stopped in a place where tall residential apartment buildings lined the road and there was minimal traffic. "All your concerns are only natural. But you forgot to add yourself and your parents to the equation. And my family as well. We'll all be there for Nadia— even Marie-Thérèse and Mathieu. And as you said, Raoul is a good man. He'll make a great father."

Rebekka again bit at the inside of her lower lip, and the action nearly drove André to distraction. He wanted more than anything to put his arms around her and offer comfort. But that wasn't going to happen. Not as long as Samuel was in the picture. Not as long as Rebekka couldn't admit to what was going on between them.

At least she had called him tonight—that in itself was a tremendous break-through. Since he had declared his feelings for her, she had never made any overtures of any kind, not even to acknowledge the flowers and plants he kept sending. But then what did he expect—a thank-you note every day? Not hardly. His offerings were solely a reminder of his love.

She reached out a hand to hold his. "Thank you for coming tonight, André. After all that's happened lately between us. . . well, I didn't expect you to . . . be a friend."

"I will always be your friend, Rebekka." He leaned closer to her, more to see her reaction than anything else because he had already promised himself he wouldn't try to force her love. She froze in his sudden spotlight. Was her breath coming faster? Or was that shallow breathing his own?

Their lips met, as first tentatively and then with more assurance. His arm crept about her and pulled her closer. *Control*, André warned himself. Rebekka meant too much to him to take advantage of her erratic emotions. When she finally did open her heart, he wanted it to be of her own free will, not because of some trauma that had occurred during the day. When she pulled gently away, he didn't protest.

She didn't look at him or speak, and for a moment, he was tempted to drag an explanation from her. "Why did you let me kiss you?" he could ask. "Or why did you kiss me like that?" But something warned him to leave it alone. He would let the kiss stand as a natural extension of their closeness. Let her begin to see their relationship did not end with friendship, but went far beyond. And above all, let her not feel threatened.

He restarted the engine without speaking, and wound his way through the dark, nearly deserted streets to her house. He had driven much further than he remembered and by the time they arrived, Rebekka had fallen asleep. The illumination from the street light cast eerie shadows on her face, making her seem fragile and ethereal. André brought the car to a halt, but kept the engine and the heater running. For a long time, he sat silently and watched her.

* * *

Rebekka tried to turn over, but something held her back. Her eyes flew open as her hands searched for the reason: the safety belt. Memory came back to her in a flood, and she glanced toward André in the driver's seat. He was twisted slightly, his back resting against the door.

"We're home," he said softly. She couldn't see his expression, but his voice sounded odd. Something about the tone made her want to kiss him again.

Then for a sudden brief instant, she saw not André but her husband in the car with her. *Marc!* her heart sang. The image faded and he was André again. Disappointment set in as the joy ebbed.

"I'd better go in," she murmured. "My parents are probably over. They'll be wondering where I am."

André nodded and opened his door. He came around to help her out, for which she was grateful. The pain in her left side was once more sharp and intense. He held her hand as they went toward her apartment building, took her keys to open the door when she fumbled at the lock, and rode up with her on the elevator. She knew he wouldn't be satisfied until she was safely inside her apartment, so she didn't bother to tell him to leave.

At the door she brought out her keys again. She paused. "André

I . . . thanks for coming. For listening."

He nodded, his face expressionless, and she knew he was purposely hiding his emotions. For a moment it made her angry. *You say you love me, and yet you stand there as though nothing happened between us.*

The thought was unreasonable, given her own feelings toward him, but Rebekka didn't care. Leaning up on her tiptoes, she whispered, "Kiss me, André. Kiss me again."

She knew she shouldn't use him like this, but she was so lonely and he was there, so handsome and strong—and so like her beloved Marc!

He was silent and for a moment she thought he would refuse. Then he put his arms around her and pulled her tightly to him. She wondered fleetingly if he could feel the bulk of the baby between them like she could, and if it repelled him.

His lips met hers—not in the gentle, comforting kisses they had shared in the car, but with a strength that both scared and exhilarated her. *I shouldn't be kissing him*, she thought. But she didn't stop. *Why shouldn't I kiss him?* another part of her returned. *We are responsible adults. Kissing is a part of a relationship.*

Almost immediately the guilt set in. Who was she fooling? Yes, kissing was part of a relationship, but should only be part of a *serious* one. And how could she be serious about André?

Marc. Oh, Marc! She pulled away and turned to the door, her mouth feeling bruised but somehow alive . . . like her heart.

"Rebekka." His voice compelled her to look at him.

"I—I'm sorry," she said. "I shouldn't have. I was just . . . I miss Marc."

He recoiled as if she had slapped him. "Well, I'm always available— for whatever you need. You only have to ask."

She bit her lip, wanting to protest, but understanding that she deserved his scorn. In these past minutes she had used him as a replacement for Marc. She had used his feelings for her to steal something that wasn't hers, nor could ever be if she were to remain faithful to her dead husband.

He sauntered to the top of the stairs leading downward to the bottom floors. "Oh, and be sure to tell Samuel hi, the next time you see him." His voice was mild, but Rebekka perceived a rebuke. André felt he had Marc's complete blessing in pursuing her, and he viewed Samuel as his competition—her boyfriend. In his mind, it was Samuel she had betrayed tonight, not Marc. He left then, taking the marble steps two at a time. As she watched, the ache and longing in her heart far exceeded the pain in her abdomen.

Behind her the door opened. "Rebekka!" exclaimed her mother in the silky voice Rebekka had inherited. "I'm so glad you got back before we left. Isn't this wonderful! We have our Nadia! Tomorrow I will bring over the crib and everything we have ready. Raoul says he wants it in his room so he can hear her if she cries. Isn't that sweet? He's going to be such a great dad."

Rebekka nodded numbly.

"Come in, honey," her father said, putting an arm around her. "Hey, you're cold. Where have you been anyway?"

Rebekka let her parents draw her into the apartment. The words washed over and around her as her family talked and made plans for the future.

Nadia had fallen peacefully asleep, and Rebekka wished she could join her. Over and over she kept feeling Andre's lips against hers, seeing his face as she told him she missed Marc. The guilt she felt at using him was compounded by the knowledge that she wanted him to kiss her again.

No, I just miss Marc, she told herself. But when she finally went to bed that night, it was André she dreamed about.

Chapter 26

Rebekka spent a busy weekend with Raoul and Nadia. She had never dreamed there was so much to learn about caring for a baby. Between feedings, diaper changes, and time in the rocking chair, Rebekka rested in her bed. She felt exhausted. The pain in her side was so great she decided to stay home from church on Sunday. Since Raoul had to teach Elder's quorum that day, he left Nadia with Rebekka.

"Are you sure you can handle her alone?" he asked.

"Yes, of course. Are you sure you can handle waiting until next week to show her around?" she countered with a smile.

He laughed. "Well, she is kind of cute. But truthfully, I'd rather we do it together. I'm afraid that one of these times, I won't be able to get her quiet when she cries.

"She's probably missing Marie-Thérèse. But you do just fine. You're a great dad."

"Then why do I feel like I'm all thumbs. You can change her diaper better than I can and you have no experience with babies."

"Well, I've helped Josette out a time or two. But mostly I think it's the mentality: I'm a woman so naturally I should be able to change a diaper."

"Hey, I believe in equal rights."

"Good," she said, passing him the baby, "because I think she just left you a present. If you hurry you'll have time to change her before you go."

After he left, Rebekka lay in her bed next to Nadia. She told herself she was too sick to do anything, but now she had begun to feel rather better. Was she faking so she wouldn't have to face André?

Rebekka groaned. *Maybe I should move away. What were Marc and I thinking staying in the same ward as both our parents and André and his family? Marie-Thérèse and Josette knew what they were doing by moving farther away.* But Rebekka didn't really believe it. She and Marc had both enjoyed being with their families and many ward members envied their close relationship.

Nadia was asleep and Rebekka let herself drift until the ringing of her bell signaled a visitor. With effort, she hauled herself to her feet and stumbled to the door. Whoever was there must have gotten in below without ringing her.

What if it's André?

She peeked though the spy hole and saw Desirée on the other side. Rebekka glanced toward her bedroom where Nadia lay sleeping. Had she come because of the baby? Reluctantly, she opened the door, but blocked it with her body. "Hi."

"Hi, Rebekka," Desirée said with a thin smile. "Is Raoul here?"

At least she hadn't purposely waited until he had left this time. "No. He's at church. I wasn't feeling well." To emphasize this, Rebekka tightened her white robe around her.

"I see," Desirée paused, apparently uncertain how to continue. Rebekka noticed she was wearing one of the outfits they had purchased last week, and she looked nice though there was entirely too much make up on her face.

"I . . . oh, Rebekka, can I come in for a minute? I need to talk."

Rebekka remembered her silent vow to be Desirée's friend. "Sure." She stepped back from the door. "I should have asked you before, but I'm not feeling well."

"It's about Nadia," Desirée said when they were seated in the kitchen where Rebekka could hear the baby if she awoke. "My parents told me Raoul called, that he'd found her."

"It's true." Rebekka launched into a full account, wondering whether she should let Desirée see Nadia. What if she were to take the baby and run? Rebekka didn't know if she was strong enough to stop her.

"Marie-Thérèse must have been very unhappy," Desirée said. "I know how much she wanted a baby."

"You do?" That surprised Rebekka. Desirée had never appeared to notice what anyone else wanted.

"Yeah. We used to talk quite a lot when Raoul and I were dating. I really like her. She never seemed to judge me the way . . ."

"The way everyone else did."

Desirée smiled wanly. "Well, they were right." She twisted her hands on the table.

"They still want to do tests to make sure Nadia is really Nadia, though there's really no doubt."

"I could tell you."

Rebekka chose her words carefully. "It's been a long time since you've seen her. She'll have changed a lot."

"I'd know my own baby," Desirée insisted. "I would. I know I was a crappy mother, that I neglected her. I know all that. But I still love her. And I need to see her."

"You'll have to go through Raoul," Rebekka said. "Isn't that what the divorce says?"

"It's not final yet. Not until we go before the judge on Monday."

Rebekka stared at her. "What are you saying?"

"Don't look at me like that. I'm not going to fight Raoul over Nadia. I know I wouldn't win. And I wouldn't want to. I'm no good—I know that. At least not now. I love my baby enough to want her to have a good life. All I'm asking is for you to arrange for me to see her. Talk to Raoul if you have to. Just let me see her and make sure she's really okay." Tears formed in Desirée's eyes. "Please, Rebekka. I can't sleep at night thinking I've killed her. All I see is coffins and dead babies in deserted alleyways. I just want to see her once. To hold her one last time and then I promise I'll stay away. I don't want my daughter to have the kind of life I do. Believe it or not, but it's true. I know she doesn't belong with me."

Rebekka said nothing as she watched Desirée, trying to measure her sincerity. Like the day they had gone shopping, she had the distinct feeling her sister-in-law was telling the truth—at least as she perceived it.

She stood. "Okay, but don't make me regret this."

She motioned for Desirée to follow her down the hall to her bedroom where the door was open. Nadia was still sleeping and hadn't budged from the place Rebekka had left her. She was lying on her back and didn't know how to roll to her stomach yet, but Rebekka had blocked the sides of the bed with a pillow just to be sure.

"We were just having a nap together when you came," Rebekka explained. "Raoul had to teach in church today so he didn't take her. You should see him, though. He just sits and stares at her. Hasn't been separated from her since Friday night. Takes her everywhere he goes. He's thrilled to be a dad."

Desirée nodded but her eyes were fixed on Nadia. "I knew he'd be a good father." Desirée moved toward the bed and picked up the baby with a sureness Rebekka wondered if she'd ever feel. Trying to be inconspicuous, Rebekka placed herself in front of the door—just in case.

Desirée made a small gasp, and for a moment Rebekka felt dread in the pit of her stomach. She almost expected Desirée to say, "This is not my baby. This is not Nadia." But instead, she murmured, "Oh, she's grown so much. She's so big. But even more beautiful. Hi, Nadia. Hello beautiful! It's Mommy. I just wanted to make sure you're okay." Desirée hugged her gently and placed a kiss on her brow. "You're going to be just fine with Daddy. He'll take good care of you. And maybe when you're a lot older, when Mommy gets things together, I can come see you again. Maybe we can go shopping or out to lunch. I bet you'll be a good girl, and smart too. I know you'll have a lot of help."

With another kiss on her forehead, Desirée walked to Rebekka and placed the baby in her arms. "Tell her I love her, would you?" she asked. "When she gets older, I mean. It may be hard for her to understand, but I really do love her."

Rebekka was touched by the ache in her voice. "If you cleaned up your act, Raoul would let you see her, I'm sure of it. You would have to gain his trust, but you could do it."

Desirée shook her head. "I can't. Not yet. I want to but I don't seem to be strong enough. Someday I'm going to be good enough for her, but until then I want her to be happy and have a good life. I don't want her to be confused, and I don't want to be a bad influence."

She moved past Rebekka into the hall.

"But—"

Desirée whirled on Rebekka, her features twisted in anger. "I can't be a mother, Rebekka! You don't seem to get it. I didn't want a baby and I don't want to change my life. Someday I will, but not now. I *like* my life."

"You're lying," Rebekka said, her own anger rising at the inconsistencies in Desirée's behavior. "I know you're lying! You want to change, but you're too lazy. Well that's just fine. Go! Get out! Take care of yourself. Nadia's no longer your problem."

For an instant Desirée's mouth gaped, but then she nodded slowly. "Just tell her I loved her. Please?"

Rebekka couldn't deny her that; for everything that Desirée wasn't, she did love her baby enough to give her up to a good home.

"I will," she promised.

Satisfied, Desirée left the apartment, leaving Rebekka to stare after her.

Only a half hour had passed when Marie-Thérèse stopped by with another bag of Nadia's things. "It's really just an excuse," she admitted. "I needed to see her. I wasn't sure if you'd be home yet from church, but I hoped you would be."

"Actually, I didn't go today. I'm not feeling that well, but church should be over now. Raoul left Nadia with me. He'll be home soon."

"May I?" Marie-Thérèse motioned to the baby in her arms.

"Oh, yes. Here. And come into the living room for a while."

"Thank you." Marie-Thérèse kissed Nadia tenderly.

"It seems our little Nadia is very popular today," Rebekka said as they sat on the couch."What do you mean?" Marie-Thérèse's brow furrowed. "Are you upset that I came?"

"Oh, no. Please don't think that. I'm glad you came. It's just that Desirée stopped by a few minutes ago. She wanted to see Nadia."

Marie-Thérèse's eyes widened. "And?"

"And she kissed her and held her and told her to have a good life. Then she left."

"Just like that?"

"Yes." Rebekka sighed. "I believe she really loves Nadia and that she wants to change, but she doesn't know how."

"Maybe this is the beginning for her," Marie-Thérèse said. "I mean, repentance works in different ways for different people. Desirée never did things the easy way."

"But to give up your baby like that!"

Marie-Thérèse lifted her chin. "It's one of the noblest things she could do. If you were in her position, could you do it?"

"I would never be in her position. *Never.*" Even as she spoke Rebekka realized she was being unfair. Who could say what she would have been like had she faced other trials? Been raised by other parents? *But I wouldn't be like Desirée*, she thought. *I would make something of my life.*

"Well, there are many thousands of children being raised in homes that are barely adequate. I think Desirée's showing great responsibility by recognizing that she can't give her baby what she needs right now."

"Or maybe she just doesn't want the work," Rebekka retorted.

Marie-Thérèse rubbed the side of her slightly upturned nose. "Maybe. Thank heaven we don't have to judge."

Rebekka grimaced. "Somehow I knew you'd say that. And you're right—that's exactly what I'm doing. But I don't understand her not wanting to have at least some part in Nadia's life, though I'm sure it'd be easier for Raoul and Nadia. I just wonder what Nadia will make of it years down the road."

"I guess we'll have to wait and see."

After Marie-Thérèse left, Rebekka fed Nadia and was settling back in bed when Raoul came home. "Sorry I'm late," he said. "We had an impromptu teacher meeting afterwards. Has it been pretty quiet?"

"Yeah, like summer at the Eiffel Tower," muttered Rebekka.

"What?"

"Nothing. Just tend your daughter. I need a nap."

"Gladly." Raoul held out his arms for Nadia. "Hello, cutie. I missed you. And so did everyone else. They all wanted to see you." He paused at the door. "Oh, that reminds me," he said. "André asked after you. He wanted to know if you want him to come over again to talk."

Rebekka remembered only too well what kind of "talking" they had done last night.

"No," she said curtly. "I most certainly do not. If he calls, tell him I'll do all my talking with Samuel."

At that she stuck her head under the pillow and tried to sleep.

Chapter 27

On Tuesday morning Raoul stuck his head in Rebekka's door as she was painfully climbing out of bed. "Hey, don't you have your appointment in a little while?"

"Yes, I do. Want to come?"

Raoul nodded. "Yes, actually. I thought we'd drop Nadia off at Marie-Thérèse's and tag along. But I'm not too sure I'd better now. My illustrious partner is out there in our kitchen waiting for you. Seems he has some idea of driving you there himself. Thank heaven we hired a COO or our business would be hurting with all these spontaneous mini-vacations we're taking."

Rebekka's heart lurched inside her chest. She hadn't seen André since Friday night, though she had thought a lot about that last turbulent kiss. "Nonsense, you work a ton of overtime, and you have great employees. Hey, Valerie could probably run the whole company alone. That reminds me—have you asked her out yet?"

"Me?" His face shown genuine surprise. "I have only been divorced a day."

"So? It's not like there's a waiting period."

"Oh. I guess you're right. Hmm. Maybe I'll do it today." He rubbed his chin in thought. "So, what do you want me to tell André? Are you going to let him drive?"

"Well, I suppose he feels obligated."

Raoul shook his head in disagreement, but he kept quiet, for which Rebekka was grateful.

"Well, I certainly want you to come." She paused. "But I don't want to hurt André's feelings."

"Then we'll both go with you. Now get dressed. I'm going to entertain our restless man out there. Right now little Nadia is doing the honors."

Rebekka smiled and shook her head. "I'm not coming out a moment before I have to. André can wait."

"Okay, but don't hold me responsible if he comes in here himself to see what's going on."

Rebekka laughed. "I can handle him." And strangely enough, she felt it was true. She would put Friday night behind them and go on as though it had never happened.

"Oh, and by the way," Raoul said over his shoulder. "He brought you a new plant."

* * *

"Hmm," said Dr. Samain.

"What does that mean?" Rebekka asked nervously. The light over the examining table hurt her eyes and the cold jelly on her stomach was uncomfortable, but neither discomfort matched the dread in her heart. If her pain was related to her intestines, why hadn't the medication permanently taken it away? What else was inside her that she should still feel so many aches? Was her baby at risk?

"Well, there's only one baby there, but—"

Only one baby! Worry consumed Rebekka. If she wasn't expecting twins, then something must be horribly wrong.

"—he's bigger than I expected. I think you must be a month further along than we thought."

"He?" André asked.

Dr. Samain nodded. "You did want to know the sex, didn't you?"

"Yes." Rebekka paused, letting the knowledge that she was having Marc's son sink in, the first grandson to bear the Perrault name. *How fitting that the oldest Perrault son should have the first Perrault boy!* "I think I knew he was boy," she murmured dreamily. "I think I knew it all along."

"Mom and Dad are going to be very happy," André said, his thoughts apparently following the same lines. "Well, they would be either way, but we really need a boy to carry on the Perrault name."

"But how could I be a month further along?" Rebekka asked, sitting up and wiping off the clear jelly on her stomach with the towel the doctor provided. "I had my cycle like normal the month before I got pregnant— at least I'm pretty sure I did. I mean, I would have noticed since we were trying to have a baby."

"Some women do have a cycle or two," the doctor said. "Usually a bit lighter than normal."

"That's right," André said. "I remember my mother telling Claire when she spotted with Ana that she had her cycle for the first three months of most of her pregnancies."

Relief washed over Rebekka. "Then I'm over five months along!

That's why I'm so big all of a sudden. But that's great! One less month to wait."

The doctor chuckled, but his face remained solemn.

"There's something else, isn't there?" Rebekka said, fighting to quell the rising panic in her heart. Fear made her mouth dry and the sound of her swallowing seemed loud in the small room.

"There seems to be another growth on your ovaries."

"A growth? Could that have caused the some of the pain?" Raoul asked.

"Actually, it is likely causing all the pain. And it could get better or become worse, depending on the hormones and other factors involved. These things are difficult to predict."

"What is it exactly?" André asked

"It appears to be a cyst on her left ovary, or two actually, partially joined."

André's mouth opened to ask another question, but the doctor rushed on. "Now don't be overly concerned. Every time a woman ovulates, she develops an ovarian cyst, called a follicle cyst, which contains an egg. When the hormones reach a certain level, the cyst breaks and releases the egg. Then the remnants of the cyst excretes progesterone which prepares the uterine lining to accept the egg sac when it tries to implant there. In early pregnancy, doctors are afraid to remove even painful cysts because it might cause a miscarriage. They always wait until at least the second trimester."

André looked doubtful. "So this is normal?"

"Oh, no. The cyst should be gone at this point. And there should be no pain. Sometimes variations occur and you get cysts that are painful or that don't go away when they should, or perhaps refill."

"So what should we do?" Raoul asked.

"Well, mostly these cysts go away by themselves and the women involved don't even know they existed—even when there is a minor problem or slight variation. But that's obviously not Rebekka's case." Dr. Samain turned his attention back to her. "I'm very concerned about the pain you're having and about the size of the cyst."

"But after the medication you gave her last week, she seemed to be feeling better," André said. "At least for a little while."

"It does feel better than last week," Rebekka agreed.

The doctor nodded. "The impacted intestine and colon could have been putting pressure on the cyst, causing additional pain. I've seen it happened before. That's why the pain is not so severe now, but hasn't gone away completely."

Rebekka finally managed to make herself ask the question that was torturing her: "It is dangerous for the baby?"

"Not presently," said the doctor. "However, because of its size and position, and the pain involved, we should probably remove it as a preventive measure. Right now it's about the size of your fist." He held up her hand to demonstrate. "The connecting one is about half that. But both could become larger and the swelling and torsion could cause very severe pain. And we have to be careful about what pain drugs you take because of the baby. I'd like to do some more tests before making a final recommendation, but my initial advice would be to remove it."

"But isn't that dangerous?" André asked. "I mean, to operate while she's pregnant."

"There is a possibility the baby could come prematurely. And at five months that wouldn't be a good thing. But the risks may outweigh the pain and the possibility of the cyst causing additional problems."

"What if we do nothing?" Rebekka asked.

Dr. Samain turned to her. "There is a chance you can go to term without complications. You could have the baby and then take care of the cyst. Or there is a slight chance that it may heal itself. Or it may react to the hormones of the pregnancy and grow incredibly large, causing so much pain that there will be no option but to remove it. Even if it bursts and starts to go away, that in itself could cause problem—a burning like you never imagined, for one. These things aren't one hundred percent sure. But I really believe you need to have it out. I've done these surgeries on pregnant women before without complications. Normally, I try to keep interference in the birth process to a minimum, but sometimes intervention is necessary."

"But the surgery could still cause an early delivery," Rebekka said. "And I might lose my baby."

"At this point that risk is still present, but less because you're already five months along," the doctor said. "I don't think . . ."

Rebekka heard the doctor continue the discussion with André and Raoul, but she couldn't concentrate on what they were saying. The idea of losing Marc's baby terrified her. This was her one and only chance to have a part of him. Besides, she had seen her baby's heart beating on the ultrasound, had felt him moving inside her. There was no way she wanted to endanger her son by having a surgery that would cause him to come before his time. But what if the growth inside her uterus continued to enlarge? What if it burst and caused more trouble? Neither choice sounded acceptable.

"I'll leave you alone to talk about it." The doctor left the room, and for a few minutes they all stared at each other in silence.

"Well? What do you think?" she asked finally.

Raoul shrugged. "I don't know."

"How do you feel about it?" André came close to the examination table where she still sat and put a tentative hand on her shoulder.

"I don't want to hurt the baby either way."

Neither said anything for long moments and Rebekka found it hard to keep from throwing herself in André arms and sobbing. Instead she clamped her lips together tightly, holding her breath.

André put his face near hers. "Maybe we should pray."

"Okay." Rebekka gulped for air, knocked further off balance at his closeness. "Will you offer it?"

"Of course."

After André locked the door, the two men stood next to where Rebekka sat painfully on the examining table. They joined hands. André said the words, pouring out his heart as Rebekka had never before heard him do. Her admiration for him doubled in that moment as he asked for the Lord's guidance. He closed the prayer and they waited in silence for an answer. The minutes ticked slowly by. *What is thy will?* Rebekka silently begged the Lord to let her feel something other that the horrible fear.

Finally, André tugged on her hands and Rebekka opened her eyes, feeling her lids damp with the tears that had already seeped down to her cheeks. André and Raoul's eyes were also wet.

"Well?" André asked.

"I think I should wait." As they sprang out of her mouth, she realized she had known what to do all along. The warmth spreading over her body verified the decision, though not completely obliterating the fear. Perhaps this would not be a comfortable choice for her, but it was the right one for her baby.

"That's what I feel too." Raoul said. "We should wait for at least a few more weeks."

André was nodding in agreement. "We should hold a family fast, too."

"Will you two give me a blessing when we get home?" Even to her own ears Rebekka's voice sounded weak.

André hugged her, the awkwardness between them completely gone. "Of course. And don't worry, it's going to be all right."

Thoughts of the losses each of them had already suffered came to her mind, but faith filled her in a heady rush as she clearly saw that their strengths had evolved because of those trials. Having made the decision with the influence of the Spirit, there was nothing more she could do. Whatever happened, she would trust in the Lord.

When Dr. Samain returned, they told him of their decision. "It's against my recommendation," he said, "but I've known your family long enough to recognize that miracles seem to follow the whole bunch of you. Why don't we just keep an eye on the situation and take things as they come? I'll run a few tests and see if they make a difference, and you can come in more often for me to check on the both the baby and cyst. Be sure and tell me if there's any change in your pain level. That will be a good indication of what we should do. I could give you some pain medica-tion—"

"Not yet," Rebekka said. "You said it wasn't good for the baby."

The doctor's smile was admiring. "The strong stuff isn't," he conceded, "though not as risky as it would be earlier in the pregnancy. But there's no reason we can't try to find something that will safely give you at least some relief."

"I'd like to try it without first," Rebekka said. "But is there anything else I should know? Things I should do or things to avoid?"

"No heavy lifting, take your prenatal vitamins, and get a lot of bed rest. Don't overdo anything. Moderation here is the key. If you feel any severe pains or burning sensations, come in immediately."

As Rebekka thanked the doctor, doubt crept in. *Am I doing the right thing?*

She took a brief cleansing breath. *Of course*, she told herself, *I received an answer. Now I just have to show my faith.* Sometimes that was the hardest part.

"Remember when we get home," she told her brother and André. "I'd like you two to give me a priesthood blessing."

Chapter 28

Both Raoul and André had returned to work, and Rebekka knew they would likely work overtime to make up for the morning's lost hour. Since she was so emotionally and physically drained after the doctor's appointment, Raoul had left Nadia with Marie-Thérèse. He told Rebekka he planned to talk to Marie-Thérèse about a more permanent baby-sitting arrangement while Rebekka was down with her cyst. Their mother had also expressed a desire to spend time with Nadia during the day while Raoul worked, and between the two women Rebekka and Raoul were satisfied that the baby would be well-taken care of and loved.

Rebekka stayed in bed that afternoon, translating new manual revisions her boss had sent over the e-mail. To her surprise, Ariana stopped by after school with André's daughters. "They made me come," she said with a wide smile. "They said they had to make sure you were all right, and I admit that I couldn't wait to come over and see you. The girls have homework to do and I thought we could visit while they did it in the kitchen."

"Ohhhh, Grandma!" the girls chorused.

"It won't take you long," Ariana said, placing a hand on each of their shoulders and propelling them gently in the direction of the kitchen. "Rebekka will still be here when you are done. And I bet she has some cookies and milk to help you think."

Rebekka laughed. "Yes—they know where they are. Help yourself, girls."

Without another word of protest, Ana and Marée raced into the kitchen.

"André called you, didn't he?" Rebekka asked Ariana, leading the way to the sitting room. She could rest just as easily there as in her bed if she reclined on the couch. "He said he would."

"Yes, he called and told me what was going on." Ariana sat on the chair opposite her. She was quiet a moment as she took in all the flowers and plants in the room. "André sent all these?" she asked.

Rebekka grimaced. "Who told you?"

"The girls." Ariana shook her head.

"I keep killing the plants," Rebekka admitted. "Marc was the one who watered the few we had. He liked plants; I never really cared for them."

"The question is, what are you going to do about it?"

"Do about what?"

"You know what I'm talking about."

"Yes, I guess I do." Rebekka felt chastened by her mother-in-law's words. "I just don't understand why this has to happen."

Ariana laughed suddenly and continued. "I seem to remember you asking that once before when Marc was in the hospital and you had just discovered your feelings for André. I told you then that the Lord knew what He was doing and that He had a reason. Do you remember?"

"Yes, I do. Or at least now that you bring it up. The other day Raoul and I were talking about the same thing in relation to Nadia—a reason for her missing, a reason for Marie-Thérèse having to give her up . . . everything."

"Well, I think I know now why you and André had those feelings." Ariana paused when she saw Rebekka's aggravated expression, but then she continued, "Of course, maybe I don't know what I'm talking about. Only you can decide."

Rebekka felt emotion building inside her. Why did everyone think she could just forget Marc and go on as though he never existed? And could she really believe that the Lord had been preparing her to live without him before they even married?

She sighed. "I am happy carrying Marc's baby," she said slowly. "Right now I can't think beyond that."

"That's fair," Ariana said. "Just remember we're all here for you if you need us. And I personally support your decisions and choices. I feel very fortunate to have you as a daughter and as the mother of one of my grandchildren."

Rebekka smiled at Ariana's sincerity. "I know that. You—everyone—has been great. In fact, after I called my mother this morning, it was all I could do to convince her not to move in with us."

Ariana laughed and the sound wiped away any of the remaining tenseness. They fell into an easy conversation that was interrupted when the girls returned, bringing a cacophony of sound with them.

"I'll leave you to chat awhile," Ariana said. "I brought some things for your dinner, and I'm going to get them started."

"You don't have to do that," Rebekka protested.

"I know. I want to. And, in fact, your mother, Josette, Marie-Thérèse, a few sisters in the ward, and I have worked out a schedule. Your mother and Raoul are going to be responsible for the grocery shopping, and the rest of us are taking turns coming in to fix dinner every day until this baby is here."

"But that's four months! That's way too much work!"

Ariana bent over and placed a hand on Rebekka's stomach. "Nothing is worth the chance of his life," she said with feeling. "You are doing your best—I know the pain isn't easy to bear. We're certainly glad to do our part by helping you stay off your feet."

Rebekka placed her hand over Ariana's, almost overwhelmed at the love and unconditional acceptance the older woman offered. "Thank you. And I gratefully accept your help."

"Good," Ariana said with a smile. "Now girls, take good care of Rebekka, okay? But keep the tone down a bit and don't make her get off the couch."

"Does it hurt?" asked Ana as Ariana left the room. Both girls came and sat on the floor by the couch.

Only when I move, Rebekka wanted to say. Instead, she said, "Not too much at the moment."

"Daddy says you need to be taken care of," Marée said, her turquoise eyes sad. "And that he doesn't know if we can come over every week like we planned."

Rebekka put an arm around the little girl as she climbed up on the couch. "Well, I think we could still manage. It's not as if you're babies that I have to take care of, right?"

Marée brightened. "That's right! We can take care of you—get you stuff, keep you company."

"We did that a lot for Mommy," Ana said. "We know how real well." The words told Rebekka how much the nine-year-old still missed her mother.

"She was sick a lot when we were little," Marée said matter-of-factly. "But now she's with Uncle Marc so she probably doesn't miss us so much. I bet he's told her all about the things we've been doing since she left."

"Well, she probably looks down on you all the time." Rebekka gathered their little hands in hers. "And until we see her again, you have me and Grandma and your other aunts to talk to."

"I wish you lived with us," said Marée. "Or that we lived here. With daddy too. That would be fun. Wouldn't it, Ana?"

There was silence for a brief moment, then a smile came to Ana's face. "I know, you and Daddy like each other, Aunt Rebekka—you're always laughing together. Why can't you get married?"

Marée's eyes seemed to grow two sizes. "Yeah! Then we could play together all the time."

"And we could take care of you always!" Ana added.

"Wait a minute," Rebekka said. "Things don't always work out like we want them too."

"But you do like Daddy?" Marée asked.

"Of course I like your daddy."

"We'll be good," Ana put in quickly. "We know how to clean up the kitchen and we keep our room clean."

"And we never talk back," Marée said. "Well, hardly ever."

Ana leaned forward conspiratorially. "Only when Daddy makes us eat peas."

"We hate peas," Marée said with an emphatic nod. "But we love broccoli and carrots and cauliflower. And salad—even with onions in it."

Marée lifted her chin. "Daddy says we're the two best behaved girls in the whole of France. Maybe even in the whole world."

Two pairs of turquoise eyes stared at Rebekka, waiting eagerly for her reply. "I agree," Rebekka hastened to assure them. "It's not you two—really. It's me. It's . . . well, you see I was married to your Uncle Marc and—"

"But he's in heaven now with our mommy," said Ana, her green eyes earnest. "So he won't mind. He'll be glad for you to take care of us and for us to take care of you. I just know it! He always liked us to come over."

Rebekka smiled. "So did I."

"See!" Marée said triumphantly. "Then you can marry Daddy."

"Girls. It's not that easy. There are other things involved."

"Like what?" came a voice from the doorway. "An American fiancé perhaps?"

"André," she said, feeling suddenly faint. She must have been so involved with the girls that she hadn't heard Ariana let him in.

He didn't smile but stared at her fixedly. "Girls," he said without taking his eyes from hers, "would you please excuse us for a minute? Your Aunt Rebekka and I need to talk."

André's expression warned that he was barely holding back fury.

Rebekka wished she was back in bed so that she could pull the covers over her head and disappear. Where was the solicitous man of that morning?

Ana nodded and scampered toward the door, but Marée looked gravely at her father. "Now, be nice," she admonished with a few shakes of her finger. "Aunt Rebekka is sick. And if you're not nice she might *never* marry you and become our mother." She gave Rebekka a wink and followed her sister out of the room.

André went to the door and shut it, making Rebekka even more nervous.

"What is it?" she asked as he came to stand by the couch, hands shoved into the pockets of his suit pants. "Uh, do you want to sit down?"

"No, I don't."

"Did I thank you for the plant you brought this morning? It's really nice."

He continued looking at her sternly and the other inane comments on her lips vanished. "So," he said finally, each word coming slowly as he struggled to maintain his calm, "did you do your talking with Samuel?"

Something warned her that he already knew the answer. "Well, no," she said. "I haven't called—"

"I figured as much. I know you don't like to make people wait on you. That's why I took the liberty of calling Samuel myself."

Rebekka's heart lurched and her throat went dry.

"And guess what? He wasn't home. He was in the Caribbean."

Rebekka had begun to feel relieved when he added, "Imagine my surprise to learn that he was there on his *honeymoon*." He took his tightly clenched hands from his pockets. He shook his head. "Rebekka, you lied to me. Not in so many words, perhaps, but the result is the same. You lied!"

"I did it for you! I did it to free you."

"Free me? Free me?" he said, running an agitated hand through his dark hair. His handsome face clearly showed his pain. "Who are you kidding? I don't want to be free! I want you! And when I think of all the wasted time. These past weeks I have waited and tried to be patient, all the while feeling tortured because I thought you had feelings for that man . . ."

Abruptly, he dropped to his knee and grabbed her hands. "You are going to marry me, Rebekka—sooner or later. I love you and whether you know it or not you love me."

She didn't say anything, unable to trust her own emotions or to bring herself to tell him the reason why she would never marry him.

"Kiss me, André," he whispered, his face drawing near. "Kiss me again. Do you remember when you said that? Can you imagine how that made me feel after waiting so long for a sign—any sign—that you cared? Something broke inside me then—something I had pent up for a long time. And imagine how I felt afterward when you implied that you kissed me only because you missed Marc." He made an impatient noise. "Now *I'm* asking, Rebekka. Kiss me—of your own will. Because you want to, not because of anything or anyone else."

She wanted to tell him to get out, but felt helpless to do so. Though she could never admit it, she *did* love him—more than she imagined possible after loving Marc so completely.

"How do you know I would be marrying you for yourself?" she asked. "And not because you look like my dead husband?"

The muscles in his jaws flexed and he swallowed hard. When he spoke, his voice was hoarse and devoid of his earlier anger. "I'll take that chance."

"Would it be enough?" Her words rose to a high pitch. "What if in my dreams, I call out his name. How would that make you feel?"

His eyes gouged into hers, as though trying to dig deep enough to spark her hidden emotions. "I would endure anything to be with you. I love you, and that means I'm here to stay." He paused and took a deep breath. "But you're wrong, Rebekka. I know you loved my brother—how could I not know that? But I see the way you respond to my kisses, I see the way you're looking at me right now. I may not be able to make you forget Marc—I wouldn't want to—but I will be able to make you happy!"

He lowered his face and kissed her. The connection between them was immediate and strong, but Rebekka's heart felt as if it were being torn in two—between the men she loved. Tears slipped down her face and soon she could taste their salt. André drew away and caught a tear on his fingertip. Then he kissed her face tenderly until the wetness was gone.

Still kneeling by the couch, he pulled her gently but firmly into his embrace, kissing her brow. "It's okay, Rebekka," he murmured. "I promise you everything is going to be all right. We'll get through it together. Trust in me a little, okay?"

Rebekka wanted to do just that. After all, she and André had been friends for many years since she was five and he thirteen. They both cared about the other and both put the Lord first. Logically, that was enough to pursue a serious relationship—even if she didn't love him, which she did. But was there any way around the guilt? Was there any way to make up to Marc the fact that if she married André, her son would grow up calling another man Daddy?

André was looking at her so tenderly and with so much love that for a moment, Rebekka believed their relationship was possible. The enormous loneliness inside her heart shriveled, leaving room for his love. "I'll try," she whispered. "I'll try."

"No more lies," he said. "I want the truth—always. I'll give you the same."

She nodded and laid her head against the warmth of his chest, feeling the comforting beat of his heart beneath his crisp white dress shirt. Oddly, he wasn't wearing a tie—something she had never thought he would forego while wearing a suit. Maybe there was a lot she didn't know about him after all . . . or herself.

"So will you marry me?" he asked.

She thought for a long moment but still came to no solid resolution within herself. "Ask me again after the baby comes. Give me until then."

"All right," he agreed. "If that's what you want, I'll wait until the baby is born."

After he left that night, taking Ariana and the girls with him, Rebekka slowly made her way to the piano bench and lifted the lid. Her fingers rippled over the keys, fumbling once or twice after the long inactivity, but quickly finding their way. Joy sprang to life in her heart. Oh, how she'd missed this! The music made her heart swell and sing, rising on a current toward the sky.

Chapter 29

Nadia was crying—again. Raoul paced the floor on Friday night, wondering how long he could keep up the vigil. He had fed, changed, bathed, and rocked the infant, but nothing seemed to improve her mood.

He went down the hall to Rebekka's room where she was lying in bed, propped up by several pillows, her laptop on her lap. An hour ago, André had been in there with Ana and Marée, playing games, but he had finally taken the girls home to bed. To Raoul's satisfaction, André had been over with the girls every night since Tuesday—four nights in a row, and Rebekka was looking much happier these days, though Raoul knew she was in constant pain that seemed only to increase with each day.

"Do you think she's teething?" he asked Rebekka, as she looked up from the computer.

"I don't know. Let's see, she's about three and a half months—do they teethe at that age? Seems kind of young."

Raoul sat on edge of the bed, staring at his screaming daughter and wondering how he could love her so much and yet be so annoyed. And how could such a small person be so loud? "Marie-Thérèse said she rarely cried—so what am I doing wrong?"

"Give her to me," Rebekka said, holding out her arms. "I mean, if you're not going to walk with her. I can at least give you a break from the crying. That way you won't get too frustrated."

Raoul shook his head and stood. He paced the room, bouncing Nadia gently in his arm. She quieted some, but the crying continued.

Rebekka watched him with concern in her gray eyes. "I wish I could help out better. Or that André was still here. If only I could stand up and walk around."

"Should I call Valerie? No, that's just an excuse to see her, isn't it?"

"Haven't you asked her out yet?"

"Yeah, on Saturday—tomorrow, I mean. Can it be Friday already? Mom said she'd baby-sit. But I don't know if she's ready for *this*."

Rebekka nodded. "I think she'll do just fine. Dad might become a little impatient, though. Maybe you could ask Ariana or Marie-Thérèse instead—they have a lot of experience with this sort of thing. I wonder what's wrong, though. This really isn't like her."

"I can't let her continue like this." Raoul put Nadia's head on his shoulder and patted her back. "She doesn't have a fever, I've checked her diaper, and I even gave her a bath. I wonder if I should call the doctor."

"Maybe." Rebekka looked thoughtful. "Hey, wait a minute! I remember Marie-Thérèse saying something about having to drive all over town to get Larissa to sleep when she was little. Maybe that'll work."

Raoul grinned. "That's it! Nadia always sleeps in the car. I should have thought of it before. Will you be okay?"

"Yes. I'll be fine. I'm just going to get a little work done before I sleep." She yawned widely. "That is, if I can stay awake."

Raoul left her, grabbing Nadia's diaper bag on his way out. In the car, she quieted after two blocks, but she didn't sleep. For one hour he drove through Paris, hardly able to keep his own eyes open. At last, Nadia drifted off, still shuddering in her sleep. Raoul drove home.

When he tried to slip her out of the car seat, she went from sleeping to screaming in a matter of seconds. With resignation, Raoul put her back into the car seat. He had been driving for another half hour when he found himself outside Marie-Thérèse's apartment building. Impulsively, he stopped. It was after midnight now, but he needed help and he was sure Marie-Thérèse and Mathieu would be able to give it. Besides, he was becoming dangerously tired and didn't want to risk an accident.

He rang the downstairs intercom three times before arousing anyone. "Yes?" came Mathieu's tired voice.

"It's Raoul," he said over Nadia's cries. "I need help with Nadia. Can I come up. Please?"

"Of course." The door clicked open.

When Raoul arrived at their apartment, Marie-Thérèse and Mathieu were waiting with the door open. Marie-Thérèse immediately opened her arms to take the screaming baby. She put her face next to Nadia's, giving her a shower of tiny kisses. "There, there," she said. "I bet it's just a touch of gas." She looked at Raoul. "Could be something worse, though. How long has she been crying?"

"Hours," Raoul said. "Not constantly, but very consistently. Do you think I should take her to the doctor?"

Marie-Thérèse removed Nadia's double-knit sweater and flipped her over so that her tiny stomach lay against Marie-Thérèse's arm. "Let's give it a moment. She's had a few nights like this with us—very few, but she's done it on occasion. Usually this calms her down enough to sleep. Larissa got colic at this age. It's not unusual."

Raoul shook his head in frustration. "She kept crying and I couldn't make her stop. I didn't want to hurt her, and Rebekka wasn't any help—she can barely get out of bed. The car calms her some, but I'm too tired to drive anymore."

Mathieu put his hand on Raoul's shoulder. "Come on in the kitchen for a drink. Let's leave Marie-Thérèse alone with Raqu—Nadia. It's possible that she's feeding off your frustration."

Raoul followed him with unveiled relief, and Mathieu grinned at him. "Hey, it's hard when there's no one else to hand off to. Larissa used to start howling every night when I came home from work, and kept it up till midnight. In fact, she'd cry all night if she woke up. Marie-Thérèse kept her right in the bed with us and the second she stirred, she'd have to feed her before she woke up all the way. If Marie-Thérèse did it quickly enough, without moving her around too much, we were okay. But if she took a moment too long—oh, we were doomed to a night of endless torture! I remember one night when she was about four months, we'd been passing her back and forth all night and we'd both had it. We placed Larissa in the middle of our bed and knelt to pray. We said, 'Father, we're too tired to do this anymore. We need Your help. You gave her to us and we've done our best, but right now we'd really like to throw her out the window. So please help us.' Of course we'd *never* really do something like that, but we were at the end of our endurance that night. We felt like terrible parents for not knowing what to do and for being so frustrated and helpless. We hadn't learned yet that every parent has really tough moments that test patience to the very limit. And we certainly didn't realize that it was okay to put our crying baby in the crib and leave the room for a while. Or to call someone for help. Anyway, after the prayer, Marie-Thérèse picked her up and Larissa fell suddenly asleep. It was a miracle. Prayer didn't usually work that quickly for us, but it did that night. Our next step would have been to call Marie-Thérèse's mother."

"Out the window, huh?" Raoul said with a grimace. He sat on a chair and put his elbows on the table, propping up his head with his hands. "Yeah, I know what you mean. I've been thinking I'm a pretty horrible father for feeling so frustrated. But I'd never hurt her, either. Not a chance."

"Of course not. That's why you're here. You learned to ask for help a lot sooner than we did." Mathieu opened the cupboard and pulled out a bottle of orange-pineapple soda. "How's this? It's my favorite. Marie-Thérèse likes well-balanced diets, so we don't drink much soda, but this is a special occasion. Your introduction, so to speak into fatherhood."

Raoul nodded his acceptance of the beverage. "But hey, I've had her a week," he said, "I'm hardly new at this."

"Well, the honeymoon is over," Mathieu said. "From here on out it only gets harder." He filled two glasses with ice and brought them to the table. "Funny thing is, it's all worth it. When they put their little arms around your neck, or when they look up at you with that trusting stare— you're a lucky man, Raoul." His voice became choked and he hurriedly busied himself with pouring the soda, not meeting Raoul's eyes.

Raoul understood in that instant how much Mathieu missed Nadia. It wasn't just Marie-Thérèse who suffered. "Thanks, Mathieu," he said, hoping to convey so much more than a simple thanks for a drink.

Mathieu smiled and leaned back. "There, see? She's done it. Marie-Thérèse is good with babies when they're upset."

Raoul hadn't even noticed that Nadia had quit crying until Mathieu pointed it out. "You don't think something's really wrong, do you?"

"No. Babies like routines and hers has been upset a lot lately. She's young but she still feels it. But you can trust Marie-Thérèse's instincts." He grinned. "My wife can smell a sick baby from across the city. Our children have been to the doctor more times than I can count, but she's kept them safe so I trust what she feels. A few times, it's been a little overkill, but I'd rather be safe than sorry."

"I understand why—Brandon's almost died several times."

Mathieu took a long sip of soda. "Yes. He's allergic to so much. It was the flour this time, and the bananas. We're hoping he grows out of some of the allergies. Marie-Thérèse sees that he gets what he should and stays away from what he's allergic to. Luckily, he's an obedient child. If Larissa had been the one with the allergies . . ." He gave a short laugh and let the subject drop.

In the ensuing silence, they heard a faint voice singing a lullaby. Both men listened for a long while without speaking until the song faded away. Then Raoul said, "I never knew silence could sound so good."

Mathieu refilled Raoul's cup. "Don't get used to it. You've got a long way to go."

Marie-Thérèse came into the kitchen, gliding along so she wouldn't wake the baby. "It's colic," she said with certainty.

"Colic?"

"Yeah. Basically the fancy name for gas. I rubbed her tummy while she was on my arm like this and I think the pressure helped."

"Will it be gone tomorrow?" Raoul asked, not daring to touch the baby who slept stomach-down on Marie-Thérèse's arm, her tiny legs and arms dangling on each side.

"I don't know. Hope so. But if not, she'll grow out of it eventually. It took Larissa about four months of nightly fits if I remember correctly."

"Only four months?" groaned Mathieu. "Don't you mean years?"

Marie-Thérèse laughed softly. "It certainly seemed like it at the time."

"Thank you so much for letting us in," Raoul said. "I'm really sorry for disturbing you. I didn't know what else to do. I guess I would have taken her to my mother or to the emergency room next."

"Any time you need help, you're welcome to show up here," Marie-Thérèse said, easing into a chair. "I really mean that."

"I know you do." Raoul felt guilty

Without disturbing Nadia, Marie-Thérèse carefully transferred the baby to her chest, stomach still facing downward. She looked at Mathieu. "Will you get me a blanket?" she asked. "Now that she's resting, I don't want her to get cold."

While Mathieu vanished into the hall, Raoul said, "I have one in the car."

"That's okay. I have plenty."

When Mathieu returned, Raoul watched them gently tuck the blanket around Nadia, still cradled against Marie-Thérèse's chest. "Well," he said with reluctance. "Guess I'd better get going."

"You can stay here tonight." Marie-Thérèse arms curled tightly around the small body.

"Well, I don't like leaving Rebekka." Raoul sighed. "Problem is, Nadia's going to wake up when I put her in the car, isn't she? Or when I take her out."

"Probably." Marie-Thérèse hesitated before continuing. "You could leave her here. Go home get a good night's sleep and come back in the morning."

"I wouldn't want to impose."

"It's okay, really," Mathieu said. "We'll take good care of her."

"Please," Marie-Thérèse added.

Raoul looked back and forth between them and understood how serious they were. Even more, he suspected that Marie-Thérèse was desperate for him to leave Nadia. Could she be more worried about

Nadia's crying than she let on? Or did she just want to make sure? Were her motherly instincts kicking in? *Probably*, he decided. *And there's not a thing wrong with that. Nadia can use all the mothering she can get.*

"You may not get any sleep," he warned.

Marie-Thérèse shrugged. "I'm used to that."

Raoul smiled. "Then, yes. I accept. And thank you. I'll sleep better knowing she's all right. But call me if anything happens, okay?"

"Of course."

At Marie-Thérèse contented expression, Raoul was glad he had allowed Nadia to stay.

"Oh, Mathieu, give him the folder from the hospital," Marie-Thérèse said as Raoul was about to leave. "I've been meaning to give it to you all week, Raoul. I might as well do it right now since I'm remembering. It's a copy of the DNA results—though they're not really needed now, and the reports and blood work from the doctor they took Nadia to before she came here."

Raoul accepted the file Mathieu retrieved from a drawer by the telephone. "Thanks. I just hope I don't lose them on the way to the car."

"You sure you don't want to sack out here?" Mathieu invited.

"No. Then I really would be intruding." Raoul gently touched his daughter's head. "Besides, Rebekka may need me. Thanks again."

Mathieu walked him to the door, and Raoul left, feeling more than a little guilty. He would have to learn to deal with Nadia if he was going to raise her. He couldn't keep running to Marie-Thérèse. "It's just this once," he promised himself. Then he laughed. "I'll call Mom next time."

As he rode down in the elevator, he searched through the medical folder Mathieu had given him. Most of it he didn't understand, but when he read the results of the blood work, he felt a sudden coldness in his heart. *No*, he told himself. *I'm just remembering wrong. There isn't a problem here.*

Nevertheless, he worried about it all the way home. Rebekka was asleep and he wasn't going to wake her, though with all her research into blood compatibility because of her husband's kidney problems she could likely resolve his concerns.

He snapped his fingers. "I know—the Internet." A person could find just about anything on the Internet.

In Rebekka's office, he switched on the computer closest to the window—the one that had belonged to Marc and that Rebekka had so graciously offered for his use since he had moved in. There hadn't been space to hook up his own equipment, and since Marc's computer was already connected to the network at their firm, and through that to the Internet, he had only needed to adjust a few passwords and transfer his own files to make the computer useful.

He drummed his fingers on the desk as he waited for the connection to go through. In a few minutes, he would learn the truth.

* * *

Marie-Thérèse lay on her bed with Nadia still on her chest. The small weight of the child was comforting to her, and the steady breathing reassuring.

Mathieu sat on the edge of the bed. "Are you going to hold her all night like that?" he asked.

"Do you mind terribly? I just miss her so much."

"Of course not. But I'd like a chance at her too."

Marie-Thérèse laughed softly. "Okay then. You can hold her while I go check on the other children, but I get her when I'm done."

"Deal." They transferred the baby to his chest.

Marie-Thérèse checked first on Brandon and then on Celisse. She even peeked into Larissa's room and listened for her breathing. "All safe and sound," she said when she returned to her bedroom. Instead of taking Nadia from Mathieu, she dimmed the lamp, curled up next to him, and put a hand on the baby's back. Full of love, she didn't think about tomorrow, about having to give Nadia up again. Tonight she would live only for the moment.

"Is it wrong to be grateful for colic?" she whispered.

Mathieu smiled. "I just had the same thought."

* * *

Raoul stared at the information on his computer screen, willing it to change. But he knew it wouldn't—he had already played out the Blood Type Calculator program five times, and each time had verified the results.

Nadia wasn't his daughter.

According to the report Marie-Thérèse had given him, her blood type was A. There was no way a woman with O blood like Desirée and a man with B like himself could have an offspring with type A blood. Period. He and Desirée could have given birth to children that were either O or B, but not A. If he'd had AB blood like his sister and Mother, then it would have been possible, or even A like his father, but he didn't. Since there was no doubt about Desirée being the natural mother, the only conclusion he could come to was that he wasn't the natural father.

The thought brought more pain than he believed possible. They were divorced, and he thought he might one day forgive Desirée . . . but for this? Not only had she hidden Nadia from him, but the baby wasn't even his!

Raoul printed up the relevant pages and broke the connection with the Internet. Burying his face in his hands, he cried. He cried for Marie-Thérèse and Mathieu, he cried for himself, he cried for Desirée. But most of all, he cried for innocent little Nadia, who had done nothing to deserve any of this chaos.

She wasn't his daughter, and yet he felt that she was. And how could he now give her back to Desirée? That was unthinkable. But to have a constant reminder of his wife's infidelities was also unthinkable

Raoul pulled at his hair, his thoughts rushing together like waves in a storm. Abruptly, he stood and ran from the room. Before he realized what he was doing, he was in his car, the urge to sleep driven from his body. He drove to Marie-Thérèse and Mathieu's, but he didn't go inside. He sat staring at the windows to their apartment, trying to feel Nadia. His bitterness grew and his tears came ceaselessly. He couldn't remember feeling so betrayed at any time during his marriage—which from the beginning had been a sham.

He shoved his car into gear and drove on, not knowing where he was heading. To his surprise, he ended up outside the apartment Valerie shared with a friend. Early morning light was beginning to feather across the sky, reflecting off the thin cloud cover.

Raoul forced himself to wait another hour before emerging from the car. The crisp morning air was cold as it always was this time of year and Raoul's thin sweater did little to protect him. He glanced in the back seat to see if he had left his jacket there, but all he saw was Nadia's car seat and her blanket. More pain knifed through him. What was he going to do?

The door to the apartment lobby had been prevented from closing with a small rock—likely by one of the inhabitants who had gone to make a quick errand nearby, and Raoul let himself in. He felt rather nervous as he rang Valerie's doorbell. She answered herself, wearing soft-looking pink thermal pajamas and with her long black hair tousled from sleep.

"Raoul?" she said in surprise. Her smile was welcoming and her beautiful hazel eyes showed honest concern.

"Val, I need . . ." He didn't know what he needed. To his chagrin, the tears returned. She opened her arms and without hesitation he fell into them. For long moments she silently held him as he sobbed in her arms.

When at last he was calmer, she led him to the couch in her sitting room. The furniture there was well-used, but clean and attractive. There were splashes of color in the room—a floral display, a wall-hanging, a hand-woven carpet—that Raoul felt sure were Valerie's contributions. They were vibrant and alive, much like Valerie herself. Suddenly, he couldn't take his eyes from her, and marveled at how beautiful she looked to him just out of bed.

"What happened?" she asked. They had separated, but she still held Raoul's arm, giving him immense comfort.

"It's Nadia," he said, launching into an explanation.

She listened carefully and then spoke in the sincere, thoughtful way that had made her so valuable at work. "You don't want to give her back, do you? And yet, you don't know if you can act like a father with a daily reminder of what Desirée did."

He nodded. "I want to raise her more than anything. She's a part of Desirée and I loved her so much—once. But when I think about Nadia not being my biological daughter I feel a huge resentment." He took Valerie's hand and began to stroke the softness. "I knew Desirée was unfaithful, but the idea of her actually having a baby with another man while we were married . . . It's just more than I can take. I feel too angry inside at her. Like it's consuming me. What if I raised Nadia and that resentment came through? What if I made her life as miserable as her mother made mine? She doesn't deserve that. None of this is her fault!" He paused, searching Valerie's face. Did she think he was a monster? He sighed. "I love Nadia. I felt connected to her and yet, now . . . Oh, I don't know! A part of me wishes that I could give her to Marie-Thérèse and Mathieu. They are already in love with her and they wouldn't have all these complicated feelings. Yet, what kind of a man gives up his daughter? Or at least a child he thought was his daughter. Besides, it's not my right to give her to them anyway."

"You're worried that Desirée will never agree to put her up for adoption."

"Exactly." He looked up from where her finely-boned hand lay cradled in his own. "Yet I know she doesn't want a baby. She told me herself that she would have gotten an abortion if not for me. So I can't let her go back to Desirée—which is exactly what will happen if I tell anyone the truth. But how can I live a lie? Every day of my life I'll see Nadia and remember."

Valerie shook her head. "I don't believe you would ever resent Nadia, though I wouldn't blame you if you did."

"But I do! I resent her!" Raoul said in agony. "That's just the point! And I feel miserable about it. All these weeks of searching and suffering, not knowing where she was, wondering if she was even dead." He gazed at Valerie earnestly, willing her to understand. "I wondered what it felt like to feel her first kick, her heartbeat, to see her born. And then in the end she's not even my child! I'm so . . . so furious at all the emotions Desirée put me through! How dare she!" He clenched and unclenched his jaws several times and then said more softly. "I don't know what to do."

Valerie was quiet as though searching for an answer. Then she said, "We'll think about it, pray about it. There *has* to be an answer—one that will give you peace and Nadia a good family."

"I don't know that I can give her that," he said heavily, "and yet there seems to be no other option." He tightened his hold on her hand. "Do you hate me for what I've said?" he asked softly.

She shook her head. "No, Raoul. I'm glad you're honest. But I still don't believe you would ever take it out on Nadia. But maybe it's too much to ask—that you raise Desirée's child when she was so terrible to you. There must to be another way."

"Then I don't know what it is."

"Neither do I. But we'll find it."

Raoul looked at her, his heart feeling warm for the first time since he had discovered the truth. Having Valerie to talk to brought an entirely new dimension into his life. He had been so alone these past years of his marriage, despite the support from family. He had attended church alone, prayed alone, and most of the time slept alone. But here she was giving him the support and companionship he so desperately craved.

Valerie's eyes widened as he closed the distance between them. Her eyes were her most vibrant feature, full of life and warmth and something else that Raoul had searched for futilely in Desirée's. "I think I'm going to kiss you," he murmured. "So maybe you'd better leave."

"I'm not going anywhere." She titled her head and her shiny black hair rippled down her back. Raoul shoved his hands in the silky mass and drew her to him.

They kissed for a long moment and when they drew apart he stared at her, amazed at the depth of his emotion. She smiled and lazily opened her eyes. "I could get used to that."

He hugged her, one hand still tangled in her hair. "Thank you for being here, Valerie. Thank you so much." He leaned forward to kiss her again.

The phone rang and Valerie broke away, laughing self-consciously. "Who would be calling so early?" she wondered aloud. "Uh, you'll have to let go of my hand if I'm going to answer. I should hurry before my roommate wakes up."

Reluctantly, Raoul let her go, knowing his problems would only come rushing back.

She retrieved the portable phone from the kitchen and returned to the sitting room. "Yeah, he's here," she was saying. She put her hand over the bottom part of the phone and said to Raoul. "It's your sister." Releasing her hand, she continued talking to Rebekka. "Oh?" Again she covered the speaker. "She was worried because she thought you hadn't come home, but then she saw the pages you left in the office and your notes. She's been worried sick."

"Let me talk to her."

Valerie spoke into the phone. "He wants to talk to you. Just a minute."

"Hi," Raoul said.

"Raoul, I've been so worried! I've been calling your cell, and I called Mom and Dad and the office. Have you been there the entire time?"

"I left the cell in my jacket—wherever that is. And, no, I've mostly been driving. I just got here about a half hour ago."

"How's Nadia?"

"Fine, I guess. I couldn't get her to stop crying last night, so I took her to Marie-Thérèse's. She fell asleep there, so I left her with them."

"So do they know?"

"Know what?"

"That Nadia's not your daughter?"

He heaved a great sigh and was gratified when Valerie took his free hand. "No. They don't. What would it help? But Rebekka, I don't know if I can do this!"

"You mean raise Nadia?"

"Yeah." Raoul repeated all the things he had told Valerie. He felt mean and small inside, but was glad Rebekka didn't seem to hate him.

"Then you wouldn't mind if Marie-Thérèse and Mathieu adopted her?"

Raoul thought for a moment, feeling pain at the words, but also a great relief. "Yes, I guess that's right. She would be close enough for me to check up on, but not so close to bring back constant pain—the hatred

I feel right now at knowing she's not mine. But it's never going to happen. The minute Desirée knows I have no claim to her, she'll be free to take Nadia, to give her to her parents, sell her to the highest bidder, or to raise her herself. And how can I resign innocent little Nadia to a life like that? A life without the gospel or any values at all—driven only by money and self-gratification? I love Nadia too much for that."

"Wait a minute," Rebekka said. "Let me think. Okay, now, in the divorce settlement, was Nadia named specifically, or did it say your child or something like that?"

"She was named. I got custody and Desirée got the trust fund I set up for her."

"Then if she fights for Nadia, she loses the trust, right?"

Now Raoul understood. "Yeah, I think that's the way we worded it. Do you think she might agree to let me find a home for Nadia if I allow her to keep the money?"

"I don't know, but I can talk to her. See how she reacts." Rebekka was silent a moment, and then, "But I really do think there's something you're overlooking here."

"What's that?"

"I think Desirée loves Nadia and wants the best for her. I think that's the real reason she gave her to you."

Raoul could see that Desirée had certainly fooled his sister, but he didn't want to hurt Rebekka by saying so. "So you think she'll give up Nadia a second time because it's the best thing for her?" Raoul couldn't help the bitterness that seeped through.

"I don't know. I hope so. And the money can be our trump card."

"What makes you think she would do the right thing?"

There was a long pause. "I never told you, but while you were at church last Sunday, Desirée came over. She'd heard that we'd found Nadia and came to ask you if she could see her—just to make sure she was all right. She was having nightmares and couldn't sleep. I—I let her hold Nadia for a minute, and after that she seemed ready to go on with her life and to stay out of Nadia's. She didn't even want to visit so she wouldn't be confused. I think she meant it."

Raoul clenched his teeth, fighting his anger. He didn't know if he was more angry at Rebekka for letting Desirée see Nadia, or for not telling him she had visited.

"Relax, Raoul," Rebekka said, sensing his mood. "She needed to see for herself that Nadia was all right. I didn't think that was too much to ask, seeing as she was willing to give her up completely."

Raoul forced his anger down. There was no use taking out his frustrations on his sister, who had done nothing but offer love and support during the past few years. "Okay, what do you think we should do?"

"Let me talk to Desirée—alone. I'll call her parents and they'll know how to reach her. You stay where you are or go get Nadia. But don't come home until I call you."

"Are you sure this is going to work?" he asked.

"If it doesn't we'll fight her with everything we've got," Rebekka said without emotion. "We have the money and we will fight. And if we have to, we will raise Nadia ourselves, and we will love every minute of it."

There was no room for arguing; Raoul knew it from her voice. "If anyone can pull this off, you can," he said. "I was always good at business, but you know people."

"I'm good at languages, that's all," she countered. "Even those people don't speak."

As Raoul hung up, he wondered what she meant. Could Rebekka really see something in Desirée that others couldn't? Something in the way she moved or spoke?

"Tell me," Valerie said, interrupting his thoughts.

"She's going to talk to Desirée. Oh, Valerie, what if this isn't the right thing to do? Desirée is so unpredictable—and this is Nadia's life we're talking about."

"How does your heart feel?" she asked.

He had to think about the question. "It feels that Nadia belongs with a family who can love her fully— not with me. And that hurts. It hurts a lot." Tears came into his eyes, blurring her face.

"Wherever Nadia ends up," Valerie said, touching his face with her soft hand, "you still saved her life. By being the person you are, Desirée let her live. That's something—even if you can't be her father."

Raoul felt infinite comfort knowing she spoke the truth. In some way he *had* contributed to Nadia's life—more perhaps than even her biological father. But this thought brought up another concern. What about the natural father? Would he have some claim to the Nadia? Did Desirée even know who he was?

Chapter 30

Rebekka spent more than an hour tracking down Desirée. Her parents gave her the number of a friend where she was supposed to be staying and that friend gave her the number of the bar where Desirée worked. The bartender in turn gave her the name of another employee he thought might know where she was. When Rebekka called there, Desirée herself answered.

"I need to talk to you right away," Rebekka said. "It's urgent."

"About Nadia?"

"Yes, actually. She's all right, but there are some complications you should know about."

"Does Raoul know you're calling me? Isn't this something he should deal with?"

"I know he has custody, but this is something you need to know. And, yes, he knows I'm calling."

"Can't you just tell me?"

"No. Please, Desirée, I need to see you. Can you come to my house? I've been put on bed rest for medical reasons, and I can't get around too well."

"I have to work at one."

"That's okay. It shouldn't take long."

Rebekka hung up and called André. As she told him what had happened, she realized how much she'd missed him in the brief time they had been separated. There was still a tension between them, but both steered clear of any discussion of their future. Rebekka knew it was only a matter of time until he brought it up again . . . and then she would have to disappoint him.

And why should I have to disappoint him? something inside her asked. *He's right when he says there's something between us. I do care about him—I love him even. I love the way he looks at me, the way he smiles, the way he takes my hand . . .* Rebekka shook her head free of the thoughts, dredging up a picture of Marc. He was her husband—she could never forget that fact . . . or him.

"Do you want me to come over?" André asked.

Rebekka started from her thoughts. "I don't think so. From what I remember, Desirée doesn't like you too well."

André chuckled. "Only because I didn't appreciate her not-too-subtle invitations."

"I think she's changing."

"Didn't you say she's still working at a bar?"

"Yes. I thought she had decided to find other work but I guess she didn't yet."

"Just be careful, okay? Call me if you need me. I have to take the girls shopping for clothes today, but I'll have my cell."

"I wish I could come with you. I'd rather shop than face Desirée any time."

"There's always next year." His voice didn't hold any innuendos, and Rebekka marveled at his assurance. How could he know there would be a next year for them?

"Well, wish me luck," she said.

"I'll call you later."

Rebekka didn't shower as it was becoming increasing difficult to do so without considerable pain. Instead, she dressed and promised herself a long leisurely bath when it was all over. She felt confused, wondering if what she planned to do was the right thing. Finally, she knelt at her bed—awkwardly and painfully—begging the Lord to help her. Nadia was her first concern, but Desirée, too, was a daughter of God.

When Desirée arrived, Rebekka was calmer. She still didn't know in what direction to lead the conversation, but she felt sure the Lord would guide her. "Come on in," she said to Desirée. "Let's go into the sitting room where we can be comfortable. Don't mind me if I hobble behind. And take the chair, would you? I need to lie on the couch."

Desirée laughed but sounded nervous. "So," she said when Rebekka was settled on the couch, "we've got to stop meeting like this."

Rebekka smiled, though she didn't feel happy. "Well, I don't suppose it will happen too many more times."

"What happened to you anyway?" Desirée asked. "What have you got?"

"I have a large cyst on my ovary. It's causing a lot of pain."

"Can't they do anything?"

"Well, they can do surgery, but it's dangerous for the baby. So are the medications to help the pain." Rebekka sighed. "So I'm waiting. There's a chance it'll go away on it's own. Or worsen. I have to go in every week to the doctor."

Desirée combed back her hair with her hands and smoothed the tight short skirt and white blouse that Rebekka assumed was her barmaid outfit. At least today her makeup was subdued. "When I was pregnant with Nadia, I quit drinking and all of that. It was hard, but I figured I owed it to her."

"You did a good thing. She's small, but very healthy."

"She was born a bit early."

Rebekka nodded. "Last night, she started crying a lot. Usually Raoul and I can get her calmed down easily, but she wouldn't hear of it. He took her driving and ended up at Marie-Thérèse's."

"I bet she got her quiet."

"That's right. Nadia's really attached to Marie-Thérèse and Mathieu, and they to her."

Desirée's brown eyes narrowed. "What are you saying?"

Rebekka gnawed on the inside of her bottom lip, not knowing how to continue.

"Tell me," Desirée demanded. Her insistence made Rebekka wonder if she had suspected all along that Nadia wasn't Raoul's. Maybe this was all a game to her.

The anger Rebekka hadn't allowed herself to feel grew in her heart. Raoul hadn't asked for anything other than Desirée's love. He hadn't made church attendance a requisite to their relationship, he hadn't forced her to dress a certain way. All he had asked was her faithfulness.

"Raoul is not Nadia's biological father," Rebekka said.

Shock ran over Desirée's face. "What! But . . . it can't be . . . I—" She broke off as the full realization of the situation rendered her speechless.

"So who is the father?" Rebekka shot at her. "And how could you have been so sure it was Raoul if you were involved in another relationship?"

"I—I . . . There was someone. A foreigner. He was only in town for a few days—I don't remember his name. We met at a bar. He was nice and Raoul and I had fought and I was lonely."

"Don't make excuses," Rebekka said. "Just answer my question. Why did you think Raoul was the father?"

"He told me he'd had an operation, and I was careful. I'm not stupid."

This was too much for Rebekka. "You're not stupid? You gave up a decent, caring man for someone whose name you don't even know?

Desirée, what were you thinking!"

"I wasn't thinking! I wasn't!" Desirée jumped to her feet, her fists in tight balls by her side. "I know that now. I was wrong. Wrong! And if I had it to do over, I would change." She began to cry. "But that doesn't do my baby any good . . . or Raoul or myself. Oh, what have I done?" The suffering on her face was unfeigned. "I've held it together thinking that at least I did something for Raoul, that Nadia somehow paid back all the bad things I did to him, but now I don't have even that!" Desirée collapsed into the chair and began to cry.

Rebekka stared helplessly as Desirée poured out her misery. She wanted to comfort the other woman, but was frozen to the couch. There was simply too much self pity in her words and actions. "Desirée," she said firmly. "Desirée, look at me."

The sniffling ceased. "I don't know where the man is," Desirée said. "Besides, I know he had a family. He wouldn't like a daughter showing up out of nowhere."

Rebekka's breath caught in her throat. She hadn't even thought about Nadia's biological father wanting her, taking her away from them. "How can you even think that way! We love Nadia—all of us. And we're not about to hand her over to some foreign stranger who cheats on his own family."

"I said I don't know who he is or where he is," Desirée said. "We couldn't find him if we tried."

Rebekka bit her tongue to stop herself from saying hateful words. How Desirée could have done something so heinous to Raoul was beyond comprehension. No wonder Raoul was reluctant to raise Nadia! How could he not be continually reminded of Desirée's betrayal? Why should he have to suffer the rest of his life for Desirée's sins? And why should Nadia?

"Now we have to decide what to do," Rebekka said slowly.

"But you said you weren't willing to give her up. So Raoul can keep her, right?"

Rebekka swallowed hard. "Is that fair, Desirée? Is it fair for him to endure a constant reminder of the pain you caused? If Nadia was his daughter, then he could find joy in their relationship, but—"

"He'll still love her! I know he will!"

"Yes, he would! But there would still be the pain. Don't you see that this isn't fair to him or to Nadia? She deserves complete love, not one hampered by memories of betrayal."

"He'd do it," Desirée said. "He won't let her come back to me. I know that much."

"Ah, that's it, isn't it? And you're right. He'll fight you for her, even knowing it isn't right for him. Because he loves her."

"Our divorce papers say that Nadia's his. It doesn't say our biological children."

Rebekka nearly choked. She'd been holding that information back, but obviously Desirée was accustomed to finding the bottom line.

"And he could take away the trust fund," Desirée went on.

"Last time you came to see Nadia, you said you couldn't be a mother. Do you still feel that way? Or has this information changed your feelings?"

Desirée looked down at her hands. "No," she said in a whisper. "I tried. I can't do it. Not now anyway."

"You also told me you don't want your parents to have her."

Desirée considered a moment. "No. They're too hard." She looked into the distance as though staring at something out of Rebekka's sight. "I wish they hadn't been so hard." Her focus returned. "No, I won't agree to have them take her. So it's either Raoul or me. And we all know who'll be the better parent."

"There is another option."

Desirée looked at her blankly. Then her eyes widened. "No. I can't give her up to strangers."

"What if they aren't strangers? What if they gave you updates and sent pictures each year? What if you gave them a letter to give Nadia when she turns eighteen?" Rebekka sensed Desirée was open to hearing more. "Remember what I was saying about how attached Marie-Thérèse and Mathieu are to Nadia? What about letting them raise her? They love her so much already—they were crushed when they learned they couldn't adopt her."

Desirée's expression grew hopeful. "Marie-Thérèse is a little bit of a neat freak, but she was always kind. She never judged me."

"Nadia would have siblings who love her. And Raoul and I see the family often. We can make sure everything is going well." Rebekka leaned forward to entreat her further. "I know that a lot of what happened doesn't seem to make sense, Desirée. But when you think about how Nadia went to stay with Celisse and then both of them went to Marie-Thérèse before it was discovered they weren't sisters. Well, doesn't it all make sense now? I believe the Lord knew exactly what He was doing and part of that was preparing us all for what would come next. I think placing Nadia with Marie-Thérèse and Mathieu would be one of the best things you could do for your daughter . . . and for Raoul."

Desirée's eyes were wet, but the tears didn't fall. "I do love her, Rebekka."

"I know that. That's why you were willing to give her to Raoul."

"He'd make a great father."

"Well, now he'll make a great uncle. Since I'd be Nadia's aunt, he's kind of an uncle."

Desirée nodded once, firmly. "Okay. I'll do it. But I get the pictures and I do want to write a letter. I want her to understand that even though I wasn't ready for her to come, I did love her enough to give her life."

"And to give her to a good family."

Desirée nodded without speaking.

"You won't be allowed to contact her until she's an adult," Rebekka said. "But I believe Marie-Thérèse and Mathieu will be very open about who you are and sympathetic when telling her about your situation. I think when the time comes, she'll want to see you."

"Okay," Desirée repeated, wiping her eyes. "Draw up the papers and I'll sign them. Just let me know when." She arose. "Don't worry, I can see myself out."

At the door to the sitting room she paused. "Rebekka, can you do one thing for me? I know I asked you before to tell Nadia that I loved her—I think you're the only person who really understands that. But can you also tell her that I took care of her for the first two months of her life, that I rocked her to sleep and sang her songs? That I . . . bought her a rattle? It said 'Mommy loves me.'" Her voice broke on the last few words. She took a deep, shuddering breath. "And tell Raoul . . . well, tell him I'm really, really sorry."

"I will. I promise."

Rebekka watched Desirée leave and then cried for a long time for the opportunities lost. But the tears were also for the hope of young Nadia's life. Then she dried her face and called Raoul at Valerie's.

"Well?" he asked anxiously.

"I ended up telling her the whole story. She said she'd sign the papers for Marie-Thérèse and Mathieu to adopt Nadia. She wants pictures and updates, but we can do that through the lawyers or I'll volunteer to be the contact since I'd like to keep track of her anyway—I sort of promised myself I'd do that. And she wants to write a letter to give to Nadia when she's older."

"Thank you. You're a miracle worker."

"It wasn't that difficult. Desirée wants what's best for Nadia."

"You mean she wants the money."

"I didn't even bring that up."

"She's no dummy. She would have made the connection."

Rebekka didn't confirm his belief. Yes, Desirée wasn't the most upstanding person, but Rebekka had found something in her that was worth saving. "I'll let you tell Marie-Thérèse and Mathieu."

"Valerie and I will go over there now." He paused. "Oh, Rebekka, this is going to be so hard. I really do love Nadia."

"I know." She let a lighter note creep into her voice. "Hey, maybe ask them if we can baby-sit once a week or something. At least for a while."

"Maybe I will."

Rebekka hung up the phone, marveling at how everything had turned out. Oh, there would likely be problems ahead, but at least Nadia would have the family she deserved, and Raoul could go on with his life.

She sighed. "If only my life could have such a happy ending."

Struggling to her feet, she shuffled down the hall to her office to stare at the painting of her and Marc by the Seine River. Since the painting was done at a distance, it wasn't too difficult to mistake Marc for André; though there was much about them that was different, the family resemblance was strong.

For the first time Rebekka wondered what would have happened if she hadn't gone to Marc that day to tell him she loved him. What if she had chosen to pursue her feelings for André instead? Almost immediately, guilt slammed into her heart.

I didn't mean it, Marc. I loved you—I still love you. And I wouldn't trade our time together for anything. Please forgive me.

Rebekka left the room, even more firm in her resolve. Somehow she would have to give up André—again. Somehow she would have to make him understand.

* * *

Raoul was glad Valerie accompanied him to Marie-Thérèse's, though he was disappointed to see her hair pulled back and the neat jeans and sweater replacing the pink pajamas. He preferred the disheveled appearance of earlier; it seemed to create an intimacy between them that he had long yearned for. Could she be feeling the same way? Was he crazy to trust another woman? He thought so, but strangely he *did* trust Valerie. At work she had never let the company down, and to his knowledge she had always fulfilled her church callings—would she treat their relationship with the same respect? Raoul wasn't sure he wanted to know. What if . . .

Stop, he told himself. *Tonight is only your first date.* He laughed aloud.

"What is it?" Valerie asked from the passenger side of his car."

"I was thinking that tonight is our first date, and I never kiss on a first date. But today we've . . ." He let the sentence dangle.

Her sweet laughter filled him with warmth. "Raoul, we already know each other well. But if it makes you feel better, we won't kiss again."

"Oh, no you don't!" They laughed together.

At Marie-Thérèse's they were met with smiles, but also with veiled reluctance. The family was gathered around the table for lunch when they arrived, with Mathieu holding the baby. Marie-Thérèse quickly took her away to hug and kiss her. Raoul could see Marie-Thérèse and the older children blinking away the tears. Little Celisse glared at him with wide, accusing eyes.

For that, he was glad at his news, but seeing Nadia and knowing he had to give her up, nearly made him change his mind. He strengthened himself by remembering the night the family had brought Nadia to him, ending the anguish he suffered. Could he not show the same courage now that their situation was reversed?

He didn't take the baby when Marie-Thérèse offered her. "I don't know how to begin," he said. "Well, I might as well just say it: Nadia is not my daughter."

Marie-Thérèse gasped, her light brown eyes growing large.

"I found out after you gave me those papers last night," he added.

"The DNA?" asked Mathieu.

"No, the blood test. Our types don't match."

In a brief, to-the-point explanation, he gave them the details of the night's discovery, leaving out his own turmoil. When he began to talk about Desirée and how she had agreed to allow them to adopt Nadia, tears poured from Marie-Thérèse's eyes. Brandon jumped up and shouted, twirling Celisse in the air, and Larissa hugged her father, wiping her tears on his T-shirt.

"I'll have my lawyer work out the papers," he said. But the family was too happy to hear the details. They were talking and laughing with one another and cooing baby talk to Nadia.

Raoul stopped talking and watched them, feeling a warmth in his chest—a confirmation that he had done the right thing. Silently, he walked up to Marie-Thérèse and kissed Nadia, not trusting himself to hold her one last time as her father, knowing he might not be able to let go. He turned to leave.

"Wait!" Marie-Thérèse said. "Thank you!"

Mathieu took a step toward him. "Yes, thank you. We know this isn't easy. We know it only too well."

"You're right," Raoul said shortly, "but it's the right thing to do."

Valerie took his hand in hers as they left the apartment. "Come on," she said, "let's get an early start on our date. I know the perfect place for lunch."

Her hand squeezed his and the broken place in his heart began to mend.

Chapter 31

December, three weeks later

Rebekka sat in the rocking chair on the cabin porch, watching Marc as he chopped wood for the fire. They were celebrating their second wedding anniversary, and Rebekka couldn't believe how happy she was. Even the fact that she had failed to become pregnant once again hadn't dimmed her anticipation of the trip with her husband.

He threw down the ax and approached the porch, wearing only jeans and a T-shirt that showed wet where his perspiration had seeped through. Bundled in a sweater and blanket, she wondered that he wasn't cold.

"Hi there," he said, climbing the few stairs. He gave her a lingering kiss and she tasted the salt on his lips from his wood-chopping efforts.

"Good work. We won't be cold tonight," she said.

"Hey, last night wasn't bad. You had me to keep you warm."

She stood and hugged him. "You're all I'll ever need." She meant it, too, but suddenly he drew away and began pacing the small porch. Rebekka sat again in the rocking chair.

After a while, she said, "Are you going to quit pacing and tell me what's wrong? Or do you like keeping me in suspense?"

"Sorry." He stopped pacing and leaned against the waist-high railing. "I was just thinking."

"Uh-oh."

He grinned. "No, it's not bad, really. It's just that everything is so excellent between us. Everything. It's better than I ever imagined—and I am pretty good in the imagination department."

"I'll say. So what's wrong with everything being so good?"

"Nothing. It's just . . . Rebekka, do you believe that anything could be too perfect? That perhaps we're being prepared for something. That maybe we don't have fights or problems because the Lord knows we won't have time to . . . well, to get through them?"

She didn't like this vein of thought. She made her response teasing. "Marc, we do have problems. Just the other day you bought another plant for me to forget to water. And two nights ago you refused to go out to eat escargot with me."

"Hey, that was your fault! If you hadn't looked so ravishing, we wouldn't have decided to have a quiet night at home."

"Marc!" Then she giggled.

"You see? We are perfect. Life is perfect."

She became more serious, "Well, we don't have a baby yet."

"So? We can adopt. I don't see that being a problem in the long run."

She stood from the chair and went to him, wrapping her arms around his now-shivering form. "It's the way we look at things, that's all. Our attitude."

He snuggled in closer. "Maybe. But there's still that feeling I had when I followed you to Utah, the one that told me I wasn't going to have you for long."

"Well, you are older than me," she tried to keep her voice light. "Now let it go. We're together and we're happy."

"There's no other donor available if I need a kidney," he said against her neck.

"Zack or Thierry could do it. Don't look for trouble."

"I'm not. I just want you to be prepared. I love you, Rebekka. I love you more than my life. And more than anything I want you to be happy. Please remember that."

Rebekka woke from the dream, startled. It had been so real. For a moment, she could almost believe that she was back in the family cabin with Marc. She wasn't surprised to be dreaming of him so clearly; today would have been their third wedding anniversary. The entire previous evening she had been thinking of him, talking aloud to him as though he were alive. She closed her eyes and tried to recapture the vivid dream, but it was gone. Tears trickled down her face and into her pillow.

The intercom by the door buzzed loudly—and again and again. Rebekka realized bitterly that the noise was what had awakened her. If whoever it was hadn't come, she could still be reliving that happy time with Marc.

The buzzer rang again.

It was Tuesday, and since Raoul had begun going to work very early in the past three weeks since relinquishing custody of Nadia, he had likely left the apartment. That meant she had no choice but to answer the buzzing or ignore it. With the persistent way the ringing continued, she doubted the person would go away.

She moved slowly, one limb at a time, and climbed out of bed. The pain today seemed bearable, though she wondered how much longer she could endure. *Three more months*, she thought, *and then he'll be born—safely*. She clung to this thought with all the tenacity she could muster.

Now at six months along, her stomach seemed impossibly large. Her inactivity had helped add to the weight and Rebekka wondered if she would ever be able to fit into her clothes again. The thought was depressing.

While putting on her robe, a sudden pain arced along her back and shuddered throughout her entire body. *Oh, help me*, she prayed. At times she was ready to go to the doctor and beg him to remove the cyst, but each time she prayed, she knew she couldn't take the risk. Not yet. She would have only one chance for Marc's baby. One chance that meant everything.

She glanced at Marc's carved clock on the wall, surprised to see that it was only six o'clock in the morning. Who could be visiting at this hour? Even Raoul might still be home. She peeked in his room, but it was empty. *Maybe he ran out for bread and forgot his keys.*

She stabbed at the intercom with an annoyed finger. "Who is it?"

"Flower delivery."

"I'll *kill* him," she muttered, pressing the button.

She fumed as she waited for the delivery man. She had been enjoying André's company these past weeks, had appreciated how he let her avoid any serious conversation, but this was going too far. This was solid proof of how he was coming between her and her memories of Marc.

She schooled herself to be polite to the man, but when he had left, she sat at the table, letting her anger and frustration rule her emotions. Tempted to throw the entire vase of three-dozen red roses out the window, she clenched her hands together until the desire passed. Finally, she grabbed the note and ripped it open. The words chilled her blood:

> *Hi honey! Three dozen beautiful red roses for three wonderful years together. I wanted to start this day off right, and knowing how forgetful I can be, I ordered in advance—way in advance. The idea of waking you with flowers on our anniversary just came to me today, and it was such a brilliant idea, I wanted to make sure I followed through. It took some doing, but I found a flower shop willing to take my order early. Okay, I paid them extra and the owner promised me he'd take care of it himself. See? No one*

could accuse me of forgetting my gorgeous wife, whom I so completely adore. Come back to bed, love, and wake me up so we can begin celebrating our anniversary! I love you with my whole heart.

Eternally yours, Marc

There was no date on the note and Rebekka wondered how long he had written it before the accident. She felt stunned—her heart simply didn't know how to react to this assault. She removed a rose from the vase and took it and Marc's note back to bed where she wept, holding them against her chest. Logically, she knew that Marc would have never done such a thing to hurt her, and yet why had this happened? She asked herself over and over. One thing was for sure, she believed this was a sign. Marc wanted her to wait for him.

* * *

André was driving to work when a strange urgency hit him. His first thoughts were of the girls who had still been sleeping when he left the house, under their grandmother's care. He called quickly on his cell phone, but Ariana assured him they were fine.

He still couldn't relax. Then the thought came again with force—this time with a name attached: *Rebekka.*

Immediately André turned the car and headed back the way he had come. He had learned to listen to the Holy Spirit and he knew Rebekka needed him. The reason made no difference; he was compelled to her side. As he drove, he prayed. His cell phone rang as he drove up at Rebekka's.

"Hello?" he asked.

"It's Raoul. Are you about here? I know we have that important meeting this morning, but I . . . I have to go home. I need to check on Rebekka."

"I'm at your apartment now," André said. "You cover the meeting."

"Thank heaven! I just had the overwhelming feeling that—"

"Me too."

"Call me if something's wrong. We can always reschedule the meeting."

"Of course. Don't worry, I'll take care of Rebekka."

André had been ringing the apartment intercom as they spoke, but there was no reply. He removed his keys and found the one he had taken from Marc's office all those months ago after his death. He should have given them back to Rebekka, but he hadn't been able to bring himself to do so—not since the time he had found her crying and staring into space the day he had come to drive her to her doctor's appointment.

He ran up the stairs, not willing to wait for the elevator. Thoughts careened about in his head. What had happened? Was she ill? She had been fine yesterday afternoon when he and the girls had checked on her after school, though she had refused their offer of attending family night, pleading a headache. Had that been the real reason for her refusal?

Again there was no answer at the door, and André blessed the fact that he had kept the keys. He nearly burst into the apartment. "Rebekka?" he called. "Rebekka!"

No answer.

He saw a vase of roses in the kitchen, but no sign of Rebekka. *Who sent them?* he wondered, knowing they were not ones he had ordered recently. He strode down the hall, his worry increasing. "Rebekka?"

He didn't stop to look in her office, but went straight to her room. She was lying in the middle of the bed on her side, curled around one of the red roses from the kitchen. "Rebekka?" Still no answer. She looked so small there, except for the mound of her stomach, small and pale and unprotected. He touched her and was shocked at the coldness of her skin. Shaking her gently, he called her name again. Relief flooded through him as her eyes opened.

"Why?" she asked. "Why did you do that?"

André had no idea to what she was referring. He pulled a blanket around her freezing body and tried to free her hands from the rose, whose thorns had pierced her fingers, bringing drops of dark red blood. Then he saw the note, pressed up against the satin nightgown covering her swollen belly. She protested feebly when he took it, but she wouldn't let go of the rose. He read the note and finally understood.

"Oh, Rebekka," he groaned, gathering her into his arms. "It wasn't me who wrote this. You aren't dreaming. I'm André. And I'm so sorry! Marc didn't mean for this to happen—for you to receive this alone. He loved you so much!"

For a very long time André kept murmuring words and rubbing her limbs under the blanket. The warmth seeped back into her body and the color into her pale cheeks. He fell silent, but still held her, wondering where they could go next. Had this event taken her from him forever?

There were tears slipping down her cheeks now, which André took as a good sign. Now she could begin to experience the emotions, to deal with them and go on. Her next words were a heartrending blow. "I can't marry you," she said softly, glancing back at him. "Not ever. You know that now—don't you?"

He took a second to steady himself before responding, praying that he could find the right answer. "I don't see that at all. I love you, Marc loved you, and you loved us both. Now he's gone and it only makes sense for us to team together for what's left of this life. To support and love one another, to raise our children together."

Rebekka drew away from him, moving slowly as though she were too weak or in too much pain to move faster. Her tears fell in torrents now as she looked blindly in his direction. "You told me to tell you the truth, but I didn't. I asked you if it was enough for you if I married you because you looked like Marc. I told you that I might cry out his name instead of yours in my dreams. But I lied." Her teeth bit into the soft inner flesh of her bottom lip, and her hands tightened on the red rose, bending and twisting the thorny green stem. "The real reason I can't marry you, that I can't have a relationship with you, is because I love you." Her voice rose an octave and continued on shakily, "And if we spend all these years together, I might just love you more. I—you would replace Marc. I made a vow to love him forever, but how can I do that if I love you? I would be unfaithful to him, and I won't do that—I promised. I covenanted not to do that."

André felt a strange hope at her words, though on the surface she was refusing him. At least she had come to the realization that she *did* love him. That alone gave him the will to continue trying. He made his voice firm. "I know that you'd rather maintain what you see as your loyalty to Marc rather that let yourself love again. I know that you'd rather let your baby grow up without a father than let go of the guilt. But you can't let that happen, Rebekka."

"His father is dead!" she shouted. "That can never change!"

"Yes, but I'm not. I love you and I love this baby. I want to be his father. Please, you can't let your heart shrivel up inside until there's no room in it for happiness. That's not good for you and it's certainly not good for your baby."

She didn't reply, but her hands went to her stomach.

"Rebekka," he said scooting closer to her. "I know this is all too sudden, way too soon after Marc's death. And being pregnant and experiencing all the emotions that involves doesn't help. By right you should have years to mourn Marc, to come to terms with your feelings and the fact that he's gone. I remember only too well these feelings—it's one of the reasons I backed off pursuing you before you married Marc. Claire had just died and I didn't want to be unfaithful to her. But Rebekka, I realize now that if I married you I *can* be faithful to her. Because you loved her and you love our daughters. Of all the women I could choose, only you can raise them to love her and to remember her. And don't you see that I can do the same for your son? And for you? If there is one person in this world that I love as much as I love you and Claire, it would be Marc. He was my brother, my friend, and business partner. Do you think I would ever try to take him from your life? No! I want us to remember him, to talk about him, and to raise your son to know him. Please, Rebekka, hear me." He was overwhelmed with emotion, and tears started to fall.

Rebekka stared at him, gray eyes opened wide, and André began to believe he was getting through the lock she had placed over her heart. "Whether this happens between us now or in five years from now is really up to you," he continued. "I'm not going anywhere. I love you and I will always love you and be a part of your life—no matter what decision you make. But what you need to understand is that it doesn't have to be Marc *or* me; you can choose both. I know, because I love you and I still love Claire. I love to talk about her and tell the girls stories about her—you've seen that."

Rebekka nodded slowly, wonderingly. "Yes, I have."

"And we'll do the same for your son. Marc would like that. You know, I think more than anything he was afraid that you wouldn't allow yourself to be happy again—stubbornly loyal, I think he once said. But he wanted you to go on. Can't you believe that? If you love me, there's no reason to hold back."

Her grip loosened from the rose and André took it from her and set it aside. Then deliberately, he reached for her hands and began rubbing the small wounds with his fingers, obliterating the blood. Her skin was warming beneath his touch.

"I was dreaming of the cabin," she said, staring at their linked hands. "Marc and I went there last year for our second anniversary. He was talking about not finding a donor when he needed another kidney and about our life being too perfect." Her eyes rose suddenly to his. "Oh, André, he did know he was going to die, sooner or later, didn't he?"

André nodded.

"Only I didn't want to hear. I just didn't want to hear." She sounded disappointed in herself.

"That's natural, Rebekka. No one would want to hear that. But it certainly wasn't as if Marc lived every day thinking about death. He just lived the best he could, enjoying the time he had with you."

Rebekka heaved a deep breath. "I thought the flowers he sent—I thought they were a request to remember him. I had been dreaming about him and then . . . Oh, it was all too much. André, I don't know if I can—"

"I was told to come here," André interrupted. "And Raoul had the same impression. I think someone up there realized you needed help."

"I wanted to die."

André didn't tell her that she might have been very close to doing just that. She had been in shock when he arrived—there was no telling what might have happened if he hadn't come. "But not now," he told her. "Now you want to live."

"Yes."

They were quiet for a long moment. André wanted to talk to her, to explain why they should marry, to convince her that Marc would want her to marry him, but he forced himself to remain quiet. He had said his piece and Rebekka was an intelligent woman. Ultimately, she would have to make up her own mind.

After a long moment she said, "Marc was trying to talk about the future, but I didn't want to hear. But I remember one thing he said then and in my dream last night. He wanted me to be happy. *My husband* wanted me to be happy. And I thought . . . I thought that I could never be happy without him. But I have been happy a lot these past weeks with you and the girls." More tears gathered in her eyes as she looked at him. "I think maybe the flowers *were* a message, André. Not to wait for Marc as I supposed, but to go ahead without him."

André reached for her, pulling her into his arms—gently so as not to aggravate the pain of the cyst. "Oh Rebekka," he murmured.

"Kiss me, André," she whispered. "Kiss me."

André grinned, hope bursting in his heart. "Only if you'll marry me."

"When?" she asked, a tremor in her voice.

"Next year? Next month? Next week? I'll take what I can get."

Her brows lifted in surprise. "That soon? I don't know. I don't think I could do that. There's still so much of Marc mixed up in what I feel about marriage. Kissing is one thing, but I don't know if I'd be ready for a real marriage."

"Perhaps that won't matter," André said. "Not when we'll have a lifetime together. We can take every step as slowly or as rapidly as you want—even if we're married. You know, from the very first I've felt an urgency in pursuing our relationship. I've fasted, I prayed—every time I still felt the urgency. Now I'm beginning to think that's because the Lord—and perhaps Marc—knew how much you would be hurting with these cysts. More than anything I want to help you through these last few months. To be there for you every day—to make your dinner, to rub your back, be there with you when the baby's born, and to walk the floors with him at night. There are so many things I could do to ease your burden right now, but some of those things really aren't appropriate if we're not married. And I'm talking about rubbing your back and holding you when you're scared or sad—not really anything more involved than that. Yes, I love you and want much more for us as a couple, believe me. I'm sure you can tell that when I kiss you. But our romance will develop in its own time and in it's own way when you are ready. I meant it when I said I'd marry you whenever you agree, but the truth is, I really want to be a father to your son—right from the very start. I want to see his first smile, to be there when he rolls over or takes his first step. I want to be there for you. But it's something you have to want too. I don't want to force you to do anything. I'm willing to listen to alternatives."

She took a deep breath and was silent a long while. "I want to be with you." She stopped talking, as though amazed at her discovery. "But before I agree, there's just one thing I want you to do."

"Anything. You name it."

"Stop buying me plants." She smiled, looking so beautiful that he badly wanted to kiss her. "I'm just going to kill them—accidentally, of course."

"What?" André blinked in surprise. "You don't like them?"

"Well, you've won, so you can quit now." Her face grew serious once more. "Marc was the one who liked plants and since he's not going to be watering them, I think it's time we found something else . . . for us. And I think we should wait at least until January to get married. I'd like our anniversary to be in a different month than the one I shared with Marc."

André saw the wisdom in her request, and if he told the truth, January was much sooner than he had ever hoped possible. "Okay, you have yourself a deal."

"Then kiss me, André." Her silky voice slid over him, an invitation he wasn't going to resist. Smiling, he gathered his future wife into his arms.

Chapter 32

After a peaceful and subdued Christmas season, January came more rapidly than Rebekka had expected. At the end of the second week, she and André were quietly married in a ceremony at the church with only family present. Because of the pain from the cyst, Rebekka needed help getting to the church and to get dressed, and she had to remain seated during most of the ceremony. Despite this, when the bishop pronounced them husband and wife, Rebekka felt happy. Wonder filled her as their kiss seemed to penetrate into her very soul, with no beginning or end. The warmth in her heart testified that marrying André didn't mean she didn't love Marc or miss him. But it did mean she could love again and that she knew he wanted her to be happy.

When the ceremony concluded, André took her to the new apartment they were in the processing of buying. Rebekka had been determined not to start their new life in a place full of memories of either Claire or Marc, but in a place where they could build their own memories. There would be no honeymoon trip until months after the baby was born; Rebekka was in so much pain now she could barely get out bed.

The weeks passed and Rebekka grew larger and more uncomfortable. At times her suffering was almost unbearable and when she cried, André would hold and comfort her. He was loving, caring, and respectful—much as his brother had been, but that's where the comparison ended. André's experience as a husband to a pregnant wife and as a father made him sensitive to things Marc had never learned to be sensitive about. Not only was André vigilant at tending her needs, he was considerate and kind about it. He was also patient, willing to be near her when she wanted him near, yet giving her space when she needed it. Rebekka was grateful for his support and was content that their relationship was moving ahead slowly. Despite her love for André and the passion she often felt for him, she still needed time to adjust to their new circumstances.

Her love for André grew, as did her love for the girls. She enjoyed having them sit on her bed while she combed their hair or read to them endlessly from books. As they had promised, they were well-behaved and even ate their peas on the one night Rebekka's mother made the vegetable.

Rebekka was glad to be living in a new ward, for while their families had been supportive and encouraging, Rebekka worried that there would be many people who would judge her for marrying so soon after her husband's death. They had no way of knowing how long she had loved André or of how the Spirit had guided their choices. André thought her fears were unfounded, that people were happy for them, but she planned to keep out of sight for a while until she felt comfortable in her new role.

In the last week of January, Rebekka was forced to ask the doctor for medication that wasn't overly dangerous to the baby. The pills did cut off the sharp razor edge of the pain, but Rebekka tried to take them sparingly.

In the second week of February, when Rebekka was eight months along, she asked Valerie to help her to the couch. Valerie had come over to make dinner since André had to work late, and the women had been enjoying a conversation in the master bedroom.

"Are you sure?" Valerie asked doubtfully.

"I've taken a pain pill, so I should be able to do it." Rebekka had learned to deal with the pain so well that sometimes during the brief moments of respite after taking the medicine, she felt almost completely well. "Please, Valerie," she said when she saw the other woman hesitating. "Everyone's coming over tonight to celebrate the adoption, and since I couldn't attend the ceremony, it would be nice to at least be lying on the couch."

"Well, that's not until later, and I'm sure André would carry you."

Rebekka frowned. "For once I would like him to see me somewhere other than in bed." Valerie's face showed sym-pathy. "Well, that I can understand." She offered her hand to Rebekka and began to help her up. Ana took the other side, and Rebekka leaned heavily upon them as they made their way out of the bedroom and down the hall. Tears leaked from her eyes at the ensuing pain—despite the medication—but she bit her lip and endured it in silence.

In the large sitting room, she sank to the couch, darting a longing glance at her baby grand—the piano she had played while growing up. Now that she lived in a large enough apartment, she had finally moved it from her parents', leaving the smaller upright at her old apartment for her brother, who played only marginally well. She longed to touch the keys, but knew the price would be too high. *After the baby comes*, she consoled herself.

She had made the effort earlier in the day to fix her hair and put on a gold-colored dressing gown that brought out the red highlights in her dark hair. The gown was at least a bit dressy and cheered her up, though she suspected she looked rather like a round, gold Christmas ball. *Don't think about it!* she thought with a sigh. For years she had taken her great figure for granted, never dreaming that pregnancy would force her to become so inactive.

It's only until the baby's born, she told herself again. *One more month. I've come so far—what could happen in a month?* Too much of course. Rebekka shook off a sudden feeling of unease.

When André came home, Rebekka heard him greet the girls and then head directly to the bedroom. "No, Daddy," Marée said, laughing. "She's in the sitting room."

"She looks pretty," Ana added.

André came into the room alone, surprise on his face. "Rebekka!" He crossed the steps to the couch, where he knelt and kissed her. "You look wonderful!"

"Thank you," she said, deciding not to mention her resemblance to a Christmas ornament. "I was tired of being in bed."

"I bet." His hands went to her stomach, smoothing the gold material over her swollen belly. "Hi, little guy," he said, bringing his head close. "Are you about done in there?"

Rebekka laughed, ignoring the additional pain the movement brought. "I wish."

"I can hardly wait for him to come out." André poked her stomach, obviously hoping to feel the baby kick back. "I mean, the girls have been great, but I can't imagine what it'll be like to have baby boy. Thierry came to me already grown."

Rebekka felt a melancholy she couldn't name. This time it didn't seem to be related to Marc missing out on his baby son, so much as André finally having one. She wiped a tear from the corner of her eye.

"Are you all right?" he asked, ever aware of her feelings.

"It's just hormones," she said. "Just hormones."

* * *

The extended Perrault family arrived after dinner to celebrate the official adoption of Celisse Marie Portier and Raquel Nadia Portier. Rebekka was glad that Marie-Thérèse and Josette kept an eye on their children and seemed to organize the desserts without any effort on her part—not that she could have risen from the couch if she had tried. During the last minutes of the party, she was seeing double with the pain and the boring solitude of her room was beginning to have its appeal.

At last André stood and made an announcement. "I think it's time we adjourned this party or moved it to another location. I need to get all my three girls to bed—especially Rebekka."

"Well, since it's Wednesday and not a weekend, we'd better call it a night," Marie-Thérèse agreed. "The kids all have school tomorrow. Thanks everyone for coming to the courthouse today and supporting us. And thank you for having us here tonight, Rebekka."

Rebekka laughed weakly. "Hey, don't thank me, it was the only way I could get in on things."

"You'll be better soon," Josette said. "But I remember that last month is the worst—even without a cyst. No way I'm *ever* doing that again!" She smiled sweetly at her husband, as if urging him to agree.

He shrugged. "Whatever you want, honey. It's up to you."

"I'll be here on Monday to help with dinner," Ariana said as she took her husband's arm.

"Thanks, Mom." André kissed his mother's cheeks. "I don't know what we'd do without you." Rebekka echoed his words.

"Nonsense, it's a pleasure," Ariana said. "I love spending time here. Well, come on gang, let's leave Rebekka to get some rest."

The family filtered out and the apartment was abruptly quiet. "Come on," André said. "Let's get you to bed. Girls, you run on ahead and change into your pajamas."

"And brush your teeth!" Rebekka called after them.

André came in from her right side and picked Rebekka up. They had learned this was the position that gave her the least pain. "I'd better stop eating or you won't be able to lift me at all," she murmured.

He snorted. "Rebekka, you don't weigh much. You just can't see beyond this stomach, that's all. And that's all baby. Well, and cyst too, I guess. It's not you."

"How do you know?"

"Because I've been through this before."

"Claire was this fat?"

"You are *not* fat. You are pregnant."

"Same thing," Rebekka muttered under her breath.

He was passing the kitchen doorway now, and she was counting the steps to the bedroom. Maybe she could take another pill. Just one more to get to sleep. Surely that wouldn't hurt the baby. Hours had passed since she had taken the last one. But no, she had better not.

Abruptly, André stopped. "Look," he whispered. Taking a few steps back, he set her down gently, still supporting a portion of her weight.

Rebekka stared into the kitchen, where her brother was kissing Valerie. "I thought everyone went home," she said softly.

"Evidently, someone forgot to tell them the party's over. Wow, that's some kiss!"

As they watched from the hall, Valerie took her hands from Raoul's hair. "Would you stop stalling already. Ask me!"

"Oh, Valerie. I love you so much. Will you marry me?"

"No," she said in a teasing tone.

"What's wr— Oh, I know." Raoul fell to his knees, his face grave, his eyes soulful. "Please? I can't live without you. Will you marry me?"

Valerie bent down and kissed him, long and hard. "Oh, yes. Now I'll marry you. Of course I will." They were in each other's arms in another instant. André whistled and Rebekka laughed.

Raoul and Valerie turned to look at them. Valerie appeared slightly embarrassed, but Raoul was triumphant. "She said yes. She's going to marry me!"

"So we heard," André said. "But when?"

The smile on Raoul's face vanished as he turned urgently to Valerie. "When?"

Valerie smiled and took his hand. "How about after Rebekka's baby comes? I'd like her to be able to come to the temple with us."

"Let's see," Raoul said. "The baby's supposed to be here in a month; that would make it the middle of March. How about the second week in April? Will that give you enough time to recover, Rebekka?"

Rebekka nodded, though the pain was so intense now that she couldn't see her brother's face. Darkness ate steadily at the edges of the light she could still see.

"Two months," Raoul went on. "That seems like a lifetime. It's too bad we couldn't—"

"André," Rebekka murmured, clutching onto his shirt. "The baby."

Abruptly, her world exploded into an endless, burning, blinding pain. Then darkness swallowed everything.

Chapter 33

Words filtered through as Rebekka's unconscious mind fought its way back to lucidity. "It's grown as big as a grapefruit now . . . partially burst . . . torsion . . . causing so much pain . . . drug ought to help . . . must have surgery . . . important not to wait any longer."

As consciousness returned, Rebekka remembered where she had heard the words. They hadn't come from a nightmare, but from the doctor. *Not now!* she thought. *Oh please not now!* She had believed with her whole heart that the cyst would go away on its own, or if it didn't that at least there would be no danger to her or the baby. Then came that terrible, blinding explosion. The memory of the agony she'd experienced brought her abruptly awake.

"She's coming around." It was André speaking, but when she opened her eyes, she saw Raoul's face.

"What time is it?" she asked groggily.

"It's near noon on Thursday," Raoul supplied. "I was here last night with Mom and Dad, but you were sleeping."

Rebekka looked around and saw that she was in a hospital bed, hooked up to several different monitors. She rolled from her side to her back, trying to sit up. "Here, let me help you," André said from her other side. "But take it slowly. It might not be good." For the cyst. Rebekka heard the words he didn't say and the reality came rushing back.

"What are we going to do?" she asked. "It's too soon."

André paused as if carefully choosing his words. "I don't feel we really have a choice. I mean, we've waited this long because the baby could have too many complications being born so early, but that risk is gone, pretty much. He still could have some complications if the surgery caused him to come, but . . ." He raised his hands helplessly. "You can't go through this pain anymore. I've questioned and questioned the doctor about all the options, and I think we should agree to the surgery." He grabbed her hand. "I know we wanted to wait, but I've been praying about it—all night I've prayed. I think maybe it's time."

Knowing André as she did—how much he loved both her and the

baby and how close he was to the Spirit—she had no doubts that he was right. Besides, whatever medication they had given her must have been very strong, because Rebekka wasn't feeling much of anything now. *How good is that for my baby?* she wondered. A tear squeezed out of her eye. "Okay, then. When?"

"Tomorrow morning."

Rebekka gave a short sob, and Raoul stepped closer, rubbing her shoulder. "Don't worry," he said. "We're all here for you."

"Thanks."

André smiled at him. "Would you go tell your parents and my own that she's awake. I think they're wearing out the carpet in the waiting room."

"Yes." Raoul gave Rebekka's shoulder one last pat. "I'll see you later."

After he left, André sat on the edge of the bed and put an arm around her. He kissed her forehead gently.

"Is he going to be okay?" she asked, desperately wanting reassurance.

André pointed to a monitor. "They turned the sound down, but that's his heartbeat. It's coming from the belt they put around your waist. Looks strong to me. I think we have every chance to get that cyst out and finish your pregnancy without a hitch. Or that if there is a complication, he'll come through just fine."

"Good," Rebekka said tearfully. "Because I'm so afraid."

"I'll be right there when you wake up," he promised. "I'll be the one holding your hand."

* * *

Waiting held an agony all it's own. André paced in the entire length of the room. *I should be there for her*, he thought. The doctor hadn't allowed his presence, though because of her pregnancy Rebekka would receive only a local anesthetic and would be awake during the procedure. André had to be content with giving her a priesthood blessing and kissing her for courage.

A hand massaged his shoulder and he looked up to see Raoul. "She's going to be okay," he said. "My sister's tough."

André smiled, but knew the gesture lacked conviction. He had felt so strongly when he had prayed that surgery was the only choice, but when he had given Rebekka a blessing earlier that morning, the reassurance he had been expecting about the baby's safety hadn't come. *Did that mean the baby would come early?*

"Come on, there's no use in torturing yourself. They'll be out soon." Ariana motioned for him to sit. André was glad his family was there and even happier that he had married Rebekka when he had. She had needed him this past month and he wouldn't trade one moment of their time together. He shuddered to think of the loneliness and despair she would have felt if she had not opened her heart to him. *We won, Marc,* he thought to his brother. *Now if only we can get through this last month.*

"Monsieur Perrault?" A nurse stood in the doorway.

"Is she all right?" he asked, nearly leaping to her side.

"The cyst is out, but there's been a complication."

André heart plunged as he listened in dread for the next words. How many times had he read stories in the newspapers about people dying from relatively simply surgeries? *No!* his thoughts screamed, *I can't live without her!*

"The baby's coming," the nurse continued. "We're not sure what caused the labor. The doctor has tried to stop it, but . . ." She shrugged delicately.

"My wife?" As much as André loved and looked forward to the birth of their child, Rebekka was his primary concern. She made him complete. He had spent many weeks carefully tending and courting her, waiting for the time when she would be healed from grief enough to give herself to him fully—mind, body, and soul. There was so much promise in their love. He couldn't lose her now!

"She's asking for you."

He sighed with relief, but his heart still pounded in his ears.

"Can I come too?" Danielle asked. "I'm her mother."

"Yes, come along, both of you."

Over his shoulder, André saw his parents and Rebekka's father, Philippe, staring after them. Danielle touched his elbow. "Babies are stronger than they appear. Yours will be fine."

Her words calmed his heart and put things into perspective. He especially liked the way she had called the baby his. "Yeah, what's a month?" he said, trying to make his voice light.

After they scrubbed and donned white paper gowns, the nurse led them to the operating room where Rebekka lay on a white-covered table, looking small in comparison to all the surrounding equipment. Dr. Samain and two nurses stood by her side.

"The baby's heart rate is rising again," a nurse was saying as they walked in the room.

Dr. Samain looked over at André. "We have to do an emergency cesarean. The labor is going fast, but the baby's under too much stress. We can't wait any longer."

André made a sound in his throat. "I understand," he said mechanically.

The doctor gave him a compassionate smile before going to work. "Don't worry, we'll take good care of them."

André walked to the front of the bed where Rebekka gazed mutely at him with large frightened eyes. He stooped and kissed her cheek. "It's going to be all right," he told her with as much assurance as he could muster.

Everything seemed to happen simultaneously. More hospital personnel entered the room, including a doctor to take care of the premature baby. The incision Dr. Samain made in Rebekka's lower abdomen fascinated and repelled André at once. Then, almost abruptly, the baby was out, scrawny, with a shock of wet, dark hair, and not yet breathing. André wasn't sure if it really was a boy because the cord blocked a clear view.

No one said anything, but the baby doctor took over, while Dr. Samain stitched the gash in Rebekka's uterus and belly. André felt torn between being with his wife and seeing what was going on with their son. His decision was made for him.

"Is he all right?" Rebekka gasped, tears escaping from her eyes. She pushed André away from the bed with surprising strength. "Go see!"

André crossed the room and stared in amazement as with gentle hands the baby doctor and checked out seemingly every aspect of the newborn. "Is he . . .?"

The doctor smiled. "He's a big little guy for coming a month early. He's got to weigh about two and a half kilos. If he had gone full term he'd have probably been at least four."

André was pleased. Two and a half kilos was small, but many full term babies were only three kilos. He remembered that one of his sisters had given birth to a baby nearly that same size and it had been perfectly healthy.

The doctor wrapped the newborn in a heated blanket and handed him to André.

He was so tiny and utterly precious. André felt an emotion in his heart that equalled the emotion he had experienced at his daughters' births. This was his brother's son, as well as his and Rebekka's, and he was privileged to be able to love and raise him. "Welcome, son," he whispered, blinking back tears. The baby nestled contentedly against his chest. Carefully, he crossed the short space to where Rebekka lay anxiously waiting.

"We have a son," he said, lowering the baby into her arms, "just like they promised. And he's completely healthy."

She gave a broken cry, half a sob, half a sigh of relief. She put one arm around the baby and twisted her head to place her lips on the baby's skull, keeping them there for a long time. Tears squeezed from under her closed lids. André knew she was praying, and he too began to silently thank his Heavenly Father.

There were more tests, but aside from a mild case of jaundice, the newest addition to the Perrault family was healthy on nearly every account. "He's blessed with his mother's endurance and both his fathers' stubbornness, that's all," André announced to the group that later gathered around Rebekka's bed.

"May I hold him?" Raoul asked.

"Sure, just don't breathed on him," André said with a grin. "The doctor says we have to keep him kind of isolated until he gains some weight."

"So what are we going to name him?" Rebekka asked. "We've never really discussed it."

André took her hand and kissed each finger slowly. "I didn't think there was any choice. He's Marc, of course. Don't you agree?"

Her eyes glistened. "Yes," she whispered. "That's exactly right."

Rebekka began humming a soft tune while gazing into their newborn's eyes. Did she feel the same compelling feeling he did when looking at their son? Or was her bond even stronger? Perhaps. What mattered was that the baby was safe and that Rebekka was his wife. A rush of happiness filled his soul. "I thought you were going to sleep," he said. "Do you want me to take the baby?"

Rebekka lifted her eyes to his. "I guess I'm too excited to sleep. He's such a miracle." Her long dark hair spilled about her shoulders and stuck to the pillow, contrasting with the stark white of her face. Her gray eyes were languid and content and André had never seen her more beautiful. He leaned down and kissed her cheek tenderly, trailing over to kiss his favorite freckle above her top lip.

"Didn't I tell you we'd get through it?" he said, sitting on the bed and snuggling up to her, the baby nestled where their bodies touched.

She smiled up at him. "I think I could survive anything as long as you're here." Her face sobered. "But I can't help thinking what might have happened if we had gone ahead with the surgery three months ago. I would have gone into labor and we would have lost him."

"We don't know that," André said. "The doctor doesn't know for sure the surgery caused the labor."

"No, but I do—we do, don't we?"

Gratitude filled André's heart. "The doctor was right," he added with a hoarse laugh. "Miracles do seem to follow our family."

"You're my miracle," she answered. "Thank you for not giving up on me when I did nothing but push you away for all those months."

"I love you," he said simply. He trailed his fingertips along her cheek and across her soft lips.

Emotion flared in her eyes. She lifted her face for his kiss, her free arm sliding around his neck, pulling him closer. "And I love you, André."

Epilogue

Because I know many of you will write to ask . . .
(Read only if you like all loose ends tied up nice and tight!)

Raoul Massoni and Valerie Bernard were married civilly in April, and shortly afterward traveled to the Swiss temple to be sealed for time and all eternity. The following year, they had a baby girl, whom they named Dietrich. Much to the company's loss, Valerie decided to quit her job at Perrault and Massoni Architecture and Engineering and become a stay-at-home mother. She quickly became pregnant again with the idea of having at least four children. For his part, Raoul began to spend less time at work and delegated more to his employees. He continued to share a special relationship with Raquel Nadia Portier, and the pain he once felt at Desirée's betrayal faded until it was completely transformed by his happiness. He and Valerie eventually had not four but a half-dozen children, four girls and two boys.

Six months after adopting Celisse and Raquel, Mathieu and Marie-Thérèse Portier had their children sealed to them in the Swiss temple. They never became very wealthy, but they had enough for their needs and to give generously to others. After the children were all in school, Marie-Thérèse began volunteering as a social worker to help save other at-risk children.

After many years of professional counseling and support from her family, Celisse gradually recovered from the abuse she suffered as a child. She served a mission in France for the LDS Church, obtained a degree in history, and later taught French history at a college in England. While there, she was called to work once a week at the temple. One day on the grounds she met a handsome Englishman whom she taught the gospel and later married. She turned thirty-one two months before their wedding, and he was twenty-seven. They had two children and adopted two more.

Larissa married a man in her stake shortly after finishing high school. After seven turbulent years, hours of professional counseling, and three babies, she learned to take responsibility for her happiness and managed to save her marriage from near failure. Through all her trials she considered her mother and Celisse her very best friends. Having survived the storm, she and her husband, a top architect, became very devoted to each other and to the Church. They served as stake missionaries and went on to complete a full time mission when they retired.

Brandon's allergy attacks lessened as he grew older, though he had to watch his diet carefully for the rest of his life. He was a great student and graduated at the top of his class. After a year service in the French army and a Church mission in France, he went to college where he studied medical science. He married a fellow student, who had been recently baptized into the Church, and ten years and five babies later, they won the Nobel Prize for their joint contribution to the science world in the field of allergy medicines.

Raquel grew up a happy child, who knew she was deeply loved. Over the years, she helped Larissa many times with her children and the two became very close. By watching Larissa's struggles, Raquel learned what was important in her own life. She decided very early to listen to her parents and stay close to the Church.

Desirée worked sporadically at bars for fifteen years after giving her baby up for adoption, living mostly on money from her divorce settlement. Occasionally, she would stop by the grade school to catch a glimpse of her daughter at play. She never approached Raquel directly or went too often. During these sad, lonely years, Rebekka continued to keep in contact with Desirée, passing along information and pictures of Raquel. Desirée wanted to change her life, but felt hopeless to do so. When personally delivering the pictures of Raquel's fifteenth birthday party, Rebekka reminded her that in only three years Raquel would receive her letter.

"If I know Raquel, she'll come looking for you." Rebekka said.

Desirée could barely see through her tears. "Okay. I'm ready."

For the fourth time she began attending a help group for alcoholics, and later that same month enrolled in a secretarial school. This time she didn't give up. Three years later, Raquel read the letter her birth mother had written and set up a meeting. At this tearful reunion, Raquel threw her arms around Desirée and thanked her for giving her life and such a wonderful family. The two became friends. Desirée never joined the Church, but at the age of sixty-one, she met and married a retired banker, who had lost his wife to cancer. She was a great support to him until his death ten years later.

Two years and a half years after meeting her birth mother, Raquel married the missionary she had waited for. She and her husband had three children, who were loved and treasured by all three of their grand-mothers.

Josette Perrault Fields became pregnant two years after Rebekka's first baby was born—despite her continual assertion that she would never have another child. She surprised herself by having not only the one little girl she had always wanted, but two fraternal sisters, thus carrying on the twin tradition in her maternal family line that had skipped only one genera-tion in the last ten. (Neither Ariana's grandmother nor grandmother's twin sister had twins.) The twins' five big brothers doted on their little sisters.

Zack Fields became very successful in his real estate business. He and Josette began taking all seven children to America every three years to visit their American grandparents and other relatives. Most of their children eventually became executive managers at Perrault and Massoni Architecture and Engineering after working their way up from the bottom of the company. Only one of their sons followed their father's profession in real estate. Both of their daughters eventually had fraternal twins of their own—a boy and a girl each.

Louis-Géralde, Ariana and Jean-Marc's youngest child, married his shy girlfriend, Sophie, and they had three children. Two years after their marriage, he became a full-fledged partner at Perrault and Massoni. Sophie finished college and in her spare time line-edited children's novels for a publishing company.

Ariana and Jean-Marc Perrault went on two missions—one to Africa and one to their native France. Though they had suffered much in their lifetimes, they had also known much joy. They never again had to pass through the pain of losing a child. They served their family and the church with joy the rest of their lives.

Rebekka's parents, Danielle and Philippe Massoni, retired and served a church welfare mission to Brazil. Philippe was so touched by what he experienced that when he returned home, he spent the rest of his life using his banking skills to raise funds to help the Church welfare program. Five years before his death, he was called to preside over the welfare program in western Europe.

Samuel and Polly Bjornenburg both became active in the Catholic religion—much to their parents' joy. They kept in touch with Rebekka through yearly Christmas cards and occasional visits when Samuel was in Paris on business. Eventually one of their three children met the LDS missionaries at a street meeting in Cincinnati and was baptized. Samuel and Polly were supportive of their son's choice. They spent the rest of their lives working hard and helping others.

And finally, André and Rebekka juggled their work schedules so that one of them was always home with Ana, Marée, and little Marc. Though they faced many emotional challenges—ones that are shared by all those who have lost beloved spouses—they took their romantic relationship slowly, growing together and banishing the sadness of the past. They came to love each other very deeply and passionately. Four years after their marriage, they had a son together, Jean-André, followed quickly by a little girl, whom they named Dani after Rebekka's mother.

Although all Rebekka's children were important and special to her, she and little Marc were always particularly close. Together she and André taught him the gospel and about his father. He never strayed from the Church, but was a constant good example to his siblings and cousins, bringing the occasional straying lamb back to the fold. André joked that little Marc was so good because he had his own personal angel and guide in his deceased father.

Little Marc, his brother Jean-André, and sister Marée served missions in France for the Church, bringing many people to a knowledge of Jesus Christ. Later, they worked at Perrault and Massoni along with Ana. Thierry, Andre's adopted son, served a mission to England and after finishing college became an English teacher as he'd always planned. All the siblings learned to play the piano well—especially Dani, who under her mother's tutelage became a concert pianist at the age of sixteen. With the exception of Dani, the children married young and lived rather ordinary but happy and fulfilling lives. Over the years Dani went on many tours and recorded a dozen CDs, but to her parent's relief she eventually settled down and married her home teacher's brother in the Swiss temple. They had two children.

Meanwhile, André and Rebekka's love continued to deepen with the passing of years until Rebekka couldn't bear to think of a time when she would be without him. But she faced the knowledge with faith in the Lord and in her first husband, finding comfort in the fact that there would be an eternity to work out relationships and to develop stronger ties with those who had gone before. *The Lord knows what He's doing*, became her life's motto.

André and Rebekka had twenty grandchildren and seventy-nine great-grandchildren. Their long and very happy life together proved that there really is such a thing as *twice in a lifetime*.

Note from the Author

I wish to thank my readers who have been so diligent at pursuing the saga of Ariana Perrault and her family. Without you, the reader, books are nothing but chicken scratches on paper! I sincerely appreciate all the support you lend to LDS fiction and to my work specifically. Those of you who have purchased my books for yourselves, for others, or have recommended them truly make it possible for me to write in the relatively small LDS market. Thank you for your continued and faithful support!

Now for some news. After much thought and nearly eight hundred thousand words, I have come to the conclusion that it's time to let the Perrault family live "happily ever after." I have, however, included an epilogue with this novel to answer some of the questions I know will arise and to give you a glimpse into what I foresee for the characters I have created.

I hope you will follow me to my next novel with anticipation. I have many great stories planned with characters I feel you will love as much as the Perrault family. Believe me, the best is yet to come!

Thanks once again for your support. As I read and prayerfully answer your many heartfelt letters and e-mails, I feel very close to you who are my sisters and brothers in the gospel. Thank you for allowing me to be a part of your lives.

Sincerely,
Rachel Ann Nunes
rachel@rachelannnunes.com

About the Author

Rachel Ann Nunes (pronounced *noon-esh*) learned to read when she was four and by age twelve knew she was going to be a writer. Now as a stay-at-home mother of five, it isn't easy to find time to write, but she will trade washing dishes or weeding the garden for an hour at the computer any day! Her only rule about writing is to never eat chocolate at the computer. "Since I love chocolate and writing," she jokes, "my family might never see me again."

Rachel enjoys camping, spending time with her family, reading, and visiting far off places. She stayed in France for six months when her father was teaching French at BYU, and later served an LDS mission to Portugal.

Twice in a Lifetime is Rachel's fifteenth published novel. She also has a picture book entitled *Daughter of a King*. All of her books have been best-sellers in the LDS market.

Rachel lives with her husband, TJ, and their children in Pleasant Grove, Utah. She enjoys hearing from her readers.

You can write to her at P.O. Box 353, American Fork, UT 84003-0353 or rachel@rachelannnunes.com. Also, feel free to visit her website at www.rachelannnunes.com.